YOU SAID I
WAS YOUR
FAVORITE

NEW YORK TIMES BESTSELLING AUTHOR

MONICA MURPHY

Entangled Publishing, LLC
644 Shrewsbury Commons Ave., STE 181
Shrewsbury, PA 17361
rights@entangledpublishing.com

Amara is an imprint of Entangled Publishing, LLC.

Visit our website at www.entangledpublishing.com.

Edited by Rebecca Barney
Cover design by Emily Wittig
Stock art by Lana1512/Depositphotos
Interior design by Toni Kerr

ISBN 978-1-64937-660-2

Manufactured in the United States of America

First Edition October 2023

10 9 8 7 6 5 4 3

ALSO BY MONICA MURPHY

THE LANCASTER PREP SERIES

Things I Wanted To Say
A Million Kisses in Your Lifetime
Promises We Meant to Keep
I'll Always Be With You
You Said I Was Your Favorite

FOR TEEN READERS

Pretty Dead Girls
Saving It
Daring the Bad Boy

At Entangled, we want our readers to be well-informed. If you would like to know if this book contains any elements that might be of concern for you, please check the back of the book for details.

CHAPTER ONE

ARCH

First day of school and this is the last place I want to be. It's my senior year and I should be feeling on top of the social ladder at the boarding school I've attended for the last three years of my life, but all I feel is…

Trapped. Tired.

Completely over it.

Despite Lancaster Prep being the most prestigious private high school in the entire country and owned by my family, I'm bored out of my skull. I'd rather be anywhere than here, but every Lancaster is forced to go to this God forsaken school because it's tradition.

I wish I could tell tradition to fuck right off, but here I am. Stuck in high school. I feel like I've been here forever. How am I going to survive one more year?

My sister attends Lancaster Prep too. Edie is a sophomore and a bit of a troublemaker, though I can't blame her for acting out. Pretty sure she's bored too. But her sometimes erratic behavior means I can't count on her for shit, which means I can't count on anyone. And as the responsible—gimme a break—oldest child and eldest son of George and Miriam Lancaster, my parents remind me constantly that I have an image to maintain.

Goddamn if that isn't stressful.

My cousins before me attended this school and ruled it with an iron fist, reigning over their peers—sometimes even the faculty and admin—however they wanted. Grant. Finn. Whittaker—the worst of them all, though Grant is a close second to Whit. Even Crew, who's the youngest son of my uncle Reggie, was known as a giant asshole.

Until he fell in love. Cue the puking emoji. That's the last thing I want right now. I'm too young to settle down and fall in love.

Sounds like a nightmare.

I tried to graduate early. I had enough credits and wanted to take a gap year, but my parents wouldn't allow it. They don't care if I'm bored and the classes don't stimulate me. They could give fuck all about my genius IQ or the fact that I could test out of here today. They claimed I was too irresponsible to travel all over Europe by myself for a year. Talk about an insult.

My parents have zero faith in me.

Doesn't help that not even a week ago, I had a huge bash to celebrate my eighteenth birthday. All of my friends—and plenty of people I don't even know—showed up at my parents' house in the Hamptons while they were on vacation in the Bahamas. We fucked that place up—it was great.

Until I got into a raging argument with my then-girlfriend, Cadence.

Someone caught us and filmed the entire fight, then proceeded to post it on social media. Mom and Dad eventually saw the post—pretty sure Edie showed them but she will neither confirm nor deny—along with the hoard of teenagers crowded in their backyard and spilling out of the house. The evidence of alcohol and drugs scattered everywhere, all over my mother's precious furniture and rugs, leaving behind a mess in pretty much every single room.

Busted.

According to my parents, that's the main reason I'm not allowed to leave Lancaster early.

"You may be eighteen and too smart for your own good, but you're still an immature little shit who can't control yourself when left alone," Father yelled at me, his face as red as a tomato.

"And someone damaged the Pollock, dear," Mother complained as she literally clutched the pearls wrapped around her neck.

It took everything I had not to roll my eyes and say something rude. There's a slight dent in the ugly ass art piece that she's referring to, but no one would notice. And my father literally has no idea what he's talking about. I can control myself just fine.

I merely choose not to most of the time.

Life is meant to be *lived*. I hate being told what to do.

"Bro." I glance up to find John Joseph Richards—my best friend, otherwise known as JJ—standing in front of me, his hand held out for a slap, which I automatically give. "What are you doing here?"

This is where things get sticky. I told everyone who mattered—only a select few—that I wasn't coming back. I had plans to get the fuck out of here, once and for all. The rolling green hills and ivy-covered buildings were going to be nothing but a distant memory if I had my way.

Unfortunately, I didn't get my way.

"Ready to start senior year." I shrug, before I roll up my sleeves. I wear only a few pieces of my uniform, leaving the heavy wool jacket back in my room. Bucking tradition when we're supposed to be fully dressed like the good little soldiers they expect us to be.

Fuck that. I'm going to do whatever I want because I'm a Lancaster.

Who's going to stop me?

"I thought you were going to spend your senior year in Europe," JJ says, still confused.

Irritated, I start walking, and JJ falls into step right beside me. "You know how it goes. Parents weren't down."

"When are they ever?" JJ knows of what he speaks. His parents give him endless shit about everything he does. Good or bad. Wrong or right. The guy gets zero breaks.

My parents look like saints compared to his.

"If they're going to force me to be here, then I'm going to make the best of it by doing things my way." I spot my sister in the near distance, surrounded by a bunch of girls while she stands tall above them. Mom wants her to model, but I don't get it. My sister isn't what I would call conventionally attractive, though she photographs well, I'll give her that.

Edie is all limbs and awkward angles. Big eyes and flat chested and a wide mouth that scowls just as often as it smiles. She doesn't look like either of our parents. It's almost as if she was an alien baby dropped off on the front stoop of our parents' old brownstone back in the day.

"Your sister is getting hotter," JJ observes.

I slap his chest, making him grunt. "Don't talk about her like that."

"Merely stating facts. You'll need to put an electric fence around her to keep the guys away."

"Don't give me any ideas," I mutter, as we make our way to the auditorium along with everyone else who attends this school. I glance around, noting that I'm the only one who's not wearing a jacket, and I stand taller, proud of myself for not giving a damn.

"Where's Cadence?" JJ asks as we draw closer to the auditorium's open front doors.

"Don't know." I shrug.

JJ says nothing for a moment and I know he expects me to explain myself further, but I don't.

What is there to say? I haven't spoken to her since the night of my birthday party when she screamed at me for two hours and ruined everything. I blocked her from my contacts, knowing that would drive her out of her mind, and I haven't responded to any of her DMs either. She deserves to sweat it out a bit.

Maybe even forever.

"She's usually glued to your side," JJ finally says.

"I haven't talked to her since the birthday party."

"Seriously?" JJ sounds shocked.

"Yeah." I spot her right then, the crowd parting to reveal her familiar long, glossy auburn hair swinging as she walks ahead of us with her friends. She filmed a shampoo commercial over the summer, her hair is that good. Too bad she's such a bitch. "We're done."

As if she can hear me talking, Cadence chooses that moment to glance over her shoulder, her eyes lighting up when she spots me. "Arch!"

"Does she know that you two are done?" JJ asks, his voice filled with amusement as I send him an irritated glare.

Cadence comes to a stop, her friends abandoning her with exaggerated groans and obvious scowls aimed in my direction, and I slow my steps, keeping the frown on my face as I draw closer and closer.

Cadence Calhoun is the epitome of a spoiled rich girl. With the gorgeous hair and the clear blue eyes, the perfect white teeth and the reconstructed—she had a deviated septum, don't you know—nose, the lips already plumped with filler, she's beautiful.

But all that beauty hides a dark, ugly soul.

She's not a nice person. I know this. Even she knows this. But, somehow, we were drawn to each other last year and we sort of formed this power couple. She ate it up, while I merely tolerated it. It's hard to resist the most beautiful girl on campus when she's sending you nudes and willingly giving you blow jobs on the regular.

But she's mean. Nothing makes her happy. She could have all the money in the world, own every Chanel bag in existence and be engaged to the hottest guy she's ever seen, and she'd still find a way to complain.

That's just her way.

I stop directly in front of Cadence, glad JJ keeps walking. He prefers to keep his distance when we're together and I don't blame him. Our conversations always end in an argument and JJ doesn't want to deal.

The moment it's just the two of us, Cadence steps closer, her hand landing on my chest, her gaze imploring. I shift back, her hand falling and her lips form the tiniest frown. "What's wrong with you?"

Fury is already bubbling close to the surface, but I swallow it down. Her snappy tone always sets me off. She talks to me like I'm her kid. I don't need another mother. I already have one and she's more than enough.

"We're not having this conversation right now." I glance around, noting that every single person nearby is watching us, even the shiny-faced freshmen and they shouldn't have a damn clue who we are. I spot my sister in the near distance with a smirk on her face and when we make eye contact, she slowly shakes her head.

Yeah. Really don't need her judgment in this moment.

"Why not?" That mock pout Cadence assumes is cute and sexy appears, doing nothing for me. She reaches for my tie, keeping me from escaping her clutches, giving the silk fabric a light tug. "I've missed you so much, Archie."

No one calls me Archie. Not a single soul because I've made it well known that I hate the nickname. I'm not particularly fond of my name in general. Archibald, after some dead ancestor who made our family a ton of money at one point about a hundred years ago or so.

Okay fine, I act like I don't know who I was named for when I do. It was my great-grandfather. My family is big on tradition. Hence the old-fashioned names and the fact that we're all named after dead relatives.

"Don't call me that," I say through clenched teeth.

Cadence's sly smile is obvious—and annoying. She knows she got to me, though she probably doesn't realize it's in a negative way. "Come on, Arch. Don't be mad. Sit with me inside."

I don't shrug her off when she lets go of my tie and curls her arm through mine. We start walking together, heading for the open doors once again.

"I'll let you finger me if we sit in the back row," she whispers close to my ear.

A few weeks ago, I might've agreed. It wouldn't be the first time I fingered Cadence somewhere in the auditorium named after yet another one of my dead relatives, but now?

I'm not interested.

"I'm keeping my hands to myself," I tell her firmly.

"God, you're no fun." More pouting but I ignore her.

Once we're inside, we sit in the senior section, which is right at the front of the stage. No fingering allowed, much to Cadence's brief disappointment. Brief because it disappears fast when she realizes we're on complete display for the rest of the student body and we're finally getting the respect that we're due.

We're seniors. We rule the school, and her being attached to a Lancaster means no other senior girl can top her. She's in charge. Or at least she thinks she is.

And she's such a power-hungry bitch, I'm sure every senior female is shaking in her loafers at the thought of potentially crossing Cadence. They're going to avoid her like the plague or kiss her ass for all eternity.

I don't have the heart to remind her we're done just yet, so I keep my mouth shut and talk mostly with JJ, who's sitting in the row directly in front of me, turned around and keeping up a steady stream of conversation while Cadence sends him the occasional glare.

"Can't he talk to someone else?" Cadence clings to my arm.

"He's my best friend, so no." I barely look at her, shooting

JJ a quick smile.

"Everyone, please come closer. Don't sit in the back seats!" Headmaster Matthews is on stage at the podium, yelling at everyone good-naturedly. I hate that schmuck. He gets off on torturing my ass and punishing me every chance he gets. I'm sure he's going to relish it more than usual since this is his last year with me.

Fucker.

"Come on, don't be shy," our headmaster yells, waving his hands in encouragement. I swear I can hear the moans and groans coming from behind me as students reluctantly get out of their seats and shuffle forward, only because he's forcing them to do so.

Every year at the first day of school assembly, Matthews encourages everyone to sit closer to the stage so it feels more inclusive—his words, not mine. The loser kids who prefer to sit in the back practically drop in the aisles. They're so distraught over having to sit near us normal people, who have functioning social lives and don't hole up in their dorms when they're not in class, too scared to mingle with their actual peers.

This morning, Matthews is more obnoxious than normal, actually sending out staff members to drag everyone closer to the stage. A few teachers and even Matthews' secretary are corralling all seniors to sit in the appointed section. There are empty seats to the right of me, but not for long. Nope, eventually there's a string of quiet, mousy girls heading down the narrow aisle, led by the quietest, mousiest one of all.

JJ snickers. "Ooh, new girlfriend alert."

"More like secret fuck bait," I return, my gaze drifting down the length of the girl who pisses me off every time I look at her.

Daisy Albright.

She's not mousy. Not even close. No, she's actually fucking beautiful and I don't get why she plays down her looks. Why no one else sees what I see. She's smart and quiet and shy and gorgeous.

I don't like her.

I don't even know her. Not really.

"Correction, bro. Jail bait," JJ says, loud and clear enough for Daisy to hear him.

She acts like she didn't, but I see the way her lips form into a frown. Her bright blonde hair is pulled into a French braid, wayward strands flying around her makeup-free face. Her cheeks are pink, like she's already hot, and I'm sure she is because she's decked out in the full uniform, jacket and all with the button-down shirt done up to her fucking chin for the love of God.

"You jail bait, Albright?" I ask her when she settles into the chair right next to mine. Her perfume drifts, something sweet and floral lingering in the air.

Fuck. She smells...

Good.

I shove that thought immediately out of my brain, reminding myself that I don't like this girl.

Daisy glances over at me, those big golden-brown eyes contemplating me for a moment before she says, "If that's your way of asking if I'm eighteen yet, then the answer is no."

JJ and I share a look and I can tell he's close to bursting out in laughter.

Cadence nudges me in the ribs and I turn to look at her. "Don't talk to her. Talk to me."

Her whining is a surefire way for me to continue ignoring her. I return my attention to Daisy, but her head is angled so all I can do is stare at her profile.

Daisy Albright is the scholarship kid. The groundskeeper's daughter, the good girl who doesn't really talk to anyone and doesn't party and doesn't get into trouble ever. She's one of those students who lacks real social skills and doesn't have a lot of friends. Most everyone on campus either feels sorry for her or they don't think about her at all.

Except for me.

I don't feel sorry for her. And I do think about her. More than I'd care to admit.

"When's your birthday?" I ask, leaning in closer to Daisy, trying to intimidate her. Putting on a show for JJ, who's currently eating it up. He knows nothing about Daisy, not like I do.

Academically, we're rivals. I'm number one in the class and she's number two—always on my heels, taking the hardest classes possible to skew her GPA and hopefully surge ahead of mine.

So far, so good. I'm still in the lead. I figure I'll graduate first in class with Little Miss Second Place right behind me, and I know that infuriates the shit out of her.

I can't help it if I'm smarter than she is. That I get better grades. She can try all she wants, but I'm not going to let her pass me up. Hell no.

Daisy turns her head, blinking when she finds that I'm closer than she realized, and she parts her lips for a moment. They're full and pink and…sexy. I jerk my attention from her mouth, my gaze meeting hers once more, noting the irritation in her eyes. "Why? What do you care?"

JJ and I share another look, the both of us making a bunch of *whoa* noises. I'm guessing he's as startled as I am by the backbone she's showing us.

Impressive.

"Only trying to make conversation, Daze." I tilt my head, my gaze zeroing in on the tiny earring dotting her ear.

A white flower with a yellow center. A daisy.

How original.

"When's your birthday?" I think she asks me. Not sure, considering she's staring straight ahead.

I lower my voice, leaning in closer. I can feel her body heat, see the way her button-down stretches tight across her tits. Looks like sweet little Daisy is stacked, though I already knew that. From what I can tell, Daisy is pretty fucking hot, though she keeps that body under wraps. "You talking to my friend there or me?"

She turns her head toward me once again, her eyes widening as if she's shocked that I'm now even closer. She even leans back a little bit. "You."

"I just had my birthday. August sixteenth," I tell her.

"You're a Leo."

"Roar," JJ adds, right before he starts cracking up.

"Is that a bad thing?" Girls are always so into astrological signs when I could give two shits. Edie goes on and on about it, boring me straight into a nap every single time she starts talking about compatible signs and who she can and cannot date. Like she actually chooses a guy based on what his sign is.

What a bunch of shit.

"Leos are notoriously obsessed with themselves," Daisy tells me.

I laugh. "Are you implying I'm egotistical?"

"I never said you were." Daisy averts her gaze, and I can literally feel the stress coming off her in waves. She'd rather be anywhere else but here.

Sitting next to me.

Another jab in my ribs from Cadence, her elbow sharp like a weapon and I'm immediately irritated. When I turn toward her, she offers a sweet smile and holds up her phone. "Want to take a selfie with me?"

"No." I turn back to Daisy, who's still staring off into the distance, her shoulders stiff. Like she's afraid she might accidently bump into me. "When's your birthday, Daze?"

"How do you know who I am?" She still won't look at me.

"Our class isn't that big." I shift in my seat, leaning toward her so my shoulder bumps into hers. She moves, her entire body turned away from mine. "Plus, we've been in…competition now for a few years. You do know who I am, right?"

Her gaze lands on mine for the briefest moment before she looks away. "Archibald Lancaster."

JJ laughs again, and I scowl at him, shutting him up with a look.

"Arch," I correct her. "And you never answered my question."

"I did," she protests, meeting my gaze yet again. "I know who you are."

"But you didn't tell me your birthday."

"Oh." She shrugs, seemingly uncomfortable. "It doesn't matter."

"So you don't have a birthday?"

"I'd rather not acknowledge it."

JJ and I glance at each other, both of us intrigued. "Why not?"

Those golden eyes lock onto mine and I swear her lips tremble before she speaks. "Because it's the same day that my mother died."

CHAPTER TWO

DAISY

There. That statement shut Archibald big mouth Lancaster up for about a minute. Even his obnoxious friend John, aka JJ, goes quiet, looking like he might've swallowed his tongue.

No one likes to talk about death, especially people my age. I don't like talking about it either, but I didn't know what else to say to get him to leave me alone.

Hitting him with the truth seemed like a good idea.

"Archie," his girlfriend Cadence whines and he turns to her, ignoring me completely and only then do I exhale, my shoulders slowly falling back into place, instead of being hunched up around my ears.

He makes me uncomfortable. Arch Lancaster. I know he prefers to be called Arch, but it was fun calling him by his full name earlier. Seeing the irritation flare in his icy blue gaze. He enjoyed giving me grief and it was nice to give him a taste of his own medicine.

I remain quiet, relieved when JJ turns and faces forward, leaving me alone as well. I shift to the right, my legs as far away as they can get from Arch's sprawled stance, though I tilt my head in his direction as subtly as possible, trying to spy on his conversation with Cadence.

The perfect, beautiful Cadence who comes from a wealthy family and wears expensive Prada loafers—I only know they're Prada thanks to the prominent triangle label right on top of her shoes—and a full face of makeup every single day. I always wonder what time she gets up in the morning and how long it takes her to get ready.

Way too long, I bet. A full face of makeup for me is mascara and a tinted lip balm, though I've always loved watching *Get Ready with Me* videos when I'm bored, which is often. I don't have a lot of money to spend on cosmetics, so I don't really buy them, though I wish I could. I'd give anything to get all dolled up in a fancy designer dress and go to the city. I follow some of the girls in my class. The exceptionally rich ones who are already living a glamorous, jet-setting life, and the majority of us aren't even eighteen yet.

"…are you still angry at me because of the party?" Cadence asks Arch.

"You chewed me out for two hours," Arch reminds her, the irritation in his deep voice obvious.

He has a nice voice. He also has a nice face.

Too bad he's a complete jerk.

"I was drunk." She makes it sound like that's a forgivable excuse. "So were you."

"Not drunk enough to forget what you said."

They go quiet, their silence tension-filled, despite everyone yelling and carrying on while we wait for Matthews to finally start the assembly.

I'm over it. I want to get on with my day and go to class.

"I didn't mean any of the things I said," Cadence finally says, full of remorse. "I was just feeling mean. You know how I get when I drink."

"You keep making the same complaints about me. About us," he reminds her. "And I can only tolerate hearing it for so long."

"What exactly are you trying to tell me?" Cadence's voice

rises, the tone sharp.

"Assume what you want." He shrugs.

"Are you trying to break up with me?"

I look away, keeping my back to them. Pretending I don't hear what they're saying because wow, she was loud.

"Keep your voice down."

"Just tell me, Archie! Do you want to break up with me?"

Everyone sitting around us hasn't uttered a peep. We're all spying on this conversation and it's so obvious.

"Jesus, Cadence…" A ragged sigh leaves him and I finally glance his way to find Arch is covering his mouth with his hand, his gaze dropped to the floor. Tension rolls off him in palpable waves and I realize that yes.

Yes, he definitely wants to break up with her.

An irritated noise leaves Cadence and she jumps to her feet, glaring down at Arch with narrowed eyes. "You're starting senior year off the wrong way, Arch. It's like you don't even remember how powerful we were together. You're making a mistake, dumping me. No one dumps me."

"What is that, a threat?" He tilts his head back, his gaze colder than usual.

"I'm merely speaking the truth. You'll regret breaking up with me. I'm going to make your life hell." She starts walking, pushing past Arch, stepping directly on my new loafer, squishing it with her Pradas and making me wince.

She doesn't care. Doesn't bother apologizing either. Cadence pushes past the rest of the students sitting in the row and makes her way out of the auditorium.

"Miss Calhoun, where do you think you're go—" Matthews' question is cut off by the loud clang of a slamming door, irritation making his eyebrows rise. His gaze zeroes in on Arch. "Are you behind this?"

"Of course not," Arch retorts, his voice loud enough that it carries across the auditorium.

Matthews stares at him.

Arch stares back, his expression one of pure boredom.

"All right then," Matthews finally says, leaning into the microphone on the podium, his voice booming. "Good morning and welcome to Lancaster Prep!"

The headmaster's voice turns into nothing but background noise when Arch glances over at me, our gazes meeting, the slow, sly smile curling his lips stealing my breath. My heart starts beating faster just from the way he's looking at me.

As if we share a secret.

I can only stare at him in return, feeling caught. Ensnared in his charming trap. Arch Lancaster has never looked at me once in all the years we've gone to school together. And he's definitely never spoken to me before either. But we know *of* each other. Not just because we're seniors and in the same class. Grade point average-wise, he is my nemesis.

My *arch* nemesis, ha ha.

But seriously, he's ranked number one in our class and I'm number two and that just…infuriates me. It doesn't seem fair that someone who is rich and good looking, whose family's name is on all the buildings on campus, also just so happens to be incredibly smart. I work so hard to get good grades and I feel like everything comes easy to him. He doesn't even seem to try. He barely shows up to class. I've had a few with him over the years and he ditches more than he attends.

But he's always there on test day. Pop quiz day. Project turn-in day. He gets his work done, receives a perfect grade and moves on with his life.

I swear the entire system is rigged.

Resentment builds within me, my constant internal struggle, but I squash it down. I refuse to let him make me feel bad about myself.

I also refuse to fall under his spell.

Rolling my eyes, I look away from Arch, focusing on

Matthews, who's boasting about the rigorous academic program at Lancaster Prep and how it's unparalleled. The best in the country, if not one of the top schools in the world. I wonder if someone is recording this to use to promote the school to inquiring parents.

I do consider myself lucky to attend this school. I'm one of the rare scholarship students who goes to Lancaster. They don't have many scholarship students—the school is that elitist and snobby. Why offer a scholarship when there's a waitlist to get in, right? In the end, it's all about the money.

That's life. Dad has told me more than once. *Money makes the world go round.*

I wish it wasn't true, but I know he's right. Spending five days a week with the offspring of extremely wealthy and powerful people will teach you a lesson or ten that has nothing to do with what happens inside the classroom.

Going here is preparing me for real life, I suppose. And how I don't want to spend my time with people who are too self-absorbed to worry about the travesties in this world. The minute I graduate, I'm leaving. I'm waiting to hear back on the application I put in for a summer abroad program in France that starts a week after graduation.

I feel it in my bones I'll get in. I'll be gone all summer. And if I get into college—no ifs, I will definitely get in, I just don't know where yet—then I will barely have to be here before I leave, once again, and start my new life. I'll miss my father, but he wants what's best for me and is encouraging me to go.

I can't wait. I need to get out of here.

Like yesterday.

The moment the assembly is over, I'm out of my chair and ready to get on with the day. See how my classes are. I wait impatiently as everyone files out of our row of seats and I can feel Arch looming behind me. He's tall and broad and I swear when he shifts closer to me, I can smell him. His cologne, which thankfully isn't too overpowering.

No, of course he smells...nice. His scent is subtle yet spicy. He flat out smells expensive.

Just as I'm about to turn into the aisle and make my way out of the building, I feel someone jerk on the end of my braid, hard enough to make me yelp. Whirling around, I see Arch standing there, his hands in his pockets, his expression one of pure innocence.

"Don't touch me," I say, hating how rattled I feel. How rattled I sound.

Ugh this boy.

"Was it true, what you said?" When I frown at him, he continues, "That your mom died on your birthday?"

I stare at him, tempted for the briefest second to tell him the truth.

Yes, she did. She died on my twelfth birthday and it was awful and traumatic and if I could forget the day ever happened, if I could have my mother back for at least one more birthday, I would sacrifice whatever I could to see her smile again. To hear her voice. To feel her arms wrap me up in a hug. Just once.

That's all I want.

Instead, I say nothing. Not like he cares. Not really.

Sighing, I turn my back to him, exiting the auditorium as fast as I can.

It's better this way, I tell myself as I walk across campus and head toward the building where my first class is. Keeping up a conversation with Arch Lancaster will bring me nothing but trouble. He doesn't like me. He looks at me only as academic competition and I feel the same way.

The same exact way.

CHAPTER THREE

ARCH

I stand there like an idiot watching Daisy hurry away from me, walking so fast her blonde braid is practically flapping in the breeze. I didn't mean to pull it so hard but it was like I couldn't help myself. And she didn't look too pleased to find me standing there like a dumbass either. What the hell is this girl's problem anyway? Seems to me she's got a giant stick lodged up her butt.

Once we've exited the auditorium, Cadence reappears, stopping right next to me and curling her arm through mine yet again. I'm already too exhausted to try and shake her off. What's the point? She'll just find yet another way to try and sink her claws into me.

She's pretty good at it—the sinking her claws into me part. In the past, I didn't care. Now though?

What we're doing isn't fun anymore. Not even close.

"Walk me to class?" Her voice is overly bright and I just fucking love how she pretends that moment in the auditorium when she was yelling at me in front of everyone never happened.

And that's what gets to me. I was ready to deal with her—if she apologized. Even an off-hand "sorry" thrown in my direction would've eased the irritation that's grating at my insides like sandpaper.

But I refuse to go through this again. Cadence took up most of my junior year with her antics and I tolerated her because we move in the same social circles so it made sense that we'd gravitate toward each other. She's also hot and always sucked my dick as her way of apologizing.

I'm tired of her, though. My dick is tired of her too.

"No." I work up the energy to slip my arm from hers and pick up my pace. Unfortunately, Cadence is tall with a long stride and walks as fast as I do. "Leave me alone, Cadence."

"You're just mad." She says it in a tone that clearly should be labeled, *silly boy. He'll get over it.*

Well, I won't. Not anymore. I'm not a 'silly boy' as I've heard Cadence reference me many times before. I'm the guy who's put up with her shit for a long time and now I'm over it. Even the promise of free pussy isn't enough to make me ignore her acting like a bitch any longer.

"Cadence." I turn to face her, my expression as serious as I think it's ever been. She watches me expectantly, her eyes still shining bright, and I'm blown away by the delusion I'm witnessing. "It's over. Really."

She frowns, taking a tiny step back. "What do you mean?"

Her voice is so soft, so fuckin' sad, for a second I feel bad. "It's been over between us for a while. We don't work together, and you know it."

"Oh." She sniffs and starts to turn away from me, her back almost to me when I can't stop myself.

"I hope you understand," I tack on, like I'm a sympathetic asshole who feels bad for dumping her in front of everyone on the first day of school.

Cadence whirls back around and lunges toward me, head butting me right in the solar plexus, nearly sending me toppling backward. Girls start screaming. I catch sight of JJ making his way toward us, reaching for Cadence and holding her back while I double over, clutching my stomach.

"You're a piece of shit, Arch Lancaster! I hope you rot in hell forever! You motherfucker!" Cadence is screaming at the top of her lungs, a string of curse words steadily leaving her mouth.

"What exactly is going on here?"

Rising to my full height, I groan when I glance up and see who's standing there glaring at us. Headmaster Matthews.

My luck is for shit today.

"Hey." I straighten my spine, wincing. Cadence's head is harder than I thought. "Everything is fine."

My voice is weak and I'm breathing hard. Matthews sees right through me. Of course, he does.

I would see right through me too.

"The two of you." Matthews points at me and Cadence. "And you." He points at JJ. "Come to my office. Now."

"JJ did nothing," Cadence rushes to say, defending my best friend, which is weird. "He was actually keeping Arch from coming at me."

"What the hell? You're the one who attacked me first!" I'm yelling, my blood pumping, and JJ grabs my arm, trying to get me under control.

"You're all still coming to my office. Let's go." Matthews jerks his thumb, and JJ and I fall into step behind him, Cadence walking alongside Matthews and making small talk.

More like sucking up to him.

"What the hell, dude?" JJ glances over at me, his eyes wide. "Why did she do that?"

"I broke up with her and she didn't like it."

JJ shakes his head, a faint smile curling his lips. I sort of want to sock it off his face but I'm not about to resort to violence in front of Matthews again. I'm in enough trouble and besides, JJ is my best friend. "You know you two will be back together next week."

"Not this time," I say vehemently, shaking my head. "I'm done."

Cadence glances over her shoulder, her expression like stone because I know she heard me.

Good.

Once we're in the administration building, Matthews has Cadence go into his office first, so she can tell her side of the story.

"I'm screwed." I groan, settling into one of the creaky old chairs that are just outside Matthews' office. They're old, extremely uncomfortable and remind me of what jail might be like.

Not that I ever plan on finding out.

"Yeah, you are," JJ readily agrees, settling into the chair beside mine. He leans back and kicks his legs out, crossing them at the ankles. "Looks like we'll be here for a while. You know how Cadence loves the sound of her own voice."

I silently agree, fuming over the entire situation. She just loves that she's fucking everything up for me and on the first day of school at that. I'm so over her games. I'm sure if my parents hear about this, they'll think I got into trouble on purpose, like I want to get kicked out of Lancaster Prep.

Hmm. Not a bad idea, though I don't want it to go down like this.

JJ and I sit there for so long waiting for Cadence to exit Matthews' office that the bell eventually rings, indicating the end of first period. JJ is slumped in his chair with his eyes closed and I envy him being able to fall asleep so easily.

All I can do is sit and think about how everything is screwed up.

Everything.

The admin office door swings open and I glance up, blinking when I realize who's entering the room with a sweet smile on her face.

Daisy Albright.

"Hi Vivian," she singsongs to Matthews' grumpy secretary, who is beaming at Daisy in return.

Beaming. I've never seen the woman smile like that ever. "Daisy. I was so glad to see you're going to be working in the office again this semester."

"You know how much I enjoy it. Plus, I've been wanting to pick your brain." Daisy goes to the empty desk next to Vivian's and drops her backpack on top of it. "I'm having issues with my roses."

"Your dad can't figure out what's going on?"

"I don't want to bother him. He's all wrapped up in the vegetables right now. The tomatoes are frustrating him to no end."

"Your father is going to have enough tomatoes to give every child at this school five each, and the staff too!" Vivian and Daisy laugh like they're old pals.

While I stare at them like they're straight-up crazy.

Pretty sure Daisy can feel my gaze on her because she glances over at me briefly, her gaze skittering away before it comes right back to me, her lips parting. I put on my most menacing smile and she turns her back to me, that braid whipping around when she moves.

I'm intrigued by that damn braid. I'm intrigued with everything about her, though I don't understand why.

But I bet her hair will be all wavy when she eventually undoes the braid. And it's soft. I could tell when I yanked on it.

The impulse to pull her hair came out of nowhere and I went with it, like I'm five and trying to get her attention. Clearly, she's not impressed by me.

Any girl that I'd show even a second of attention toward would be interested. With the exception of this one.

I don't get her.

Matthews' door suddenly opens and I kick JJ in the shins, making him grunt and sit up straight. Cadence appears in the doorway, her head tilted back as she calls to Matthews, "Thank you so much, Headmaster. I appreciate you listening to my side of the story."

I make a retching sound, while JJ starts to laugh. Cadence stops in front of both of us, her hands on her hips, her gaze downright evil.

"I hope you get suspended," she whisper-hisses.

"Please. They won't suspend me." I rise to my feet, standing tall over her. "Besides, you're the one who attacked me first."

"Like they'd believe that. Look at you. You could break me in half." She says the last four words extra loud, bringing Matthews to the door.

"Lancaster. Get in here," he snaps, glaring at me.

Heaving a big sigh, I step over JJ's outstretched legs and head for the headmaster's office, slamming the door behind me. God, I hate this guy's office. It's small and overly-crowded with books and papers and it's a mess. I don't know how he runs the entire school being so damn unorganized.

"Sit down," he says like I'm a fucking dog.

"I'd rather stand." I lift my chin, glaring at him.

He glares at me in return. We go like this for what feels like five minutes but is probably only thirty seconds before his shoulders fall and he settles into the chair behind his desk.

"I spoke with Miss Calhoun and she claims that you attacked her after she told you she doesn't want to date you anymore." Matthews crosses his arms in front of his chest and leans back in his chair, which makes a horrible creaking sound. Is nothing new in this building? "Care to elaborate?"

I start pacing, which is near impossible because there's hardly any space in this closet of a room. "Sir, if I can be frank with you, she's lying."

"Really." Matthews' voice is flat.

"Absolutely. I was trying to break it off with her as nicely as possible when she lost her mind and charged me like a bull. She head-butted me." I come to a stop, curling my hands around the back of my neck, and grip it tightly as I study him. "She almost took me down too. She's stronger than she looks."

"So you didn't try to slap her?"

"Hell no!" When Matthews glares, I clear my throat. "Sorry. No. I didn't try to slap her. I didn't touch her. She's the one who came at me first."

The skeptical look on his face clearly says he doesn't believe me but I forge on.

"Ask JJ. He'll vouch for me."

"He's your best friend."

"So? He's a witness."

"He'll always vouch for you. You and your buddies have some sort of unwritten bro code you always stick to." Matthews drops his arms and scoots forward, the chair squealing in protest. "Regardless of who started it, we do not tolerate violence on this campus."

"Good," I retort. "I assume she'll get in trouble for trying to take me out?"

"You are both participants in the altercation, so you'll both be…in trouble, as you call it."

Groaning, I fall into the chair directly behind me, resting my elbows on my knees and holding my head in my hands. "You've got to be kidding me."

"First day of school and you've caused a ruckus from the moment you entered the auditorium. I can't have you disrupting school-sanctioned functions like this. You're a distraction, Arch, and I'm tired of it. We're all tired of it."

I lift my head. "Who's we?"

"Everyone on this campus. You think you're untouchable because you're a Lancaster and I suppose you're right. But I'm going to put a stop to your deviant behavior once and for all."

I stare at him, shocked at the anger in his voice, the way his mouth is drawn tight. This dude is actually pissed at me. And I don't think it's because of what just happened during the assembly or afterward.

This feels like it's three long years of pent-up anger and

frustration directed right at me. My friends and I have given this guy endless shit since we started here. And he's finally got me where he wants me.

At his mercy.

"Tell me my punishment then." I sit up straight, my expression stoic. "I can take it."

I mean, come on.

How bad can it be?

Matthews turns to his computer and starts tapping away on the keyboard, his dark brows drawn together in utter concentration as he reads whatever is on the screen. "Your open period is now."

"Right." I actually had two open periods in my schedule, but they forced me to take a study hall to fill one of them. Considering it's in the library and that old battle ax librarian Miss Taylor loves me, I'll just need to check in with her before I slide out the side door and go about the rest of my afternoon.

"You can work here then." He glances up, his gaze meeting mine. "In the office."

I frown. "You sure you want me around you regularly like that?"

Sounds like a nightmare. Locked up in this musty old building and doing whatever his secretary demands I do five days a week?

Awful.

Matthews appears to be actually considering what I just said. I know exactly how to drive him crazy and I would do my best to make his life miserable for approximately fifty minutes Monday through Friday.

"You already have someone working in here during this period anyway," I point out. "Daisy Albright."

Matthews' face actually lights up. "That's right. Sweet girl. She might be a good role model for you. You could learn a thing or two from her."

I snort. "Please. Little Miss Sunshine is full of shit."

She has to be.

Matthews scowls. "Watch your mouth."

"Come on." I roll my eyes. "No one can be that sweet all the time."

"You're going to find out if it's true or not." Matthews smiles, and I swear it's the evilest I've ever seen him look. "You're on office duty for second period for the entire year. Welcome to the admin building."

CHAPTER FOUR

DAISY

I lean in as if I'm conspiring with Vivian, murmuring, "What did he do?"

"You mean Archibald?" Vivian rolls her eyes and I muffle a giggle with my fingers. I'm guessing she gets a thrill out of calling him by his full name too. "What does that child not do to aggravate the headmaster on a daily basis?"

"But it's only the first day of school." Arch's reputation is known around campus. He's the troublemaker. The reckless one. The impulsive one. He gets caught in stupid stunts all the time and it's a wonder he hasn't broken a bone or done some sort of permanent damage to himself by now.

He may be intelligent, but he can act stupid with the best of them too.

"Oh, he started it off in typical Archibald style." Vivian rises from her chair and bustles around her desk, heading for the counter so she can lean over it and talk to JJ. "What exactly happened with your best friend, John?"

JJ turns to look at Vivian, his expression incredulous. "First, no one ever calls me John but you."

"It's your name," she states, her voice flat.

Vivian doesn't always have the best sense of humor, but I

don't think she's as mean as everyone says.

He blows out a breath. "And second, nothing happened."

"Nothing?" Vivian's brows shoot up.

JJ nods, his expression solemn. "That's my story and I'm sticking to it."

Vivian sends me a look and I shrug. JJ's gaze slides to mine and he smiles. "Oh hey, jail bait."

Vivian's gaze narrows. "What did you just call her, young man?"

"It's fine." I plop my butt on top of the empty desk that all of the office aides sit at and swing my feet. I'd give anything to get out of this itchy skirt and it's only second period. The jacket is hot too. So hot, I shrug out of it, dropping it on top of the desk. "JJ and I go way back."

JJ grins. "Yeah, we do."

Vivian glances over at me. "How far back?"

"All the way to about an hour ago, in the auditorium. That's his little nickname for me." I smile sweetly, still swinging my feet, silently daring him to call me jail bait again.

Vivian watches him as if she fully expects him to say it too.

"You're ballsier than I thought," JJ finally says, and I swear there's a touch of respect in his tone. "You can hold your own, Albright."

The door suddenly swings open and Arch appears, his hair seeming to stand on end and his tie hanging crookedly from around his neck. His biceps strain against the white cotton of his button down and he stops when he sees me, his expression downright murderous.

No one says a word. Not JJ, not Vivian and not even Arch. Eventually, an exasperated breath leaves him and he tilts his head, JJ jumping to his feet, and the two of them silently flee the office, the door slamming behind them.

"Did Arch actually leave?" Headmaster Matthews calls from his office.

"Yes, sir, he certainly did, along with JJ," Vivian says with relish. I'm sure she'd love for both of them to get in trouble.

Matthews appears in his office doorway, his expression even when he says, "It's fine. JJ can go. He'll only defend his best friend anyway, so it's not like he'll tell me anything new."

JJ didn't mention anything to us either, so I'm thinking Headmaster Matthews is right.

"Daisy, go follow them and grab Arch for me, will you?" Matthews smiles at me. "I need you to bring him back here."

I gape at him, my swinging legs coming to a stop. "You want me to go get him?"

"He'll now be helping out in the office during second period, and I'll need you to teach him what to do." Matthews inclines his head toward the door. "Go on."

"But—" I pause, swallowing hard. "I'm the only office aide for second period."

"And now we have two. Hurry and go chase him down before he disappears." I can tell by the tone of his voice, Matthews isn't going to back down.

I'm going to have to go find Arch and bring him back here.

With reluctant steps I exit the admin building and walk outside, wincing from the intensity of the sun and how my new loafers rub against the back of my ankles. There isn't anyone else outside except for two tall shapes moving across the campus at a pretty good clip, headed toward the parking lot.

Arch and JJ.

I launch into a jog, wincing when my loafers pinch my feet but I push through. I'm grateful I dumped the jacket because it's so hot outside that I can feel sweat dampening my shirt and the back of my neck.

"Hey," I call when I draw closer to them, though my voice is weak and they don't hear me. "Hey!"

JJ glances over his shoulder, nudging Arch in his side as he says something.

Arch doesn't even bother turning around.

"You guys!" I pick up the pace, ignoring the way my loafers rub against the back of my ankles. "Stop!"

They actually listen to me this time and turn around, matching bored expressions on their faces as they watch me approach. I come to a stop directly in front of them, trying to hide the fact that I'm panting, but they can tell.

"Out of shape much?" JJ asks. He's an excellent lacrosse player and probably doesn't know what it feels like to be winded.

"I just—it's hot." I smile, brushing wayward strands of hair out of my eyes. I put my hair into a braid to keep it out of the way and it's all falling out regardless. "Matthews asked that you come back to the office, Arch."

"He did, huh?" Arch shoves his hands in his trousers, contemplating me, that bored expression still on his handsome face. With the haphazard hair and partially undone tie, he's giving disheveled chic, and I have to admit, he looks great. Which is infuriating. "You can tell him I'm not going to be his second period office aide. He's already got you."

"Trust me, I really don't want you to be the office aide either," I retort, absolutely hating the idea of being in close proximity of Arch Lancaster five days a week. Besides, I'm sure a Lancaster would never want to be a lowly office aide.

The boys share a look, Arch's lips curling into a faint smile before he returns his attention to me. "You don't like me, do you?"

"Not particularly." The words fly out of my mouth with no warning, and for a second, I wish I could take them back. I'm not outwardly mean. That's not my style.

"Love your honesty, because the feeling is mutual." His smile is sweet despite his venomous words, and I can only stare at him in shock.

No one has ever told me to my face that they don't like me. I don't have a lot of friends here and part of that is my own fault, considering I prefer to keep to myself. People who work at Lancaster Prep adore me thanks to my father. I've lived on this campus for years, and many of the teachers and staff have witnessed me growing up. They feel connected to me, and I feel the same way about them. Like we're one big happy family.

But my fellow students? They don't think about me much at all. I don't fit in, no matter how hard I try. I can't ski in Gstaad over winter break and I don't summer in the Hamptons or travel all over Europe. I've been nowhere because we don't have a lot of money. I went to New York City a couple of times as a kid with my parents to see a Broadway show, but after Mom died, Dad didn't have much time for Broadway. Or trips.

He prefers to stay here on campus. Where it's quiet and peaceful and he can putter around in his garden or in his workshop.

"Y-you really don't like me?" I ask Arch, still in shock.

To hear someone—the most popular boy on campus—say that to my face is…

Painful.

"No. I don't. You think you're better than everyone else. And you're too quiet, like you're full of secrets. What are you hiding, anyway? Because you're definitely hiding something. Right, JJ?"

JJ seems uncomfortable, keeping his gaze cast downward on his feet. "Yeah, right," he grumbles.

Secrets? I'm not interesting enough to keep any secrets. What is he talking about?

"Plus, you keep gunning for the number one position like we're in actual competition with each other," Arch explains, his intense gaze locked on me. "Get comfortable being number two, Albright. There's no way I'm giving up the top spot. My GPA is solid."

I wasn't even sure he was aware that I was right behind him, GPA-wise. He rarely acknowledges me, not that I need his attention. I'd rather fly under the radar.

And I fully planned on trying to surpass his GPA this

semester. I took two college credit courses over the summer and everything is advanced this and advanced that. My only relaxing period is in the office and I'm not about to let him disturb my peace. "Isn't that the whole point? That we're in competition with each other, trying to do better?"

He makes a scoffing noise. "You're *not* competition. You're just that try-hard girl who thinks she's better than me."

Anger fills my blood and I take a step back, trying to calm my breathing. "More like you think you're better than me."

"Guess what?" His brows shoot up. "I am."

Seriously? Did he really just say that?

"You're a monster." My words are a knee-jerk reaction and I immediately wish I called him something stronger.

Something worse.

Arch actually grins. "You're right. Don't ever forget it."

"Oh, trust me. I won't." I lift my chin. "I'll let Matthews know you refused to come back to the building with me."

With those final words, I turn on my heel and head back toward the administration building, my anger growing with every step I take. How dare he describe me like I'm some annoying gnat that irritates him every time I come around. Like I don't even matter to him. As if I'm somehow...subhuman.

How dare he dismiss me with a few words and a sneer on his lips. Who the heck does he think he is?

Well, I know who he is. And so does everyone else on this campus. He's a Lancaster.

Meaning he's untouchable.

I'm almost to the building when I feel someone whoosh past and suddenly Arch is right in front of me, a placating smile on his handsome face. I come to a stop and I'm tempted for the briefest moment to stomp my foot on top of his.

But I don't. Instead, I say in the most demanding voice I can muster, "Move."

Arch rears his head back, as if he's startled by what I said and this...pleases me.

I hate that I've stooped to his level but he gave me no choice. And now he's smiling at me like we're best friends and this conversation we're having is completely normal when it so isn't.

"Hey, we don't need to keep up this war between us." He shifts out of my way, keeping pace as I head for the double doors that lead into the admin building. "Let's present a united front to Matthews. What do you think?"

I come to a halt directly in front of the doors, whirling around to face him. "I think you should take that united front and— shove it up your ass."

He laughs as I push my way through the double doors, but I keep my back to him and my head held high.

I rarely curse. I don't say rude things to people and I'm not confrontational. Truthfully, I'm shocked I came up with all of that but wow.

It definitely felt...

Good.

CHAPTER FIVE

DAISY

No matter how hard I try, I can't get over what Arch said to me. How he's intent on remaining ranked number one in our class, and how he doesn't consider me competition. It irked me, how dismissive he was. He didn't take me seriously, not that I expected him to, but I figured he would at least be...I don't know. Polite?

The fact that he practically laughed in my face is what goaded me into action.

After our run-in, I poured over the class schedule, looking for those classes that weighed even heavier than usual, that would give me more points toward my GPA. By Tuesday morning, I was in my guidance counselor's office, going over everything with Mrs. Peebles and explaining to her my intention without ever mentioning Arch Lancaster's name once.

I'd like to forget all about him, though I know that's impossible. He's the only reason I'm doing this. Pushing myself harder, determined to prove to him that I'm a viable threat. That I actually am competition.

"Are you sure you want to take advanced physics?" Mrs. Peebles peers over her readers, her gaze meeting mine. "That's a tough course."

"Are you saying you don't think I'm capable?" I sound a little more hostile than I mean to and I soften my words with a faint smile. "I'm just striving to be my very best for my senior year."

"I know, Daisy. But you've been on a pretty intense track since your freshman year. I thought you structured it that way to ease up a little now, so you can relax during your last year in high school," Mrs. Peebles reminds me.

"I've changed my mind." I sit up straighter, determination filling me. "I want to do this."

"And advanced statistics?" Her eyebrows shoot almost comically high. "Adding those two classes equals what I would consider a very tough school year."

"I can do it," I say with all the confidence I don't necessarily feel. I am really faking it this morning. "I want to do it."

Mrs. Peebles watches me for a moment, her gaze softening just before she pushes her glasses up the slope of her nose. "Be honest with me, Daisy. Are you trying to outdo a certain someone in your class?"

My cheeks go hot at her question. She knows I've struggled to outdo Arch Lancaster since midway through our sophomore year. I was the one originally on top—until he took over the number one spot. "I want to beat him."

"His schedule is just as intense as this."

I feel like she just gave me enemy information and I lean closer to her desk, eager for more. "Is he taking the same classes?"

"Not quite." She smiles, clasping her hands together and resting them on top of her desk. "I think this will work for you, Daisy. I just want to make sure this is what you actually want to do."

"I do."

"And what does your father say about this change?"

I didn't even mention it to Dad yet. He'd probably try and convince me not to do it, knowing him. He encourages me to be an overachiever but he's also a big believer in remembering our limits. I think my mother's untimely death made him cautious about a few things, including being a workaholic. He thinks I have that issue. Schoolwork consumes me all the time and he doesn't love it.

If I told him I wanted to make my schedule even harder, he probably wouldn't approve. That's why I haven't said anything to him.

"He thinks it's a good idea," I lie smoothly, surprised at myself.

Ever since that conversation with Arch, I've been doing things out of the norm. Not that I'm pleased about it.

Mrs. Peebles finalizes a few things on the computer before she prints out my new schedule and hands it to me. "If the classes start to overwhelm you, let me know, okay? We can make a few more changes if necessary. I don't want you getting in over your head."

"Thank you." I take the schedule from her, wondering if she gave Arch the same warning.

Probably not. She most likely believes he's capable of such a tough class load and has zero doubts. Where I'm looked at as weaker.

Or maybe I'm projecting my own insecurities on this poor woman. I'm not sure.

I escape the building seconds later, headed for my first class, which hasn't changed. It's advanced English, and he's in that class.

Arch.

The moment I walk in, it's like he knows it, his head lifting, his gaze meeting mine. I glare at him, clutching my new schedule between my fingers and he actually smiles, reminding me of a shark. Not that sharks smile, but oh my God, he looks like he'd derive great pleasure from sinking his teeth into my flesh and shaking my helpless body back and forth in the water until all the life drains out of me...

Taking a deep breath, I tear my gaze away from Arch's and head into the classroom, plopping into the desk that's front and center. Where I normally sit in any class.

Every class.

When I try to unzip my backpack, I realize I'm shaking. Trembling. My overactive imagination has sent me spiraling and I exhale as steadily as possible, closing my eyes for the briefest moment. Desperate to calm my frazzled nerves.

"Meditating?"

That now familiar deep voice curls around me and I crack my eyes open to find Arch standing in front of my desk, watching me with an amused look on his handsome face, his hands shoved in his pockets, as casual as ever.

"Go away," I mutter like I'm five.

He frowns. "I wanted to talk to you."

"I have nothing to say to you." I rest my hands on top of my desk and curl my fingers together, wishing he'd just go away.

"I don't want you to say anything to me. I want you to listen." Arch watches me for a moment and it's impossible to tear my gaze from his. I hate how he looks at me. As if he can see right through me and knows what's hidden beneath. I've never felt like I have deep, dark secrets I'm keeping from those who surround me, but when it comes to this boy?

He makes me feel like I'm a puzzle he's dying to figure out. And I don't like it.

"You're so rude," I murmur, the words he said finally sinking in. What, he wants to yell at me? Berate me for whatever reason? It's like he gets off on talking down to me and I'm not going to tolerate it.

"Mr. Lancaster." We both swivel our heads to see our English teacher Mr. Winston enter the classroom. "Please tell me you're going to sit in the front alongside Miss Albright."

From the expression on Arch's face, I think that's the last thing he wants to do. "I prefer learning from the back of the classroom, Winston."

Our teacher walks over to his desk and settles his book bag

onto the empty desk chair. "Somehow, I knew you'd say that."

Arch sends me a look I can't decipher before he turns away and heads to his desk, leaving me alone. I should feel relieved. I should talk to Mr. Winston, who's one of my favorites. He replaced the last guy—who got busted for having an inappropriate relationship with a student—and he's a great teacher. I think it helps that he's young. He's only like twenty-three or twenty-four and I think it makes him more relatable.

The bell rings and Mr. Winston immediately starts talking, pacing the front of the classroom like he always does, becoming quickly impassioned while speaking on the subject of romance in literature. It's literally my favorite topic, and I try my best to focus on the words our teacher is saying and how excited he is about it.

But all I can feel is a certain someone's eyes on me. Watching me. Making the hairs on the back of my neck stand on end. I don't dare to look back, too afraid to see the judgment in his eyes.

The amusement.

By the time we're in second period and I'm sitting in the office while Arch is late doing whatever it is he does when he's off screwing around, I'm positively fuming. Vivian leaves me alone as if she knows I'm mad, and while I feel bad that my mood is permeating the entire office, I also sort of don't care.

I'm not normally a moody person, but there's something about Arch Lancaster that gets under my skin. Only when he focuses on me and opens his mouth though. Yes, he was an irritant before but nothing too bad. I could forget about him fairly easily.

Now though? He's infuriating. After our initial conversation the first day of school, it's like I've become a target for him. I hate it.

I don't like him. At all.

When Arch walks in ten minutes after the bell with a smile on his face, he's actually whistling.

Whistling.

I can't take it.

"You're late," I bite out the moment the door shuts behind him.

He comes to a stop, leaning against the door, contemplating me with a sly gleam in his eyes that makes me uncomfortable. "And you care why?"

"I care," Vivian pipes up, her voice stern.

He barely looks in her direction. "You going to tell Matthews?"

Vivian lifts her chin. "Of course, I am."

"Let him know I had to take a call." He strolls deeper into the office, heading right toward me. I'm sitting at the desk all office aides use, and there's only one chair. "Move out of my seat, Albright."

Vivian sucks in a sharp breath at his rude demand, while I spin the chair around to face him, glaring up at him defiantly. "Make me."

He doesn't slow his approach, only stopping when his feet are practically on top of mine, his eyes blazing with anger. At least there's some emotion there. Usually, his eyes are either blank or full of contemptuous amusement. Like the world is a joke and we're all here to entertain him.

God, I really can't stand this boy. I'm the nice girl. The person who smiles at everyone, even though most of the students on this campus barely acknowledge me.

I don't understand why I care what others think about me, or why I waste my time, but here I am, nearing my breaking point, ready to unleash all over Arch Lancaster.

"You really want to mess with me right now?" His voice is low. I'm not even sure if Vivian could make out what he said and she's only standing a few feet away from us, but I can definitely hear the threat in his tone. See the venom in his eyes.

The phone rings and Vivian rushes to answer it, leaving Arch and me to talk freely.

"I thought I didn't matter to you." I arch a brow. "You don't consider me a threat, remember?"

"I don't consider you at all," he drawls as his gaze sweeps over me, lingering.

Making me squirm.

I jump to my feet, irritated with myself and my reaction. Startling him since I moved so fast and he doesn't have the time to step away from me. We're so close, I can feel his body heat, smell his scent and I mentally brace myself.

Again, I can't help but think he smells...good. And I hate it.

"For someone who claims he doesn't think about me, I suddenly catch you staring at me all the time," I taunt.

Arch makes a dismissive noise. "Please. You wish I was staring at you. You're just pissed I never considered you in the first place."

"You're rude."

"And you're a pick-me girl," he throws back at me.

I go silent, confused. "What do you mean?"

"Oh, come on. You've never heard that phrase before? You're the type of girl who always acts like, 'pick me, pick me.' You're dying for someone to pay attention to you, to talk to you, hell, even to *look* at you. Because no one notices you, Daze. You walk around campus with your sunshiny attitude and your stupid braid." He literally flicks it off my shoulder with his fingers. "But no one really *sees* you."

My chin is wobbling and my eyes are misty, but I refuse to cry. I absolutely refuse. There is no way I'm going to fall apart and let him see me in a weak moment. I'm the one who started this fight.

I need to finish it.

He leans in closer, his mouth at my ear, his breath hot on my skin when he speaks. "But I see you. I see exactly what you are. A little nobody who doesn't matter. A lost little girl with severe mommy issues."

I don't even remember it happening. It's as if I blink and suddenly my palm is stinging and there's a red mark on Arch's cheek in the shape of a hand. A stunned expression on his face.

I slapped him.

CHAPTER SIX

DAISY

"Are you serious? You're going to *suspend* me?" I'm crying. More like sobbing. Clutching a gob of crumpled, damp tissues in my fist, the endless tears streaming down my face.

"You give me no choice, Daisy." The pained expression on Matthews' face is little consolation to the turbulent emotions currently swirling inside me. "School policy is that a student cannot put hands on another student." I start to protest, but Matthews is one step ahead of me. "It doesn't matter what he said. Words are one thing. Physical violence is another."

What Arch said was the most hurtful thing someone could've *ever* said to me, and I'm sure he knows it. That's why he said it. He knew it would get to me.

Mommy issues. He doesn't even know my story, but he knows enough to hurl those two words at me and stab me right in the heart.

He's a prick. A dick. An asshole.

All words I don't normally like to use, but he deserves to be called them. Every single one of them.

"Why didn't he get suspended for what happened between him and Cadence?" I ask, feeling defiant.

Matthews' eyebrows shoot up, as if he's surprised that I would question him. "I investigated that matter further and it turns out Mr. Lancaster didn't touch Miss Calhoun."

"She head-butted him." I'd heard the stories whispered around campus and regret I didn't actually get to see it.

"And she's been properly punished, just like Mr. Lancaster has. This matter between the two of you is completely different." His expression turns the slightest bit pleading. "You leave me no choice, Daisy. You *slapped* Arch. Right in front of Vivian. She saw the entire incident. I have to suspend you."

Sitting up straight, I try my best to keep my composure as I whisper, "For how long?"

"Two days."

Two entire days. "And will this go on my school record?"

He nods, remaining quiet. Looking helpless.

I crumple, the fresh tears coming, and I bury my face in my hands. The headmaster lets me cry it out, tapping away on his keyboard, and I wonder where Arch is.

Probably laughing at this very moment while my life has been ruined.

"Will he get in trouble?"

"Who?" When I lift my head and glare at him, Matthews clears his throat. "You mean Arch Lancaster."

I nod, steeling myself for his answer.

"He'll be written up and given a week of detention."

"That's it?" I'm incredulous.

"It's standard for his behavior."

"He's a menace." I leap to my feet, suddenly too irritated to sit still. Not like I can pace around Matthews' cramped and crowded office. There are books and things everywhere. "He needs to be stopped."

"Slapping him in the face isn't the way to stop him."

I pause, staring at the headmaster, whose hands are probably tied because the boy I slapped just so happens to be part of the family that owns the school. The boy who comes from immense wealth, while I'm the girl with the dad who is the school groundskeeper, and to the Lancasters, we're nothing but lowly servants who work for them.

"When does my suspension begin?" I lift my chin, desperate to be brave.

"Right now. You can come back to class first thing Thursday."

Without a word, I grab my backpack and sling it over my shoulder, turning my back to Matthews and heading for the door.

"You're going to be okay, Daisy," he calls after me, his tone soft and I suppose reassuring. "This suspension won't hurt your record. Not too badly. You'll still get into a good college."

If he really cared, he wouldn't suspend me at all. He'd fight for me.

Without a word, I exit Matthews' office and find that no one is around. Not even Vivian and thank God, not Arch either. I make my way out of the admin office and walk down the hall, keeping my head down, grateful it's empty.

I can't believe this is happening to me.

The moment I'm outside, I burst into a run, heading for the cottage on the outskirts of campus I share with my father, knowing I should probably seek him out first and let him know what happened.

But I'm sure Matthews will tell him. I doubt I'll get punished by my father for what I did, but I hate the thought of disappointing him. Because he will be disappointed.

I can guarantee that.

By the time I'm in my tiny bedroom and shedding my uniform, I'm crying again. Mad at myself for losing control. Madder still that Arch can get away with pretty much anything, while I'm over here suffering. Dealing with the aftermath.

There's no point in working hard and trying to get a better grade point average compared to him. He's got me beat.

At least he doesn't have a suspension on his record.

...

"Ah, Daisy."

I glance up from where I'm lying on the couch, my dad standing in the open doorway. I must've dozed off or else I would've prepared better for him returning home from work.

I can see it in his weather-worn face and his tired eyes. He knows what happened and his disappointment in me is written all over him.

"I'm sorry." I sit up, tears prick the corners of my eyes, and I'm so sick of crying.

The tears come anyway, streaming down my face.

He slowly shuts the door and makes his way into the living room, settling on the edge of his recliner, so he can study me. "Want to tell me what happened?"

Taking a deep breath, I launch into my story, trying not to leave too many details out. He wants to know the truth and I will give it to him.

Dad winces when I mention the mommy issues' statement. "How did that boy know about your mother?"

I was dumb enough to tell him, I want to say, but instead, I shrug. "I might've mentioned it once."

"You actually talk to Arch Lancaster?" There's shock and awe in his voice, like I'm referring to a celebrity.

"Only recently." Another shrug. I'm uncomfortable talking about him with my father, that's for sure.

"Mmm hmm." That simple sound is full of doubt. "I would recommend…staying away from that boy."

"Why?" I know my father is overprotective of me, but he doesn't tell me to stay away from anyone. He's always encouraging me to try and make friends but for whatever reason, no one wants to get close to me.

Well. I know the reason. I'm not on their level financially.

"He's trouble. Wild. Reckless." Dad shakes his head. "He's done some things on campus that I've looked the other way about, but no longer. It shouldn't matter what his last name is. That boy is a terror."

I almost smile, remembering how I told Matthews that Arch was a menace. "You don't need to fight my battles for me, Daddy. What happened, happened. I shouldn't have slapped him."

"He's cruel."

"And I should've told him so. I didn't need to hit him. Resorting to violence isn't the answer," I say, hating the shame that rushes over me.

My father studies me, his gaze kind, despite the hint of disappointment I see there too. He just wants what's best for me. We're all each other has, and I know he wants me to continue pursuing my education and become someone he can be proud of. That's all I want too.

Slapping a boy and getting suspended isn't the path to success. I need to remember myself around Arch Lancaster, and not give into my impulses. Impulses I didn't even know I had until I actually spoke to this boy.

"Have you gone outside and tended to your roses? They looked a little thirsty last I checked," Dad says, gratefully changing the subject.

We had a few rose bushes in our backyard that were originally planted by my mother, whose name was Rose. A couple of years ago, I got into helping my father maintain the rose garden on campus. One, because they remind me of my mom, and two, because I actually enjoy taking care of them. There's something so rewarding about watching a rose grow and bloom into something so beautiful, and so fragrant. Dad even planted a row of roses just for me next to his garden and they're my own little project.

A project I might have to neglect here and there, thanks to my school load. Soon fall will be fully upon us and the cold weather will sweep in. With that, the bushes will go dormant for the most part until spring.

But right now? The branches are still heavy with blooms as they usually are late into summer, and I should probably go clip them.

"Might help take your mind off your troubles," Dad adds, like he knows I needed to hear that.

A sigh leaving me, I rise from the couch and go to my father, bending over and dropping a kiss on his cheek. "Thank you, Dad."

"For what?"

"For not being mad at me."

"I think you're mad enough at yourself already, sweetie." His smile is gentle and I rush out of there before I do something silly.

Like burst into tears again.

Once I'm outside, the heat hits me like a furnace. The temperature has been extra high lately and it's awful. Thankfully, I'm in a pair of cotton shorts and a tank top, my hair still in a now messy braid, bright pink slides on my feet. I grab my bucket and clippers and wander over to the rose bushes, smiling when I see the deep red blooms wave in the gentle breeze.

My dad was right, I think as I concentrate on clipping off the dying roses, dropping them into the empty bucket. This was just what I needed to clear my head. Being outside—despite the heat—taking care of the roses my father planted just for me. The flowers that make me feel close to my mom. I have homework waiting for me, but I've got plenty of time to work on it. Besides, I needed this. My ugly thoughts are slowly leaving me with every breath I take.

I'm so into my little clip and toss rhythm, I don't even notice someone approaching until I hear a voice.

His voice.

"Hey."

I lift my head, tightly clutching the clippers in my fingers when I see who it is.

Arch.

He shouldn't get too close. I might want to lunge toward him like Cadence did, but I have the advantage. A weapon in my hand.

"What do you want?" My voice is as cold as I've ever heard it. I could tell Arch he's on our property but that would be a lie. We don't own this patch of land within the Lancaster Prep campus.

Arch's family does.

He stares at me for a moment, quiet for once in his life and I realize that he looks…distraught.

Oh please. I must be reading him wrong.

"I tried to get Matthews to relax on your suspension but he wouldn't listen to me," Arch says.

"I slapped you. I deserved to be suspended," I say flatly, repeating what Matthews told me. I know what the headmaster said is true, but it still hurts.

A lot.

"I provoked you." Arch shakes his head. "I went too far."

Notice how he doesn't apologize. "I think that's a trend."

He frowns. "What do you mean?"

I don't like that he's here in my territory. Being in his presence leaves me uneasy and I don't understand why. It's not just anger either. There's a weird tension that grows between us any time we're close to each other and I don't get it. Maybe he's just my enemy and my body recognizes when he's near. I don't know.

"From what my dad just told me, you're pretty reckless. You don't think before you speak," I explain.

His smile is faint and I hate how my heart seems to trip over itself when I see it. He shouldn't affect me. Not like that. "That's been a constant issue for me since I started here. Pretty much my entire life, actually."

"Well, now your issue has become mine and I've been suspended for two days, so thanks for ruining my life." I offer him a sugary sweet smile and resume my task, grabbing at a perfectly good rose and clipping the stem with extra force, realizing my mistake too late. This is what I get for being too dramatic.

Guess I'll take that one inside and put it in a vase with some water and enjoy it before it dies.

I know people love to fill their homes with real flowers and enjoy receiving them as gifts, but I prefer my roses to stay in the ground and live for as long as possible. Where they show off their beauty and put a smile on my face every time I go outside.

I'd probably be sad if a boy brought me flowers, though I'd try my best to never let him know. But those flowers?

They're only going to die anyway. And I don't like it when things die.

Or people.

"I didn't mean for that to happen," Arch says, his voice soft.

"Right. Mean things just come out of your mouth without warning. Noted." I nod, turning my back to him and concentrating as hard as possible on the rose bush in front of me. The roses are this peachy-orange color that were my mother's favorite color. She said it was sunshiny and bright, like me.

More tears threaten and I muster all the strength I've got to fight them off. I refuse to cry in front of Arch. And he's still there. I can feel him standing on the edge of the garden, watching me. Probably wondering why I'm not reacting to what he says. He deserves to be kneed in the balls.

"Why do you hate me so much?" he asks, genuine confusion in his voice. When I look at his face, I see the confusion in his gaze too. He doesn't get it.

He probably never will.

"Oh, I don't know. Maybe because all you have to do is exist and everything is handed to you? I bet you've never had to work for a single thing in your life. You say awful things and you don't even get in trouble for it. I'm the one who's being punished." For slapping him, but after what he said and what I've been through, I think my reaction was justified. "You're not a nice person, Arch. Not even close."

"Everyone loves me—"

I interrupt him. "Everyone is scared to cross you. Or they're kissing up to you to stay on your good side. Big difference." I glare at him for a moment and all he can do is stare back, his eyes wide. Like I just shocked him with the truth.

Good. Maybe he needed to hear it.

Ignoring him, I return my attention to the roses, my hair streaming across my face when the breeze kicks up. I bat it away, the bucket dropping from my hand and landing on its side, all of the old, dead roses rolling out, their petals scattering everywhere.

"I'm going to talk to Matthews again," Arch finally says, raising his voice to be heard above the wind, which kicks up another notch. The pine trees that surround our cottage sway, creating a white noise that I love to listen to when I'm trying to fall asleep and I keep my bedroom window open. "Be prepared to come back to class tomorrow, Daze."

My skin prickles with awareness at hearing him call me that. I don't like the nickname. Makes it seem like we're friends when we are absolutely nothing like that.

I know one thing for certain.

Arch Lancaster and I will never be friends.

CHAPTER SEVEN

ARCH

I'm waiting outside of Matthews' office first thing Wednesday morning, ready to plead Daisy's case again. I pushed her too far and I know it, and damn if she didn't get to me yesterday afternoon, clipping roses in her dad's garden and looking pitiful as fuck. Her face was pale and her eyes were swollen, like she'd been crying nonstop since second period, which she probably had.

Seeing her like that made me feel bad—and renewed my intentions. I refuse to let this girl remain suspended for another day. I basically asked for that slap. I provoked her into violence and I'm more than willing to own it. Couldn't even tell anyone why I did that. Something about her sets me on fire, and not always in a good way. It's annoying, how she doesn't seem to like me. And then what do I do?

Push her limits and make her hate me even more.

God, I'm stupid sometimes.

But ultimately, I'm a fucking Lancaster and I know I can convince Matthews to revoke the suspension or whatever he has to do to get it off her record. He adores Daisy. Thinks the sun rises and sets on her pretty blonde head. He doesn't want his favorite student to be among the degenerates of the school, which she sort of is right now.

Kind of hot, I cannot lie. The girl definitely has spirit inside her. She had no qualms slapping me yesterday morning. No hesitation either. One second, she's staring at me in disbelief and the next, her hand is cracking across my cheek, making it throb.

The moment Matthews enters the admin building and sees me standing outside his closed office door, he comes to a stop, his shoulders sagging as he tilts his head back for a moment before he zeros that gaze of his directly on me.

"What are you doing here?"

He knows what I'm doing here. I don't know why I have to bother explaining.

"Daisy Albright," I answer, shoving my hands in my pockets.

I went full blown Lancaster Prep today, wearing every piece of my uniform. Even the goddamn jacket. I wanted to look like the perfect little student in the hopes it would convince Matthews I mean business.

"You can't change what happened." He strides toward me, walking past me to unlock his office door. "Only a few days into the school year and look at the chaos you've already caused."

"I want to make it right," I tell him as I follow Matthews into his cramped office.

He completely ignores me, turning on the lights and dropping his battered leather book bag on top of a pile of file folders. Hasn't the man heard of digital filing? Storage? iClouds?

"There's nothing you can do to change the situation," Matthews says once he's settled into his creaky old chair. "She has one more day of suspension and then she'll be back at school tomorrow. It's fine. She's going to be fine."

I feel responsible for her getting in trouble. I should've never said she had mommy issues. I pushed and pushed until she broke and after seeing her yesterday, I realized she's not just broke, she's broken.

Maybe she's always been broken. I don't know. Deep down, I feel like shit for it. I've done her wrong and I need to fix this.

And I never want to fix shit.

When I remain in front of his desk deathly quiet, Matthews finally sighs, leaning back in his chair as he watches me. "You're not going to give up, are you?"

I shake my head. "No."

"Why do you want to help her anyway?"

"It wasn't her fault, what happened."

"She's the one who slapped you."

"I said something shitty to her to make her react like that," I say.

Matthews' brows shoot up. "What exactly did you say?"

I shake my head, my lips pressed together. I'm not telling him because hearing me admit it out loud will make me feel even shittier.

A sigh leaves Matthews. "Are you willing to take on her punishment?"

Icy tendrils of shock slide down my spine, but I remain as stiff as a board as I murmur, "Maybe."

Or maybe not. Fuck, what will that do to me? I'm already in detention. Newsflash—it sucks. Taking a mandatory day off of school because I got "suspended"? My parents, specifically my father, might want to kill me, but what's really going to happen in the long run?

Absolutely nothing. If I want to go to college, my dad will just buy my entry anyway. Via paying for a new dorm building or whatever. It'll be no problem.

While Daisy is over here toiling away, trying to earn good grades so she can get into a good school and become a good little tax-contributing citizen for the rest of her life. She'll work a boring job and marry a boring man and have a couple of boring kids.

Sounds real fucking great.

So why the hell do I care? Why do I want to help her?

The look on her face when I said she had mommy issues

haunts me. The shock in her gaze, the pain. I hurt her with two carelessly said words and I can't take them back.

I may be reckless and impulsive, but I never want to intentionally hurt someone. And that's what I did to Daisy.

What I keep doing to her.

"How about this. I'll suspend *you* for two days and scratch Daisy's suspension off of her record. Not like the suspension will hurt you," Matthews mutters.

It's like he read my mind. I need to make it up to her so I automatically say, "I'll do it."

"Why?"

I blink at him. "Excuse me?"

"Why are you willing to take on her punishment? You're not what I would call a martyr, Arch. You're probably one of the most selfish Lancasters I've run into, and trust me, I've dealt with a lot of you," Matthews says vehemently. "Not a single one of them has taken on someone else's punishment as their own."

"Like I said, I made her do it," I admit. "I goaded her into slapping me."

"You goad everyone into doing what they do when they're around you. You do realize this, right? You need to learn how to control yourself." Matthews leans forward and reaches for his desk phone, picking up the receiver and punching a few numbers on the keypad before it starts ringing. "Hey, Ralph. Will you let Daisy know she can come to school today? Yeah, I know I had to suspend her, but there was some, ah, confusion regarding the situation."

He goes quiet and I can hear the school groundskeeper, otherwise known as Daisy's father, berating Matthews for making such a huge mix up. The headmaster glares at me as he takes his verbal beating, finally able to speak after a few minutes.

"I apologize for any misunderstanding. Have Daisy come to my office as soon as she can and then we'll let her go on to first period. Yes, I'll be waiting. I apologize again. Thank you." He hangs up the phone, his gaze finding mine once more. "You owe me, Lancaster."

I stand up straighter. "I know."

"The dad is angry, as he has every right to be. Did you hear him? Daisy cried buckets yesterday after what happened."

"I know." Seeing her yesterday, her pale face and bloodshot eyes, told me as much. I felt like absolute shit after what she said to me. How people don't really like me, implying that they all just kiss my ass because they're afraid to cross me. She's full of shit. I have friends. I run this fucking school. "I owed her this for what I said."

I can't believe those words just left me, but damn, it's true.

"I'm suspending you for five days." I'm about to complain, but he holds up his index finger, silencing me. "Even worse, I'm going to make you go to school anyway. I'm just marking on your permanent record that you have a five-day suspension. That's what you're going to do as payback for whatever it was you said to her. What you do to everyone. Stop torturing people, Lancaster. Especially sweet, harmless girls who are good students and who've done nothing wrong. Daisy's only mistake is somehow getting in your crosshairs."

I school my features into complete neutrality, not about to show him even a bit of emotion.

His words are like a punch to the gut. What I do to *everyone?* I don't torture people.

Well. Maybe I tortured Daisy. But we're even now.

She tortures me all the damn time, though she's completely unaware of it.

I exit the admin office minutes later, running into JJ in the senior hallway where our lockers are. He flicks his chin as he makes his way toward me, his lazy swagger enough to make me want to roll my eyes, but I keep my expression straight. Serious.

"What's up?" is how JJ greets me, reaching for the lock on his locker, twirling it open.

"Nothing much. Same ol' shit, different day." I open my locker and stare inside, not shocked whatsoever to find it empty. All of my books are back in my room.

God, my teachers must hate me.

"Saw Cadence last night," JJ drops as nonchalantly as can be as we start walking down the hall.

"So?" I can't even work up enough emotion to care. I know they don't get along, but I'm sensing Cadence might've put JJ up to say this to me. Unlucky for her, I don't give a damn what she's doing or who she's doing it with.

"We were chilling in the common room at our dorm hall. If you hung out with us normies every once in a while, you'd get to see her too." JJ grins.

"I don't want to see her. That's the issue. Next time I run into her, I'll go running and screaming in the opposite direction." I laugh, but there's no humor in the sound so I immediately stop.

"Ouch, harsh." JJ rubs at his chest, as if my words were a direct hit on his heart and not Cadence.

"You know what I mean. When I said I was ending things, I meant it. She's nothing but trouble, and now she wants me back? Forget her." I slow my steps as we draw closer to my English class, surprised when I see the familiar blonde head walking down the hall from the opposite direction, her long hair pulled back into that ever-present braid. It's neater this morning, not a hair out of place, and I sort of want to mess it up.

"Well, I talked to her for a while last night, and she's really upset, A. I don't know why, but she misses your mean ass and wanted me to tell you that," JJ says, getting to the crux of the conversation.

Thinking of Cadence supposedly suffering over our breakup makes me feel nothing at all. That's a serious indicator that I'm completely over her. "Tell Cadence I don't miss her."

JJ rears back. "I can't say that to her face."

I send him a look. "I know. But you should anyway. See ya."

Leaving JJ where he stands, I dash into English right at the same time Daisy enters the room. I'm directly behind her and she has to know it, but she doesn't look back. Doesn't say hi or say my name, or offer me a thank you or anything.

That kind of…what? Hurts?

Nah. Nothing hurts me. I'm impenetrable.

I watch her settle into her usual desk right at the front of the room, dropping her backpack at her feet. She shrugs out of her jacket, the front of her button-down straining across her chest and my gaze drops there, staring for a second too long at her tits. I wonder what they look like without the shirt on. Without a bra on. This leads me to wonder what she looks like completely naked.

I bet she looks pretty fucking great.

She glances over at me, doing a double take when she realizes I'm standing there staring at her like a dumbass, people entering the classroom and pushing their way past me as I somewhat block their entry. Her lips form into a slight frown, her brows drawing together and she looks away, focusing on unloading her backpack of everything she needs for class.

Like I have no control over myself, I go to her. Settle into the desk behind her, dropping my backpack at my feet as well. Extra close to hers, so I have no choice but to bend over and practically invade her space as I unzip the top and blindly pull out a notebook.

I have no idea if that notebook is for English, but I'm running with it for now.

"What are you doing?" Her tone is soft, yet vaguely hostile, and when I chance a glance at her face, I see the pain in her gaze. The wariness.

She should be wary of me. According to her and Matthews, I'm a piece of shit that gets a tiny thrill out of torturing her and everyone else at this school.

"Getting ready for class," I tell her, wondering if Matthews mentioned the reason why she's back in school a day early. Did he tell her that I'm the one who's taking the punishment now? Does she know that her suspension is off her school record?

Probably not. I bet money Matthews made it seem like he's the hero and he bailed her out.

Such shit.

"You don't sit here," she points out.

"It's a free country. I can sit wherever I want. And I don't think Winston's gonna protest." I say his name extra loud because he just entered the classroom, and by the pleased smile I see on his face, I can tell he agrees.

"If Arch Lancaster is choosing to sit at the front of the class, I can't complain," Winston says as he makes his way to his desk. "What's brought you closer?"

"I'm enraptured with your scintillating lectures," I tell him, laying it on thick.

I can practically hear the aggravated noise that leaves Daisy. A few other people in class laugh too.

"I appreciate it. Don't think they've ever been called scintillating but if you're this enthusiastic and we're only starting the semester, I know I'm on the right track." Winston grins before he ambles over to his desk.

Daisy turns in her seat the moment he's gone, her narrowed gaze only for me. "What, now you're the suck-up?"

"He loves it." I shrug. "He's a good guy."

"I really like him," she admits softly.

A surge of emotion fills me, something I don't recognize, and I sit with it for a moment, wondering what the fuck.

Am I...jealous? Of her saying she really likes Mr. Winston?

No. Impossible.

CHAPTER EIGHT

DAISY

I still don't know what happened to make Headmaster Matthews call my father a few days ago and let me know that my suspension was up early, but I didn't question his decision and Matthews never offered any more information about it either. It's almost as if he was trying to pretend the entire moment never happened in the first place, which is weird.

But I'm never one to push so I went about my business, relieved it was over.

Except for the slightly confrontational moment in English that first morning I returned to class, I haven't really spoken to Arch again. Oh, I notice him all the time because now that we've had actual interactions, he's hard to unsee. Plus, he's in practically every single one of my classes, save for a couple. Once lunch hits and we have the two remaining periods afterward, I don't see him for the rest of the day.

I would never admit this out loud, but I sort of miss him paying attention to me.

I know, I know. It makes no sense. I can't stand him. He's so entitled and arrogant and mean. What he said to me, how he got me suspended…I swear in English that morning when I came back, he was trying to tell me something, but he couldn't come up with the right words to say it. The imploring looks and sitting extra close to me wasn't enough to get his point across. We don't know each other that well, and it's not like I can read his mind.

Though it's probably better this way, him leaving me alone. That's what I tell myself. He hangs out with a very privileged crowd, and I've noticed that Cadence has inserted herself back into it. Not that she ever really left, but they did break up.

I've seen the two of them in the hallway walking side by side every morning for the past week. Cadence's gaze is adoring as she chats him up, while he just stares straight ahead, the stony look on his face making me wonder if he's even listening to her.

I couldn't stand that. He acts like he can barely tolerate Cadence and she's perfectly fine with it? That's not a relationship. That's not love.

Though what do I know about romantic love? Not like I can judge. I've had a few minor crushes over the years but nothing serious. I had a boy ask me to the winter formal my freshman year and I got all ready for the dance in a dress that cost my dad a lot, only for the boy to cancel at the last minute because he got sick. He was even hospitalized for a short time, he was so ill.

Some things are just…not meant to happen.

I enter the dining hall with apprehension because I hate it in there. But I'm in the mood for something healthy and the salad bar here is pretty great. Besides, I didn't bring anything from home to eat. So here I am, clutching a tray in my hands and going down the line at the salad bar, putting together my lunch and praying no one mean looks at me or says anything rude.

And when I refer to someone mean, I'm talking about Arch or any of his friends. Mainly JJ. Though he's relatively harmless. Truly so is Arch, at least lately. He doesn't utter a word to me when we're in the admin office together during second period. Vivian won't let him. She puts him straight to work, usually enclosing him in an unused office that's about the size of a closet, where she makes him staple papers together into packets. I'm sure he hates it.

I'm just glad I don't have to do it. Instead, I monitor the phones while Vivian and I talk about gardening. She's always got a few tips to offer.

God, I'm turning into an old lady. Could my life be any more boring?

It is a relief not to have him around in the office though. His mere presence unsettles me. When he walks into the admin building every morning—and he's always late, it's like he does it on purpose—it's as if he sucks all the oxygen out of the space. Leaving me breathless and extremely aware of him. Everything about him. He's so handsome I can barely look him in the eye, and he's so tall and broad and muscular. His jawline and his eyes and basically his entire face—

It's a problem. For me, it's a monumental problem. I've never reacted to anyone like this before and the fact that it's Arch Lancaster who makes me feel this way? I don't like it.

At all.

"God, the tomatoes are so ugly, they look like they've been punched in the face," the girl standing behind me in line mutters.

I glance over at her at the same time she looks at me and she smiles. My heart drops when I recognize her.

Edie Lancaster. Arch's little sister.

"I don't really like tomatoes," I manage to say, my voice so soft she probably didn't hear me over the noise that fills the dining hall every day at lunch.

"I do, but only if they're fresh off the vine." Edie wrinkles her nose. "Those look straight out of a can."

I can't help but laugh. "None of the vegetables in the salad bar are canned."

"How do you know?" She doesn't say it as a challenge. She sounds genuinely curious.

"My dad works here." Heat creeps up my neck and into my cheeks.

"Oh, so you're Daisy. I should've known." Her smile remains friendly, as does her tone, but I don't know.

I don't like how she said that.

"Why should you have known?" I'm wary, my hand shaky as I reach out and grab the tongs to dump a pile of red onion on top of my salad.

"The earrings are a dead giveaway," Edie says.

My wariness melts at her referring to my tiny daisy earrings and I offer her a smile. "My mom gave them to me."

"They're cute. Your mom has good taste."

I don't correct her by saying had. There's no need to let Edie know my mom is gone. I've already made that mistake with her brother and he totally used it against me.

We make small talk as we work our way down the bar, and once we're done, I'm about to go my own way when Edie says, "Where are you sitting?"

"Oh." I clear my throat, shocked she'd ask. Doesn't she have a pile of friends she can sit with? Maybe she hangs out with her brother's friends. That current group is a mixed bag of grades. "I usually sit over there."

I incline my head toward the small tables that only have two chairs.

"Do you mind if I join you? Or do you already sit with someone? It's cool if you do. I just thought I'd ask." Edie's smile is small and if you look a little more closely, it's also fragile.

Like she's afraid I'm going to reject her.

"You can join me," I offer, shocked by the blinding smile she flashes in my direction.

We go and sit at one of the tiny tables and I watch as Edie grabs her fork the moment we're in our seats, diving right into her salad. I follow her lead, suddenly ravenous, and for a few minutes, we're silent as we eat. The loud crunch of my chewing the only thing I can focus on.

"You know my brother," is what Edie finally says to restart

our conversation.

I practically choke on a cucumber at her statement and immediately reach for my water tumbler, taking a long sip from the thick plastic straw to get the rest of the cucumber down before I can speak. "I know *of* him." I pause. "Everyone does."

"True." Edie tilts her head, her examining gaze making me want to squirm. She has the same eyes as Arch, though hers are a little darker. A lot friendlier. "You're the girl he got suspended for."

Surprise fills me. "He didn't get suspended."

Edie is nodding before I can finish my sentence. "Yes, he did. Well, part of his suspension is he still had to go to class, which is just the ultimate punishment for Arch. He hates it here."

"Why?" The word pops out of my mouth like I have no control, but what she said is so shocking. "He's a Lancaster. He should be having the time of his life."

"He's bored. Too smart for his own good." Edie ducks her head, staring at her salad for a moment before she lifts her gaze to mine once more. "Your dad is Ralph, right?"

I nod.

"I have a question."

I wait, apprehension filling me.

"When is he going to hook the kitchen up with those juicy tomatoes growing in his garden, huh?"

I'm laughing. And I'm also having a realization. She's known exactly who I was since the moment she stood behind me in line at the salad bar.

"I don't know," I tell her truthfully. "But he's good friends with Kathy who works in the kitchen, so I'm sure he'll provide them with tomatoes soon enough."

Edie is grinning. "Good."

We eat in silence once more, curiosity gnawing at my insides until I can't take it anymore.

"Can I ask you a question?"

"Sure." She waits expectantly.

"What exactly were you talking about, Arch being suspended because of me? And that he still had to go to class?"

"He confessed all at our most recent family luncheon." Edie shrugs one shoulder, seemingly uncomfortable. "I guess Matthews let our father know what happened and Arch got drilled about it."

"Matthews let your father know what?"

"That Arch said something rude to you and you two got into an…altercation, I believe is the word he used to describe it. And that Arch was suspended."

I'm gaping at her, her words on repeat in my mind. "I was the one who was suspended."

Her eyes go wide with shock. "No way. What did you do?"

I squirm in my seat, not wanting to admit what happened. Is she drilling me for information? Is she going to take what I say and somehow use it against me? I don't know her. I shouldn't trust her.

"I slapped him in the face."

Yet here I am, making my confession like she's my closest friend.

Edie's eyes go even wider. "You slapped him?"

I nod.

"You look like the type of person who wouldn't harm a fly."

Something keeps me from admitting what he said. How far he pushed me. Instead, I offer up a shrug, just like she did only moments ago. "Arch deserved it."

"I'm sure he did," Edie murmurs, her gaze lighting up with an unfamiliar gleam. "Impressive."

Is that respect I see glowing in her eyes? For slapping her brother?

Yes, I think it is.

"Is that why you approached me in the salad bar line?" I brace myself, ready to be hurt by her words. Worse, ready for her to leave me and I'll go back to eating lunch alone.

Like usual.

"Because of your brother?" I continue when she still hasn't responded.

"I was curious to talk to the quiet girl who got my brother suspended," she admits. "And now that I have, I must admit, I'm surprised."

"Surprised by what?"

"You. You're not what I expected."

"I'm still confused over how he got suspended when I'm the one who hit him."

"Sounds like that's something you need to take up with Matthews," Edie suggests.

"I should." I'll talk to him tomorrow morning, during second period. I need to know what happened.

I deserve to know.

"Edie, what the hell are you doing?"

We both jerk our heads up to find Arch standing beside our table, the anger on his face unmistakable.

"Oh, mind your business, Arch." Edie flicks her fingers in a dismissive gesture. "Go back to Cadence."

Hearing her name said out loud to Arch makes my stomach ache for some weird reason.

"Fuck off, Edith." Arch turns to me, unleashing his furious gaze in my direction. I remain rigid in my seat, desperate not to cave. "You get nowhere with me so you thought you'd hang out with my sister instead?"

His words are offensive, no surprise. "She approached me first."

"Right." He snorts, his disbelief obvious. "Next thing I know you'll be hanging out with my friend group and going out with JJ."

I wrinkle my nose. Edie bursts out laughing.

"Gross. JJ is disgusting. She would never stoop so low," Edie says.

"You don't know her that well," Arch says, never taking his gaze off me. "JJ might be more her style. And he's always enjoyed slumming."

Edie makes a disgusted noise while I leap to my feet like I have no control over myself, thrusting my face in his. Which is difficult because he's so much taller than me.

"You're an asshole," I murmur between clenched teeth, hating how my heart is in freefall at his nearness. At the unmistakable anger blazing in his beautiful blue eyes.

Why does he provoke me all the time? And why do I enjoy arguing with him?

"So you keep telling me," he returns, sounding pleased. "I know just how to get under your skin, don't I, Daze? Guess it doesn't take much to trip up the school's golden girl."

My breaths come heavier and my mouth grows dry, making it difficult to speak.

"What, no fighting words? I figured after the slap you'd learn how to defend yourself better, at least verbally." He steps even closer, his body nudging into mine and a rush of tingles sweeps over my skin at the contact.

I back away, unsettled. Shaky. "I hate you."

His grin could belong on Satan's face. "Good. I don't like you either. Stay away from me. And my family."

I glance over at Edie, who's mouthing the words, *I'm sorry*, her eyes full of sadness. She bends her arm and jabs her elbow into her brother's side, but he doesn't even flinch.

He's heartless. Cold. Unstoppable. And when he's got his sights set on me?

I'm meaningless.

Nothing.

Holding back the sob that wants to escape, I turn around.

And run out of the dining hall. Never once looking back.

Too afraid to see the devil laughing as I run away from him.

CHAPTER NINE

ARCH

I'm such an asshole, I disgust myself.

Yesterday in the dining hall, I became infuriated seeing my sister with Daisy. Why the hell is she invading every part of my life? My thoughts, my dreams, practically every fucking class, she's right there. Blonde and quiet and always watching me with those big golden eyes. I tell myself I can't stand her.

Yet I can't stop thinking about her.

And I don't understand why.

It felt good, being mean to her. Pushing her away. The moment she ran, Edie turned on me, giving me endless shit about what a classless human being I am.

I said nothing. Didn't protest, didn't argue with her description. Every word she said was true. I'm a mean piece of shit who deserves every bit of grief Cadence gives me—a direct quote from my little sister.

Fucking Cadence. She's another problem, one I can't shake. Constantly following me around and inserting herself where she's not wanted, just like Daisy but worse.

So much worse.

Couldn't sleep for shit last night, the confrontation with Daisy running on repeat in my head. How I crushed her spirit all over again with a few choice words. How good it felt for a brief moment, watching the pain flit across her face. She tortures me so it's only fair I give her some torture back, is what I tell myself.

Petty. Shitty. Immature. That's me.

I gave up on trying to sleep and decided to go for an early morning run instead. It's something I find myself doing more and more lately. Helps clear my mind, leaving it blessedly blank and not thinking about anything but the pounding of my feet on the ground. The steady pace of my breaths. The amped up speed of my heart.

And when I stop, it all comes flooding back. How Cadence won't leave me the hell alone. The way Matthews sneers at me every time I so much as glance in his direction. How his mean secretary makes me staple endless packets of bullshit every day during second period, locking me away in a stifling office the size of a cardboard box while I can hear her and Daisy laughing at their desks.

Fuck, the sound of Daisy's laughter. It's light and pretty and... perfect. It lightens my heart and eases my morose thoughts, even when I'm stuck in that office doing mindless work and mentally cursing Matthews for putting me through this torture.

The sweet torture of Daisy's laughter and not being able to see her when it happens? That's even worse.

I scrub a hand over my face, my steps faltering. I almost trip over my own feet and I come to a stop, breathing heavily as I rest my hands on my hips, quickly realizing that I'm not too far from the garden Daisy's father keeps.

Those damn rose bushes sit in a line on the other side of the garden, the branches still heavy with blooms. I stare at them, idly wondering which color is Daisy's favorite.

I'd go with the yellow roses, but that's too obvious. The red ones are beautiful. Deep in color and giving me blood vibes, which means I'm demented and sick and I need to think about sunshine and sweet things, not death.

Maybe it's the orange roses. I didn't even know they could be that color, but there they are, waving at me on their branches when a gentle breeze sweeps through, ruffling my hair. Drying the sweat that coats my skin.

I hear the sound of hinges creaking, the slam of a door, and within seconds, there's someone walking toward the rose bushes, a giant floppy hat covering her head, the handle of a bucket clutched in her hand.

Fucking Daisy.

Like a perv, I sneak behind a nearby hedge, peeking around it so I can spy on her. There's no one around. The entire campus is eerily silent and I slip my phone out of my pocket to check the time.

It's not even seven yet.

I return my gaze to Daisy, watching as she moves down the row of rose bushes, a pair of clippers in her hand as she snips off the dying buds. She never cuts off the newly-bloomed flowers and I wonder why. My mother always has the gardener bring in fresh flowers that she would arrange in vases throughout our house in the Hamptons during the summer.

Daisy leaves them to grow, though I can tell she likes them. She bends over one of the deep red ones, breathing deep and inhaling the scent, a shocked sound leaving her when she backs away with a breathless laugh.

A bee flies out of the flower, buzzing away and Daisy pushes the hat out of the way so it falls to rest against her back, holding on by a string around her neck. She tilts her face toward the sky, closing her eyes and something tugs at my heart. At the way she enjoys the early morning light bathing her face. How she's completely alone and absorbing the beautiful morning, while I stand behind a shrub like a goddamn stalker watching her.

Turning, I walk away, disgusted with myself. With the choices I've made and the attitude I have. I should change. I should be better.

But I don't want to. This is who I am.

Whether I like it or not.

. . .

"Who reads during lunch?"

JJ makes this observation in his usual sardonic tone, but no one else is paying attention to him. I guess except for me.

"What are you talking about?" I ask because I know he wants me to. Truly, I don't give a damn.

We're in the dining hall for lunch, sitting at our usual table, surrounded by others from our social circle, including a few girls, such as Cadence. She's sitting on the opposite end of the table though so at least she's not trying to catch my attention or worse, touching me. I don't know how many times I have to blatantly ignore her or tell her to her face that I'm not interested—she doesn't get the hint.

Her persistence is almost admirable.

"That one. Over there." JJ inclines his head in the direction he wants me to look and I almost groan out loud when I see who he's talking about.

Daisy sitting alone at a table, her face buried in a book. The cover is illustrated with what looks like a couple wrapped up in each other in a tight hug, and though it's colorful and bright, that is definitely not a children's book.

At least she's not sitting with my sister.

"Wait a minute. That's jail bait." JJ laughs and I glare.

I don't like him calling her that. Inferring that he might be interested in her sexually—he needs to take his diseased dick and keep it far, far away from Daisy.

"Oh God. He's talking about Daisy Albright." This comes from Cadence, who was eavesdropping on our conversation. Typical. "She's so annoying."

"She's so *nice*," Mya adds. She's Cadence's best friend and I can tolerate her a little more than Cadence. Barely. "No one is that nice."

She's not, is what I want to say, but that would be a lie. The only time she's mean is when she's dealing with an absolute asshole who's pushed her to her limits and that would be me so...yeah.

"Isn't her dad Ralph?" JJ grins. "I love that dude."

Cadence wrinkles her nose. "His hands are always so dirty."

"He's the fucking groundskeeper," JJ says, tearing his gaze away from Daisy. "Of course, his hands are dirty."

"Like under his nails, there's constant dirt." The grimace on Cadence's face isn't attractive. Matches her ugly soul, though outwardly, she's a complete knockout. I can't deny it. Naked, she looks pretty good too but shit. She's not worth the headache she gives me. "It's gross."

"He has a garden," I say in Ralph's defense.

They all look at me with blank expressions on their faces, like they can't grasp the concept.

"What? I'm serious. He has a garden out back, behind my building. He's growing vegetables. Has a few fruit trees and flowers. Rose bushes." I shrug, hating how closely they look at me. Like they're surprised I'm talking about gardens and shit, but I've always noticed the garden. It's so large, it's difficult to ignore. I can stare at it out my room window whenever I want.

Lancaster children don't stay in the dorms on campus, which gives us a little more freedom, though not much. We have our own suites where we get to live during the school year. Where we can come and go as we please—to a point. "He's always out there puttering around. Planting shit. Digging up shit," I continue to explain, realizing I need to shut the hell up so I can be done with this conversation.

Cadence giggles. "I hope you're not being literal."

Mya joins in, the two of them laughing, though it dies when

they both finally notice the scowl on my face. "God, you're so moody lately," she mumbles.

She's not wrong.

"I don't mind," Cadence says brightly and that's it.

I'm done.

Pushing my chair back, I rise to my feet. "I'm out of here."

JJ stares almost lovingly at his tray full of food before he glances up at me. "You want to leave now?"

"You can stay," I tell him, my gaze seeking out Daisy despite my negative feelings toward her.

No one has joined her for lunch. Not my sister and not anyone else. Does she really not have any friends? While we've gone to school together the last three years, I've never really paid attention.

Now it's like she's all I can think about and I hate it.

Hate. It.

She seems perfectly content alone though. Her gaze is fixed on the book, her delicate brows drawn together in concentration. The tray in front of her has a plate on it with a sad looking sandwich and an apple. She's got one of those giant pastel-colored—a turquoise shade, big surprise—steel water tumblers sitting to her right. Either she's on trend or she truly likes to stay hydrated because that cup is huge.

"You sure, bro?" JJ asks.

"Yeah." My gaze never strays from Daisy as I grab my backpack and sling the strap over my shoulder. "I'll see you after school."

I'm gone before he can say anything, Cadence shouting goodbye at me as I walk away from the table. I don't turn back and acknowledge her—what's the point? I'm too intent on something else anyway.

Someone else.

It's weird how Daisy has become a constant presence in my life. I mean she's my academic rival so of course I was always aware of her. And I've always thought she was hot, though I don't discuss her with anyone.

Not even JJ.

Who's part of Daisy's group? Who does she hang out with? I really hope her only friend isn't Vivian, Matthews' secretary. Talk about pathetic...

Daisy is definitely a loner.

Drawing closer to her table, I stare at the back of her blonde head, the way the ends of her hair curl perfectly. The ponytail is a sweet touch.

Maybe even cuter than the braid.

I'm close enough to smell her when she tilts her head to the side, her ponytail sliding over her shoulder as she reaches behind her and grips the back of her neck with her left hand. I note the way her fingers press into her flesh, as if she's massaging herself, and I hear a sweet sigh come from her.

That sigh settles in my dick, making it twitch.

What the hell?

She must sense I'm behind her because she glances to her right, her gaze landing on me, recognition dawning in her eyes. The friendly look on her face disappears like magic. "What do you want?"

"Ease up, Grumpy." I do the chin nod thing, playing it cool. Hating how riotous my pulse turns at her nearness. "Whatcha reading?"

Her cheeks color and she slams the book shut so it's lying face down on the table. "Nothing."

"Must be good if you'd rather read than hang with your... friends at lunch."

Her expression remains impassive. Hard to read. "I don't have a lot of friends."

The words hit me right in the chest, stunning me silent because what do you say to something like that?

She shoves the book in her backpack and reaches for the

sandwich, bringing it to her mouth so she can take a bite. I watch her, transfixed as she chews and swallows, then grabs her tumbler cup and takes a sip, her perfect lips wrapped around the straw tight.

Jesus. I need to get away from her. She's making me feel things I'm not used to.

"Are you just going to stare or do you want something?" she asks once she's let go of the straw.

"I should go." I don't budge.

Her lips curl in a tiny smile that's full of relief. Like she can't wait to get rid of me. "See you later then."

Realizing I need to leave, I turn on my heel and exit the dining hall without another word, frustrated.

Confused.

Why did I even bother talking to her yet again? She's not my type. I'm not interested in charity cases. Sweet girls who would put way too much faith in me when all I'd do in the end is disappoint them.

Fuck that.

CHAPTER TEN

DAISY

My entire body relaxes only after Arch Lancaster walks away. I reach for my travel cup with shaky fingers and take another fortifying sip of icy cold water, frowning down at the plain sandwich I've barely eaten. It wasn't that good.

I grab the apple instead of the sandwich, sinking my teeth into it, savoring the satisfying crunch when I bite into the fruit. I keep eating, glancing around at the full tables, everyone seeming to sit with their backs to me. I'm at a table in the middle of the dining hall, yet not a single person talks to me, or even approaches me. No one ever really looks at me.

Except for Arch. Oh and his sister.

This is all so new, and I'm not sure if I like it. Have I become so accustomed to being invisible to everyone that it now feels strange having someone—especially a Lancaster someone—notice me?

Yes. I think so.

I'm comfortable in my invisible existence. I know what I look like to the people who attend this school. I've even heard it murmured here and there over the years. It's no secret, how they all feel about me.

I'm beneath them. I think I make them uncomfortable

whenever I come around, and while at first it hurt, I've slowly grown used to it.

Grabbing my book, I try to resume reading but all I can think about is Arch sneaking up on me. Catching me reading it. Oh God, maybe he read a few snippets over my shoulder. That would be embarrassing. The cover is relatively harmless—more like it's downright cute—but the contents inside are pretty spicy.

After I give up on trying to read, I quickly polish off the apple and gather my things, tossing my trash in the bin before I leave the dining hall. No one pays attention as I exit. Not a single person makes eye contact with me or says hello or calls out my name and yet again I feel like a ghost.

Once I'm outside, I spot Arch sitting at a picnic bench under a massive tree, a boy sitting next to him. They're both handsome, but my gaze is stuck on Arch.

He doesn't see me, too busy chatting with his friend—I don't recognize him and it's definitely not JJ. They're talking animatedly, their combined laughter lingering in the air and I almost smile at the sound.

Reminding myself I can't smile about anything in regards to Arch Lancaster, I keep walking with my head down, going the long way to my next class so I don't have to walk directly by him. Doing whatever I can to avoid another interaction with him.

Gee, how mature of me.

I clutch both shoulder straps extra tight as I enter the building and make my way toward my class, the nylon fabric straps cutting into my hands. The hallway is mostly vacant since the bell hasn't rung yet, and I'm grateful for the quiet.

When I reach my classroom I test the handle, finding the door is unlocked. I enter the room, thrilled it's blessedly empty. I settle into my desk and crack open my book, excited to get back to the story now that no one is around.

I may enjoy the classics and there are some quality YA books and series out there that I've devoured, but there's nothing like a thrilling romance that gets my blood pumping. Not that I would ever say that out loud. Dad knows I read romances but he doesn't know exactly what the content is like inside the book. Because the books I like to read, while also swoony and romantic, they're also very, very...

Sexy.

Within minutes, I'm digging in my backpack again, pulling out my favorite teal blue pen and coordinating sticky tabs that match the cover of the book. I've totally gotten into annotating books lately, highlighting or underlining my favorite parts. My favorite lines.

The main male character in this book says the best things.

I read over the last few pages I consumed while in the dining hall, drawing lines beneath the sentences. Adding a few small hearts around his name. I get so lost in annotating and rereading my favorite parts, I don't realize the classroom is starting to fill up until a few minutes before the bell rings.

Taking a deep breath, I gently shut my book, putting away the tabs and my pen. Our statistics teacher enters the room, walking right past my desk since I sit in the first row and she smiles at me.

"I read that book over the summer." She inclines her head toward the very book sitting on my desk. "It's a good one."

My cheeks feel as if they turned twenty shades of pink and I grab it, shoving it into the open slot of the desk that none of us really ever use. "Oh yeah?"

Mrs. Nelson smiles. I will say this—the staff always acknowledges me but that's probably only because I'm a good student who never causes any problems and does well. "Yes. Kind of sexy though."

Now my face is turning various shades of red, I swear.

Mrs. Nelson laughs. "Don't worry. Your secret is safe with me."

...

After school is finished, I head back home to find my father is already in the garden, which is surprising since he's usually still on the clock at this time of day. He's among the rows of vegetables, kneeling in the dirt and plucking the ripe tomatoes, carefully setting them in a basket that's already full.

I immediately think of Edie and how she wants my dad's tomatoes in the salad bar. Should I mention it to him?

"Daisy Mae," he calls when he sees me, a big grin on his face.

I smile, remembering how only a few years ago, I thought my first and middle name made me sound like a country bumpkin. Now I like it. Only because it brings my father so much joy to call me by both names. "Hi, Dad."

"How was school?" he asks as I deposit my backpack on the potting bench, careful not to set it in the soil that's spilled all over the surface.

"It was good." I wander over to my rose bushes, smiling at them like I can't help myself. Their fragrance tickles my nose and I lean over one perfect, deep red rose, breathing in its scent. Savoring it because this won't last much longer.

A sigh leaves me and I grab my pruning shears and bucket like I usually do and resume clipping off some of the old, dying roses, dropping them in the bucket. "Soon the roses won't bloom anymore."

"And we'll have to cut back the bushes to get them ready for next spring." Dad's voice never wavers. Always cheerful, always positive, when he's got plenty to be sad about.

I stand amongst the row of rose bushes, taking in their beauty. I helped him plant them when I was ten, alongside my mother, who chattered happily the entire time, telling me how roses made her think of her great-grandmother, who died before I was born.

Swallowing past the sudden lump in my throat, I try to shove the memory from my brain. Back when we all lived on campus together. Our own little family. Dad was the groundskeeper and Mom worked in the dining hall and I was the little girl who would help out in the late afternoon anywhere I was needed.

"I hate the winter," I say, my voice soft, my mood shifting as it often does when I get caught up in thoughts of the past. My mother's face looms in my memory, so much like mine. I don't know how my father can stand looking at me sometimes. The older I get, the more I resemble her, and that can't be easy for him.

"It's needed," Dad says, rising to his feet, clutching the basket handle as he starts to make his way toward me. A tomato falls out, rolling onto the dirt, and he shakes his head, not bothering to pick it up. "I'm going to take these to the dining hall. Kathy was asking me about them."

"Really? I was just talking to someone who wanted to know when your tomatoes would end up on the salad bar."

"Who was it?"

Should I tell him it was a Lancaster? He might run to the kitchen right now and make sure the tomatoes make their appearance first thing tomorrow just to please Edie.

Arch though? More like he'd throw tomatoes at him, aiming at his handsome face.

Or he might want to please Kathy. I think he likes her. She works in the kitchen, just like Mom did and she seems nice enough. She's around my father's age and she's divorced. Though I don't know her that well, my father acts like he's more than a little enamored with her.

Which is...odd. I can't lie. It's weird to think of my father with someone else that's not my mother.

"Edie Lancaster," I finally admit.

"You friends with the sister now?" His brows shoot up and I can see the concern swirling in his gaze.

"We talked for a little bit. It was no big deal." I shrug, trying to play it off. I didn't see her at all today. I'm sure it was a one-off moment. Like I'm an animal in a cage at the zoo and she wanted to check me out to see what all the fuss was about.

Guess she wasn't impressed.

"Well, Kathy likes the fresh veggies and we've got more than we could ever eat so I'm going to give her a bunch. I'll be back." He starts to walk away and I watch him go.

"Will you be back by dinner?" I call out to him.

He turns, shading his eyes from the sun with his hand. "Go ahead and eat at the dining hall tonight, or make yourself something at home. I have some work to catch up on."

Disappointment fills me but I wave at him before he turns and heads toward the center of campus. I'd sort of wished we could eat together tonight. I was craving some of his cooking or at the very least, would've cooked something for both of us myself, but I guess he's working.

More like he's spending extra time with Kathy.

Once I've finished trimming the rose bushes, I go to my backpack, eager to grab my book and sit in the sun at the café table Dad set up a few years ago just for me. I like to read there, especially in the late afternoon, though it's still kind of hot.

As I rifle through my backpack though, dread settles in my stomach, slowly spreading until it coats my insides.

I can't find my book.

Determined, I dig through my stuff again. The papers and the notebooks and the pens and the book I'm supposed to read for English that I'm already putting off. But it's not here.

And then I remember.

I left it in my math class after Mrs. Nelson distracted me with her commentary about said book.

A groan leaves me and I hang my head, hoping it'll still be there when I check tomorrow. No one uses those storage compartments at our desks anyway. We're always getting moved around to different desks when we're in class and we all either use our backpacks or our lockers. I'll check in the morning, before school starts. Hopefully the classroom will be open.

I just don't want to lose my book. They're not cheap and I only allow myself to buy paperbacks of my favorite authors.

Dad always makes sure to give me gift cards for my birthday and Christmas, but money is tight. I worked part-time during the summer at the coffeeshop downtown and while I didn't get a lot of hours, I do my best to save as much money as possible. Not only do I not want to replace the book by buying another one, I also wasn't finished with it yet. That's the most frustrating part of it all.

What am I going to read tonight?

Taking out one of my notebooks instead, I grab a couple of pens and start doodling. I'm no artist but I do enjoy drawing sometimes. I find myself sketching a face. A boy. With longish hair and intense blue eyes, a scowl on his handsome face.

Ugh, I'm drawing Arch Lancaster. I don't even like him and I'm sitting here mooning over him like he's my secret crush. All because he pays attention to me—and it's mostly bad attention too.

I must be starved for human interaction, I swear.

As if I conjured him up from my brain, I glance to my right to see him approaching the closest building. The one that's used by the Lancaster family instead of the dorms. They don't sleep with the little people. They have their own suites to stay in.

Remaining very quiet, I watch him stride down the sidewalk, his head held high, his hair blowing away from his face with the breeze. I stare at that handsome face, really taking him in, marveling at how freaking attractive he is.

Straight out of a romance novel.

Thankfully he doesn't notice me and within minutes, he disappears inside the building and I release the breath I didn't realize I was holding. I can't let this boy distract me.

He's not worth my time.

CHAPTER ELEVEN

ARCH

The next day I do my best to keep my cool and act normal around everyone but it's fucking tough. I'm not in the mood for any type of interaction with anyone, and what makes it worse? The one person I'm trying my damnedest to forget seems to have already forgotten me.

Daisy.

The moment I stormed into the admin building, Daisy had her back to me, completely ignoring me. She didn't even look in my direction when Vivian called out my name, or when I snapped at Vivian in return and she asked what crawled up my rear?

Direct quote. Stupid quote. I just stared at her without saying a word, and Vivian waved her hand toward my favorite office, sending me in to perform my favorite task.

No eye contact from Daisy, no nothing. I stapled papers so hard, I think I broke the fucking stapler, but I didn't give a damn.

In the classes we share, she wouldn't look at me. During lunch, she was nowhere near the dining hall.

Where the hell did she go?

I wandered around outside, my gaze constantly searching for her despite my animosity toward her. Despite the burning in my gut and the way I clenched my fists every time I thought about her. I never saw her blonde head when I was outside. Hell, I even went to the library early since I spend sixth period in there, but she wasn't hiding among the stacks either.

I could almost believe she's purposely avoiding me and it's driving me out of my mind.

My last class of the day is statistics and it's my least favorite. I hate the classroom. It's old and musty and I can imagine one of my dead relatives going here back in the early nineteen hundreds, mouthing off and acting like he owns the school.

Just like me.

This period though, instead of glowering and daring anyone to even look at me, I keep my gaze fixed on the desk, listening to Mrs. Nelson talk about meaningless topics. I don't have the energy to listen, to pay attention, to work on the sample problems she mentions.

God, I hate statistics. Math. All of it.

The day is dark and I swear it's only because I haven't looked into Daisy's eyes. Crazy, right? My mood is for shit and I wonder if seeing her, hearing her voice—fuck, getting her to actually acknowledge me—will make me feel better. She's bright and pretty, a flower shining in the sun and I feel like I need some of that brightness shining on me.

The hair and the face and the smile and the sunny disposition, it all works for her. While that is some corny shit and I don't normally think like that at all, but for some reason, I can't shake her.

I'm desperate to shake her.

I tell myself it's just a passing phase. I'll forget all about her by the weekend. If I'm lucky enough, I'll wake up tomorrow not thinking about her at all and when I see her during first period maybe I'll think, oh yeah. There's Daisy.

Big deal.

And then again, maybe not. Because it doesn't feel like I'm going to shake her any time soon. I'm...consumed.

Obsessed.

Pissed about it too.

I normally like girls who are dark-haired and mysterious. Girls who play it cool and don't fawn all over me—with the exception of Cadence, who makes me feel like a rock star with the way she pays far too much attention to me. Her fangirl behavior is obnoxious.

Girls who don't consider me anything special are usually more my speed because they're wealthy too and the money part doesn't impress them. Yes, I'm a Lancaster and richer than all the rest, but they come from wealth and prestige as well, and while a lot of them have been trained to be husband hunters, they don't push too hard or make too big of a deal about who I am. They're hoping I choose them, and none of them, not a single one of them is who I want to choose.

A ragged sigh leaves me and I scrub my hand over my face, hating how twisted my gut is. I can't eat. I can't focus. I can't sleep for shit.

Girls with money should be the ones that interest me but that will never be Daisy because she's broke as a joke and comes from her groundskeeper father. And her dead mother.

What happened to her? Why did she die? How? When did it happen? Is that why Daisy keeps to herself? She may think she's friendless and that none of us like her but I see how she is. How she puts up that wall and doesn't let anyone penetrate it.

I want to. God help me, I want to even though I know it's a giant mistake and she's the last girl I should be interested in.

"Open up your textbooks to page twenty-six," Mrs. Nelson announces, and I hear the shuffle of books opening, pages being turned. "That includes you too, Mr. Lancaster."

Ah, called out. I appreciate Nelson's imaginary balls. Most of the staff have been afraid to speak to me today and I appreciate her acting like I'm just another student. When I look up, I catch her watching me, slowly shaking her head, and I flash her a rueful smile before I duck down, reaching for my backpack.

Pausing when I spot a book sitting in the open slot beneath my desk.

I reach inside and pull it closer, recognizing the cover immediately. This is Daisy's book. The one she was reading at lunch. I bet she has this class during sixth period, and for whatever reason, she left her book behind.

Huh.

"Arch." Mrs. Nelson's sharp tone causes my head to snap up. "Your textbook, please?"

"Sorry," I mutter, reaching for my backpack and pulling out the math textbook, setting it on my desk and opening it to page twenty-six like she asked.

She goes over the lesson and then asks us to work on some problems, which I do in what feels like two minutes flat, even though she lectured for at least ten minutes and I never listened to a single word she said.

All the while I'm working on the configurations, I think of Daisy's book in the desk, calling my name.

The moment I finish the assignment, I'm reaching for the book, cracking it open at the spot where she placed a flower-themed bookmark. Frowning, I notice there a few sentences underlined. There are even hearts drawn on the page, around the dude's—Aaron—name.

Huh. That's weird. She doesn't seem like the type to doodle on the inside of a book. I'd guess she'd believe that was wrong, messing up a book's interior.

I read the lines she underlined, noting how romantic the words are.

He looks at me as if I'm the only thing he sees and my heart swells with a foreign emotion. I think this is what it feels like to be...

Loved.

But maybe I'm mistaken.

I flip through the book, noting that it's heavily annotated only about a third of the way in.

"Have you finished your assignment, Arch?"

I glance up to find Mrs. Nelson smiling down at me, her eyes sparkling with amusement when she notices the book in my hands. I snap it shut and grab the lined piece of paper I used to complete the problems, holding it out toward her.

She takes it from me and glances over my work, nodding slowly. "Looks like you don't have any difficulty with this."

"Nope."

"I suppose I should let you get back to your reading then."

Shit. "It's not my book."

"I know." When I meet her gaze, she explains further, "It's Daisy Albright's. She was reading it earlier and must've left it behind."

Confirmation that I didn't really need.

"Why don't you give it to me and I can make sure she'll get it tomorrow." Mrs. Nelson holds out her hand and I clutch the book tighter, not about to let it go.

"I can give it to her. I'll see her after class." I say the words with utter confidence. As if it's perfectly normal that I'll meet up with Daisy when Nelson knows—everybody knows—the two of us don't socialize.

At all.

Nelson frowns, suspicion filling her eyes. Like she's onto my scheme. "You will?"

Nodding, I sit up straighter, resting my forearms on top of the book. "I've got it handled."

"If you say so." Her voice is full of doubt, but she walks away, stopping at a desk to help someone else.

Exhaling loudly, I reach for the pack of Post-it notes I keep in my backpack, grabbing my pencil and scrawling a few words across it before I tear it off and attach it to the inside of the book, placing it right on the bookmark.

Smiling, I close the book and deposit it back into the desk slot, wondering if she'll answer me.

She better.

CHAPTER TWELVE

DAISY

Today hasn't been great.

I had a paper due first thing in English this morning and while I turned it in on time, I had second thoughts about how I wrote it from the moment I handed it to Mr. Winston. But it was too late.

What's done is done.

In American Government, we had a pop quiz I wasn't prepared for. Everyone could leave early when they finished, and of course, Arch Lancaster was first out the door. I even heard Mr. Briggs tell him, "One hundred percent. Impressive," before Arch flashed him a smug smile, turning his attention toward me—why, why, why—and then promptly exited the classroom.

I skipped second period—office duty—claiming I needed to catch up on homework. Vivian told me that was fine, and I hid out in the library, unable to concentrate on anything but my thoughts.

Like how I was purposely avoiding Arch and I didn't understand why. Just the idea of being near him made me nervous. Confused.

Worried.

Lunch was miserable too. I stood my ground by remaining in the dining hall versus running away and hiding, which was what I really wanted to do. I got another salad but sat with no one. Was ignored by everyone and for whatever reason, that hurt more than usual. I don't know what I did wrong, or what I did to deserve this, but it's starting to hurt more and more. That I have no friends. That no one seems to like me.

Am I snobbish? Unlikable? I try so hard, but maybe Arch was right? Maybe I try too hard? I don't know.

I can't wait to get out of here. Go somewhere new. Start my life over.

By the time I'm in statistics, I'm settling in at my desk with complete relief, knowing there are only two more classes and then I can finally go home. All I can think about is hiding away in my bedroom, wrapping a blanket around me and hopefully reading my book that I've missed since I forgot it in this class yesterday.

Setting my backpack on the floor, I duck my head and peer into the storage cubby beneath the desk, relief flooding me when I see my book. I pull it out, ignoring the people filing into the classroom, cracking open the spot where my bookmark is nestled, frowning when I see the blue Post-it stuck in between the pages.

What's your favorite part?

I lift my head, glancing around the room. Who wrote this? This means someone was thumbing through my book and saw all the pages I annotated and highlighted.

That's…embarrassing.

"Oh, you found your book. I'm so glad," Mrs. Nelson says as she stops by my desk.

"Yes, I forgot it here yesterday," I tell her, wondering if she knew who had their hands on it. Who might've written the note. "Do you happen—"

"Mrs. Nelson, I have a question," another student calls, distracting her. She offers me a quick smile before she takes off, eager to help whoever it was that asked.

Leaving me alone with the book. And the note.

I crack it back open and stare at the words. How they're written. Very brash and bold, which I didn't realize handwriting could be. Like a boy wrote it.

My entire body flushes at the realization. This is so embarrassing. Why would he want to know my favorite part?

That's just…weird.

I look at the last words I highlighted, reading them again and again.

He looks at me as if I'm the only thing he sees and my heart swells with a foreign emotion. I think this is what it feels like to be…

Loved.

But maybe I'm mistaken.

Swallowing hard, I scan through the pages, looking for my favorite part. I don't want to leave the book behind but maybe… maybe whoever it is will read it and see me for who I really am. Maybe it's a way to make a friend.

This might not be a guy who left the note. It could be a girl. A fellow bookworm who enjoys reading romances on the spicier side. Wouldn't it be fun if we could bond over that and eventually start a book club together?

My heart skips a beat at the promising thought.

Deciding I can sacrifice one more day without my book, I choose the section that's been my favorite so far and stick the Post-it note on that page, adding my own words to the note before I shut it and discreetly stash it away in the desk.

If they don't respond tomorrow, then it's fine. My hopes will be dashed, but I'll take my book home and finish it. But if they do answer…

Then maybe we can continue our conversation.

• • •

"Aw Daisy Mae, why do you look so down?"

I smile at my father when he enters the house, but it feels forced so I let it fall, glancing back down at the book I'm supposed to be reading for English.

I'm not reading it at all. I stare at the pages and the words become distorted. Fuzzy. I'm too distracted by everything going on in my life. The attention from Arch. Whoever's writing secret notes in my book. All of the homework I still need to do. I'm so caught up in my thoughts I didn't realize how late it actually was and I promised my dad I would fix dinner tonight.

"I'm just tired," I tell him as I shove the throw blanket aside and stand, stretching my arms above my head and yawning as loudly as possible. None of that is forced. I haven't been sleeping great lately either. "Sorry dinner isn't ready yet."

"I can wait." Dad smiles. "I can even help you."

"That would be nice."

We move about the kitchen smoothly, the two of us used to dealing with each other over the past almost six years. His mood is somber tonight too and I know why. It's probably why mine is as well, though we're both loathe to admit it.

It's almost my birthday.

The anniversary of my mother's death.

The day isn't special for me anymore. It's a sad day. A remembrance of how tragically we lost her. I can't celebrate on that day. It just doesn't feel right, and while Dad always tries to make the day a positive one, it never works.

We're two weeks away and look at us. Already quiet, the air tinged with sadness. All of the unspoken things hanging between us, heavy and foreboding. He'll eventually want to ask me what I want to do for my birthday and I'll insist on nothing. He'll get me a cake and try to make my favorite dinner but the night will end in tears.

It always does. For the both of us.

But tonight we're pretending, offering each other quick smiles as we pass in the tiny kitchen. I boil water for the noodles while Dad browns the meat for the sauce. A homemade sauce we can together, using the vegetables from the garden. His mother, my grandmother, was Italian and handed down her recipe to Mom, but she could never make it right. Dad though? He makes it perfectly, and he taught me how to as well.

Twenty minutes later and we're seated at the table, both of us silently eating our spaghetti, the only sound the crunch of our salads or Dad tearing into the garlic bread. I finally start asking him questions, hating how thick the silence is, needing to break it for a bit.

"Did you give Kathy any more tomatoes?"

He swallows down a big bite of garlic bread. "I sure did. Brought her a whole bucket earlier this afternoon. She said they'll make their appearance in the salad bar tomorrow. They'll also be offered on sandwiches and if I keep her supplied, they'll be available for Taco Tuesday."

"That's great." I smile at him, taking another bite of spaghetti.

"We'll have to keep some more for ourselves, of course. So we can can up the sauce for next—" He ducks his head for a moment and I stare at his graying hair, my heart panging. He's getting older, and I worry about him being alone when I leave. "You won't be around next year."

"I'll be here until June," I remind him, my voice soft. "I can eat plenty of spaghetti between now and June."

He smiles, but his gaze is tinged with sadness. "I'm going to miss you, Daisy."

"I'll miss you too." Reaching out, I settle my hand over his, giving it a squeeze. "I got a B on my American Government quiz."

"That's great."

"It's okay." I shrug, wondering why I told him.

"It's great," he repeats, his gaze fixed on me. "You're too hard on yourself."

"I want to be the best I can be." He already knows about my extra hard class schedule. I came clean the day after I made the changes because I can't keep secrets from this man. He's the only family I've got. "And a B isn't the best."

"It's better than failing."

"Arch Lancaster got an A. He didn't miss a single answer."

"He's inhuman," Dad says vehemently, making me giggle.

"Like a robot," I add.

"A troubled one." Dad shakes his head, stabbing his fork in his salad bowl almost viciously. "You're leaving him alone, aren't you?"

I nod, my voice solemn. "Yes, Daddy."

"I'm glad." He chews, his expression thoughtful. "You're too good for that boy."

"I'm not interested in him like that," I say too quickly. "And he's definitely not interested in me."

"He's a damn fool if he's not. Look at you, Daisy. You're a beautiful girl. Sweet and smart and kind. All the boys you go to school with are blind idiots." He averts his head, staring out the window, wincing against the waning sunlight. "Maybe I should be glad they don't notice you. None of that lot is worthy of you."

I know he's trying to make me feel better but all he's doing is reminding me that no one really cares about me. Just the faculty and staff, and most of their care is probably out of obligation. Out of loyalty to my father, who's been such a good employee over the years. Someone they can all count on.

Including myself.

I give up on eating because my appetite still isn't the best and I clean up the kitchen, loading up the dishwasher as full as I can so I don't have to hand wash anything tonight.

"I'm going to take a shower," Dad says as I'm finishing wiping down the counters.

"I'll be outside," I tell him, almost rolling my eyes when he stops short at my reply.

"It's almost dark."

We both glance toward the window. "The sun is still out."

Kind of.

"It's dangerous after dark."

"It's a gated campus," I point out, but his voice is firm.

"Still dangerous. Too many boys out roaming around in the night."

I burst out laughing at how ominous he sounds.

"I'll stick around the house. I promise."

Once he's gone, I rinse out the wash rag and leave it in the dish drain, then make my way outside. I don't really want to take an actual walk. More like I just need fresh air to clear my head for a bit.

Without even planning on it, I find myself in the gardens behind the library, where all of the ancient statues stand. Most of them are of old Lancasters, and I stop in front of one in particular, staring at the man's face. He looks young. The name etched below his feet surprises me.

Archibald Lancaster.

Not the Arch I know, but I can see the family resemblance, even etched in marble. I drink him in for far too long, staring at his face. The hard set of his jaw. The firm line of his lips. His stare is cold, even though he's not real, and it's as if the longer I look at him, the more he seems to come to life. Leaving me completely unsettled.

With a little shake of my shoulders, I leave the gardens in a rush, practically tripping over a striped ball of fur that runs beneath my feet. It's a thin tabby cat that goes hiding behind good ol' Archibald, its golden eyes staring at me as the cat tilts his head to the side.

"Aw." I kneel down, holding my hand out. "Come here, kitty kitty."

The cat stares and I swear I can feel its silent judgment.

"Come on." I rub my fingers together in a soft snap and make a tsking noise like I remember my mom doing when I was little. We used to always have cats because Mom loved them. Once she was gone, Dad gave them all away.

Every single one of them.

I keep calling, to the point that the sun is mostly gone and the sky is glowing a mix of purple and pink, tiny stars twinkling. I shift closer and closer to the kitty, until I'm actually touching it—I wish I knew if it was a boy or a girl.

"Come here, cutie," I murmur, pleased to hear the soft, low rumble of a purr. "You are so sweet, aren't you? Oh yes, you are."

I'm even petting the top of its head, eager to coax it into my arms when I hear a deep voice boom from behind me.

"Are you actually communicating with that cat? Pretty sure you're a fucking fairy princess, Daze."

Gasping, I leap to my feet and whirl around, the cat scampering off, disappointment filling me for a brief moment at the loss. Just when I was making progress too.

But then I lift my head and find that it's Arch standing in front of me. Clad in sweatpants and...

Oh my God, nothing else.

He's all sweaty and there are AirPods in his ears. Very expensive looking Nikes on his feet. It's obvious he was running and I do my best to keep my gaze trained on his face, but it's like I can't. Not when there's so much bare skin on display.

He appears even bigger without a shirt on. Muscles everywhere the eye can see. His thick shoulders and bulging arms. His firm pecs and flat stomach with a hint of a washboard.

Wait, that's no hint. His abdomen is at least a six-pack and oh my God, I don't think I've ever seen such a fit specimen in the literal flesh in my life. I know we're basically the same age but he seems so much bigger, so much older.

He looks like a man, while I feel like an inept child.

"You're staring," he snaps when I don't respond.

My gaze flies to his and I see irritation there. With a hint of something else. Something unfamiliar, but somehow, I recognize it. Because I have the same feeling tugging deep in my belly, reminding me that I'm a female and he's a male and while we may bicker and fight, there's something else brewing between us that is getting harder to deny.

Attraction.

Chemistry.

Whatever you want to call it.

It's there, like an invisible string tugging, pulling me closer to him. I take a step forward, like I can't help myself, and he doesn't move, his gaze sweeping over me. Lingering in places that leaves me tingling.

"What are you doing out here? Looking for pussy?"

I rear back a little at his dark tone, at the words he just said. "Why are you always so crude?"

"I don't know." He shrugs, his expression almost blank. "I think you bring it out of me."

"So, it's my fault that you act like such an ass?" I can't believe that question just flew out of my mouth, but when I'm around him, it's as if I can't help myself.

I just say what I feel, consequences be damned.

The faintest smile curves his lush lips and I swear my heart skips a beat. "Yeah. I'd definitely say it's your fault."

"You're ridiculous." I roll my eyes and wrap my arms around myself to fight off the sudden chill that wants to steal over me. Or maybe it's his nearness that's affecting me, making me all shivery. Pretty sure my nipples are hard too because they're literally aching and it makes no sense. So, he's shirtless.

So what?

I can't stop letting my gaze roam over him. His skin looks so smooth. I bet the muscles beneath all that smooth skin are hard as a rock. I wonder what it would feel like, being pressed up against him. Or having him pin me, my body beneath his—

"Tell me what you're thinking. Right now."

The knowing in his voice makes me uneasy and I shake my head.

"N-no way." He chuckles, the rich sound washing over me,

leaving me achingly aware of his nearness.

His near nakedness.

What's he got on under those sweats anyway?

My entire body flushes hot at the thought.

"Where were you today?" he asks, changing the subject. Leaving me confused for a moment.

"I was at school." I say it slowly, like he might have trouble comprehending me.

Arch makes a dismissive noise. "You weren't at the office second period."

"Oh." He realized that, hmm? What, did he miss me? If I had more courage, I'd ask him if he did. I'm sure he would have no qualms asking me that question, but I can't seem to work up the nerve. "I was in the library."

"Why?"

"I needed to study." I shrug, hating my lie.

More like I needed to stay far away from him.

"You missed out. Vivian trained me on the phones." He makes a disgusted face and I almost want to laugh. "That is the very last thing I ever want to do."

"Answer the school phone?"

"Yeah. I asked Viv if I could change up the script but she said hell no."

I very much doubt she literally said the words *hell no* to him. And I know for a fact she wouldn't let him get away with calling her Viv either. "How exactly did you want to change the script?"

"Thank you for calling Lancaster Prep. Arch Lancaster speaking." He grins. "She said no one would believe an actual Lancaster would answer the phone, and I argued that's my point. But she still wouldn't let me say it."

"Is she going to continue to let you answer the phone?" Sounds risky. He might say or do something that could cause trouble. Something he loves to do apparently.

"No way. She'll shove me back into that coffin of an office

tomorrow and have me stapling useless packets until the end of time. You do realize what they're doing, right?"

"What are they doing?" And who is *they?*

"Keeping us apart."

It's the way he says it. Like he hates the fact that Matthews and Vivian are the ones keeping us apart when maybe...

Maybe he doesn't want to be kept away from me?

No. I'm reaching. Seriously.

"I should get back home," I say as I start to walk right past him, but he reaches out at the last second, his fingers locking around my wrist, keeping me in place.

The moment he puts his hand on me, my heart starts to race, and the blood rushes through my head, pounding in my ears. His touch is firm yet somehow still gentle. He's barely touching me at all, but I can feel his hands on me as if he were running them all over my skin. Lighting me up inside.

Reminding me that I'm small and delicate and he is very much...

Not.

"Where's your dad?"

"In the shower," I say, breathless.

"He knows you came out here by yourself?" Arch's brows shoot up.

I'm rendered silent. All I can do is nod.

"Go back home, Daze," he murmurs. "Bad things happen out here after dark."

I stare at him for a moment, my head buzzing. Filled with lurid thoughts of bad things. Naughty things.

Every single one of those 'things' starring Arch Lancaster.

And me.

"I'm serious." He loosens his hold on my arm, his thumb brushing the sensitive skin on the inside of my wrist, and my full body shudder is hard to hide from him. His predatory smile tells me he noticed. "Go home. Hide away in your bedroom and read one of those romance books like you do, instead of living your actual life."

I gape at him, shocked he knows I read romance. "How do you—"

"You were reading it in the dining hall yesterday at lunch," he fills in for me. "Is the story juicy? Full of dirty sex scenes?"

My hot cheeks give my answer away and he smiles.

"That's what I thought." He tugs me close, my body colliding with his, his mouth at my ear when he whispers, "Next time you read one of those scenes in your book that gets you so hot and bothered that you're sticking your fingers in your panties, maybe you can imagine it's me doing those things to you instead of some fictional character."

"Wha—" My voice drifts when I realize he's gone. Leaving behind no trace except for the scent of clean sweat lingering in the air.

And the ghost of his hot words throbbing between my legs.

CHAPTER THIRTEEN

ARCH

I should've never said what I did to Daisy. I probably blew her mind, saying something so dirty to her, and it wasn't even that dirty.

Okay, it was a little bit, but I bet I shocked the shit out of her, encouraging her to think of me.

Sexually.

Can't get the image of hot little Daisy Albright lying in her narrow bed, her busy hand between her thighs, fingering herself into total bliss over some corny dialogue in a sexy book. Fuck that. I would rather she think about me whispering something way hotter in her ear while she fingered herself. Or even better...

Letting me finger her.

Once the image takes hold in my brain, I can't let it go. No matter how hard I try. I run another mile just to sweat it out. Sweat *her* out.

It doesn't work.

My mind is filled with thoughts of Daisy. Naked Daisy. All golden limbs and rosy nipples, shyly kissing me. Scared to take it any further because she's innocent and sweet and no one else has ever touched her.

Not like I want to touch her.

I bet she'd be hot. And wet and creamy, with a swollen pussy and a greedy little clit just dying to find release. I could give it to her. I could make her feel so good, but she's not meant for me.

And I'm not meant for her.

Didn't stop me from going back to my room and taking a hot shower though. Jerking off under the blast of steamy water to thoughts of Daisy on her knees, her lush lips parted and ready for my cock.

I come so hard at the imaginary vision I end up slumped against the wall, breathing hard. Heavier than I did when I pushed myself running only moments ago. Harder than I ever did when I've had sex with other girls.

There have only been a couple, but all of them fade away. They were nothing. Meaningless. Pointless.

Jesus, I've got a serious issue.

And her name is Daisy.

. . .

The next day at school I prowl around the campus like a predator on the hunt for its prey. Cadence says hi and I growl at her. Mya calls me an asshole and I give her the finger. JJ keeps his distance, as do the rest of our friends, and when I enter my first class of the day, I settle into a chair in the very back of the classroom, my gaze fixated on the back of Daisy's head.

She doesn't even turn around to look at me.

Of course, she doesn't.

Today she's wearing a short sleeve button-down shirt, her slender golden arms on display. Her skirt is hiked up, showing off her firm legs and she's got ankle high socks on with her loafers. The socks are trimmed with lace and give off that good girl vibe she's got going on. And then there's her hair.

Don't know why I'm so fascinated with it, but she's wearing

two braids this morning, the ends tied with a snippet of silky blue ribbon. Any other girl I'd find it too cutesy. On Daisy, it's adorable.

Adorably sexy.

I watch the back of her for the entirety of class. To the point that I notice every little twitch. The way her shoulders rise almost to her damn ears when Winston starts talking about the essay that's due soon.

Wonder if that stresses her out.

She toys with the end of her right braid at one point, twirling the wisps of hair over and over again around her finger and I'm fascinated. Desperate to do the same thing to her. Touch her hair. Ignore her protests that I'll only mess it up. I won't. I'll be careful. I just want to touch her. Hear her murmur with pleasure when I hit a spot that she likes. Maybe I could kiss her behind her ear. Breathe in her sweet scent. Try to control myself because the girl is like a drug that hits my bloodstream, making me crave more, and I don't want to scare her—

The bell rings and I blink, shocked I let my thoughts be filled with Daisy and nothing else for the entire period.

By the time I'm out of my desk and slinging my backpack over my shoulder, Daisy is already gone.

My steps determined, I follow after her, breaking out into a jog when I spot her just ahead. I catch up with her easily, slowing my pace so I'm walking right beside her and she glances over at me, shock dawning in her golden eyes.

"Morning," I greet, staring at her pretty face.

When did I realize she was so damn pretty anyway? Before, I thought she was mousy and plain, but I was wrong. So fucking wrong.

"Hi." Her voice is soft, her gaze skittering away like she's scared to look at me for too long.

"You going to the office today?" Apprehension clutches at my heart, preparing for her to say no.

"Yes." She nods and the relief that hits me is like a punch to my solar plexus, leaving me breathless.

This is fucking ridiculous. All over a girl.

"Think Viv will let me answer the phone?" I raise my brow, noting how her eyes dance with amusement.

"You probably shouldn't call her Viv."

"She doesn't mind." She'd probably give me detention if she heard me call her Viv, but it's worth the risk just to see Daisy almost smile at something I said.

"I very much doubt that."

"Hey." I touch her arm and she comes to a stop like I do, and I turn to face her. She tilts her head back so our gazes meet, her braids falling behind her shoulders and the urge to touch her hair is so strong, I have to clutch my hands into fists to stop myself. "Do me a favor and try to convince Viv to not stow me away in that shitty office today."

"Why?"

What would she say if I told her I just wanted to sit with her at the desk and pretend that Viv likes me, while I listen to them talk about gardening? I could give absolutely zero shits about gardening and soil and flowers but it would be the perfect opportunity. I'd let myself look my fill of Daisy's face without any interruptions. Watch her mouth move as she speaks. Enjoy the sound of her laughter.

Yeah, that's what I want to do the most. Listen to her laugh. She's always so quiet everywhere else she goes. In class. In the dining hall.

In the office, she's more relaxed. Open. Even animated.

"I'm tired of stapling. I've built a callus from that damn stapler." I hold up my uncalloused hand, running with my excuse.

Her gaze shifts to my palm, her lips barely curving into a smile before she looks at me. "I don't see a callus."

"I'm lying, Daze. I'm just—I'm tired of sitting alone in that office. I think I've done my penance. Let me hang out with everyone else."

She starts walking and I do too, staring at her profile, willing her to say something. Anything.

"That's not up to me," she finally murmurs.

"You have influence. Pull."

"I should still be mad at you."

My heart trips over itself and I'm surprised I'm not sprawled on the ground. The pain in her voice is obvious. I'm such an asshole.

I should probably apologize for everything I've said and done, but it's like I can't. It's humanly impossible for me to say the words, *I'm sorry* to anyone. Not my parents, not my siblings, not my friends or former girlfriends. I've never had to apologize for who I am, and why should I? I'm not sorry for the things I've done.

With the exception of what I've said to Daisy. I hurt her.

And she didn't deserve that.

"You probably should be," I agree with her, rushing forward when we get to the admin building to hold the door open for her. "But let me make it up to you."

"Make up what?" She enters the building and I follow behind her, restraining myself from tugging on one of her braids. What am I, six? "The horrible things you keep saying to me?"

"Horrible things I *keep* saying?" I repeat back to her. "Like what?"

I know what she's referring to. Last night when I said the word pussy to her.

When I told her to think of me when she masturbates.

Does she even masturbate? Or is she too freaked out by the thought of touching herself there? Is she one of those girls who can't even say the words out loud? I'm guessing yes. I'd probably drop dead before I ever heard sweet Daisy Albright utter the words pussy or cock or cunt.

Pretty sure those words aren't part of her vocabulary.

"You were rather inappropriate toward me last night, Arch,"

she says, her voice wry. The pointed look she flashes me over her shoulder as she keeps pace ahead of me is intriguing. I want to see it again.

"Inappropriate? Are you talking about when I asked if you were looking for pussy?" I say the last word a little too loud and I'm surprised she doesn't shush me.

Her cheeks turn the palest pink. "I forgot you even said that."

Uh huh. So, she's definitely still thinking about *my fingers in her panties* remark then.

I shift closer to her, so close my front bumps against her back, her ass brushing my junk for the briefest moment. Enough to make my eyes want to cross. "You're referring to the hand in your panties comment then, hmm?"

She sucks in a sharp breath. I hear it. Practically feel it. I reach around her and open the admin office door for her and she scurries forward, creating distance between us like she needs it, and I stroll inside after her, feeling high on fucking life.

High on Daisy.

"You want me to say nice things to you?" I ask as she hurries toward the empty desk next to Vivian's—who's nowhere to be found, thank God. "How about this?"

She whirls on me, her eyes wide and unblinking. "Don't say anything inappropriate. *Please.*"

"I was going to tell you that I like the braids." My gaze drops to them, how they lie across her tits. "And the socks."

My gaze drops to her feet.

"Oh." A shuddery breath leaves her. "Thank you."

"You're welcome."

Tension slowly fills the room, heady and thick, and I take a step toward her, eager to...what? Touch her?

Yes. I want to touch her. At least her hair, and at least for a second. Maybe two. I'm not asking for much.

Daisy visibly swallows and her lips part, as if she might want to say something. I wait, curiosity paralyzing me completely.

The moment is ruined by Vivian dashing into the office, hip checking me as she walks past. "Good morning, children!"

Nothing like a middle-aged high school secretary calling Daisy and me children to ruin the mood.

Thanks, Viv.

CHAPTER FOURTEEN

DAISY

'm still turning over in my mind what Arch said to me. Over and over again, his deep voice on repeat.

I was going to tell you I like the braids. And the socks.

I haven't worn my hair in two braids in years. I figured they looked too childish but this morning, something told me to put my hair in two French braids versus only one and so I did.

The socks? They're new. I bought a variety pack of cute socks to wear with my uniform when I did a little back-to-school shopping and immediately felt silly for purchasing them. And mad at myself for wasting money on them too.

Again, something compelled me to put the socks on this morning. They're cute. Even a little sweet.

That Arch noticed something different about me—two things that are different—makes my heart expand.

And this boy should absolutely not have that sort of effect on me whatsoever. He's cold and cruel and he says the worst things.

He says nice things too though. Interesting things.

Still can't get the words he said to me last night out of my head either. The pussy remark? I'd completely forgotten. It was the other words he said. The tone of his voice. His breath hot in my ear, his presence looming. Warming me from the inside out.

Maybe you can imagine it's me doing those things to you instead of some fictional character.

He probably believes I'm scared of my sexuality and was disgusted by his remark, but I wasn't. No, I did exactly what he said last night before I fell asleep.

Instead of the usual, faceless fictional character I imagine doing—things to me, I thought of Arch. It wasn't my fingers moving between my legs last night.

They were Arch's fingers. His mouth on my ear and his hand in my panties, touching me while he said unholy things to me that left me a shuddery, exhausted mess.

"Why are you two staring at each other?" Vivian's voice breaks through my Arch-induced fog and I glance over at her to find her watching me, concern in her eyes. "Please tell me he's not starting another fight with you."

I slowly shake my head. "He's being a perfect gentleman."

I steal a look at Arch, who's grinning.

Vivian snorts in disbelief.

"Archibald Lancaster, do you know how to be a perfect gentleman?"

"My mama enrolled me in etiquette courses when I was ten," he says with the utmost seriousness. "I can manage to be a gentleman when it's called for."

"Well, when it comes to our Daisy, it's always called for," Vivian says, harumphing as she drops herself into her desk chair.

"If I promise to be on my best behavior, will you let me hang out with you two instead of shoving me away in that damn closet you call an office?" Arch raises his brows.

Vivian studies him for a while, chewing on her lower lip. I think there's a part of her that enjoys bantering with Arch. Just like I do. There's something about him. Even when he's mean and awful, he's also still somehow…appealing.

Charisma. That's what he has. Tons of it. He has a magnetic presence that draws people to him despite themselves. I'm just one of many who's intrigued by him. I'm definitely nothing special.

That's what I'm trying to tell myself.

"What do you think, Daisy?" Vivian turns to me, as does Arch.

Power surges through me as I study him, knowing I'm the one who will make the final decision whether he stays or goes. The rational part of me says he should absolutely go. Make him suffer in that stuffy, awful office. But he doesn't like closed-in spaces. That much is clear. And neither do I.

But my soft side, the one that leads with my heart and various other parts of my body, wants him to stay.

"You can hang out with us," I finally say.

Vivian mutters *oh dear* under her breath while Arch grins, the sight of it dazzling.

Leaving me dizzy.

"Vivian." Matthews enters the office, all of us swiveling our heads in his direction. "I'm about to hop on a call in ten minutes and I was hoping you could join me. I need you to take notes in case I miss anything."

Vivian stands up straighter. "Of course. Daisy can be in charge. Let me gather my things and I'll be right in."

He smiles and nods, his gaze sliding over Arch, with no acknowledgment whatsoever, before landing on me. "Good morning, Daisy."

"Good morning." I smile at him. Can practically feel the snarl on Arch's face for being ignored.

Another thing he doesn't like. He prefers all eyes on him.

Once Matthews is in his office and Vivian is about to join him, she turns on us, her index finger out and wagging. "No funny business from you, Arch."

"What about Daisy? What if she's up to funny business?"

I almost laugh. He's so antagonizing.

"I don't expect it from her. She'll be fine. You? I don't trust you." Vivian's gaze narrows. "Be good."

He throws his hands up as if he's about to be arrested. "You can trust me."

"Ha!" She turns and enters Matthews' office, closing the door behind her.

Leaving us alone.

I go to the empty desk and settle in, dropping my backpack on top of it. Arch makes his way toward me, leaning against the desk, standing right next to my chair. So close I could reach out and touch his hip. His thigh.

But I don't. I could never.

"Want to get up to some funny business?" He waggles his brows at me and I finally let go of the laugh that I've been holding in.

He seems pleased. I can see it in the way his eyes glow. The faint smile that tugs at the corners of his mouth. I shake my head, still laughing, probably laughing too much, but he doesn't seem bothered by it.

"We have to answer the phones since Vivian is in the office with Matthews," I point out.

"Will you show me how?"

"I thought Vivian showed you yesterday."

"I already forgot." He goes and grabs a chair, pulling it right up next to me and sits, his shoulder brushing mine. "You don't have a problem answering the phone?"

"No." I shake my head, wondering what he might do if I crawled into his lap and settled in. "Is that shocking?"

"Yeah. You always seem so nervous."

"I do?"

"Definitely. But maybe that's because I make you nervous." He turns his head toward me, his gaze locking on mine. "Is that it? Do I make you nervous, Daze?"

Yes. One thousand times yes. "Sometimes." I shrug.

"Why?"

"I worry about what you might say." Okay, that's not a lie.

"Oh yeah." He leans back in the chair, kicking his legs out in front of him. "That makes sense."

This boy. I don't know how to act around him. Or what to say. He definitely makes me nervous and jumpy and even a little nauseous. Lightheaded. Overwhelmed.

Overcome.

The phone rings and I automatically answer it. "Thank you for calling Lancaster Prep. How may I direct your call?"

I can feel Arch's eyes on me as I listen to the older gentleman ask to speak with Headmaster Matthews. "I'm afraid he's in a meeting right now. Would you care to leave a message and I can give it to him when he's available?"

I take down the man's name and number and hang up the phone. Tearing the message off the sheet, I rise up, leaning over the desk to leave it on top of Vivian's.

Arch's gaze drops to my skirt. I can feel it. Hot and curious. And when I glance over my shoulder, his gaze lifts, meeting mine, and I know for a fact he was staring at my butt. The back of my thighs.

My entire body feels as if it caught fire.

"You sound like a professional," he murmurs.

"You make that sound like a bad thing." I'm breathless over his compliment, which is ridiculous.

"It's not. You have a phone voice." I glance over at him, frowning. "You do. It completely changed when you answered that call."

"I sounded like a dork, didn't I?" This is embarrassing. A bad idea, having Arch sit right next to me. Critiquing me. I will never measure up to this boy's standards. He is on a whole other level compared to me. An unreachable level.

"Not at all." He's shaking his head, catching his lower lip with his teeth. "Doesn't this school have an automated phone system?"

I nod slowly, my gaze caught up in his. "If they hit zero, they get me."

"If I hit zero, will I get you?" The words fall from his lips with no care and they make no sense. Not really. Though I get this sense that he's trying to see if he can...

Get me.

No. Absolutely not. I'm reading too much into this.

"I'm ungettable," I tell him, my voice firm.

"You are?"

I nod, trying to calm my accelerated breaths.

"Is that why you keep to yourself, Daze? You're not interested in human interaction of any kind?"

I'm desperate for human interaction—of any kind. Does that make me pathetic?

Probably.

"Pushing everyone away is a lonely existence," he continues, shifting closer. Close enough that I can smell him and feel his body heat radiating toward me. He's not wearing the uniform jacket—when does he ever? And neither am I and it feels like layers have been peeled back between us. It would take nothing for me to touch him. Or for him to touch me.

I'm not brave enough to try and touch him so we know that's not going to happen.

"It's easier though. Letting someone get too close is only opening yourself to heartbreak, you know?" A shuddery breath leaves me and I regret saying those words immediately.

"You'd rather be lonely than heartbroken?"

"I'm currently dealing with both emotions, but yeah, I'd rather forget the heartbreak and be lonely forever. Keeping to myself is easier than letting someone in."

His gaze roams over my face, like he can't quite believe I just said that.

"Who broke your heart?" The fierce way he says the words has my brittle heart dropping and I stare at him, realizing that he sounds almost...

Protective.

"My mother's death," I whisper. "And I don't think there's any way I can put it back together again."

The pain on his face is obvious. Is he thinking about what he said to me? How I have mommy issues? He's not wrong. I do have mommy issues. And that's why his words struck such a chord with me. They hurt because it's true.

And I hate that about myself. I wish I could say I was healed and open and willing to love and be loved. But people my age scare me. They're so careless with their emotions and words. Like Arch.

Like everyone.

I'd rather retreat and watch life unfold than participate in it. It's easier.

The phone rings and I answer it automatically, like I'm a robot. I can still feel Arch's gaze on me, heavy with questions, but I don't look at him. Instead, I focus on the call, and the next one after that, grateful for the deluge. Trying my best to ignore him when he shifts closer, his arm brushing mine before it settles.

Resting right next to mine, his warmth bleeding into me. Leaving me breathless.

Reminding me that I'm not as robotic as I'd hoped.

CHAPTER FIFTEEN

DAISY

I walk into my statistics class eagerly, the first one here, as usual. At least this time the teacher is already in the room, sitting at her desk while she absently pops grapes into her mouth, her gaze fixed on her phone.

"Hi, Mrs. Nelson," I greet as I sit at my desk, refusing to look inside the storage area to see if my book is waiting for me.

Savoring the anticipation curling through me instead.

"Oh hi, Daisy. How are you?" she asks absently, her gaze straying once more to her phone.

"Great," I chirp, dropping my backpack at my feet and taking a deep breath.

I bend my head to the side, spotting my book, and I reach for it, pulling it out. Flipping it open and reading the note I left behind in the section that I like the best so far.

This is my favorite scene, especially the part I highlighted.

My gaze drops to the highlighted section, reading it again.

We sit next to each other, our bodies straining. Achingly aware of how close we are. I set my hand on the seat, stretching my pinky finger out as far as it will go and he does the same.

The exact same.

Our fingers brush. Once. Twice. And then he retreats,

removing his hand completely. The disappointment that leaves me hollow is overwhelming and I release a shaky breath, scared he might not notice.

Smiling when I realize he did.

The chatter as everyone starts to enter the classroom after lunch is extra loud and I lift my head, blowing out a harsh breath. That is still my favorite scene, but it doesn't look like my anonymous friend left me a note in response.

The disappointment I feel is crushing.

I turn the page, my heart lodging in my throat when I realize there is a response. In that same bold, masculine handwriting.

You like it subtle.

A smile touches my lips. Yes, I do like it subtle. And this isn't a girl. A girl wouldn't say *I like it subtle*. She'd say, *that's my favorite part too*! Or something like that.

This is a boy who's trying to figure out...what? What I like? What I don't like? Why does he care? What does it matter?

I flip through the book, finding another Post-it note in a section I haven't read, a few sentences underlined with pencil accompanied by the note.

I like this.

My gaze drops to the lines he haphazardly underlined, my heart rate accelerating.

Her lips are pink and all I can think about is kissing them.

I do exactly that. I kiss her with everything I've got and she opens to me easily. Too easily. I cup her cheek, streak my fingers across her soft skin as I slowly circle my tongue around hers.

Slow. Searching. Tasting. Learning.

Until she's moaning. Whimpering. Clutching the front of my shirt. Begging for it without saying the words.

She wants me.

"Okay, Michael, will you shut the door, please? It's so loud out there," Mrs. Nelson says, startling me.

I glance up and around me, but no one is paying attention.

Not a single soul. Not even Mrs. Nelson, who currently has three students surrounding her desk, all of them asking questions about last night's homework assignment.

I finished it—not with ease, but I eventually got it and completed the assignment. Stayed up way too late working on homework so maybe that's why I keep finding myself in my head. Having thoughts of a certain someone kissing me just like the passage I read.

Scrambling, I get my textbook out, along with the bag I like to keep my pens and pencils in. I unzip it, digging through all the pens until I pull out a pastel blue highlighter pen from a set Dad gave me for Christmas.

I grab my Post-its next, scribbling a note across it, my pulse racing like I just ran a mile. I'm breathless, excited and when I slap the Post-it on the page within, I shut the book and shove it in the desk cubby, along with the pen.

And then, like the good girl I want to be, I sit up straight and flip open my textbook to the pages we discussed yesterday. Hand my homework to Mrs. Nelson when she asks for it after doing roll call. Pay attention to everything she says, dutifully taking notes. Squinting at the problems she writes out on the white board, getting them almost immediately.

Thank goodness.

All the while I'm aware of the book inside the desk. The words he underlined in my head. The string of four words getting to me the most.

Slow. Searching. Tasting. Learning.

What would it be like, getting kissed like that? So thoroughly, so deliciously, you'd be left a shivery, overwhelmed mess? I want to know.

I want to know if Arch kisses like that.

My guess is yes.

Yes, he does.

When class is over, I take my time to gather my things, my

pace unusually slow. To the point that Mrs. Nelson notices.

I'm always out of the class quick. I don't like to be late to anything.

"You okay, Daisy?"

"I'm fine." I send her an encouraging smile, shoving my textbook in my backpack at a turtle's pace. Students from the next period start filing in, one after the other, but no one approaches my desk.

No one says, hey that's my seat.

Reluctantly, I leave, wishing I knew who sat there.

Wishing I knew who underlined that part. Who said it was their favorite.

Wishing more than anything that it was Arch who wrote that. Who liked that.

In my dreams...

CHAPTER SIXTEEN

ARCH

I wait for Daisy to leave the damn classroom, wondering what's taking her so long. She's always the first person to shoot out of her desk, running off at high speed so she won't be late.

Me? I take my time and am late for pretty much every class. Teachers don't even mark me tardy because what's the point? I won't really get in trouble.

For the most part.

This afternoon though, I'm eager to get into statistics class. I want to see if Daisy responded to my note. What did she think of my scene choice? I thought it was pretty tame, but there was something undeniably hot about the way the author described the kiss. Slow and searching and shit.

Wouldn't mind kissing Daisy like that. Still worried she might slap me if I try though.

Did she notice what I did in the office? I tried my best to recreate that scene from the book where the couple touched pinkies. I mean, that's not even close to sexual, but it's a tension thing so I see the appeal.

That's why I shifted close to her while she remained on the phone for so long. Pressing myself against her. Absorbing her. Did she realize it? She seemed extra focused on those phone calls so maybe not. She's not sexually experienced at all and I'm assuming she doesn't think I like her because of that.

I shouldn't like her like that.

She's all I can think about.

Finally, she exits the classroom, turning her head left, then right, causing me to duck, tucking myself on the other side of the line of lockers I'm standing by so she doesn't see me. I wait a few seconds, my heart pounding before I finally peer around the lockers once more.

The coast is clear.

I sneak into the classroom just as the bell rings, settling into my desk. Mrs. Nelson watches me, her lips curved when our gazes meet.

"Look at you showing up on time. I'm impressed."

I flash her a smile. I've always liked Nelson. She doesn't give me too much shit. "I aim to please."

"You're also a flirt." She grabs an eraser and taps it loudly against the white board. "Okay, class! Time to get your homework assignments out and pass them to the front."

I've already got my assignment out, and since I'm sitting in the first seat of the row—channeling my inner Daisy Albright before I even realized it, go figure—I wait to collect everyone else's, ignoring the way the girl who sits behind me smiles. Like she's interested.

No thanks.

Once Nelson has started her lecture, I reach for Daisy's book, curious to see what she said. What she wrote. The book is still there and I take that as a good sign. Slowly, I pull it out, resting it in my lap and flipping it open to the place I notated.

I smile when I see she drew little pink hearts all around my favorite part of the section I highlighted.

Slow. Searching. Tasting. Learning.

Glancing up, I make sure no one is paying attention to me before I read what she wrote on the Post-it.

I like that part too. It made me shiver.

There are lots of ways I could make this girl shiver.

I left you a pen so you can highlight whatever you want. A favorite line. A meaningful one. I highlighted what I liked in chapter fifteen in pink.

Without hesitation, I flip to chapter fifteen in search of what she liked, finding it quickly.

With sweaty palms I exit the dressing room, clad in the red dress he chose for me. He stands the moment he sees me, his eyes darkening I can tell.

He likes the dress.

He likes it on me.

"Get it," he says.

"But—"

"Get it," he repeats.

I smile and he smiles in return. He wants me.

I want him too.

So much.

Ignoring the book, I lift my head and stare off into space, thinking. Daisy opened up to me earlier, in the office. Explaining why she's so closed off. Why she wants to protect her heart. My mommy issues comment was right on the mark, but that doesn't make it okay that I said it.

I should've never said those words to her but I'm a heartless dick who speaks before he thinks, like I can't help myself.

Most of the time, I can't. My impulse control is nonexistent, according to my parents.

This passage I just read tells me she wants to be beautiful for someone else. She wants to be noticed. The earlier passage tells me she wants to be kissed.

I'm willing to do both for her—tell her she's beautiful and kiss her. But she acts so damn scared most of the time, I'm worried she'll bail the moment I try.

Nelson calls my name and I slide my attention to her, my

brows up in question.

"Do you understand this segment?"

Nodding, I say, "Absolutely."

Her smile is pleased and she doesn't challenge me further. "Good. Let's continue."

I thumb through the book when I can, trying not to look suspicious, and I finally find a scene I like. I grab the pen Daisy left me and uncap it, then carefully underline the sentences I like the best.

I am no artist so I don't bother drawing anything on the page. She's lucky she's getting the highlighter. That's about as far as I'll take it.

And I can't believe I'm taking it this far. I would never do this kind of sappy shit for a girl. Not a single one of them means anything to me enough to want to do this. I'm putting in a lot of effort when in the past, I've put in zero.

They all just come running. Surrounding me. Clamoring for me. Wanting me.

Look at Cadence. I could go to her right now and tell her to spread her legs and she would. She's that into me. That eager to please me.

But it doesn't feel real. It doesn't feel right. Cadence and the rest of them don't give a shit about me. Not really. They care about what I can do for them, being seen with me. My last name and the money and prestige that comes with it. To spend time with a Lancaster makes people feel special and I guess I get it.

I think about Daisy, and how she doesn't act that way around me at all. My name definitely doesn't impress her, and I'm pretty sure she hated me on sight. And while I sound like a complete douche even in my own head, I can't help but find that refreshing.

It's not that she's one of those "not like other girls" girls. It's just that she has zero tolerance for me. She's not interested. I'm not even on her radar.

She was aware of me, of course, because of our academic

situation. And while I've noticed her and always thought she was pretty—fine, she's beautiful—I didn't think of her like that. She's a good girl.

And I've never bothered with good girls before.

The more I think about her, the more I want to get to know her. I want to find out what she likes, what she doesn't like. Her favorite food. Her favorite color. What does she want to do once high school is over. She's a total overachiever so I'd guess college is on the agenda.

Would she think less of me if I told her that doesn't interest me? Would I sound like a spoiled rich prick if I admitted I just want to travel around for the next few years and see the world?

I sound like a rich prick in my own head so I'm sure the answer is yes to that last question.

I grab a fresh Post-it and slap it on the page I just highlighted, then grab my pencil and write a little note for Daisy. Wondering if she's figured out who she's communicating with yet.

Probably not. Will she be pissed when she finds out it's me? Probably.

I'm willing to take the risk.

Once school is over and I'm exiting the building, I spot my sister walking just ahead of me. I call her name and she glances over her shoulder, stopping to wait for me as I approach.

"Lowering your standards to be seen with me, hmm?" Edie tilts her head, her assessing gaze landing on my face.

I scowl. "Come on, Edie. Lowering my standards? Give me a break. You're the one who's never around."

"I'm hanging out with my friends and you're hanging out with yours. Though I've noticed you've been ignoring them more and more lately."

She's right.

"Cadence texted me last night," Edie adds.

Damn, why can't she leave this—me—alone? "What the hell did she want?"

"Tips on how to get back into your bed." Edie laughs when I sputter. "She didn't say those exact words, but she implied it. She's so sad, Arch."

"She can remain sad. I'm not interested in her." If Edie really fell for Cadence's lies, then she's more gullible than I thought she was.

"Who are you interested in?"

"No one," I lie. "What about you?"

"Not a single student on this campus could interest me," Edie says, her voice downright smug. "They're all so immature. Even guys in your class. *Especially* guys in your class."

"Right and all of those assholes in your class are far superior," I say sarcastically.

"I never said that. They definitely aren't."

We give each other shit the entire walk back to the building where our rooms are. She's right down the hall from me and it's kind of nice, knowing she's there with me. I can't imagine being on this campus alone, the only Lancaster in this old, creepy building. Once I graduate, Edie will be the only Lancaster left standing on campus.

Wait. Our little brothers will be freshmen next year so she won't be a complete loner. I'll be the one who's out and the rest of my siblings will be here.

My steps slow when we pass by the Albright's garden. Row after row of vegetables, mostly tomatoes. And the rose bushes. Funny how they don't grow daisies.

I take it all in, wishing she was there so I could go to her and talk to her, just so I could hear her voice, but there's no one out there.

Just that damn cat I scared off last night. Sniffing around the vegetables right before it sinks its teeth into a fat tomato, makes a hissing noise and then runs off.

"You know back in the day the Italians wouldn't eat tomatoes because they tasted too acidic. They thought they were poisonous,"

Edie says, dropping a little factoid like she often does.

"No shit?"

"Yeah. I don't think that cat liked the taste."

"That cat is kind of a dumbass."

"You know this cat?" Edie sounds amused.

"We've had run-ins before, yeah."

"Oh really?"

I change the subject, not about to mention who else I ran into.

There's something about Daisy that I want to keep all to myself. Not that I'm ashamed of her or anything. More like I want to protect her. No one else needs to know about us. Our interactions. Nothing can come of this. It's more than likely that nothing at all will come of it and that'll be that.

But right now, while I can cling to these moments with her, I'm going to. I sound like a sappy asshole even in my own head, but I can't help it. This girl...

Feels special.

I don't want to fuck it up.

CHAPTER SEVENTEEN

DAISY

I have a crush on Arch Lancaster.

I know, it's so stupid. He's completely unattainable and out of my league and all of those other things, but I can't stop thinking about him. Remembering how he looks at me. The things he says. He's not romantic. Not even close. He's blunt and borderline crude.

Not sure why I soften it with the word borderline. He *is* crude. He's also outspoken and we're nothing alike. Not at all.

But he looks at me and my heart beats faster. He smiles at me and I'm breathless. And when he touches me?

I feel like I could melt.

I truly believed I wanted a romantic love like what I read about it in my books, but that's not what's happening with Arch. At least, I don't think it is. I'm not even sure anymore what's real and what's fake. It's like I'm superimposing the situation with my book upon Arch, as if it's him who's annotating the book and highlighting his favorite parts.

The boy highlights all the sexy parts. The ones that make me blush. He started out tame enough but he's taking it further with every day that passes, to the point that he highlighted the sexiest scene yet, where the guy went down on the girl in a rather descriptive manner.

After that moment, I took the book with me, not leaving it behind for him. I was too embarrassed to continue, I suppose. Ending our little game once and for all. Was he disappointed? Probably. But I don't want to lead someone on. I don't like whoever it is I'm talking to. Not like that.

I like Arch. Whenever I read the highlighted parts, I imagine Arch doing those things to me.

His lips find the spot between my legs, sucking me. Licking me. His tongue slides inside of my pussy, essentially fucking me with it and that's all it takes.

I'm coming. All over his face. Making a mess. Normally I'd be embarrassed but not with him.

Never with him.

I slam the book shut and shove it under my bed before I leap off the mattress, going to the mirror that sits over my dresser and staring at my reflection, not impressed.

I look like a little girl with the stupid braids. I rarely wear makeup and my face is plain. I like my hair, it's probably my best feature but I hide it by putting it in braids all the time. It's like I don't want anyone to notice me.

It's dumb.

Annoyed, I change out of my clothes and don a bright pink sports bra and matching pair of shorts that I got for my birthday last year. A set I desperately wanted and that wasn't cheap. I was surprised my father bought it for me and I'd been so excited when I opened the box.

Then I promptly shoved the clothes in my dresser and never wore them. Too embarrassed, afraid the color was too bold. Like I would draw unwanted attention if I wore it.

Who's going to see me? I don't take P.E. anymore and I'm not in any sports. The only place I can wear it is our yard. Or walking around campus after hours. I could run down to the beach but it's kind of far and I don't like to go there alone.

I tear off the tags and toss them in the trash, then slip on a pair of no-show socks on my feet. Put on my newer Nikes and head outside, determined to get a little sun and wear this damn "too revealing" outfit. Who deemed it too revealing anyway, huh?

Me, that's who. I'm my own harshest critic. No one is as cruel to me as…me.

Not even Arch, and he's said some pretty crappy stuff to me.

My phone buzzes and I check it to see I have a text from my dad.

Going out to dinner with Kathy tonight. Want to join us?

Frowning, I immediately type out the word NO but then backtrack, thinking about what I should say.

I can't begrudge my father for wanting to go out and find female companionship. Kathy is nice. She seems to like and appreciate my father and he enjoys spending time with her. I know he's been fairly quiet about his intentions toward her and that's because of me. He's worried about how I might react.

He's lonely. I'm lonely. He wants a girlfriend. I want friends.

Fine, I want a boyfriend.

But I don't think I'm going to find one in the boy I like the most. He doesn't seem like he's boyfriend material.

Sighing, I type out a nice, encouraging response to my father.

Have fun. Don't stay out too late!

There. That's good. I sound like a parent, which he might appreciate.

He responds quickly.

Dad: *I'll be home before curfew.*

Smiling, I leave my phone on the dresser and head outside, eager to soak up the sun at least for a few minutes. I don't bother putting on a hat either. I walk right outside, squinting from the sunlight, grabbing my shears and bucket and start working on the roses, clipping all the dead leaves and dying blooms, murmuring to the pretty new buds. After a few minutes I feel something soft brush against my ankles and startled, I glance down to see the cat I tried to get a few days ago. Purring and rubbing against me as if he—or she—owns me.

"Look at you," I say, pleased. "Are you my friend now?"

The cat glances up at me, golden eyes glowing as it meows.

I sort of ignore the cat, going about my business, wanting the kitty to be comfortable with me. Eventually I set down the bucket and she doesn't run away. I bend down, rubbing my fingers together and the cat butts her head against my hand, purring loudly.

"Oh, we're truly friends now, huh." I scratch the cat under its chin, rubbing. Smiling at the loud motor sound of its purr. The cat wanders off, its tail standing straight up and I can tell it's a boy.

"What's your name, huh, buddy? Where did you come from? Are you hungry?"

"You talking to yourself out there, Daze? Or are you talking to the roses?"

I rise up, startled to find Arch standing on the edge of the garden, his hand at his eyebrows, shielding his eyes from the sun.

"What are you doing here?" I fight the humiliation spilling over my skin at him finding me like this. Talking to a cat and wearing this outfit.

This outfit that's not me.

"I was about to go for a run but I thought I heard your voice." I drink him in, noting the shorts and T-shirt he's wearing. He's staring at me too. I can feel his eyes skimming over me. His hot gaze lingers on my chest for a beat too long and I swear I can feel my nipples bead tight. "You look like you're about to go for a run too."

"I don't run."

"Is that your rose cutting outfit, then?" He's smiling, but I can't tell if he's making fun or not.

"It's too bright, huh. The color. I thought I would like it but I don't know. I feel stupid." I'm this close to bolting for the back door of my house, embarrassed I would admit this to him.

"I like the color." He takes a step forward, his voice gentle, his expression...sincere. As if he can sense my panic and wants to reassure me. "You look good, Daisy."

"I-I do? You're not just saying that?" My heart beats extra fast as he draws closer, and I tell myself to calm down. It's going to be okay. It's just Arch.

But that's the problem. It's Arch. And I'm all alone. Dad is gone. School has been out for hours. Most of the admin staff is gone, only the dorm advisors are left behind. Oh, and that one old, chubby security guard, who even I could take down if I wanted to.

Not that I want to take down Cliff, but he doesn't instill any sort of safe feelings inside me when I see him.

"I would never just say that. When it comes to you, I mean every word I say." He stops, an entire row of vegetables between us and I'm tempted for the briefest moment to throw myself at him. Just so I could feel his arms close around me.

Just once.

"I have a question for you," he says, his voice calm. Like he's not trying to talk me down from a full-blown panic attack.

"Wh-what is it?" I hate that I'm stuttering, but he just makes me so nervous.

"Why do you never clip any of the live roses and bring them inside?"

I stare at him, stunned he would ask. Surprised he noticed. Not even my father pays that close attention to me.

"What do you mean?" I ask warily, my defenses up.

As usual.

"I've noticed that about you, whenever I catch you cutting roses. You only take off the dead ones and trim back the branches. The dead leaves. You always leave the roses that are budding, letting them bloom fully instead of cutting them and putting them in a vase to enjoy inside," he explains.

Should I be worried he noticed all of that? Because I'm not.

A flush of pleasure washes over me at his words, at his attention to detail.

He notices me.

He sees me when it feels like no one ever does.

"I enjoy seeing them here. In their natural element." Swallowing hard, I decide to be real with him. "When you clip them, they're essentially dead. You kill them for what? To put in a vase and water so they can look pretty on a kitchen counter or a table for a few days? No. I'd rather keep them alive for as long as I can. Everything deserves to live."

Arch stares at me, seeming to take in what I just said, and I can't help but worry he might think I'm...I don't know. Weird? I have issues. Don't we all?

My issue is with death.

Time is fleeting. One moment you have someone in your life, and the next they're gone. Why not enjoy everything you can in its natural element? Like roses?

"Daze..." His voice drifts and I watch as he tilts his head back, his hands shoved into the pockets of his shorts. I stare at the strong column of his neck, noting the bob of his Adam's apple when he swallows. He's scaring me. This long pause, like he's trying to work up to say something.

What is it? What's wrong? What did I do?

All those questions run through my head, bringing that panic attack roaring back to life. Bigger than before.

"I need to tell you something." He says this to the sky and my heart is in my throat, I swear. "But I don't want you to get mad."

His words make my head spin and I close my eyes for the briefest moment, swallowing hard. I'm swaying on my feet, finding it difficult to stand up straight and there are dots flashing before my eyes. "Arch."

My voice sounds like it's coming from far away, his name a croak on my lips.

He's there, right when I begin to crumple, his strong arms

coming around me, catching me before I fall. I don't completely black out, but I was about to. I know I was. I've done this before, especially when I was younger. Right after Mom died. I was so fragile then. Never eating, not really taking care of myself.

When I blink my eyes open, I find Arch's face is in mine, worry etched into his handsome features, his hands gentle as he holds me.

So gentle.

"Shit, Daze, are you okay?" He sounds worried.

Scared.

My gaze searches his and I don't know when things switched. When he became my savior instead of my enemy, but I'm grateful he's here. Right now.

I need him.

"Take me inside," I whisper. "Please. I need to lie down."

He gathers me in his arms, carrying me as if I don't weigh a thing and I cling to him, my arms slung around his neck, my head resting against his chest. I can feel the pounding of his heart beneath my ear and I close my eyes, a shiver stealing over me when his fingers press into my bare skin.

If he never stops touching me, I'll die happy.

Arch makes his way inside our tiny house and I can't even work up the energy to be embarrassed over how old everything looks inside. How threadbare. Dad doesn't like spending money on what he calls useless things. Knickknacks and new furniture or the latest in electronics doesn't matter to him. It never really has. He's saving just about every dime he makes on a retirement plan for him and a college plan for me.

I love him for that and don't really need the finer things in life, but right now, I'm a little mortified by how old our TV is. And our couch, which sags in the middle.

But I can't worry about any of that now. Not when I've got Arch in the middle of my living room, gently settling me down on the couch like I'm made of glass and I might shatter at any moment.

"You want something to drink? Water?" he asks, rising to his full height and glancing around the tiny living room.

Everything seems small when Arch is in the room. He fills the space with his overwhelming presence and all I can do is stare at him in disbelief.

He's in my house. He's trying to take care of me.

What is this life?

"Daisy." His voice is firm and my gaze snaps to his, taking in the serious line of his mouth. How he's watching me with lowered brows and an almost frantic light flickering in his brilliant blue eyes. "I'm getting you something to drink."

"My water bottle is in my bedroom," I admit.

His gaze goes to the hallway. "Down there?"

"First door on the left."

He's gone in an instant and I sling my arm over my eyes, closing them. Sort of wanting to die. This is so embarrassing. I almost fainted—something I haven't done in a long time—right in front of him and now I'm acting like a damsel in distress. This is awful.

I'm sure the moment he can get out of here, he'll go running and never look back.

Arch returns in seconds, my pale peach colored Stanley clutched in his hand and I sit up, pausing when my head starts to spin. I blink slowly once, twice, and thankfully, the spinning stops.

"Here." He thrusts the tumbler in my face, the straw right at my lips. "Drink."

I do as he says, taking long sips, the icy cold water cooling my heated skin. I eventually take the tumbler from him, our fingers brushing, sending a scattering of tingles up both of my arms.

All over me.

It's like I can't help but react to him every single time he so much as looks at me, let alone touches me.

"I feel better," I admit once I guzzle a bunch of water. "I don't know what happened just now."

"You almost fainted," he says, filling me in on exactly what happened. "Even your eyes rolled into the back of your head."

"Oh God." Fresh humiliation seeps in and I cover my face with my hands, wishing he wasn't here.

Also, incredibly grateful that he is here.

"Have you ever fainted before?" he asks.

"A few times," I admit. "When I was younger. After..."

I don't finish the sentence. I don't think I have to.

After my mom died.

He's quiet for a moment and when I drop my hands, I see that he's watching me. His expression is incredibly serious. "You freaked me out."

"I'm sorry."

"Don't apologize," he's quick to say. "It's not like you did it on purpose."

Not sure what I should say, I grab my tumbler and take another sip. Shocked when he settles his big body on the other end of the couch, lifting my feet and settling them in his lap before he proceeds to untie my shoes.

"What are you doing?" I squeak, leaning over to set the Stanley cup on the coffee table in front of us.

"Taking off your shoes," he says, as calm as ever. He slips each one off, then my socks, and I try to jerk my feet out of his lap, but he clamps down hard on my ankles, keeping me in place.

"They might stink," I warn him, my cheeks, my entire body flushed with embarrassment.

"They don't." He literally brings one of my feet up to his face and breathes deep, like he's trying to inhale my toes. "Not at all."

A nervous giggle leaves me, and I'm jumpy when he curves his hands around my feet and starts to massage the insole, his touch light.

Perfect.

"You're tense," he murmurs, his gaze on mine. "Everywhere."

I swallow hard.

"Including your feet."

It's your fault, I want to tell him. I get in your presence and I almost faint.

But I don't say that. How could I? Confessing all is…

Scary.

And I don't even know what I'm confessing. Everything that's happened between us since the first day of school has been so confusing. Conflicting. He's mean, he's nice. He's hot, he's cold.

I don't get it. I don't get *him*.

"Where's your dad?"

The question is casual, but the way he's touching me is definitely not. He might only be rubbing my feet but who does that? No one. No one really touches me ever. I get the occasional hug from my father but that's it. I am starved for physical touch and obvious displays of affection. The way that Arch has his hands on me…

I never want him to stop.

Should I tell him the truth about Dad's whereabouts?

"He went out to dinner." My voice is hollow, a scrape against the dry skin of my throat and I take another sip from my Stanley cup. "With Kathy."

Arch's brows draw together. "Kathy from the dining hall?"

I nod. Sip yet again.

"They like each other?"

"I think so."

"That's…" His gaze finds mine again. "You're okay with that?"

"I want to be."

"Are you though?"

"I will be eventually." I shrug. "He's lonely."

"So are you, Daze."

My heart drops into freefall.

What did he just say?

CHAPTER EIGHTEEN

ARCH

I probably shouldn't have said that. I've completely overstepped my boundaries and she's most likely going to tell me to go to hell. Kick me right out of her house and tell me to never look at her again.

But damn, it's the truth. This girl is so damn lonely she aches with it and you know what?

So do I.

"You think I'm lonely?" Her voice is so soft I can barely hear her.

Nodding, I loosen my touch on her foot, drifting a single finger up the center of the bottom of her arch. She shivers. I feel it. That little shiver has my dick fucking throbbing.

"You are. You talk to no one. Hang out with no one. Just the admin staff and your dad and the roses and now the cat."

Her lips part and she takes a deep breath, like she might want to say something in protest over what I just told her. But she clamps those lips shut and leans back against the old gray couch, crossing her arms in front of her chest, plumping up her tits.

Slowly killing me in that pink sports bra and shorts is what she's doing. She got all freaked out earlier asking if she looked stupid in that outfit but hell no.

She looks fucking hot.

"Arch…"

"Yeah?" I release my hold on her foot once again, drifting my fingers up the back of her calf. Her skin is so damn soft. Silky smooth. Fragrant with some sort of lotion that has my mouth watering.

This isn't good, me being alone in this house with Daisy. Her barely clothed and her feet in my lap. The two of us on the couch staring like we'd give anything to touch each other for real. Like we mean it.

"Thank you for coming to my rescue." Her smile is small. Pretty. Everything about her is so damn pretty it hurts. "But you should probably go."

My fingers go still on her skin for a moment and I drop my head, staring at her tanned shin. She's right. I should go. I should walk right out of here and leave her alone because whatever it is this girl wants, I can't possibly give it to her. Not like she deserves.

"Do you want me to leave?" I lift my head to find her watching me with so much longing shining in her gaze, I already know the answer.

Slowly she shakes her head, her braids sliding across her bare shoulders. My gaze drops to her chest, noting how hard her little nipples are and fuck.

Fuck.

"Daze…"

"You can go if you want," she rushes to say, like she's trying to give me an out. "I'm sure you have somewhere else to be. Someone else to see."

"Daisy."

"And it's okay if you do. I get it. You're popular. Everyone loves you. No one knows me." Her laughter is broken, caught on a sob, and she clamps her hand over her mouth, silencing herself.

The tears in her eyes shine like glittery diamonds and I can't take it anymore.

Without a word, I haul her into my arms, tucking her into my lap, her head beneath my chin, her face pressed against my throat. Her tears dampen my skin and I squeeze her, smoothing my hands up and down her back, my fingers drifting across her bare skin. She's warm and soft and I just want her to feel safe.

I want her to feel wanted.

She cries for I don't know how long, sniffing into my neck, slinging her hand so her fingers curl around my right shoulder. My skin burns where she touches me and I'm desperate for more.

But I restrain myself. Keep my mouth shut. Let her cling to me like I'm her lifeline and I'm the only thing keeping her afloat.

"This is so embarrassing," she eventually croaks, and when she tries to pull away, I stop her.

Daisy leans back, her bloodshot eyes open, her tear-stained cheeks making my chest ache. "I cried all over you."

"It's okay."

"I'm sorry."

"Don't apologize." I touch the side of her face, drift my thumb across her cheek, catching a couple of stray tears. She releases a shuddery breath and closes her eyes, and I give into what I've been wanting to do for who knows how long.

Leaning in, I brush her mouth with mine. Featherlight. Barely a kiss at all.

She goes completely still. Rigid in my arms. As if she didn't like what I just did at all.

Shit.

I'm about to pull away but she reaches up, her hand curling around the back of my head, keeping me in place. Her fingers sink into my hair at the same time she presses her mouth more firmly against mine, with more purpose.

It's like I can't breathe. Pretty damn sure my heart stopped beating as she kisses me again and again. I let her take over completely, giving her all the power, afraid if I make one wrong move she'll stop.

And I never want her to fucking stop.

Slowly I return her kisses, my lips clinging to hers. Her lips parting more with each pass. She shifts in my arms, facing me more fully and when she takes a breath, I sneak my tongue out, licking at the corner of her lips.

A shuddery exhale leaves her and she pulls away slightly, her wide eyes meeting mine. Both of her arms are slung around my neck and I've got my arms around her waist. She's basically straddling me and she readjusts herself, her ass brushing against my dick, making me hiss in a breath.

"Arch..."

"If you tell me you want to stop, we'll stop. But just know it'll be the hardest thing I've ever done in my fucking life," I proclaim through gritted teeth.

"I—" She pauses, and I close my eyes, tilting my head back in complete agony. "I don't want you to stop."

A feral growl leaves me like I'm a fucking animal and I cup the back of her head, drinking from her lush lips. Her tongue meets mine and I think of that damn romance book and the line she liked so much.

Slow. Searching. Tasting. Learning.

Taking my time, I search her mouth with my tongue. Tasting her. Learning what she likes. Her tongue licks against mine and she scoots closer, her perfect tits crushed against my chest and I wish I could rip my shirt off so I can feel her skin on mine.

This will have to do for now.

I break the kiss first, dipping my head, licking my way down her neck. She tilts her head back, her hands in my hair, her chest heaving. Slowly I run my hand up her side, along her rib cage, my fingers tickling the edge of her sports bra and I'm tempted.

So damn tempted to touch her. Slip my fingers beneath the bra and cup her bare flesh.

I refuse to push her though. To move too fast. This girl needs me to take things slow and I'm going to.

For once in my damn life, I'm going to put someone else's feelings above mine.

She lowers her head as I pull away, our gazes meeting and I stare at her swollen mouth. Her flushed cheeks. Her still bloodshot eyes.

"Are you okay?" My voice is rough and I clear my throat, trying to calm my racing thoughts.

I want her naked. I want inside her. I want to fuck her hard and make her come all over my cock again and again but I can't.

I can't.

She nods, her expression hazy. A little lost. "I'm sorry I cried."

"I told you that you don't have to apologize."

"I feel bad. It's just—this is a tough time for me." She presses her lips together, her eyes falling shut for the briefest second. "It's almost my birthday. In two days."

Meaning it's the anniversary of her mother's death. Shit. That had to have fucked her up somewhat. "You'll be eighteen?"

Her eyes pop open and she nods, her teeth sinking into her lower lip. "I could've almost said eighteen and never been kissed but you just took care of that."

"That was your first kiss?" I'm incredulous, but then again, I'm not. This girl is untouched. Completely innocent. Sweet as can be.

A jackass like me has no business dirtying her up.

She nods, her chin trembling. I hate how scared she looks. "Was it bad?"

I groan at her question, pulling her in close, my hands locking around the ends of her braids, gathering her hair in my fist and giving it a light tug. "It was perfect."

You're perfect, is what I almost say, but I don't.

"Are you going to celebrate?" I ask after I kiss her soundly, releasing my tight hold on her hair. "Your birthday?"

Daisy shakes her head. "It's just another day. Sort of a bad day. My father is always so sad on my birthday. It's hard to celebrate, you know?"

That is so messed up. I'm not him and I have no idea what it's like to lose the love of my life on the day the child you share was born, but seriously. I would do everything in my power to make it a good day for this girl.

She deserves nothing but the best.

My phone buzzes in the pocket of my shorts and I pull it out to see I have a text from JJ.

Where you at fucker?

Irritated, I shove my phone back in my pocket, leaning against the couch and breathing deep while Daisy remains on my lap, wide-eyed and unsure.

"You're so fucking pretty, it hurts to look at you," I tell her and she blinks at me, shocked by my outburst. "What? Don't look at me like that. You don't believe me when I say you're pretty?"

Her lips part. I can practically taste the protest she's about to give.

"Fuck that," I rush to say before she speaks. "You're not pretty, you're goddamn gorgeous."

"Arch..."

"It's true, Daze. Look at you right now." My gaze wanders, touching all over her. "I should go."

She climbs off my lap in a hurry, keeping her face averted, and when I stand, I reach for her, cupping her chin and forcing her to look at me. I see the hurt in her gaze and I know my abrupt statement is what's bothering her.

"If I don't leave now, I can't be held accountable for what I might do to you if we keep this up," I admit, my voice low, my gaze locked on hers.

Daisy swallows hard, her shining eyes never straying. "What do you want to do?"

"To you?" I lean in close, my mouth at her ear, my voice harsh when I whisper, "Everything. Every fucking dirty thing your sweet mind can come up with, that's what I want to do to you, Daze."

I take a much-needed step back, noting how she trembles.

"And don't say you'll let me do whatever I want to you. You're not ready yet," I say firmly.

"But…"

"You're in a vulnerable spot," I say, cutting her off. "Just—I'm going to leave. It's what's best."

"Okay," she whispers.

We walk to the front door together, her trailing behind me, her sadness and confusion palpable. When she reaches around me to unlock the door, I sweep her into my arms and kiss her. Hard. With lots of tongue.

She gives in easily, whimpering into my mouth, her arms coming around my neck and then I'm shoving her away, hating how out of control she makes me feel.

"I'll see you tomorrow," I say with all the conviction I can muster because that's something I can guarantee.

I will see her tomorrow. In class.

And after class too, if I'm lucky.

CHAPTER NINETEEN

DAISY

I enter my English class the next morning in a daze, my head still swimming with thoughts of Arch. What we did last night. How he touched me. How he kissed me. How he left me.

That hurt the most, but he did it for me. At least that's what he implied. And when he whispered in my ear before he kissed me, those words still live inside me, just like everything else he says to me.

Every fucking dirty thing your sweet mind can come up with, that's what I want to do to you, Daze.

I have a pretty vivid imagination, thanks to the romance books I read. And while I've never done any of the things I read about, beyond kissing Arch for the first time last night, I can come up with all sorts of…sexual situations. Involving me and Arch.

My entire body goes liquid at the mere thought.

Glancing around the room, there are only a few students sitting at their desks. Two girls sit close, talking in hurried whispers, and when I walk by, one of them glances up, her gaze meeting mine.

"Hi," she says, surprising me.

"H-hi," I return, scurrying away before I say something stupid and falling into my desk at the front of the class.

Why can't I be normal? Why can't I just be friendly and not worry over it all the time?

I really need to work on my social skills.

Minutes later and the bell is about to ring, but still no Arch. This isn't unusual. He runs late always. He has his own clock and doesn't care what anyone thinks, while I'm early to the point of ridiculousness.

Mr. Winston enters the classroom, whistling under his breath, cheerful as usual. He flashes me a smile and a few days ago, I would've thought he looked handsome. I still sort of think that. He's young and attractive and a lot of girls on campus have a crush on him.

But now when I think of someone handsome, I immediately think of Arch. I think of the way he kissed me with this almost— desperate quality. Like he somehow knows whatever it is we're doing won't last and he needs to get as much of it, as much of *me,* as he can.

I feel exactly the same way.

A sigh leaves me and Mr. Winston gives me a funny look.

"Morning, Daisy."

"Good morning, Mr. Winston," I say just before I glance toward the door.

Still no Arch.

"Distracted?" my teacher asks.

I turn back toward him. "A little tired, I guess."

I didn't sleep well, my head too full of what happened. Reliving those moments over and over.

The taste of Arch's hot, wet mouth. His tongue. His hands. How he touched me, his fingers eliciting fire everywhere they landed…

The bell rings, interrupting my thoughts, and Winston goes to the door, about to pull it closed when Arch slips inside, flashing our teacher a rueful smile before he glances around the room, his blue gaze landing on me.

"Glad to see you're on time for once," Mr. Winston greets him with a shake of his head.

"Barely," Arch tells him with a laugh, making the rest of the class laugh too.

A slow smile spreads across Arch's face and he heads straight for me, settling into the empty desk directly behind mine. I angle my body toward his, unsure of what to say, taking him in silently.

His hair is damp, as if he barely just got out of the shower, and his tie is looped haphazardly around his neck like usual. He is wearing the navy blue uniform jacket though, which is different. He never wears that thing.

"Morning, Daze," he says, his deep voice washing over me, landing in a low throb between my thighs.

"Hi," I squeak, whirling around to face the front when Mr. Winston starts taking roll. I'm the first name he calls and I murmur, "Here."

I'm achingly aware of Arch's presence, Winston's voice fading into nothing but unintelligible noise. I remain still, my head tilted slightly to the right, as if I can see him out of the corner of my eye.

He shifts closer after Winston calls his name, his presence only amping up the wild beating of my heart. "Only one braid today, huh?"

Nodding, I turn a little more, meeting his gaze briefly. "Yeah."

He smiles, his gaze on my mouth. Like he's remembering kissing it. "Why don't you ever wear it down?"

"Mr. Lancaster, are you really going to sit behind my best student and disturb her?" Winston's voice rings across the classroom and I sort of want to die.

"I thought I was your best student." Arch shifts away from me, kicking out his legs, his feet touching the front legs of my chair.

Gosh, he's long.

"You're one of them." Winston sounds amused. "Think of what you could be if you actually applied yourself."

I'm almost offended on Arch's behalf but he just laughs like it's no big deal. They've had this sort of conversation before and it used to irritate me. How hard I would work to earn my grades while it feels like Arch just strolls in and does well without having to think about it.

I need to talk to him about this. Is he a complete genius or what? I'm smart. I know I am. But I also put a lot of effort into my studies, my papers, my tests. I want to be the best I can be.

It's like Arch is just…the best with little to no effort. That's sort of infuriating.

But now I'm intrigued.

Winston starts talking about our reading assignment, analyzing passages and questioning the motives of the author. This is usually my favorite sort of lecture, because I love looking deeper into what an author writes, though I'm guessing a lot of the time, there's no real meaning behind the words. They're just telling a story.

Right now, though? I can't focus on anything else but Arch's nearness. His scent. His feet touching the legs of my chair. What is he thinking? Is he thinking about me like I am him?

After a few minutes of listening to our teacher, I feel something. The light touch of Arch's fingers toying with the end of my braid. He tugs on it, gently at first.

Then a little harder.

Only to curl my hair around his finger, his thumb rubbing against it slowly. Back and forth. Tingles spread over me, starting at the top of my head and working their way down until I feel like I'm covered in goosebumps. I hold still, my breaths coming faster, my lips parted.

He's going to kill me if he keeps this up. His innocent touch that doesn't feel innocent at all. Like he's trying to drive me out of my mind with…lust.

It's working. The emotions rising within me are unfamiliar but welcome. I feel downright giddy, even when he stops touching me. When he lets go of my hair and leans back in his chair, his legs still sprawled. I wish I could look at him. Just blatantly stare at him for the entirety of the class period.

Ducking my head, I blow out a breath, vaguely annoyed with myself. I've got it bad for this boy and I...I shouldn't. He's dangerous to my wellbeing. He's careless and thoughtless. A troublemaker. And rich beyond anyone else I've ever encountered. Once he graduates, he'll be gone and I'll never see him again.

Just the thought of that...hurts. More than I want to admit. Even to myself.

By the time the bell is ringing, signaling class is over, I'm in a full-blown funk thanks to the turn of my thoughts. Who am I fooling, thinking Arch Lancaster is really interested in me? So we kissed yesterday. Big deal. I'm sure he goes around kissing girls all the time.

All. The. Time.

I am nothing special.

Without a word I exit the classroom, leaving Arch behind, and of course, me being me, I immediately feel terrible for being so rude.

But that doesn't stop me from fleeing. Besides, he'll just follow me because we're both going to the same place.

By the time I'm reaching the admin building, Arch's fingers are curling around the crook of my elbow and he hauls me around the side of the building so I end up with my back against it, Arch standing directly in front of me, his expression thunderous when I look up into his eyes.

"What's wrong?" he demands.

I blink up at him, at a loss for words. All I can do is shrug one shoulder.

"Talk to me, Daze." He touches my face and I melt like the weakling I am for him. "You just tore out of there and I was hoping you'd wait for me."

"You want to be seen with me?" I whisper, staring at him in disbelief.

"What the fuck are you saying? I don't have a problem being seen with you." His hand drifts down to curve around my neck, his fingers exerting just enough pressure to tilt my head back.

And then his mouth is right there, on mine. Brief and soft and just long enough to have me closing my eyes, desperate to savor the moment.

"Think Viv will notice if we both don't show up to second period?" He murmurs the question against my lips.

"Yes, she definitely will," I say when he pulls back.

He frowns. "Guess you'll have to instruct me on how to answer phones then."

"Again? You haven't picked it up yet?" I can't believe I'm teasing him after having a minor meltdown not even five minutes ago.

I really need to get myself together. I'm making everything worse when in reality, nothing is wrong.

Everything is scarily going my way.

Can't help but think something horrible is going to come along and ruin everything though.

"I can't help that I'm easily distracted." He's staring, not saying a word, and I realize he's referring to me. That I'm a distraction.

"Arch…"

"Why don't you ever wear your hair down, Daze?" He reaches out, tucking a few stray tendrils behind my ear, his finger brushing against my skin and setting off a fresh scattering of goosebumps.

"It always gets in my way," I say with a little shrug. He's asked me this question before. Like he's fixated with my hair or something. I don't get it.

"I want to see it down." His gaze is intense, his voice extra deep. "Would you ever do that? For me?"

For him. Right now, and the way he's watching me, I would do anything for him.

Anything.

The bell rings and I literally squeal, pushing past him and running toward the double doors. Arch is right behind me, both of us entering the office seconds later, me offering an apologetic smile in Vivian's direction.

"I'm so sorry I'm late," I tell her, my words sliding all together.

Vivian waves a dismissive hand, bustling past us as we make our way toward the desk where we usually sit. Lately together. "Don't even worry about it. I need you two to do something a little different for me today anyway."

"What's up, Viv?" Arch asks, cheeky as can be.

The look she sends him would level a normal person, but Arch just slips his hands in his pockets and smiles at her. "I need you both to go to the library where the storage area is. We're looking for a couple of boxes full of old photos and I haven't had a chance to try and dig them up yet."

I'm surprised she hasn't asked my dad to grab the boxes, but his duties are mostly outside so maybe that's why.

"What do you need the old photos for?" Arch asks, because of course he does. He has no qualms questioning things because this institution is his heritage. His family.

Me? I would've just done what Vivian asked with no questions.

"The school website is being redone and the web designer wanted to use old photos. I knew we had a bunch and thought they were somewhere in here, but Miss Taylor said they're probably stored away in a couple of boxes in the library. But she's too frail to dig through them," Vivian describes.

"Miz Taylor is older than dirt," Arch agrees, earning an annoyed glare from Vivian.

"She knows far more about this campus than anyone else here," she says. "You could probably learn a thing or two from her."

"I already do," he says solemnly. "We chat every day during sixth period."

"You're in the library during sixth period?" I ask him.

He turns his gaze on me, and I lock my knees so they don't wobble like they want to. "It's a free period for me. So I hang out with Taylor every day. We talk it up."

I find that hard to believe. The woman is slightly terrifying. Always shushing students even when we whisper. She barely tolerates us. Imagining her chatting away with Arch doesn't seem possible.

"Daisy, I trust you to carefully look inside the boxes and find the ones with the photos. Arch, you're going because you've got the brawn to carry the boxes and this is your family's school so you might discover a thing or two going through everything," Vivian explains.

I'm surprised she's letting us do this—alone. Hasn't she noticed the tension growing between us? It's quiet and private in that old room. We could get up to whatever we wanted and no one would know.

From the dark look Arch sends my way, I'm guessing he's thinking the same exact thing.

I've been in that back storage room in the library only once in all the years I've gone here and lived on campus. Dad took me there when he had to drop off a couple of boxes and I was surprised at how large the room was. At one point it was a part of the library and was even used as a classroom, but eventually, they shut it down and kept it as storage. Something about the wall of windows being too distracting.

Sounds like an excuse but whatever. That expanse of windows is pretty impressive. It overlooks the entire gardens.

"Let's go," Arch says, his gaze only for me before it slides to Vivian. "We'll be right back."

"Don't bother returning here if you can't find any photos today. Take your time. You can look tomorrow if you need to, but we need those photos—at least a few of them—by Friday," Vivian says, handing me a keychain with only a single key on it.

"Will do." Arch salutes her and I roll my eyes, yelping when he grabs my hand and drags me out of the office along with him, never letting go of my hand the entire way as we walk across campus.

If he gives me nothing for my birthday—and I don't expect him to give me a single thing, we barely know each other and my birthday is tomorrow—I will be satisfied with this. Him holding my hand and smiling at me, his fingers intertwined with mine.

This is more than enough.

It's everything.

CHAPTER TWENTY

ARCH

We make our way through the aisles of bookshelves in the library, Daisy's hand still in mine as we head for that door in the very back, the one she has the key for. Excitement sizzles through my veins and I remind myself to calm down. We're on a mission and Daisy is a good girl. She won't want to mess around in the cavernous storage room, no matter how badly I want to persuade her.

We come to a stop in front of the door, Daisy slipping her hand from mine as she takes the key and shoves it in the lock, turning it slowly, like it's difficult. I step closer, my body brushing hers, helping her shove the door open and we walk inside. I shut the door, shrouding us in darkness, a tiny beam of light in the distance the only thing allowing us to see.

"Come on," I tell her, taking over the situation as I once again take her hand.

She walks with me not saying a thing and I realize I'm so damn grateful she doesn't feel the need to fill the silence with nonsensical, pointless chatter. Any other girl I've ever known would do exactly that but not Daisy. She's so damn quiet. I'm curious about her but she doesn't reveal much.

I wish she did.

The beam of light gets brighter the deeper we move through the room and then we're in front of the infamous mass of windows, the ones that face out over the gardens. I stop in front of it and so does she, our hands still connected. I can see her little house to the right in the distance. I can even see a couple of her rose bushes, the blooms waving in the breeze.

"There's your house," I tell her, my voice barely above a whisper.

"I see it." She turns to me at the same time I look at her and I wonder if she's as tempted as I am to just fuck responsibilities and make out instead. "We should look for the boxes."

Damn. There's my answer.

Letting go of her hand, I wander over to the other side of the room, wincing at the stack upon stack of boxes that line the wall. Most every one of them has writing on the box, telling us the contents inside but not all of them.

Shit.

"No wonder Viv keeps putting this off," I mutter, craning my neck to read what the boxes say at the top. "This school seriously needs to move into the digital age."

"As a Lancaster, you could probably make that happen," she says, her voice light. Like she might be teasing me. And when I glance over at her to find she's smiling at me, I shake my head.

"I'll let someone else take care of that," I drawl.

Standing up straighter, she rests her hands on her hips, drawing my attention to how they flare. She's not wearing a jacket—I shrug out of mine, dropping it on the ground without a care—and she's got her shirt tucked in. We all wear these damn uniforms and everyone looks the same on campus.

But there's something about Daisy that stands out over everyone else. At least to me. She's fucking beautiful and sweet. Sexy. I can't stop staring at her, like she's my favorite thing to look at in the entire world. The way that pleated plaid skirt flirts around her thighs...

I want to slip my hands under it.

"Where should we start?" she asks, glancing over at me.

"Do we have to start now?" When she raises her brows, I go on. "We've got tomorrow to do this too. Let's just chill."

"Arch..."

"Daze..." I grin.

She shakes her head, looking at me like I'm a naughty boy and she's going to bust me. "Vivian trusts us to do this."

"What Viv doesn't know, doesn't hurt her." I go to her, snatching her around the waist and making her shriek. "Come on, let's go check out the view again."

I haul her into my arms, tipping her halfway over my shoulder and she's literally screaming. Her skirt rides up high and I clamp my hand on the back of one smooth thigh.

She goes silent.

My dick twitches.

Shit.

This girl is dangerous. She fucks with my head and everything else too. If I don't watch it, she might up end up fucking with my heart.

Not that I have one. Not really.

There's a table right by the wall of windows, and it's covered with a thin, old tablecloth. Bending down while keeping a squirming Daisy balanced over my shoulder, I snag the tablecloth off and drop it onto the ground before I deposit her on top of the table, leaving her sprawled across it.

She's sputtering, her hands braced behind her, her legs slightly spread. Looking like a sexy little snack I want to feast on. "What in the world are you doing, Arch?"

"Tell me to stop and I will." I bend over her, my hands braced next to her hands, my face level with hers. She's breathing faster, her eyes searching my face, falling closed right as I touch her lips with mine.

A quiet moan leaves her when I part her lips with my tongue, her head falling back, her tongue tangling with mine. I shift closer, tempted to crawl on the damn table myself and crush her, but I'm afraid it can't take my weight so I remain restrained. Kissing her lips but touching her nowhere else.

She doesn't like it. I can tell by the needy noises she makes. How restless she becomes. She wants to feel my hands on her as we continue to kiss and I refuse to touch her. Getting off on seeing how much she wants me.

How much she needs me.

At one point, I bite her lower lip gently, sinking my teeth into the plump flesh and giving it a tug, and she darts out her tongue, licking at my lower lip.

Look at that. My Daze is getting braver.

"Did that hurt?" I whisper against her mouth after I let go of her lip.

"No," she whispers back, pausing before she admits, "I liked it."

I deepen the kiss, my tongue licking everywhere I can reach, her tongue sliding against mine. I could kiss this girl for what feels like forever and never get tired of it. But I can't keep this up or I will end up fucking her on this table and so I end the kiss, noting the way she leans into me as I pull back, like she doesn't want to stop.

Pushing away from the table, I rise to my full height, licking my lips. Tasting her on them. She watches me, her hungry gaze tracking my tongue and I realize she's hot for it.

Hot for me.

"You've really never kissed anyone before?" I ask like a dumbass.

Her gaze narrows and she sits up, brushing the flyaway hairs away from her face. "Are you trying to accuse me of something?"

"What? No way. I just—it's good, between us."

How underwhelming I described what we share. It's better than good. It's amazing.

Unbelievable.

Her face turns redder than it already is, which seems impossible. "You bring it out in me."

"Oh yeah?"

She hops off the table and stops directly in front of me, yanking on the end of my tie. "Don't let it get to your head though."

Her sassiness is a surprise and I like it. So much that when she lets go of my tie and starts to walk away, I reach out and swat her on the ass.

"Hey!" She glances over her shoulder, her eyes wide. Like I shocked her. "What was that for?"

"Your sassy mouth," I say without hesitation. "Come on, Daze. Let's go find those boxes ol' Viv wants."

We dig around among the haphazard stacks of boxes, Daisy peeking inside the unmarked ones before pushing them aside. I take them from her and restack them, my nose itching. Everything in this place is covered in a thin layer of dust and it's stuffy as hell too. To the point that I undo my tie and shove it in my pocket. Unbutton the cuffs of my sleeves and roll them up to my elbows.

Daisy watches me do that particular task with extra interest, her gaze tracking my every movement and I'm tempted to flex just for her, but I restrain myself.

Barely.

"Oh, look at this!" she exclaims when she lifts the lid on one particular box. Inside are a ton of photos, the ones on top mostly in black and white. She pulls one out, staring at it for a second before she shows it to me. "That's out in front of the entrance."

I take the photo from her, staring at it. The row of men standing on the steps that lead to the main entrance of Lancaster Prep. It's from a long time ago. Late eighteen hundreds maybe? Early nineteen hundreds? The men are dressed impeccably and there's a single woman standing there amongst the men in the middle of the front row.

"I'm related to her." I tap the woman, showing the photo to Daisy. "She's a great-great-great grandma. Maybe a couple more greats, not sure."

I'm exaggerating with the greats, but I am definitely related to her.

"Wow, really?" Daisy takes the photo from me, staring at it again. She lifts her gaze to me, studying my face before she returns her attention to the photo. "You look like her."

I scoff. "Do not."

"Do so," she returns, holding the photo away from me so I can't grab it. "Face it, Archibald, you're a Lancaster through and through."

"Do not call me Archibald," I threaten, my voice dark.

"Or what?" she challenges, her eyes twinkling. "What are you going to do?"

"You don't want these dirty hands on you." I hold them up, though they don't look that bad. "Not when you're wearing that pristine white shirt."

She laughs. "I get the sense that all you ever want to do is dirty me up."

"You don't even know the half of it," I murmur.

Her laughter dies, her expression turning serious. "What are you doing, Arch?"

"What do you mean?" I frown.

"What are…your intentions? Toward me?"

I gulp, turning her words over in my mind. Intentions? Such an old-fashioned word. "I thought we were just living it day by day. I'm not the type to think about the future."

"Ever?"

I slowly shake my head.

A sigh leaves her and she averts her gaze. "It must be easy, to feel so comfortable in your existence that you don't have to plan for anything coming up."

My frown returns. "What are you saying? That I've got it easy?"

She shrugs. "Easier than anyone else I know. You just… exist, and everything falls into place. There are no challenges, no worries. You are the perfect eldest Lancaster son. The sun rises and sets on your head."

"You have no clue what my life is like. And it's nothing like that." I'm fucking offended she would assess me like that. "My life isn't that easy all the time. I'm dealing with a tremendous amount of pressure. My parents have expectations on me that I will never meet, no matter how hard I try."

"I'm guessing you don't try very hard."

Anger rises, and I tell myself to calm down. Don't blow up on this girl. "What does that mean?"

"You're so smart, Arch. You barely apply yourself and you get perfect grades. You're number one in the class and you make it look so easy, while I'm over here working my butt off by studying day and night, trying to keep up." Her voice rises. Clearly, she's a little heated too.

"Are you accusing me of coasting?"

"I'm not accusing you of anything. We all know you're totally coasting! Handsome Arch, charming Arch, smart Arch. No one is going to argue with the Lancaster. No one dares cross him. Your life is easy."

I'm shaking my head as I walk away from her, bending down to grab my jacket where I left it on the floor. "You don't like it when I assume things about you, Daisy. I don't like it either."

Before she can say a word to me, I'm out of there, practically running to the door. Pissed that she would be so dismissive of me. Like I don't have any feelings. Like I'm inhuman.

I may act that way sometimes, but it's easier to be the smart, untouchable Lancaster than let my guard down and let anyone in.

See how it worked out just now? I try to give this girl a glimpse of my real self.

And she stomps all over me.

Fuck that.

• • •

By lunch I've calmed down, but I'm still hurt by what Daisy said. I avoided her earlier in class, which isn't hard because she avoids me as well. No wonder I never really had any interactions with this girl until recently. She slips in and out of the classroom like a ghost, never uttering a word or even looking at anyone the entire time.

Must suck to move through life like you don't exist. I can't even imagine. I'd rather have all eyes on me at all times then that sort of lonely existence.

Shaking my head, I walk into the dining hall with JJ, pasting on a smile and laughing at the stupid joke he just told.

"You better now?" he asks me after my laughter dies.

"I'm good," I confirm with a nod.

"You sure? You were in a foul mood earlier," JJ mutters as we check out lunch options.

I grab a tray and set a plate with a cheeseburger on it and then grab a small basket full of fresh french fries. I can practically taste the salty goodness, I'm so fucking hungry all of a sudden. "I was just hungry."

"More like hangry!" says a familiar female voice.

We both turn to see Cadence and Mya standing there, matching hopeful expressions on their faces. I groan inwardly, but JJ smiles like he's a host on a game show, eager to please.

"Ladies," he says, bowing at them before he reaches for his own cheeseburger.

"We haven't sat together in a while," Mya says, sharing a look with Cadence. "Can we join you guys?"

They haven't sat with us since last week, which means it hasn't been that long. I wonder at their motive, but I shrug, not wanting to give them any encouragement. "You can sit wherever you want."

Another shared look between the girls but I ignore them.

"Join us," JJ says, his focus only on Mya. "But only if you share your fries with me."

"Deal," Mya says with a giggle.

Cadence falls into step beside me as we walk out into the dining area, JJ and Mya following behind us. She sends me a knowing look, and I almost roll my eyes at her in return but restrain myself.

This is what I need to do with Daisy too. Restrain myself. But I overreacted because her comments touched a nerve. I need to find her and apologize, but I don't see her pretty blonde head anywhere.

She's probably hiding from me, and I can't blame her.

"I've missed you, Archie," Cadence says as we approach our usual table.

"Don't start," I warn her. "I'm not in the mood."

"You're never in the mood anymore." She settles into a chair and I purposely choose one that's not right next to her to sit in.

"Because we're done," I say with a finality I hope she picks up on.

But she doesn't. Mya and JJ are flirting it up throughout lunch, with Cadence sending me meaningful looks every time I so much as glance in her direction.

"What are you guys doing this weekend?" Cadence asks at one point, her extra cheerful voice grating on my nerves.

"We've got no plans," JJ says, glancing over at me. "Right, Arch?"

I nod. "I was hoping for a low-key weekend. Plus, I gotta go see my parents Sunday."

"How are they?" Cadence asks me. "I miss them."

What a lie. They didn't particularly like her and she didn't like them either.

"They're fine," I say, my voice clipped. I think about what I've got due in class next week. "I also need to write a paper."

"Ugh, that's so boring," Mya says, giggling when JJ pokes her side with his index finger.

They're into each other, and I envy how easy it is for them to kid around and flirt. Like it's no big deal. It makes sense considering we're all a part of the same friend group.

I wish it was that easy for me and Daisy.

"Well, we're getting an Airbnb," Cadence proclaims, glancing over at Mya, who nods encouragingly. "We're having a big party Friday night."

Tomorrow. Daisy's birthday.

"What for?" I ask.

"Does there need to be a reason?" JJ asks me before he turns to the girls. "We'll be there."

"Yay!" Cadence claps her hands, her gaze stuck on me. "Maybe we could all hang out."

"At another one of your big bashes where you've probably invited the entire school?" I raise my brows.

"I didn't invite the *entire* school." She shakes her head, that smile still on her face. I gotta give it to her, she doesn't give up. "Just a few people from our class. It's nothing too crazy. Last time we tried to invite a bunch of people, the neighbors called the cops and they shut the party down."

I remember that. Late last year, right before school was done. One of Cadence's senior friends reserved the house for her and we partied like fucking crazy that night. I was naked in the pool with a pair of sunglasses on and a cowboy hat on my head when the cops rolled up.

Talk about ruining the party vibe.

"We had fun that night," Cadence murmurs just for me, JJ and Mya involved in their own conversation.

"We did," I agree because yeah, we did. But I'm not willing to have fun with her anymore.

I wish she'd get that through her head.

"We could have fun again, you know. I miss you."

I blow out a harsh breath, about to lean back in my chair, but Cadence's hand darts out, landing on top of my forearm. I don't push her away, testing it out. Her touch makes me feel nothing and I think of how it feels when Daisy touches me.

Like I want more. I need more. I want to feel her hands all over me.

Cadence's fingers curl and she walks them up my arm, like that's cute. Like I might enjoy it.

I still feel nothing. When it comes to Cadence, it's like I'm dead inside.

"Knock it off, Cadence. You don't really miss me," I tell her, wishing she'd stop touching me. "It's not the same anymore between us."

"Is there someone else?" Her fingers go flat and she starts tracing them up and down my arm. Still nothing. Zero reaction. "Who is she?"

"There's no one else," I lie, hating that I said those words out loud.

There is definitely someone else. I might be mad at her but I am far from over her.

It's not even that I'm mad. Daisy hurt my feelings.

And that's a new thing for me to deal with. Not many people get close enough to actually hurt me. I barely know this girl and look at the power she wields.

"If there's no one else, then come to the party." Cadence smiles, her fingers curling around my forearm. "Please?"

Every single hair on my body seems to stand on end and it's not because of Cadence's pleading voice or how she can't stop stroking my arm. I glance up, meeting Daisy's gaze from across the dining hall. She's clutching a tray in front of her, so tight I can see her knuckles turning white, and there's a single sandwich on a plate. A shiny red apple sitting next to it.

We stare at each other, and I see it. The flicker of disappointment. It disappears in an instant, replaced by disgust.

For me.

Lifting her chin, she grips the tray and heads straight for us. My heart starts to hammer in my chest, Cadence's insistent voice fading the closer Daisy gets.

Until she's walking right past our table with her head held high, not even looking in our direction as she sails by us and settles into a chair at one of the smaller tables nearby.

Frustration flickers in my gut, churning. My appetite is long gone.

"Jail bait is looking better and better every time I see her," JJ drawls, like he's trying to provoke my ass.

"Stay the fuck away from her," I bite out, jerking my arm away from Cadence's hand. I stand, contemplating the three of them. JJ's amused. Mya's confused, and Cadence is hopeful.

Better than bitter and pissed, which is how she usually looks when she's dealing with me.

"I'll go to your party," I tell her just before I leave the table. I stalk my way out of the dining hall, passing directly behind Daisy's chair.

Streaking my fingers across her back from shoulder to shoulder as I go.

Don't need to look back to know she's watching me leave.

CHAPTER TWENTY-ONE

DAISY

feel terrible for what I said to Arch. But it's almost like he needed to hear it too? I don't know. I probably overstepped my boundaries. I'm guessing no one talks to Arch like that. He's the privileged eldest son of an esteemed family and in everyone's eyes, he's untouchable. Inhuman.

But he is a human. He hurts and bleeds like the rest of us. He also has faults. No one is perfect, least of all him.

I wanted to share with him that I go through struggles when it comes to school, and I ended up talking down to him and calling him out for his faults instead. Probably wasn't the best approach to take with the only person on this campus who talks to me, but I couldn't help it.

He needs to realize that to everyone else, he looks like he's living a perfect life. And if he's not?

I wish he would tell me. Share his secrets. His hopes and his fears. Though I need to do the same. I've barely told him anything.

Yet it feels like he's got me all figured out.

It killed me to see him sitting with Cadence and her hand on his arm like she owns him. He was kissing me only an hour ago. Devouring my mouth like he was starving and oh God, it woke up all sorts of unfamiliar feelings buried deep inside me. He didn't even touch me. Just his hungry mouth on mine, kissing me so thoroughly I could barely breathe.

Hot. The man knows how to heat me up and make me want more.

More, more, more.

When he left the dining hall and traced a line across my shoulders, I almost melted with relief. It was a reminder that just because Cadence had her hands on him, he still wanted to put his hands on me.

Or maybe I'm sick and twisted and completely wrong. Why would I be glad a boy let another girl touch him before he touched me? After he kissed me? I should be angry.

Instead, I feel bad.

Sixth period and I can't pay attention to what Mrs. Nelson is saying, no matter how hard I try. I think about the boy who highlighted his favorite parts in my book. Who was it? Does he know who the book belongs to? I doubt it. If he did, he wouldn't keep up this conversation with me. No boy is interested in me. Not until Arch.

And he wouldn't do something like this. This isn't his style.

I wish I knew who it was.

Courage gathering within me, I grab a piece of paper and start writing. I don't stop until I get it all out, my every request. I read over what I wrote only once, telling myself I can't regret it.

I just need to do it.

I want to know who you are. You might be disappointed in me and maybe you will be when you see it's me, but I want to meet.

After your class. Right after school. Wait outside of Nelson's classroom. Please? It's my birthday tomorrow and…I just want to know who you are.

Maybe we can be friends. I don't have a lot of friends here and I'm always open to making a new one. Besides, I can't stand the suspense any longer.

I need to know your name.

I fold the note and stuff it in the desk, my heart racing wildly. If it's JJ, I will die. But I know it's not JJ. The possibilities of who it might be are endless. There are a lot of guys in my class who I've never spoken to before. Nice boys who come from good families. Rich boys with impeccable genes and pleasant smiles. Overachievers who might be intimidated by a girl who's considered smarter than them. A quiet girl who's too shy to talk to anyone, let alone a boy she doesn't know.

Inhaling deeply, I hold my breath for only a moment before I let it all out in a shuddery, agitated exhale. Mrs. Nelson catches me, her brows lowering in concern, but I flash her a quick smile, letting her know I'm okay.

Everything's going to be all right.

I know it is.

. . .

I feel like I'm going to throw up.

Thank God it was quiet in my last class. Advanced physics, which is such a difficult subject. Our teacher gave us free time to catch up on our assignments and ask him any questions we might have. Which was nice. I appreciated the catch-up period but oh my God, it also left me with way too much idle time on my hands and all I can think about is what's about to unfold.

Right now.

My feet feel like I have lead weights on them as I head for Mrs. Nelson's class. The halls are mostly empty, everyone having taken off and headed back to the dorms or they've gone outside or to whatever practice they need to attend.

I have nowhere to go. Well, except I'm about to meet the

person who was highlighting the sexy parts in my book.

I spot Mrs. Nelson's door, which is closed, and I stop in the middle of the hall to catch my breath, resting my hand on my stomach. It twists and turns, like I could throw up at any second and I swallow hard, trying to regain control.

This is the moment and I'm acting like I'm walking to the death chamber. It's not going to be so bad.

It's not.

Taking a deep breath, I drop my hand and march toward the door, looking around. I told him to wait outside but there's no one here.

Not a single soul.

I open the classroom door, and not even Nelson is inside, which is unusual. My gaze goes to my desk—his desk—but it's empty.

Someone—a male someone—clears his throat, and I turn around, the shock and relief I feel when I see Arch standing in the doorway nearly has me sagging.

"You're kind of pushy." This is all he says to me.

Then he holds up the note. My note.

"It's you?" I breathe, staring at him in disbelief.

"Yeah. It was me." He carefully refolds the note and stashes it in his pocket as he strides inside the room. I can see by the guarded look on his face that he's still wary with me.

"I'm sorry for what I said earlier." I throw it out there before he can say anything. I don't want us to argue. "It was uncalled for."

He shoves his hands in his pockets. "You were right."

My mouth pops open. "Huh?"

"You were right," he repeats. "I deserve to be called out for my shit. No one ever does that."

I snap my lips together, listening.

"Things do come easy for me, but not everything, Daze. My life isn't sunshine and roses. You're the one who acts like you're a Disney princess."

"With a tragic backstory," I mutter.

"Yeah. About that. You should share some of those details. If you ever want to," he tacks on.

I should. I need to. But not right now. "Why didn't you tell me you were the one highlighting my book?"

"I liked the mystery of it." He shrugs. "Plus, it was a great way to pick your brain."

"Pick my brain?"

"And see what you like." The knowing look on his face has me blushing.

Profusely.

Arch starts walking, until he's standing directly in front of me. He reaches out, his fingers slipping beneath my chin, tilting my face up to his. His thumb streaks back and forth along my jaw. Down my throat. Making my stomach flutter with nerves. And something else.

Desire.

"You're kinkier than I thought," he drawls, and if my cheeks could catch fire, they would be doing exactly that right now.

"I am not kinky," I insist, my protest weak.

"You like the dirty stuff though. Which is surprising."

"It's easier to admit when it's done anonymously." My breath hitches when he continues to stroke my throat with his fingers. "You like dirty stuff too."

"Of course, I do. What guy doesn't want to shove his cock down his girl's throat?" He says the words so matter-of-factly, but my brain is still stuck on the last part of the sentence: *his girl's throat.*

It's not even the mention of cock that has me all fluttery and weak.

It's the way he said *his girl.* As if that's what I am to him.

Before I even realize what he's doing, he grabs my hand, tugging me closer, our bodies colliding, sparks seeming to light up between us. It is such a complete relief that we're on good terms once again that I'm tempted to melt into him and beg him to never let me go.

But I don't. It's still so hard for me to admit I have feelings for him—feelings that I don't even fully understand.

Feelings I've never confessed to anyone before. What we share is...special. Overwhelming.

Does he feel the same way? About me?

"I want to give you an early birthday present," he announces with a smirk.

I tilt my head back, smiling up at him. "What do you want to give me?"

He tilts his head close to mine, his mouth brushing my ear as he whispers, "An orgasm."

Giving in to my urges, I lean into him, tilting my head to the side, wishing he'd keep talking.

"Have you made yourself come before, Daze?"

I close my eyes, trembling. This is even harder to admit than how I feel about him.

"You can tell me," he reassures. "I won't tell anyone else."

Slowly, I nod. I can feel him smile and sort of want to die.

"With your fingers?"

"Yes." I swallow hard.

"What if I said I wanted to give you one with my fingers." Those same fingers are streaking down my side, toying with the hem of my skirt.

"Not here," I whisper.

"Definitely not here." His mouth finds my neck, his lips warm and soft and I tilt my head back on a sigh. "There's somewhere I want to take you."

"Where?"

"Do you trust me?"

I shouldn't. I absolutely, one hundred percent should not trust this boy as far as I can throw him. I will end up giving my entire heart and soul to him and he will hurt me. That much is guaranteed.

"Yes," I whisper like the fool that I am.

He pulls away so he can look me in the eyes and all I see is lust. He wants me. Maybe as badly as I want him, and I don't think I ever believed I'd see someone like Arch Lancaster looking at me like this.

Wanting me like this.

"Ready to go?" he asks, his brows shooting up.

"Right now?"

"Yeah." His smile is faint.

"Should we change?" I'm always eager to get out of this uniform by the end of the day and put on something more comfortable.

"No." He tugs on my hand, leading me toward the door. "The skirt will give me better access."

CHAPTER TWENTY-TWO

DAISY

He takes me deep onto the school's property, far from campus until we're close to the woods that divides the property from the beach. We're so far out, I can hear the ocean roaring in the near distance. The breeze is cooler out here, directly off the water, and I shiver despite the warm sun shining down upon us.

When the old ruins appear, I know where he's taking me. To the building that used to house staff on campus before it burned in a fire years ago. The annual Halloween party is held out here for students. It's all student-run, the school doesn't sanction it, and I know for a fact they hate that this party happens, but since it's normally a Lancaster organizing it—or a friend of—they look the other way and pretend they don't know about it.

I haven't gone to the party, so I don't know what it's like. I've never been to this burned-out building at all. Not even my dad has taken me out here, but from what I can see, it's kind of beautiful.

A little sad but still beautiful. You can tell the building was stately before it burned. There are crumbling old bricks still covering part of the front, and what was once white clapboard is now withered wood with peeling paint. The building is nothing but a shell. There's no roof, and only some of the walls still remain standing, though enough was left behind for it to protect us from spying eyes.

Somewhat.

Would anyone even think to follow us out here? I doubt it.

Arch is holding my hand—I really love it when he does that—and he squeezes my fingers as we both come to a stop in front of the rickety staircase that leads to the front door, which is really just a frame. An outline of a door.

"Have you ever been out here before?"

I shake my head. He has to already know that answer.

"You'll have to come to the Halloween party this year. It'll be a rager."

"I don't really go to parties." I try to hide my disappointment that he didn't say he wanted me to come with him to the party. That's still so far away. Who knows where we'll be by the end of October?

"You'll go with me." He says this like a statement, as if I don't have a choice, and my worry from only a few seconds ago evaporates. Just like that.

He tugs on my hand and I follow him up the front stairs, careful where I step. We walk through the open doorway and my gaze is everywhere, touching on everything. I can't make out what anything is supposed to be anymore. The wood is weathered with a silvery gray hue to it and I go to where a window used to be to look out. The glass is mostly gone but the frame is still there and I peer through it, watching the sun shine upon the water in the distance.

"It's pretty out here," I murmur, sucking in a breath when Arch stops behind me, slipping his arms around my waist. "The view."

"It's a great view," he says, his voice muffled against the side of my neck. "I mean, look at you."

I rest my arms over his, my hands on top of his. I'm shivering. Cold despite the sun and Arch's big body wrapped around me. And so, so nervous. "I wasn't talking about myself."

"I know, Daze." His hand slips from beneath mine, reaching

for the hem of my skirt and I wait, breathless as his fingers slide up the outside of my thigh. "You're trembling."

I close my eyes, fighting my nerves. "I've never done anything like this before."

"Never been kissed?" He presses his mouth against my neck. "Never done anything? Ever?"

"Only been kissed by you," I whisper, a dull ache starting between my thighs at his touch.

"Gonna be the one who takes every single one of your firsts, Daze, but not all of them today." His hot breath fans across my neck, my ear, and I close my eyes when he bites it. Nibbles on the lobe, his fingers drifting up and down the outside of my thigh.

Guilt trickles through me, brief and startling, and my eyes fly open. I shouldn't be doing this. I shouldn't let Arch do this to me. My father always said I should save a moment like this for someone special.

For someone I love.

But I'm almost eighteen—in less than twenty-four hours, I will be eighteen. An adult. If I choose to let Arch slip his hands into my panties like I've fantasized about for weeks, then I'm going to do it.

He's special. He makes me *feel* special. And besides...

I can't save myself forever.

Arch grabs hold of my shoulders and gently spins me around, crushing me to him, his mouth on mine. His lips and tongue busy. Messy. It's an out-of-control kiss, both of us frantic, panting, our tongues battling, my hands somehow finding the front of his shirt and undoing the buttons with shaky fingers. I wasn't even conscious of my doing it until I break away from his still seeking lips and spread his shirt open, my lips parting at all that warm, hard flesh on display and I do what feels natural.

Leaning in, I press my mouth against the center of his chest, breathing in his scent. His warmth. The pounding of his heart matches mine and I close my eyes, my mouth running over his skin. I want to consume him.

I want to feel him inside me.

Groaning, he slips his fingers beneath my chin and tilts my head up, his mouth finding mine once again. I let him kiss me, overwhelmed by his constantly moving mouth and tongue. I can feel his hand wander down my side. From my rib cage to my waist to my hips. Down along the side of my skirt, his fingers curling. Gathering the fabric.

His fingers slip beneath my skirt, his tongue circling mine, making me groan. All while his fingers drift across the side of my panties, toying with them, tugging on them. Teasing me.

I'm wet. I can feel it. And his touch is making me even wetter. I didn't know sex—foreplay, whatever you want to call it—could feel like this. All-consuming and scary and wonderful all at once. I'm tempted to both push him away and beg him for more. It's too much.

Not enough.

His fingers slip beneath the fabric of my panties, drifting along my hip and I'm restless. Desperate for him to touch me where I really want.

"Are you wet for me, Daisy?" His fingers get closer and air lodges in my throat, making it hard for me to breathe. "Are you?"

"Y-yes," I stutter, a gasp escaping me when he gently shoves me against the wall, the wood rough on my back. His fingers never stop moving, sliding closer. His other hand rises up, gently holding my throat, pinning me in place and I wait there. Helpless.

Desperate.

"I want to watch your face the first time I touch you," he whispers, making my legs wobble. Thank God I'm leaning against the wall, his big body holding me up. "But if I take it too far, tell me. Okay? I want this to be good for you."

I nod, my hair brushing against the splintered wood, strands getting stuck on it, yanking on my braid. I keep my eyes closed, holding my breath as I wait. It feels like even my heart stops for a moment, hanging on that edge, desperate to feel his hands on me.

His fingers move, encountering pubic hair before they slide down, fully cupping me. I suck in a breath, my eyes still closed, everything focused on that one spot where he's touching me. He removes his hand from my neck and I exhale, a whimper leaving me when his fingers press, splitting me open.

A rough sound leaves him, making me throb.

"Soaked," he murmurs, sounding pleased. "Damn, Daze."

I should probably be embarrassed, but I'm not. I like that he found me wet, and that it pleases him. I like the sound of his fingers searching me. Testing me. I spread my legs a little and crack my eyes open, keeping my head bent down so I can watch. His arm and hand shifts beneath my skirt, his fingers sliding back and forth just before his thumb presses against a spot that has me moaning.

His mouth lands on mine, swallowing the last of my moan, his tongue thrusting. I return the kiss, clinging to him, spreading my legs farther, his busy fingers rubbing, his pace increasing before he shifts downward. He teases my entrance, slipping just the tip of his finger inside and I squeeze my thighs together, trapping his hand.

"Does that hurt?"

"N-no." I shake my head, wincing when my hair snags on the wood.

He pulls away so he can stare into my eyes and we watch each other, his finger still inside me. The reality of what we're doing smacks into me like a punch, and I can feel my entire face turn hot. "I don't want to hurt you."

"You're not," I whisper, struggling with embarrassment.

He pushes his finger deeper inside me and I part my lips, exhaling softly, my tongue sneaking out to touch my upper lip. The embarrassment dissipates, and I am wholly concentrated on that spot where we're connected. His thick finger curling. Slowly sliding out before thrusting back in. I whimper when his thumb brushes my clit again and he keeps doing it. Faster. Harder.

A gathering sensation starts in the pit of my stomach, my breaths coming quicker. Harder. He kisses me again, his lips and tongue all over me. My mouth and cheeks and chin and jaw. My neck, my ear. Hot and frantic and all-consuming. When his hand drops away from me, the disappointment nearly swallows me whole.

And then he slips both of his hands beneath my skirt, gripping my butt and lifting. Without hesitation, I go willingly. His mouth thankfully on mine once more, he pulls me close, my center pressed against his unmistakable erection and I go still, startled.

Though I have zero experience in situations like this, he seems huge. Thick and hard and intimidating. Fear creeps over my skin, along with a healthy dose of nervousness, and I tilt my hips forward almost mistakenly.

The strangled groan that falls from his lips has me feeling brave and I do it again.

Again.

"Fuck, Daze." He sounds dazed. Consumed. With me?

That's how I feel with him. Consumed. Obsessed.

Arch begins to move his hips, nudging against me in the most perfect way possible and that feeling is back, tenfold. The gathering sensation low in my belly. The throbbing, the heat pouring through my veins. I move with him, against him, the friction between that one spot where our bodies rub and strain making me hotter.

I'm burning up.

My climax smacks into me out of nowhere, so strong it's like I can't even breathe. It goes on and on, my lips parted on a silent scream as I clutch onto him. Until I'm finally slumped against him and he gathers me closer, the shudders wracking my body for what feels like forever.

"Happy Birthday," he whispers against my ear when my orgasm is over.

Making me smile.

CHAPTER TWENTY-THREE

DAISY

My alarm wakes me, my eyes popping open. I stare at the ceiling for a few seconds, my brain hazy with sleep and the memory of what Arch and I did yesterday.

A smile curls my lips and I close my eyes, stretching my arms and legs out with a small groan. A quick knock on the door has me sitting up, pushing my hair out of my eyes as I stare at my closed bedroom door.

"Good morning, Daisy Mae," Dad calls from the other side. "Happy Birthday."

He sounds oddly...cheerful. Which isn't a bad thing, it's just unusual. Today isn't a good day for him. For us.

Six years ago today, we lost her. The most important woman in our lives.

"Thank you," I tell him, clearing my throat.

"I've made you breakfast," he says, and I can tell he's walking away. Most likely heading back to the kitchen. "Your favorite, so hurry up if you want to eat."

I leap out of bed and go to my mirror, staring at myself. Do I look different? Changed? Not because I'm eighteen now, no. I feel changed because of what happened yesterday between me and Arch.

The longer I stare, the more I realize I look no different. Just the same old Daisy, my blonde hair spilling past my shoulders in a haphazard mess, clad in a thin tank top and a pair of panties because it gets hot in my bedroom, even at night.

There is nothing sexy about me that I can see, yet Arch stares at me like I'm the sexiest thing he's ever seen. And the way he kisses me...

I touch my lips, tugging on the lower one. The same. Everything's the same.

But I feel so incredibly different. Not like myself at all.

Wait, I take that back. I feel like myself—but a heightened version of myself. Like I've discovered things about me that I didn't know existed until now.

Smiling at my reflection, I run my fingers through the ends of my hair, deciding that today is the day I wear it down. Maybe I can even curl it, if I have enough time...

"Daisy! Your pancakes are ready!" Dad calls, launching me into action.

By the time I'm entering the kitchen, Dad is already sitting at the tiny table close to the window, forking up a mouthful of pancakes, his gaze sticking on me.

"You're wearing your hair down," he says after he swallows.

I sit across from him and pick up the syrup, drizzling it over my stack of pancakes, careful not to add too much. "I felt like doing something different."

If he knew I was doing this for Arch, he wouldn't be pleased. He doesn't like him, while I'm afraid I like Arch a little too much.

"You look pretty, sweetheart." He studies me for a moment and I can tell by the look on his face that he's caught up in his memories. Thinking of another time. "I can't believe you're eighteen."

"I can," I tell him with a little laugh, digging into my pancakes. I don't want to reminisce over past birthdays or tragedy and loss. The fierce way I miss my mother is a physical ache that lives inside me, but I know she wouldn't want me to be sad about losing her on a day that should be for me.

He smiles at my answer. "Are you feeling every one of those eighteen years?"

"I suppose." I take another bite of my breakfast, chewing and swallowing it down. "Thank you for breakfast. It's delicious."

"You're welcome."

We eat in comfortable silence, him reading the local newspaper on his iPad and me checking social media on my phone. I follow people I go to school with but not a lot and I don't know why I never thought of it before, but I go and check Arch's profile.

It's public, because of course it is, and he has an outrageous amount of followers. Over fifty thousand, which is like…crazy. Though I assume they follow him because of who he is.

A Lancaster.

I realize the follow button on his profile actually says "follow back" and I'm surprised I didn't get a notification that he requested to follow me. I hit the button, accepting his follow and wondering if he'll be disappointed.

My posts are boring. Mostly photos of roses or a bird sitting on a branch in a tree. Semi-artsy stuff when I thought I wanted to be a photographer for all of a minute.

There are no photos of me with friends or a past boyfriend. Oh, there's a photo of me and my parents from the Christmas when I was eleven.

The last Christmas we got with her.

"You have plans tonight for your birthday?" Dad asks when we're almost done with our breakfast.

I stare at him in disbelief. What friends would I celebrate with? "No."

"Ah." He squirms in his seat and I wonder what his problem is. "Kathy asked if I wanted to get together for dinner and I told her maybe."

Well, at least he's thinking of doing something else on this day versus reliving the moment that changed our lives forever.

"I can cancel on her and tell her we need to save it for another time," he's quick to say when I don't respond. "We can go out instead. Just the two of us."

And be sad all night? "You can go out with her."

He tilts his head. "You sure about that? I don't want to leave you alone, sweetheart."

"It's okay. Really. I might have plans." I think of Arch. He doesn't even have my phone number, so it's not like he can text me and ask if I want to do something on my birthday. Does he even remember that it's my birthday?

I remember how he said happy birthday in my ear yesterday afternoon after he made me come, and I'm guessing yes.

He remembers.

But that doesn't mean he'll want to spend his Friday night with me. I shouldn't expect anything from him.

"You might, huh?" His smile is wide and I can tell my response pleases him. All he wants is for me to be happy. To make friends and live a normal teenage existence. Instead of the life I'm actually living, which is nothing normal.

It's not that I think I'm special or above anyone else. I'm just introverted. Shy. I find it freaking impossible to make small talk. I wish I was better at that sort of thing. More social, more easygoing. More open and flirtatious and cute.

Like Cadence. She's perfect. A little whiny sometimes but I don't think any of the boys at our school mind too much. She's beautiful and confident and has lots of friends. She's the most popular girl at the school and this isn't the first time I've thought about her and felt…

Envious.

Arch used to be her boyfriend. If—somehow—Arch and I become a public thing—I can't even imagine that happening but maybe it could—how will she react? Will she hate me?

Maybe.

Probably.

See, this is why I don't let myself get close to anyone. Problems come with that. It's so much easier just keeping to myself.

Dad leaves the house before I do and I dash back into my bathroom, grabbing a hair tie and pulling my hair up into a high ponytail, glaring at myself in the mirror the entire time. Hating myself for wanting to change. I don't bother putting on mascara like I'd planned. Instead, I brush my teeth, grab my stuff and leave the house, walking with determined steps toward campus.

I'm running a little later than normal and I stop short in the open doorway of my English class, surprised to see Arch is already sitting in the desk directly behind mine, having a conversation with Mr. Winston.

It's a miracle. The bell hasn't even rung yet.

Arch notices me the second I step into the classroom, his eyes lighting up, following my every move as I approach, despite Winston still talking to him. Arch keeps up the conversation, sitting up straighter as I settle into my desk, unzipping my backpack in my lap and pulling out my things.

He tugs on the end of my ponytail, his fingers brushing across the back of my neck, and I quickly whip around, studying him in surprise.

"Happy Birthday to my favorite person." Arch smiles and all I can do is stare mutely back at him. As if I've lost all ability to speak. His smile fades and he rests his forearms on the desk, leaning closer as his voice lowers. "You okay?"

I nod slowly, touched he called me his favorite person. Touched even more that he would ask about my well-being. He knows the truth of this day and I'm glad he checked in without blatantly mentioning what happened. "I'm great," I say, breathless.

His smile returns, fainter this time, concern lighting his blue eyes. "You sure about that?"

"It's just another day, right?" I turn away from him, pulling a pen out of my backpack and setting it on top of my notebook. Trying to act normal, though I can feel his eyes on me. Cataloging my every move.

"Not really," he finally says, his deep voice causing me to pause. "It's special—the day you were born. And you're eighteen now."

My gaze locks with his and he's watching me with this intensity I can feel down to my bones. "I am."

He leans even closer toward me, his voice low when he confesses, "I can't stop thinking about yesterday."

The bell rings before I can respond and Winston is already talking. Taking roll like usual, as if he gets a thrill from calling out our names. I offer up a weak *here* when he says my name first, still not looking away from Arch.

Only when Winston starts actually lecturing do I turn and face forward, my mind anywhere else but on what the teacher is talking about. And when I feel Arch wind my hair around his finger, I know he's thinking about the same thing that I am.

Me. And him.

Together.

. . .

We walk together to the admin building because we always do and it doesn't feel like we're causing any sort of fuss. No one is paying attention to us anyway, and I prefer that. Even though it's not Arch's style.

In the not-so-distant past he always seemed to enjoy being the center of attention. I used to find his antics so annoying and completely over the top.

Now I feel like I've got him figured out—well, not completely but somewhat.

"I got you something," he says as he rushes forward to hold

the door open for me.

I murmur a thank you as I walk past him, pleased when he rushes to make sure he's walking beside me as we head for the admin office. "What did you get me?"

"It's a surprise," he says with all of that quiet confidence I wished I had even an ounce of.

I hate surprises. That's what happened when Mom died six years ago. A complete surprise. Totally unexpected.

Totally awful.

We both stop in front of the closed office door and I turn toward him, my shoulders falling. "Just tell me what it is."

He's frowning. "No way. Not like it's a bad surprise, if that's what you're thinking."

With a rough sigh, I push the door open, Arch trailing right behind me and I come to a stop when I see what's sitting on top of the desk we sit at.

A miniature rose bush in a galvanized steel pot. The flowers are the beautiful pink-peachy color that was my mom's absolute favorite.

"Oh." My voice is soft and I rush toward the desk, picking up the pot and sniffing the tiny blooms. The familiar scent fills my senses and I set the pot back onto the desk, reaching out to trace over the petals of one of the roses. "They're so pretty."

"You like it?"

I turn to face Arch, frowning. "What do you mean?"

"My surprise." He shoves his hands in his front pockets, looking...

Nervous.

"This is my surprise?" We both glance over at the pot. "I thought Vivian brought it for me."

"Nope. This is all me. I wanted to get something bigger for you but I didn't have much time." He's smiling, his hands still in his pockets, a funny light in his eyes. Reminding me of someone trying to balance on a tightrope and not sure if he's going to tip over to the left or to the right and fall off, plunging into darkness. "I know how much you like roses, and this way, you can keep them in your house. Your room or whatever, and you don't have to cut them off. They can grow and live inside, you know?"

My heart aches. Feels like it is going to burst out of my chest as I go to him and throw my arms around his middle, pressing my face against his chest as I murmur, "I love them. Thank you."

His arms slowly come around me and his big hands run up and down my back, comforting me. Yet also firing me up. "You're welcome."

"What in the world is going on here? Oh, the roses! So beautiful!"

I jerk out of Arch's embrace, my cheeks hot as we both turn to face Vivian, who's watching us carefully.

"Arch got them for me," I say, trying to play it off. Failing miserably. "For my birthday."

"Well, isn't that thoughtful of you, hmm?" Vivian's gaze narrows as she studies Arch with a scrutiny I don't think I've seen from her before. "How interesting, that the two of you have become—friends."

Friends. Friends who kiss. Friends who dry hump each other because that's what I did to Arch yesterday.

It's what I want to do again. I'm willing to take it a step further even, and I feel bad that he didn't get any sort of satisfaction yesterday. Though I have no idea what to do with a penis. I've never seen a naked one in real life before and I wouldn't know the first thing of how to touch it.

Well, that's not true. I've read plenty of romances. They're like a learning book for romance. Sexual activity. Maybe I do know how to touch one.

Maybe I should test it out and see what Arch thinks.

CHAPTER TWENTY-FOUR

ARCH

I walk alongside Daisy as we head toward the library to continue working on the project that Vivian asked us to do yesterday, me basking in the glow of Daisy's good mood. She was pleased by my gift and I sweated over that for way too long, so thank God, she liked it.

That hug she gave me more than proved she liked it.

This girl though. I can't quite figure her out. She runs hot and cold. Standoffish or all over me. Currently, I'm thinking I could get her all over me and I'm down for that. Down for anything she wants to do.

Watching the orgasm sweep over her yesterday when we were at the ruins was one of the hottest things I think I've ever witnessed. The way her skin flushed, her gaze going unfocused when it first hit, her lips parting. Kissing her, touching her, letting her rub all over me—Jesus.

I wonder if she'd want a repeat performance in the library. No one would be around. No one would catch us. We could find a dark spot behind a shelf or a stack of boxes and I could press her against the wall, just like I did yesterday, slide my fingers inside her welcoming hot pussy and stroke her until she's shouting my name. So loud I'd have to put my hand over her mouth, muffling her cries and…

Yeah. I need to keep my thoughts under control.

We don't talk at all when we enter the library, where I shout a hearty greeting to Miss Taylor. She merely glares, not shushing me like she does everyone else, and I flash her the most charming smile I can muster.

The librarian merely scowls as we walk by her desk, Daisy sending me a nervous glance from over her shoulder.

I let Daisy lead the way through the library, enjoying my view as I trail behind her. The way her blonde ponytail swings. How straight her shoulders are, how perfect her posture is. The length of her neck. How soft her skin is there, how fragrant. That damn skirt and how it moves when she walks. The back of her thighs. Thighs that were wrapped around my hips only yesterday. Thighs I want to caress with my fingers. My lips.

I scrub at my face, mentally reminding myself I need to calm down.

By the time we're in the back storage room, I give in to my lust-filled thoughts and grab Daisy from behind, whirling her around in my arms and kissing her. A noise of surprise leaves her right before my lips touch hers and I plan on keeping it quick. Simple.

But when it comes to Daisy, I can't do quick and simple. The kiss turns deeper. Longer. Until my hands are wandering and she's whimpering and my tongue is thoroughly searching her mouth. It's only when I slide my hand up her skirt is she pulling away, shaking her head.

"We can't," she says, her voice weak. Like my resolve. "Come on, let's find the photos first."

"First? And then what?" I follow her toward the stack of boxes, hating the thought of digging through those again.

I'm already over it. All I want to do is get my hands back on Daisy.

"If we find what Vivian wants, then you can do…whatever

you want." Her smile is shy. A little sexy.

"Whatever I want?" I lift my brows and she nods. "But it's your birthday. Shouldn't it be whatever *you* want?"

"I have no idea what to do…next." She shrugs helplessly.

"Oh, give me a break, Daze. You read those sexy romance books. You have a few ideas running around in that pretty little head of yours." My words make her blush.

This girl. She can play shy all she wants, but I read the passages in that one book with the cutesy cover. There was nothing cutesy about the contents though. Those sex scenes were pretty descriptive.

She ignores me and cracks open a box, searching through it. We keep this up for at least a half hour until we come across another box full of old black and white photos, mostly of campus and the buildings. I put it aside along with the first one that had a few photos in it that we found yesterday.

"I think this is good enough," I tell her as I shove a lid on a box and stack it back into place. "We've found a decent amount of photos."

"I'm sure Vivian will be pleased." Daisy brushes her hair away from her face, trying to tuck it back into her ponytail. I'm disappointed she didn't wear her hair down today. For some reason I thought she might. "Should we take the boxes back to the office?"

"I thought you were going to let me do whatever I wanted now."

"But we're all dusty," she protests.

True. "How about lunch?"

"What about lunch?"

"Let's sneak off somewhere. Just the two of us."

"Um…"

"Maybe your place. Your dad will be on campus, right? Working? Or does he eat lunch at home?"

"No, not really. Especially not lately. I think he takes a later lunch so he can spend time with Kathy." She makes a little face, and I wonder how on board she is with this new romantic relationship her dad is embarking on.

"Then let's go back to your house for lunch."

She shuffles her feet, her teeth sinking into her lower lip and I can tell she's nervous. "I don't know…"

"I won't do anything you don't want to," I rush to say. "I won't push, Daze. I just like—spending time with you."

She actually laughs, like she can see right through me. "Spending time with me? Is that code for kissing me?"

"Well, yeah. Like I told you earlier, I can't stop thinking about yesterday."

"I can't stop thinking about it either," she admits, her voice soft.

"Yeah?" I lift my brows, pleased at her confession. I've already conjured up all sorts of mental images of what we can do next. How much further we can take it. There are what I consider natural steps to the process and I'm perfectly okay with making them. I'm not about to push this girl too hard. Even though I'm always impatient, always eager to get to the good stuff. The main thing.

Sex. Boning. Penetration. Whatever you want to call it. That's what I'm down for always. Fucking.

With this girl, every experience, every interaction, touch, kiss and stroke I qualify as the good stuff. When she touches me, my entire body lights up as if she hit a damn switch and turned me on.

"Yes," she says, standing up straighter and looking all prissy and hot. Odd combo but it's working for me. "Can you grab the boxes and carry them to the office for me?"

"Whatever the birthday girl wants," I drawl, teasing her.

She rolls her eyes, laughing, and as I grab the boxes and start to head for the door, I realize something.

I like making her laugh. Seeing her smile.

I like it—her—a lot.

We go back to the office and deliver the boxes to Vivian, who examines the contents with a pleased smile on her face. "You two did great."

"I need to wash my hands. Do you mind if I go to the restroom?" Daisy asks Vivian, who dismisses her with a wave of her hand.

The moment Daisy is out of the office, Viv is turning on me with a frown. "What are you doing, young man?"

I rear back a little at her tone. "What do you mean?"

"I sincerely hope you're not toying with Daisy's heart." I open my mouth to protest but she talks right over me. "I see the way you look at her. How you grabbed her hand yesterday and brought her a birthday gift today. If this is some sort of game to see how far you can take things with Daisy, may I strongly suggest you stop now before you do real, permanent damage?"

I'm actually fucking offended. And more than a little hurt. "I'm not playing a game with Daisy. I-I like her."

The skeptical look on Viv's face is telling me she's not falling for my schemes.

But for once, it's not a scheme. I do like this girl. A whole fucking lot.

"Really, Arch?"

"Really, Viv." I let the nickname drop and irritation flares in her eyes. "And I don't need you telling me what to do or how to treat her. I know how to respect someone and their boundaries. And that's what I'm doing with our girl Daze."

Viv snorts. "Our girl. She's never been your girl before, Arch. You've never even looked twice at her before and now all of a sudden, you've got moon eyes and you follow her around as if she's got you on a leash."

"I do?" Shit, I didn't think I was that obvious.

"Yes, you do, and if what you're feeling is real, then more power to you. Daisy is a delightful, giving girl and she deserves the world. While most of the time you've spent here at Lancaster

Prep, you've proven to be a spoiled brat and nothing else. Learn a thing from her."

"Like what?" I ask, annoyed.

"Like how to be a decent, thoughtful person."

. . .

"The house is kind of messy," Daisy warns as we approach the front door. She glances over her shoulder, an unsure look on her face. "No judgment. We don't have a team of maids like you do."

I roll my eyes, hating how she always feels like she's gotta remind me of our differences. "I'm sure it's not that bad."

"I never cleaned up our breakfast dishes." She opens the door and steps inside, me right on her heels, following her into the house, closing the door behind me.

She's got the miniature roses I gave her tucked in her arm and she sets it on a shelf that's beneath the front window, arranging it carefully so it's facing the light. I glance around the living room, taking in the shabby couch, the scratched-up coffee table. I didn't even notice the furniture the last time I came in here, when Daisy just about fainted.

The house isn't a mess like she said. More like it appears lived in. Like a home versus a museum, which is how my mother keeps our house. Not that she ever lifts a finger to clean.

We have a staff of housekeepers, just like Daisy said.

The scent of maple syrup lingers in the air, making my stomach growl even though the last thing on my mind is actual food. I'm hungry all right, but not for a meal.

I'm hungry to get my hands and mouth and whatever else I can get on Daisy.

"You going to leave the roses right there?" I ask, watching as Daisy darts around the living room and straightens things up.

"For now," she says, grabbing a throw blanket and folding it carefully before she places it on the back of the couch. "My bedroom can be kind of dark throughout the day and the roses need light."

I'd sort of hoped she'd keep it on her nightstand and always think about me when she's in bed, but I guess beggars can't be choosers or however that saying goes.

"Do you want something to drink? Or eat?" She twists her hands together, her fingers curled, her nervousness radiating from her.

Slowly I shake my head, making my way toward her. Drawn to her like a moth to a flame, a magnet to steel. Sappy thoughts run through my head when it comes to Daze, and I blame the damn romance book I read. The one that fueled my imagination and made me think of all the things I can do to Daisy. Things she'd like.

Things she might do to me.

I stop only when I've got my arms around her waist, my hands splayed across the narrow expanse of her back. She's a tiny thing. Not very tall and she weighs nothing. I remember how I slung her over my shoulder yesterday and wonder why she hasn't told me to kick rocks already.

But she doesn't tell me to leave when I get my hands on her. Nope, she puts her hands on me, resting them on my chest, her fingertips burning through the layers of clothes I've got on. I want to feel her hands on my bare skin and I want to put my hands on her too.

I want to make her mine. Mark her in places no one else can see. Hell, mark her in places everyone can see so they know she's my girl. I want everyone to smell me on her.

I want to smell her on me.

"Arch..." Her voice trails off and she takes a deep breath, like she's trying to work up the courage to speak. "I'm nervous."

I kiss her forehead. "I already said you don't have to worry about it. The moment you say stop, I'll stop."

"I just—I don't want to take it too far yet. Like what we did yesterday."

I frown. "You regret it?"

She slowly shakes her head. "No, but I don't know if I'm ready for all of that. Can't we just kiss for a while instead?"

Yep. Yes. Whatever she wants, I'll give her.

"You wanna make out on the couch."

We turn to look at it at the same time and she wrinkles her nose. "It's so saggy. No."

"No?"

"How about we go to my bedroom?" Her delicate brows lift.

Triumph surges through me. I get her on a bed and who knows where things will go. "Okay."

CHAPTER TWENTY-FIVE

DAISY

I'm a nervous wreck and I hate how jumpy my emotions make me feel. Guilt swamps me at having Arch in my house without my father's knowledge. If he knew we were here unsupervised, he wouldn't like it. It feels like I'm breaking all sorts of rules, letting Arch into our home. My room.

The moment he enters the tiny space, it's as if he sucks up all the air, leaving me breathless. His tall, broad frame seems even taller and broader in here with me, and I stand there helplessly, while he looks his fill, seeming to drink in every detail of my private sanctuary.

"I like your room," he declares once he's facing me. He shrugs out of his jacket, dropping it on the desk chair that's right next to him. "It feels like you."

"Feels like me how?" I'm curious at his choice of words— specifically the feel part.

"All warm and cozy, I don't know." He shrugs, seemingly uncomfortable, and I marvel at this for a moment. Is he nervous too? He's always so confident and sure of himself. Charming and irresistible.

"You think I'm warm and cozy?" I don't take the words as an insult.

"You're all sorts of things, Daze." He stares at me for a moment, his gaze tracing over my face as if he's trying to memorize it. "I have a request."

"What?" I whisper.

"Will you take your hair out of the ponytail for me?"

A simple request that I can manage. Automatically I lift my arms, fingers tugging on the hair tie, pulling it from my hair, wincing when it snags on a few stray strands. My hair tumbles past my shoulders and I'm sure there's that annoying bend in it from the hair tie, but from the way Arch is watching me, I don't think he minds.

I shake my hair out before I start to finger comb it but suddenly Arch is there, standing directly in front of me.

"Let me do it," he says, his voice husky.

I drop my hands to my sides when he runs his fingers through my hair, exhaling softly when he massages the back of my scalp, sending tingles scattering all over my skin. His touch feels so good, making me want more of it.

"So pretty," he murmurs, and I lift my gaze to his, noting how heavy his lids are. The hot, intense way he's watching me. "You need to wear it down every day."

"It gets in the way," I protest weakly. "And it's so hot still."

"Your hair is beautiful." His fingers sift through the strands and I lean into his touch. "Wear it down. For me."

When he says it like that, I want to do whatever he asks of me.

He gathers my hair together in his fist, his knuckles brushing the back of my neck as he tugs me closer to him, and I go willingly, as if I'm in a trance. His other hand rests on my hip, his touch light, almost as if he's not touching me at all, and when his mouth finds mine, his lips sear me where I stand. Hot and damp and persuasive, his tongue sliding inside.

I give in like the weakling I am when I'm in his presence. There is something about the way he looks at me, touches me, kisses me.

All I want is more.

As we kiss, he guides me across the room, until the back of my legs hit my bed and then I'm falling, landing on the mattress with a soft thud. He follows me, somehow scooting me up the bed with his persuasive hands and soft mouth and hard body. Until I'm lying in the center of my double bed, my head on the pillow, my hair spread out everywhere. I part my legs, my skirt riding up, most of my thighs on display, my knees bent and feet planted on the mattress, Arch lying between them.

Our mouths fused.

"Tell me to stop," he murmurs against my lips, his breath hot, his weight solid as he lies on top of me. I can already feel him, hard beneath his uniform trousers.

I slowly shake my head. "No."

He kisses me, his lips soft and warm and oh so persuasive. "You sure?"

"Yes," I whisper, a shuddery breath leaving me when he traces my lower lip with his tongue.

I told myself—I've even told *him* that I didn't want to go too fast and here we are, going too fast and I'm willingly along for the ride. I want him. I wanted him all over me and he granted my wish. We're kissing and kissing and it's as if I can barely breathe, but I somehow am. His tongue is a hot, wet brand and when he breaks our kiss to slide his lips down the length of my neck, his tongue licking at my skin has me shivering. Wanting more.

Always more.

He doesn't say a word as he nibbles on my neck, his fingers pulling on my tucked-in shirt until it slips out of the waistband of my skirt. His hand tunnels beneath the cotton shirt, his fingers hot and rough on my skin and I lift up, seeking more.

Disappointment slams into me when he removes his hand, replaced by relief when his fingers find the front of my shirt and he slowly undoes each button, his fingers brushing against my exposed skin. He lifts away from me so he can watch what he's doing, and when his fingers hit the last button, his gaze lifts to mine, questioning.

Can I go further? Is the silent request.

My answer is a barely-there nod.

That last button is undone and then he's spreading open the fabric, his gaze locked on me. My plain white bra with the tiny bit of lace trim. The goosebumps on the tops of my exposed breasts. He reaches out, tracing the lace with his index finger and I bite down hard on my lower lip, a soft noise sounding from deep in my throat.

"You sure you want to do this?" He slides his fingertip back and forth across the front clasp of my bra. "If you don't, I'll stop right now and we can go get one of those pathetic sandwiches you're always eating in the dining hall."

I almost laugh at his words, but I'm too caught up in the fact that he notices I eat a lot of those pathetic sandwiches in the first place. He notices everything about me.

And I love it. For once…

I feel seen.

His gaze finds mine, hot and unfocused, his features strained. He's doing his best to keep himself in check and that is a thrilling realization. That I somehow undo him like he does me.

"I don't want a sandwich," I tell him as sincerely as I can.

His smile is slow. Devastating. With skilled fingers he undoes the snap, the cups of my bra loosening but not quite exposing me. I wait with my breath lodged in my throat as his big hands brush the first cup aside, and then the other, his gaze never straying from my chest.

I went from let's take this slow to letting him get my bra off in about fifteen minutes. Maybe less. Does this make me amoral?

I don't even care anymore. I want his hands on me. My nipples are hard, stiff peaks that ache to the point of pain and if he doesn't touch me there soon, I might scream.

"You're beautiful," he rasps and I can hear the sincerity

ringing in his words. In the way he looks at me, his head's slow descent, the back of his hand drifting across my right nipple, making me gasp.

He does the same thing to my left breast, that barely-there touch twisting my insides, leaving me throbbing between my legs. His mouth is back on mine, his touch becoming bolder, his hands squeezing my flesh, thumbs brushing my nipples and I whimper against his lips, wanting more. Greedy with it.

Arch ends the kiss, his mouth finding my neck, drifting down. Across my collarbone, my chest. The tops of my breasts. I sink my fingers into his hair, holding on to him lightly, afraid he might pull away, though he doesn't. He kisses my breasts, all around my nipples, and I bring my legs in, pressing my thighs against his hips, frustration streaming through my blood.

When his tongue darts out and licks at my nipple, I almost fall apart. And when he draws it into his mouth, sucking it deep, I cry out.

The insistent pull of his mouth creates an answering pull low in my belly and I wind my legs around his hips, clinging to him, his erection brushing against me. He presses closer, his weight settling more firmly on top of me and I welcome it.

Crave it.

He crawls up my body, his hungry mouth on mine, the kiss almost feral. Sloppy. Teeth and tongue and gasps and spit and groans. His hand drifts, his fingers skimming my skin, disappearing for a moment only to return, sliding up my skirt, my thighs, streaking across the front of my panties.

"This isn't taking it slow," he murmurs against my lips and I can't help it.

I laugh, spreading my legs wider, eager to feel him there again. And he doesn't disappoint. His fingers test me, stroking. Teasing. Sliding inside me until I'm clinging to him, a gasping, writhing mess. Coming so hard I swear I see stars.

· · ·

Long minutes later and we're walking back to campus, Arch wearing a knowing smile the entire time. Me with a haphazard, sloppy bun on top of my head, still dazed from the orgasm he gave me. I don't even know how I'm upright. My legs feel like wobbly noodles, barely able to stand.

He sends me a look at one point, so much heat and promise in his eyes that I swear my skin catches fire. How I don't just burn up in flames where I stand, I'm not sure.

"What are you doing tonight?" His voice is casual, his hands sliding into his pockets as he walks and I stare at him, unsure how to answer.

Dad won't be around. He's going to dinner with Kathy. The distraction he's looking for I suppose. This is what I'd hoped for. That Arch would ask me to do something to celebrate my birthday. And what I want to do might shock him, but for once in my life, I'm going to be brave.

I want to give him what he's given me. An orgasm with my hands or maybe even…my mouth?

Nervousness races through my veins and I don't know if I'm that brave. Yet.

"Nothing," I answer, hating how breathless and hopeful I sound. I shouldn't be afraid to show my emotions to this boy, but I still sort of am. It's a hard habit to break.

"Cadence is having a party," he starts, and the disappointment that crashes into me is strong enough to make me stumble.

That was the last thing I expected him to say.

"Oh yeah?" I try to sound as casual as I can.

He nods. "Let's go. You've never been to a party before, right?"

I shake my head. "Not the parties you go to."

"Well, let me take you then." He smiles, and in this moment,

I refuse to fall under his sway.

"Arch..." I come to a stop and so does he, confusion on his handsome face. "She's your ex-girlfriend."

"Uh huh."

Is he being purposely dense?

"She might not want me there." I hesitate. "With you."

"She won't care." He waves a dismissive hand.

"Cadence will care." I'm a girl. A woman. I know she will care. I know she still has a thing for him. It's obvious. "If she invited you to this party, I'm guessing she didn't plan on you bringing a guest."

"It won't be so bad. Other people are going and she'll have food. Liquor. Dr—" He snaps his lips shut, his expression one of pure innocence. I know what he was going to say.

Drugs.

I am not about that. I don't really want to drink either. Alcohol and drugs alter your mind and that scares me. I don't like the idea of losing control.

"Look, Daze. I gotta say—if we're going to become something, then I want to bring you around my friends, you know? You should get to know them so you can hang out with us more. At lunch and whatever." He shrugs, his expression earnest.

I know he means well. He somehow believes his friends will accept me into their fold easily and we'll hang out for the rest of senior year. I'll be known as Arch Lancaster's girlfriend and I can't lie.

That is about the most exciting thing that's ever happened to me. He's the most popular boy on campus and I'm an absolute nobody.

I'm also not stupid. His friends won't easily accept me into their group. Why would they? I've gone to school with all of them for the last three years and they've barely acknowledged my existence. Why would they now? Because Arch says so?

Maybe. He does have a lot of influence...

"I want to hang out with your friends," I say, though I'm sort of lying. "But it's my birthday, Arch. I'd rather we spend it by ourselves."

He's nodding, reaching for me, pulling me into his arms and giving me a squeeze. I let myself enjoy the feel of his arms wrapping around me, cradling me tight, not caring that we're on the edge of campus and anyone could see us.

"You're right," he murmurs into my hair, his voice so low it feels like it's vibrating through me. "We'll do something tonight. Just the two of us."

I nod, pressing my face against his shirt, inhaling his clean, soapy scent. "Just the two of us."

When we pull away from each other, I turn my head, spotting a cluster of girls blatantly watching us, shock registering on their faces when they realize who Arch is hugging. One of them is Mya, and standing right next to her is Cadence.

Who doesn't look pleased.

At all.

CHAPTER TWENTY-SIX

ARCH

I'm an idiot for suggesting to Daisy that we should go to Cadence's party tonight. Of course, she doesn't want to go. What was I thinking, that Cadence would welcome Daisy with open arms and be okay with her being there? What the hell am I smoking, believing that would work out?

I'm high on my feelings for Daisy, that's what the problem is. I'm so into her, I'm automatically believing everyone else will be into her too. Despite knowing that deep down, my friends are kind of shitty and my ex is *really* shitty and bringing Daisy to Cadence's party would most likely turn into a complete nightmare.

No, thank you.

Instead, Daisy and I made plans to go out for dinner in the next town over. Her dad is going somewhere with Kathy tonight and she doesn't want to run into him, not that I blame her. I'm sure it's weird that they're not spending this day together, but I think they're both looking for a distraction from what the day truly signifies to them. The unavoidable sadness that comes with it. Kathy is Ralph's distraction.

I'm Daisy's.

And I don't mind. Whatever distraction she needs from the

reality of this day, I'm here for it. Here for her. Just thinking about what happened between us earlier, my fingers sinking inside her as I swallowed her moans, kissing her deep. Shit.

Why would I share her with others when I can keep her all to myself?

After I made her come and she was still in a blissed out, Arch-can-do-no-wrong state, she reached for me, her shaky fingers skimming across my dick, making it leap to life.

"I want to make you feel good too," she'd said with a little pout when I removed her hand from my junk.

"Later," I told her, punctuating the promise with a deep kiss.

Yeah. It may be her birthday, but if I get it my way, I'll have her hand wrapped tight around my dick, giving me the hand job of my dreams later tonight. Though I'd prefer her mouth, not gonna lie. But again, let's remember.

The natural progression. Hands, then mouths, then the real fuckin' deal.

I'm distracted in my last class and it doesn't really matter because Nelson is cool and doesn't make us work too hard on a Friday. I sit at my desk like a complete dope, lost in thought. My thoughts only filled with one person.

Daisy.

"Hey."

I glance up to find JJ standing in front of my desk, a devious smile on his face. "What are you doing here?"

JJ settles into the desk next to mine. It's empty because the dude who usually sits there is somewhere else. Nelson gave up on trying to teach us anything new about ten minutes ago and is letting us do whatever we want. She hasn't even batted an eyelash at JJ walking in here, and he's not even in this class.

"I wanted to talk to you since you weren't at lunch." JJ's gaze stares at me extra hard. "Where were you?"

I shrug and look away. "Around."

I can't tell him where I actually was. Or who I was with. Not yet. It feels too new, too private, what's going on with Daisy.

"Uh huh. Listen, I want to make sure you're coming to Cadence's party tonight."

"Can't make it," I say cutting him off. "I already have plans."

"Who the hell do you have plans with tonight?" JJ sounds shocked.

"You don't know her." I offer him a mysterious smile.

Shaking his head, JJ whistles. "What, you found yourself someone new? Cadence is going to lose it."

"I'm not hers to lose it over, so she'll have to deal." I'm already bored with this conversation. "I don't want to talk about Cadence."

"Too bad. She sent me to look for you. She's dying for you to come tonight. I don't know who you're seeing now, but I can guarantee she won't put out like Cadence is talking," JJ says with a sly grin, like he's trying to sell me on the idea of Cadence.

Weird.

"Wait, is she telling you what she plans on doing to me? Like in descriptive detail? That's fucking weird, bro." I lean back in my seat, sprawling my legs out like I do, fighting the annoyance that sweeps over me.

Fucking Cadence. I am not in the mood for this.

"She didn't tell me shit, but come on. You've given me plenty of deets about her over the last few months." JJ leers and this is why I refuse to mention Daisy to him. I'm not about to have him throw whatever bits of info I give him back into my face. Besides...

What Daisy and I share is—special. I'm not about to taint it by giving up all the dirty details to my friends.

"Yeah, well..." I drop my gaze to the desk, tapping my fingers on it. "Tell her I can't make it."

"What's wrong with you, huh? You haven't been the same since the first day of school. It's like you're preoccupied all the time. You never want to hang out with us. With me. Do you think you're, what? Better than all of us somehow?" JJ taunts.

He knows I don't like being treated special just because I'm a Lancaster. I may take advantage of my last name here, but I also try my hardest to keep it real with my friends. I may come from a ridiculous amount of money but that isn't who I am. Not really.

"I don't think that and you know it, ass wipe," I mutter, shaking my head. "Stop trying to start a fight."

JJ leans back in his chair, contemplating me for a few seconds before he begins slowly shaking his head. "I'm disappointed in you. It's our senior year and you've turned into an old man."

Don't care who you are, peer pressure always works. I'm realizing that in this very moment because his words are a challenge. His obvious disappointment, a chance for me to make it up to him. I don't want to let this guy down. JJ has been my best friend throughout high school and he's right. We always promised each other we'd have the best senior year together. I didn't plan on falling for a girl—I need to spend a little time with JJ too.

"Fine," I say with a sigh. "I'll go. But only for an hour. And we're going early, bro. Like I said, I have plans tonight."

JJ holds up his hand with a grin and I slap my hand against his. "Player. Getting some with Cadence first before you get some more with your mystery girl."

"That's not what I meant—" I snap my lips shut, realizing JJ doesn't give a damn what I meant.

He's already made his assumptions about me. There's no point in correcting him.

The moment school is over I make my way to my room, sending a quick text to Daisy. We finally exchanged phone numbers when we were at her house—can't believe it took us that long—and I want to check in with her and see if she doesn't mind going out to dinner a little later.

Me: *Can we push back our dinner plans to nine?*

Can I really get out of there by nine? Probably not but I'll try my hardest.

She responds almost immediately.

Daze: *That's so late. I'll be starving. The eight o'clock reservation was late enough.*

I come to a stop and glance around, wishing she was right here with me. I feel like a schmuck for asking her to wait.

And I refuse to be a jerk toward her on this day. It's too momentous for her. She shouldn't be alone.

Me: *Should I change it for seven then?*

Daze: *If you can! That'll give us more time to be alone after.*

It's the word *after* that fills me with promise.

Me: *Maybe we should skip dinner.*

She sends a string of laughing emojis.

Daze: *No. I need food to keep up my strength.*

Me: *Yeah, you do. What time does your dad expect you home?*

Daze: *He didn't really give me a time.*

Me: *You don't have a curfew?*

Daze: *Not really. I don't go out with anyone to need a curfew.*

This girl needs to get out more.

And I'm going to be just the guy to make it happen.

Switching gears, I text JJ next and back out of the party.

Me: *I can't make it tonight after all.*

I'm almost in my room before I finally hear from my friend.

JJ: *You gotta be shittin me. Cadence is going to freak the fuck out.*

Me: *She'll get over it. I'm nothing special.*

JJ: *Not according to her.*

JJ: *Sure hope this mystery girl is worth it.*

Smiling, I tap out a simple two-word response.

Me: *She is.*

CHAPTER TWENTY-SEVEN

DAISY

I'm second-guessing my every decision tonight. From how I do my hair to how much makeup I put on my face to the dress I'm currently wearing, which feels like too much. I'm completely overdressed and I probably look stupid.

Staring at my reflection in the mirror above my dresser, I rub my sweaty palms on the skirt, then shake my hands out, afraid I'll ruin the dress.

I'm a mess. An excited, overwhelmed mess who's about to go on a date with a boy who I've let finger me to orgasm not just once but twice.

Who am I? What happened to the Daisy I used to be?

I'm not that girl anymore. I'm someone different now and I don't know if I like it. The new me is a little terrifying. But the idea of going back to the old me, who spoke to no one and never caught the attention of a certain boy?

That terrifies me even more.

Sliding my fingers through my hair, I tuck one side behind my ear, liking how it looks, cascading down my back in loose waves. It took forever to curl my hair and get the waves to stick since my hair is always so bone straight. I've got my daisy earrings in my ears because when do I not? But today, tonight, I have to wear them. My mother gave them to me. They're special.

The ring on my finger is from her too. It belonged to her and my dad gave it to me after she died. I stare at the ring. A simple thin gold band with a tiny pearl sitting right in the center. It was the first piece of jewelry my father gave to my mother as their first wedding anniversary present.

I rarely wear it. I don't wear a lot of jewelry at all but tonight I even have a necklace on. I'm dressing up.

For Arch.

The dress I'm wearing is made of the softest denim and has a deep V neckline, though it's not very wide so it doesn't expose much skin. The skirt is tiered, ending at about mid-thigh and while I'm not showing that much skin—no more than I would on a regular school day—I feel almost...sexy in this dress. It's simple and cute and the platform sandals I'm wearing are the perfect touch.

At least, I hope they are. I hope Arch sees me and thinks I'm beautiful.

There's a knock on the front door and I run out to the living room, coming to a skidding stop before the door and smoothing my hands down my skirt, reminding myself I need to be calm.

It's just Arch.

Taking a deep breath, I paste a small smile on my lips before I unlock and throw open the door.

He's standing on the doorstep, clutching a pot full of daisies in his arm. Reminding me of the other pot he gave me earlier today. "These made me think of you."

Thrusting the pot out toward me, I take it from him, smiling like a loon. "They're beautiful."

"They're daisies."

"I know." We share a look and I'm tempted to toss the pot aside and throw myself at him.

But I don't.

Instead, I look my fill for a few seconds. He's so handsome in the pressed khakis and blue button down that's open at the neck, showing off the strong column of his throat. His hair is damp and pushed back from his face and he appears freshly shaven.

Just staring at him makes my chest—and other key body parts—ache with longing.

"Let me put this away." I hold up the pot and turn to go set it in the kitchen, nervousness buzzing through my veins when I realize he's followed me into the house. It's when I'm at the kitchen sink about to run a little water in the soil that I feel him, pinning me in place, his front to my back. Solid and warm.

His arms sneak around my waist from behind, delivering a soft kiss to the side of my neck that leaves me a shivery mess. "Did I tell you that you look beautiful, especially with your hair down?"

I shake my head, smiling as I reach out and turn off the water. "No, you didn't."

"Well, you do. Happy Birthday." Another lingering kiss on my neck and I'm afraid if he keeps this up, we won't leave the house.

"You spoil me."

"You deserve it." His arm shoots out next to mine, fingers drifting over my mother's ring. "Is this new?"

"It was my mom's." I go silent.

So does Arch, though he keeps his hold on me, his arms still wrapped around my waist. All I can hear is the steady beat of my heart, ratcheting up the longer we remain quiet.

"Are you ever going to tell me what happened?" he finally asks, his voice a gruff whisper.

I shrug. "Maybe."

He doesn't push. Instead, he asks, "Are you hungry?"

I close my eyes for a moment, grateful for his change in subject. "Yes."

"We should go."

"How are we getting there?"

"I'm driving you."

"You have a car?"

He spins me around in his arms so I'm facing him, a smirk on his handsome face. "Yeah, I have a car."

"I never see you drive anywhere." I shrug. I guess I assumed he had a car but then again, he's a Lancaster so maybe he has a hired driver who takes him everywhere he needs to go.

"Because I haven't driven anywhere with you before." He reaches out, brushing the hair away from my face. "I like your hair down."

"Thank you." I smile.

"You ready to go, birthday girl?"

I nod, tingling where he touches me. Shivering at the way he looks at me. His gaze hot and full of promise. I have a feeling this is going to be the best night of my life.

All thanks to Arch.

. . .

We end up at a steakhouse Arch made reservations at that's about forty minutes from campus. Arch's car is nice—a Mercedes G Wagon—and he drove a little too fast for my taste, though I get the sense he took some of those curves extra fast on purpose to make me squeal. He's got a naughty streak that means he's always up to no good, and while there's something endearing about his mischievous ways, it's also a little terrifying.

When we're seated and I crack open the menu, I almost fall out of my chair at the prices. I look up, trying to get his attention, but he's too busy concentrating on the menu, his brows drawn together in concentration.

"I think I'm getting the ribeye. What do you want?" He glances up real quick, doing a double take when I'm hurriedly shaking my head. "What's wrong?"

"It's so expensive here." I set the menu down and lean across the table, lowering my voice even more. "It's too much, Arch."

"No, it's not," he says firmly, returning his attention to the menu. "Get whatever you want. It's your birthday. I want to spoil you."

I can't even afford a salad in this place and I scan over the various options, chewing on my lower lip. I'm so hungry and can't deny a steak sounds delicious. I don't eat a lot of red meat normally but when I do, it feels like a treat.

But a steak here is well over my budget and I feel bad, having Arch pay for something so pricey.

"I can practically feel the worry pouring off of you." I glance up to find him watching me. "Order what you want, it doesn't matter about the price. I can afford to pay for every single person's meal in this place."

He's right. I know he can. But still—

"Daze." My gaze jerks to his, noting the seriousness I see shining in the blue depths. "It's a special night. Don't ruin it."

I smile at him and nod once. "I want steak too."

"You should get the ribeye," he says without hesitation.

I glance at how many ounces the ribeye is and wince. "I don't think I could eat that much."

"Get something smaller. Like a filet."

I have no idea what sort of steak I should get because I don't go to fancy restaurants regularly so I go with the one that's the smallest, which means it's the cheapest. When the server appears, Arch tries to order a beer but the server just shakes his head at him slowly and instead, he gets a Coke. I order a glass of water and the moment the server is gone, Arch is shaking his head.

"Live a little, baby." My stomach tumbles pleasantly at him calling me baby. "You don't have to stick with water."

"Want me to try ordering a beer like you?"

He bursts out laughing. "He might serve you a beer. You're cuter than me."

I don't know about that, but I don't say it out loud.

When the server comes back with our drinks, Arch orders a couple of appetizers and I ask for a strawberry lemonade, which pleases my date.

"That's my girl," he says when the server is gone, a faint smile curving his lips. "Living it up with a lemonade."

"Stop." I mock glare at him and he chuckles. "I like lemonade."

"Of course, you do." He shifts forward, leaning his forearms on the table. "What else do you like?"

I frown. "What do you mean?"

"What's your favorite color?"

"Yellow."

"Food?"

"Pizza."

"Class?"

"English."

"Flower?"

"Roses. That was my mom's name. Rose. Rosalie actually, but everyone called her Rose." My voice drifts and I tell myself not to think about her too much.

He nods, his expression serious and I get the sense he's glad I gave him that tidbit. That I told him something personal. "I thought you'd say daisies."

I slowly shake my head. "I like them too, but roses are special to me."

"I understand why now," he murmurs, his gaze never straying from mine.

"What's your mom's name?" I ask.

"Miriam." He rolls his eyes. "No nickname. She's always just Miriam."

"You don't like the name?"

"It sounds formal. Like her." The server arrives at our table, handing me my drink while Arch sips from his. The moment he's gone, Arch resumes talking. "My parents are big on rules and appearances."

"What do they think of you?"

"What do you mean?"

"You don't act like someone who cares much about rules or appearances."

Arch grins. "I don't. Maybe that's why I am the way I am."

"Always pushing the limits?"

"You know it," he drawls, his foot nudging mine beneath the table. "Unlike you. My little rule follower."

"I've never felt the need to push the limits." I shrug one shoulder. "Though I've been doing it more since I started spending time with you."

He's grinning, extremely pleased with himself. "Isn't it liberating?"

"Maybe." I tilt my head, studying him. "Is that your issue? Do you feel caged in?"

"Being a Lancaster means there are certain...expectations put upon me." He leans back in his chair, his foot still resting against mine. Like he needs to maintain contact. "Especially since I'm the oldest."

"There's Edie and who else?"

"There's me, Edith, Jameson and Aidan." A sigh leaves him. "We're all given old family names and we all sort of hate it."

"Like Archibald?" I lift a brow.

"Don't make fun. We've already had this conversation," he warns, his tone fierce, though he's still smiling.

I like it way too much when he teases me.

The server returns yet again with our appetizers and Arch plucks a stuffed mushroom off the plate, shoving it in his mouth and immediately exhaling, his lips parted. "Hot."

"That's what you get." I fork up a mushroom and set it on my tiny plate, letting it cool for a moment. "I'm guessing you're hungry?"

He gulps the mushroom down. "Starved."

We eat for a while, the mushrooms and the cheesy garlic

bread Arch also ordered absolutely delicious. I listen to him talk about his favorite foods. The list is long. The guy is fixated on food, and I suppose I can't blame him, especially since he's traveled all over the world and has sampled some of the best cuisine out there.

"Italy?" I ask after he mentions the Amalfi Coast. "You've been to Italy?"

"A few times. I've been all over Europe," he says.

"I would love to go there someday." A dreamy sigh leaves me and I let my mind drift. Images I've seen on the internet flit through my mind. I even have a European travel dream board on Pinterest. "I've always wanted to see Europe. Especially Italy."

"It's gorgeous. You'd like it." His smile is small, his gaze never straying from mine. "Maybe someday I could take you."

I nod, dropping my gaze to the plate in front of me. He—we— shouldn't talk like this. I have no idea if we'll be in each other's lives later. Everything is still so fresh and new between us.

But I love the idea of traveling all over Europe with Arch as my tour guide. Money would be no object. He could take me anywhere, everywhere. Maybe we could take a gap year and travel the world. My dad would be so angry but that sounds…

Fun.

Okay, I need to calm down. I am getting way too ahead of myself.

When dinner finally arrives, I'm worried I won't be able to eat another bite thanks to the stuffed mushroom appetizer and our salad, but the second I take a bite of the steak, it melts on my tongue, making me moan out loud.

"Good?" Arch's eyebrows are high enough to hit his hairline and I realize I probably moaned a little too loud.

I nod, swallowing the bite down. "Delicious."

Throughout the meal, I can't help but feel like a grown up, which is silly. To feel like one means I'm not one yet and I suppose that's okay. But going out with Arch, ordering an expensive dinner and making conversation with a handsome boy, who keeps looking at me as if he wants to eat me alive, is definitely the sort of night that makes me feel very much like an adult.

It's when the server clears our dinner plates and leaves behind a dessert menu that Arch sets something in the middle of table, causing me to look up from what I was reading. My gaze snags on a small box wrapped in gold paper, a white bow on top.

"What's that?"

"A gift." His tone is nonchalant but when I look at his face, I can see a hint of nervousness in his eyes.

"For what?"

"Your birthday."

"You already gave me a gift." I stare at the wrapped box, a heady mixture of anticipation and nerves twisting my insides.

"It wasn't enough."

It was more than enough. His gift was thoughtful. Sweet. I don't need anything else, but I don't say that, worried he'd take it as an insult.

I reach for the box and carefully undo the wrapped paper, slipping my finger beneath the tape, grateful nothing tears. Arch watches me, his body vibrating with impatience and I'm sure he thinks I'm being ridiculous.

Once the wrapping paper is gone, it's obvious that it's jewelry. The box is small, and when I take the lid off, I see black velvet nestled inside.

My heart hammers in my throat and when I wordlessly stare into his eyes, he murmurs, "Open it."

I pull the velvet box out and crack it open to see a pair of earrings inside. They glitter and shine from the subtle overhead lighting, and I realize they're in the shape of a flower.

Daisies.

"They're beautiful," I murmur, tracing the edge of the petals. The stones are clear, the center stone yellow and my breaths start to come faster at the realization. "Are these diamonds?"

He's quiet for a moment and when he finally answers, "Yes," I set the box on the table, pushing it toward him with a flick of my fingers.

"I can't accept this."

"Daisy—"

"It's too much. *Diamonds?*" I stare at the still open box, the stones twinkling. Like they're winking at me. "How much money did you spend?"

"What I spent doesn't matter." He shrugs.

It doesn't matter to him. He could've spent a million dollars on those earrings and it wouldn't affect his bank account whatsoever. But me?

Even a thousand dollars is too much. Five hundred. I don't have that kind of money to just toss around. I'm not like him. Rich beyond measure.

I continue staring at the earrings, longing rising within me despite my protests. They're beautiful. And from the slightly hurt expression on Arch's face, I know I messed up. I shouldn't turn down a gift, no matter how uncomfortable it might make me.

"Daze." He reaches across the table and takes my hand from where it rests, intertwining his fingers with mine. "I wanted to give you something special."

"You already did," I croak, my throat suddenly thick with tears.

"Yeah, but those flowers right there?" He nods at the box. "They'll never die. You'll always have them."

I'm smiling despite the way my heart aches at his sweet words. They're the most thoughtful, romantic thing anyone has ever said to me. "They are beautiful."

His smile matches mine. "They are."

"But roses are my favorite." I'm teasing him now, reaching for the box with my free hand, pulling it closer to me.

"Well, daisies are my favorite. One in particular." His expression turns serious. "I'm not trying to replace the daisy earrings you have. Just so you know."

Did I tell him my mother gave me those? I can't remember. "They're definitely an upgrade."

"I saw them and thought of you."

"You just randomly go into jewelry stores?" I raise a brow, slowly withdrawing my hand from his so I can cradle the velvet box in my hands.

"Only when I'm looking for a birthday gift."

When would he have had the chance to buy them? Maybe when he spent a weekend with his parents?

It doesn't matter. What matters is he bought me this gift and I tried to tell him it was too much instead of gratefully accepting my gift. I hope he doesn't think I'm rude.

I trace the stones again before I take out the old daisy earring from my ear, then the other, replacing them with the new ones, which are much heavier. I place my enamel daisy earrings into the box and snap the box shut. "I love them. Thank you."

His relief is palpable, his gaze lingering on my ears. "You're welcome. They look good on you."

I slip the box in my purse, wondering how I'm going to explain these earrings to my father. He can't see them, and even if he does, I'll have to lie and say they're costume jewelry. He'll believe that.

Probably no one would believe they're real.

By the time we leave the restaurant, it's late and the air has turned cold. Arch slips his arm around my shoulders as we head for the parking lot, tucking me into his side and I go willingly, absorbing his warmth.

The entire night feels like a dream and I'm scared to wake up. Face the harsh realities of the day because I'm worried this… whatever it is between me and Arch? It won't last.

How can it?

"You're awfully quiet," he observes, his arm squeezing my shoulders as he steers me toward his car. "You in a beef-induced coma or what?"

I can't help the giggle that escapes. "Maybe."

"Or maybe it was the dessert." We shared a slice of cheesecake drizzled with raspberry sauce and it was delicious. "Too rich?"

"It was amazing. All of it. Thank you." That's probably the tenth time I've thanked him but I can't help myself.

I'm grateful for the night. The dinner. The earrings. Just being with him.

"Want to go for a drive?" He pulls his key fob out and hits a button, unlocking the G Wagon.

"Maybe we should get back to campus. I don't know when my dad will be home," I remind him, touching one of the diamond daisies again. It's like I can't help it. They're all I can feel, their weight still so obvious.

My words are like a splash of cold water in his face, ruining his mood. "Yeah. Okay."

On the drive back, we're quiet and I swear I even doze off at one point, startling awake only when the car swerves right extra hard, jerking me in the seat.

"Everything okay?" I ask, breathless.

The grim look on Arch's face as he grips the steering wheel tells me that no. Everything is not okay. "Guy was driving extra slow back there so I passed him." He sends me a look, the tension seeming to ease out of him. Maybe he sees the panic on my face. "It's all good."

My heart is racing and my body shaky from the abrupt way I woke up. Swallowing hard, I close my eyes, fighting the thick wave of melancholy that threatens to suddenly swallow me whole.

It's weird, how fast it comes, seemingly out of nowhere. My head is full of memories of a past birthday where I was a little girl secure in the knowledge that she had two parents who loved and took care of her, and then all of a sudden, I only had one.

I try to keep it together, fighting the grief. The sadness. The tears. I'm not crying at this exact moment, but I'm on the verge and I feel…tense.

I wonder if Arch can sense it.

Opening my eyes, I watch him. How assured he looks driving the car, one hand on the steering wheel and the other resting on his thigh. He's so handsome and capable and strong.

I'm filled with the sudden need to confess what happened on this day. How that moment changed my entire world.

"Can I tell you something?" I whisper.

He glances over at me, his expression soft. The softest I think I've ever seen him look. "You can tell me anything, Daze."

I believe him. I do.

Taking a deep breath, I begin telling my story that I've never said out loud to anyone else. Not really. I've given a few details to grief counselors. I've talked about her death in therapy. But never really with my father.

Never really with anyone.

"I was turning twelve, and I was going to have a party. I had some friends at the middle school I went to, and I was excited to have them over. I was getting ready with two of my friends in my bedroom. Kayla and Hallie. I lost touch with them after I started high school at Lancaster…"

My voice drifts and Arch remains quiet. I can tell he wants to prompt me. Push me to continue but he restrains himself.

Pushing me would only make me clam up more.

"Anyway." I press the back of my head against the seat and stare out into the darkness. "We were in my room and I was trying on different outfits for them. I wanted to look good for my party, you know? Anyway, I heard a strange thud come from the dining room or kitchen, I couldn't tell. I went running out there, thinking my cake fell off the table, which is just the most selfish thing, you know? But I was twelve and all I could focus on was my party. What I was getting. What we were doing."

I pause, trying to gather my thoughts. Control my memories. "I actually found her in the living room, right behind the couch.

It took me a minute to realize that my mom was lying on the floor on her back, her eyes wide and unseeing. She couldn't see me. It's like she couldn't hear me because I kept saying Mom to her over and over. Then I said her name. It's like I couldn't stop saying it. Rose. Rosalie. Rose. She never answered me."

More silence, the only noise the tires on the road. The steady hum of the engine.

"My dad came into the house at the same time I started screaming and he ran into the living room. So did Kayla and Hallie. They witnessed everything. My mom looked like she was dead. I thought she was. I couldn't stop screaming and crying. It was terrible." A single tear falls down my cheek and I wipe it away viciously, annoyed that it made an appearance. "She had a brain aneurysm. She was pretty much brain dead by the time the ambulance took her to the hospital. She was on life support but when the doctors told my father there was no hope, he made the agonizing decision to take her off the machines. She died a day later. I know I said she died on my birthday when she actually didn't, but it was close enough. I lost her that day, and she never came back."

Without a word Arch reaches out and settles his big warm hand on my knee, giving it a squeeze. His touch is gentle. Reassuring, and I don't know why, but the dam breaks.

And I cry like a baby.

CHAPTER TWENTY-EIGHT

ARCH

The sound of her sobs twists my insides into knots, and the moment I spot the darkened building up ahead with the giant parking lot surrounding it, I pull over, stopping in front of the breakfast house. I throw the car into park and undo my seat belt before I reach for hers and do the same thing.

And then I haul her into my arms and she doesn't protest. She goes willingly, somehow curling into my lap, her arms coming around my neck, her face buried against my chest. Her tears soak through the front of my shirt and I don't even care. All I can do is stroke her hair and murmur reassuring noises, feeling helpless. Useless.

My family? We haven't suffered much tragedy. We also don't handle our emotions very well. As in, we don't really show them at all. There weren't a lot of 'I love yous' spread around my household and while we're definitely not the coldest Lancaster branch that I know, we're still pretty cold.

Emotionless.

Doesn't help that my mother is British. Stiff upper lip and all the shit that comes with it. My father married a cold fish and man was he angry about it—enough to tell me all about his troubles last winter break, when he was drunk and they'd just gotten into a huge argument.

I was seventeen. The last thing I wanted to hear about was my father complaining how he never had sex with my mother anymore. That she felt the act was an obligatory duty and she gave him four children, so why is he protesting?

He's had a few affairs—confessed to that too. Discreet indiscretions that didn't amount to much, though he always made sure my mother found out. She never seemed to care, which infuriated him even more.

"All I want is acknowledgement," said the very man who's not very good at acknowledging any of his children. The irony.

Pretty sure my mother could've birthed him a dozen warrior sons and I don't think he would've been pleased. Not fully. But we're not the disappointment in his life.

Dear old mother is.

I don't talk about that conversation, or our family troubles. Just like Daisy doesn't talk about her mom or her emotions. She keeps them all stuffed deep inside, only letting them pour out this one singular day a year. When she can mourn the death of her mother that just so happened on her twelfth birthday.

That is some fucked-up shit. And so random. A brain aneurysm. One second you're there, next second you're gone, though I thought they at least got a warning sign with headaches and stuff. Not that I'm going to ask. If Daze wants to share any more details, I'm willing to listen, but she's too busy crying currently to speak.

She's still crying into my shirt and I tangle my fingers in her soft hair, resting my chin on top of her head as I stare out into the dark night. The clock on my dashboard says it's almost eleven and I hope to hell Ralph doesn't pitch a fit when he realizes his sweet, virginal daughter isn't home yet. Though his night with Kathy might still be going on…

Wonder how he'd feel about me being with his daughter. Would he approve?

Probably not.

No one seems to approve of me being with her.

"Oh my God." She moans as she tries to pull away from me. I keep my hold firm on her but she tilts her head back, her luminous gaze meeting mine. "Your shirt is soaked."

"It's okay." I tuck a few strands of hair behind her ear. Draw my thumb across her bottom lip. "You're okay. Right?"

She's still for a beat too long for my comfort before she nods hesitantly. "I've never shared that story with anyone before."

"No one?"

Daisy slowly shakes her head. "Nobody."

I'm blown away that she would share it with me. "I hate that your mother's death happened on your birthday."

Her face begins to crumple. "It wasn't her fault."

"I'm not saying it was. I just—I don't like that your birthday has been tainted forever because of it. She wouldn't want that for you."

"I know." Daisy sniffs, nodding. "I know."

"I tried to make today good for you." I really did. I wanted her distracted and happy but in the end I failed.

And I don't like failing.

"You did a great job, I promise. Dinner was wonderful." She rises up a little, her lips brushing mine and I cup the back of her head, keeping her in place.

Kissing her because I can't resist. It's my favorite thing to do.

She's tentative at first. Like she doesn't want to do this. Not here. Not now. I realize it quickly and am about to pull away when she kisses me again, her lips clinging. Again.

And again.

Until my lips coax hers open and my tongue is touching hers. Lightly at first. I don't want to push.

Fuck that. All I want to do is push when it comes to Daisy. The second she gets close, our bodies brushing, touching, mine is set on fire for her.

No one else. Just her.

I continue to kiss her. Light, sweet kisses with a hint of tongue. Just persuasive enough until our tongues are tangling. Our breaths accelerating. My heart racing.

My cock fucking throbbing.

Daisy's sweetness is what does me in. Makes me crave more. I use so much restraint when it comes to these private moments with her. My need to possess her grows and grows every time I kiss her.

Every damn time.

I drop my hand so it rests on the outside of her thigh. *A purely innocent touch*, I tell myself. I'm not going to try anything else.

But the kiss deepens. The moan sounds low in her throat. The groan rumbles in my chest. Without thought, my hand is sliding beneath her skirt, fingers skimming across her soft flesh until they encounter the side of her panties, right at her hip.

I give them a tug and she gasps. I slip my fingers into the front of them and she whimpers. She's wet. A few kisses and she's ready for me and Jesus, I shouldn't do this. Shouldn't take advantage of her when she's in such a vulnerable state but here I am with her on my lap in my car, my fingers sliding into the wet heat of her pussy. Back and forth, featherlight, making her shiver.

Making her hips push forward, eager for more.

A soft sigh escapes her when I begin to stroke and her hips shift with my hand, seeking more. I keep my mouth on hers, my fingers busy, the sounds of her wet pussy filling the close confines of the car. The scent of her.

God.

I get her off quick, her orgasm hitting her at the exact moment she breaks our kiss. Her hot breath bathes my neck as she pants into my skin, her body shaking. I kiss her forehead and hold her close, trying to give her whatever she needs. Comfort. Caring. A shoulder to cry on.

An orgasm.

She slumps against me, her face still buried against my neck, her body soft and pliant as it melts into mine. I tighten my arms around her and when she starts to move, I try to let her go, but she stops me.

Daisy lifts her head, her golden eyes shining in the dim light from outside. "It's always about me and never about you."

I'm frowning, brushing my fingers through her hair because I can't resist. It's soft and silky and I love it down. "It's your birthday."

"I mean—sexually." She swallows hard, like that was difficult for her to say.

My smile is sly. A little devious. "I'll come collecting here eventually."

She doesn't even crack a smile. More like she looks terrified. "I have no idea what I'm doing when it comes to…this."

"You don't have to worry about it tonight." I lean in to kiss her and she backs away a little, which is fucking disappointing, not going to lie.

"Maybe I want to," she murmurs.

"Daze," I start to say, but she readjusts herself on my lap, until she's straddling me. The skirt of her dress hiked up over her hips, offering me a glimpse of her simple pale pink cotton panties, which are currently pressed firmly against the ridge of my cock poking against my khakis. "You don't have to—"

"I want to," she whispers against my lips as she slowly rubs her panty-covered pussy against my crotch. "Show me what to do, Arch. Teach me."

Oh fuck. How can I resist that?

"Back up a little, baby," I tell her and she scoots backward, hitting the steering wheel with a wince. I reach down and adjust the seat, giving us more room, and I can tell she's excited. Looking for a distraction, maybe?

Probably. But I don't care. I'll give her what she wants.

Gladly.

With her straddling my thighs and her ass basically resting on my knees, there is room between us. Room for her to stare blatantly at the front of my khakis, which is exactly what she's doing. Without warning she reaches out, drifting her fingers along my erection and I hiss out a breath.

She jerks her fingers away, her gaze lifting to mine. "Did that hurt?"

"No." I shake my head, deciding to be truthful with her. "You should unzip my pants."

"Should I?" Her voice is shaky. I can tell she's nervous.

"If you want." I clear my throat. Shift in my seat.

I'm dying to feel her hands on me.

Daisy undoes the button. Slides the zipper down, spreading the material open wide. Somehow, I'm able to lift my ass and shove my pants down while she lifts up, and I push them farther until they're bunched around my calves. My cock strains against the front of my boxer briefs. I'm throbbing with the need to feel her touch me, and when she settles her hand on top of my dick, I close my eyes and lift my hips a little, seeking more.

Needing more.

"Don't be shy," I rasp. "Pull it out if you want."

CHAPTER TWENTY-NINE

DAISY

I need this from Arch. Kissing him and touching him. Having him touch me. It's an escape. One I desperately sought, and while I told myself when I was crying that there was no way any of this was going to happen tonight, now I'm glad it did.

And it's still happening.

My gaze sticks on his erection, straining against the front of his black boxer briefs and with tentative fingers I touch him, tracing the length of him. His words echo through my head and I want to do what he suggested.

Pull it out. Touch his bare skin. He's warm, I can already feel his heat seeping through the cotton and I can't resist any longer.

I tug on the front of his boxers, indicating what I want to do and he eagerly helps out, lifting up and helping me pull them down. His erection springs free, thick and long, the crowned head waving a little.

"Umm…" My voice drifts and he grips the base, giving himself a single stroke, his head falling back against the seat as his eyes slide closed.

Something tugs deep inside me at the sight of him like this. It's hot. A word I don't ever use for anything, but seeing Arch with his fingers wrapped tight around his shaft, his throat stretched and his breathing ragged, that's the only word floating through my mind.

Hot. He's so hot.

And when I reach out to touch him, I find that he's hard yet soft, almost velvety. But I can feel the ridge of steel beneath his skin, fear trickling through my blood at the thought of him pushing inside me. Sometimes his fingers can feel like too much.

How is he supposed to slide inside me with ease? I've read enough romance novels featuring both virgins and non-virgin characters and they make sex sound so easy. Even with the scared-out-of-her-mind virgin, which is who I am right now.

"Fuck, Daze," he bites out at one point when I begin to stroke him.

I pause. "What? Am I doing it wrong?"

"No." He frantically shakes his head. "You could never do it wrong. Just—you can go a little faster. Squeeze a little harder."

I do as he requests and he groans, the ragged sound settling between my thighs, making me pulse. Making my panties flood with moisture. I stroke him faster. Squeeze him harder, fluid appearing in the slit of his cock's head.

He grabs hold of me, his fingers tangling in my hair when he kisses me with a ferocity I've never experienced before. His tongue lashes against mine, circling. Thrusting in time with my strokes and I squeeze him as hard as I can, earning a groan against my lips.

"Feels so good," he whispers into my mouth, his tongue licking. "Don't stop."

I don't stop. My fingers move faster and eventually he joins in, gripping the base, his mouth devouring mine. Until he pulls away with a muttered, "Oh fuck."

His erection jerks in my hand and he's coming, semen spilling all over my fingers, his shaft pulsating. I watch in complete fascination, my gaze hurriedly switching from his face to his cock and back to his face again.

This moment feels almost...sacred. The most intimate thing I've shared with another person ever. I just made him come. After he made me come. We now share something that I have with no one else.

"I made a mess all over your hand." He blows out a long breath, closing his eyes and pressing the back of his head against the seat. "There are napkins in the glove compartment."

With my clean hand, I reach over and fumble with the latch before it falls open and I'm digging up a couple of napkins, cleaning off my fingers before I try to wipe away the semen still on him. He takes the napkins from me and finishes off the rest, balling them up in his palm before he tosses it in the back seat.

Then he's reaching for me, kissing me for long, tongue-filled moments, like he's channeling his gratitude for what I just did from his lips to mine. I cling to him, rocking against him, my clit on fire for contact with his bare skin though I'm still wearing my panties.

He eventually pushes me off his lap, his touch gentle, his smile full of regret when I plop back onto the passenger seat. "I should get you home."

"Why?" I'm truly confused, my brain still fuzzy from what we just did.

"Your dad is probably wondering where you are."

His words sober me right up and I worry for the rest of the drive home, nibbling on my lower lip, still tasting the ghost of Arch's touch on my skin. His mouth. I glance over at him as he pulls into the long driveway that leads to Lancaster Prep. How relaxed he looks, how utterly in his skin he appears as he drives. Without a care in the world.

While I sit here and fret over my father's reaction to coming home and discovering I'm not there.

"I can feel your stress," Arch says once he's parked his car in the east lot. Not many students can have a vehicle on campus, but of course Arch does. "Do you think your dad will be mad at you? Me?"

"I don't know." I shrug. "I've never done this before."

I settle my hand on the door handle, ready to climb out of the car, but Arch is reaching for me, pulling me into his arms, delivering the softest kiss ever to my lips. "Don't worry," he murmurs, his gaze lingering on my mouth. Like he's dying to devour it again. "I'll walk you to your house."

"You don't have to—" I start, but he shakes his head, kissing me again.

"I want to." His voice is firm and I can tell I won't be able to argue with him.

So I don't.

We walk back to my house hand in hand, the chilly air making me shiver. Eventually he wraps his arm around my shoulders and keeps me warm as we walk and I feel protected.

Safe.

If I didn't feel safe with Arch, I would never do any of this with him. But I trust him. He seems to care for me and wants to make sure I'm okay, which is the absolute best feeling in the world.

My father has been my protector for the last six years, while I basically let no one else into my life and neither did he. Oh, I became friendly with the staff here at Lancaster Prep but that's different. They don't feel like friends, no matter how many conversations I find myself in with Vivian or whoever else. They're authority figures, not my friends.

Arch feels like a friend, but more than that.

He feels like he could be my everything.

"Hey." He tugs me closer with his arm, pressing his lips against my forehead as we walk. "You're awfully quiet."

"Thinking," I tell him, my voice soft.

"Hopefully about nothing bad." He's trying to play it off but I can tell.

He might be a little worried.

"Nothing bad at all," I agree, refusing to let my sad memories and emotions weigh me down. "You really did make today pretty great, Arch."

"Yeah?" He glances down at me with the faintest smile on his perfect lips.

"Yeah."

We approach the house and trepidation fills me. I left a single lamp on before I left and I can tell it's still lit, its light shining from behind the closed curtains. I turn to Arch as his arm slips off my shoulders and give him a quick hug. "Thank you."

"Happy Birthday." He presses his mouth to the top of my head in a soft kiss before making a sweet offer. "Want me to go in with you?"

Who is this person and what has he done with the flippant, arrogant boy I despised for years?

Shaking my head, I reluctantly pull away from him. "I'll be okay."

"Can I confess something to you?"

I'm frowning. "Of course."

"I told JJ I would go with him to that party tonight," he admits, his voice low. "The one Cadence is throwing. Remember?"

My frown deepens, hating how I feel when her name drops from his lips.

Jealous, when I have no reason to be. He's not with her tonight.

He's with me.

"But then I turned him down. I didn't want to go to that party. I'd rather be with you. Alone." He grabs my hand and pulls me close, whispering in my ear, "Tell your dad you were at Cadence's party if he asks where you were. That might make things easier on you."

He pulls away before I can reply, offering a sweet smile as he starts walking backward. "Go inside, Daze."

Smiling faintly, I watch him, realizing he's not going to turn

and walk like a normal person until I'm in the house so I do as
he says: unlock the door and hurry inside, leaning against it for
a moment and closing my eyes once I'm inside the house, trying
to calm my racing heart.

"Where in the world have you been?"

I crack my eyes open to find my father sitting on the edge of
the couch, his hair standing up on end as if he's been tugging on
it for the last few hours.

"I told you I was going out," I say, my voice trembling.

He jumps to his feet, concern etched in his features. "I was
worried about you."

"Did you text me?" I glance at my phone to find I have no
texts from anyone. Nothing unusual.

"No. I only got home about thirty minutes ago and when I
realized you weren't here, I started to panic. But then I checked
Find My Phone and saw you were driving home. Or more like
someone was bringing you back here."

"Yeah, I got a ride back. I went to a, uh, a party." I nod,
remembering what Arch said. Using his excuse.

"Oh." Dad's face brightens. "Was it in celebration of your
birthday?"

"No, Dad," I say softly. "It was just a Friday night party, you
know? But I had fun."

"You did?" He sounds hopeful. I thought he'd be mad I was
out, but he's not. He wishes I was more social and had friends
so this aligns with what he wants. "I'm happy to hear that,
sweetheart. You only deserve the best on your birthday."

His words don't match his previous years' thoughts and I
wonder if we're actually making progress for once. Mourning
my mother—his wife, the love of his life—has consumed us every
year at this time for the last six years.

While I had a moment in the car with Arch, it feels like telling
him the story of that day was almost like a purge. The sadness
that always lingered in my chest and made me push everyone

away isn't as strong.

"I had fun, but I'm tired." I push away from the door, pausing at the mouth of the hallway. "Did you have a nice night with Kathy?"

"I did." His expression grows distant, a tiny smile curving his lips, and I wonder if he's thinking of her. I can't imagine him feeling the same way about Kathy as I do about Arch. That's just…no.

Impossible.

"I'm glad you had a good time with her," I say as I head for my bedroom. "Good night, Daddy."

"Night, sweetie."

I lock myself away in the bathroom seconds later, breathing a sigh of relief as I slump against the door. I don't like lying to my father, but I was too afraid of how he might react if he found out I was actually with Arch. He doesn't like him. At least that one time we talked about him, I got that sense.

And I like Arch. A lot.

Probably more than I should.

Staring at my reflection, I wash my hands, staring at myself hard. Looking for a difference in my eyes, my face, my anything.

But again, there's no difference. I'm just me. After everything I did earlier tonight—my cheeks literally turn pink at the memory, I am witnessing it happen in the mirror—with Arch, I figured I would maybe look like a new person. Older. More mature.

My hair is down. That's really the only difference but as I dry off my hands, I realize something.

I *feel* different. There's more to my world now than just me and Dad and the roses and school. There's Arch. Arch and me.

Me and Arch.

My heart thumps harder than usual and I rest my hand over my chest, inhaling deeply. It's scary, thinking of us together. Publicly. I don't know if I'm ready for that.

Is he?

CHAPTER THIRTY

ARCH

The secret is getting to me. Our secret. Mine and Daisy's.

Don't get me wrong, there's something exciting about sneaking around, hoping we don't get caught. The knowledge that we might giving both of us an indescribable thrill, one that keeps me coming back for more. Pushing our limits.

We've been seeing each other for almost a month. Nonstop. The moment I get her alone, my hands are all over her, our mouths fused. I've kissed this girl more than anyone I've ever kissed in my life and we've never taken it beyond getting handsy. As in her giving me hand jobs and me fingering her. Oh, and plenty of grinding on each other. That's about it.

Daze is a good girl and I have to be patient with her, but it's slipping. My patience. I think about mauling her. Tearing her clothes off and going down on her and fucking her. Hearing her whimper with my every thrust, her golden eyes trained on me and nothing else, her lips parting on my name as I make her come.

It's constant, the thoughts in my head. I can't concentrate for shit. My grades are slipping and I swear to fucking God, she's doing better. Better than me.

"Arch, I hate to tell you this but…" My guidance counselor Mrs. Peebles lifts her gaze away from her computer screen to study me. "Currently you're number two in your class."

There's the confirmation I already knew.

"Daisy beat me, huh?" She is going to love this. Hell, she probably already knows. A few weeks ago, the beginning of school, this would've pissed me off mightily.

Now all I can do is shrug at Peebles when she stares hard at me, like I might've sprouted a second head.

"She's currently beating you, yes. What's going on? Are your classes going well? Or are you struggling?"

My counselor's fake concern almost makes me roll my eyes. It's not that I think Peebles is a straight-up liar. I just know she doesn't worry about me in the normal context. Hell, she doesn't worry about any of us at this school. We're all guaranteed a more than decent future as long as we don't fuck anything up.

Daisy though? She's working hard and striving and fucking thriving, that girl. She deserves to be number one.

Okay, clearly I've lost my mind because I'm willingly rooting for the girl who's taken over my spot at the head of the class.

The girl who I can't stop thinking about.

"I'm not struggling," I tell Mrs. Peebles when I realize she's waiting for my answer. "I just—"

"I know it's tough. Senior year and you want to be free. You've been saying that for a while." Peebles' expression is full of understanding and I think of all the times I've gone to her before. When I demanded she talk to my parents and tell them how I should have already graduated. That I don't need to be here.

I can't imagine leaving now. Leaving Daisy. That is the last thing I want to do.

"I'm cool with it now," I tell her, sitting forward in my chair. "I should live it up my senior year, right? My last chance at a life with zero responsibilities."

The look she gives me tells me she knows I could most likely live the rest of my life with zero worries. Or at least that's what she thinks. It's what everyone thinks.

The pressure my parents put on me has ramped up lately. They want to know what my plans are for after I graduate. When I tell them I want to take a gap year, that answer isn't good enough for them. They both want me to go to college, but damn.

That sounds like a trap. Another four years in an institution like this?

No thank you.

"I'm happy to hear you've reconciled with the fact that you're here for the rest of the school year. It's not such a bad place to be, you know." She smiles and I nod, already distracted. I'm missing first period, meeting with Peebles, and I want to get back to English. Not that I'm interested in listening to Winston drone on like he usually does in another boring lecture.

I want to sit behind Daisy and play with her hair. Breathe in her sweet scent. Does anyone notice me? Notice us? I've always been flirtatious. This isn't new behavior for me, but I've never been so fixated on one girl in particular before.

That's new. And that might be drawing attention.

JJ was pissed I ditched out on Cadence's party the night of Daisy's birthday, but he eventually got over it. He never holds a grudge for too long.

Cadence and Mya though? Those chicks avoid us. Me in particular, which I prefer. Though if looks could kill, the evil glares Cadence sends my way would slay me dead.

Still don't feel bad though. Our relationship is history. The past.

"Anything else you want to talk about?" I ask Peebles, my knee bouncing with impatience.

"Have you considered what colleges you want to apply to yet?" Mrs. Peebles asks, her voice extra cheerful. She knows this is a touchy subject for me.

"Nah."

"You should." Her response is quick. "If you start applying now, you could get accepted on early admission at certain universities."

"Uh huh." I nod, tapping my knee with my fingers, checking the clock on the wall right above Peebles' head.

I need to get out of here. First period is over soon and I don't want to miss even a minute of second period. Where Daisy and I are in the office and Viv mostly leaves us alone so we can flirt and talk and I can openly watch Daze blush when I murmur something inappropriate to her.

"Think about it." She drops a pile of brochures on her desk, nudging them closer to me with her fingers. "I believe you could get into any of these colleges."

They're all Ivy League schools and I can't help the chuckle that slips out. "My dad can buy my admission to any of those places."

"I know, but wouldn't it be great to get in on your own merits?" Peebles' smile is serene as she folds her hands together, resting them on top of her desk. "Have you ever stood on your own, Arch? Or do you always get by on the Lancaster name?"

Anger rushes through my blood as I snatch the brochures from her desk, rising to my feet. "Thanks for the guidance," I say, my voice full of sarcasm.

I'm out of the office in seconds, frustrated with my outburst. Frustrated more with how her questions hit home.

Maybe I've never stood on my own in life because I'm barely eighteen. Has she ever thought about that? Or how damn hard it is to shake the reputation the Lancaster name brings with it?

The ease of everything it brings? Being a Lancaster opens doors. Opens eyes. Opens legs.

I could have whatever I wanted with a snap of my fingers. I've never had to work hard for a single thing in my life. Not even school. I'm smart as fuck and barely have to apply myself. Hell, I don't apply myself and I'm still ranked second.

The realization smacks me in the chest as I head across campus, the trill of the bell sounding, indicating first period is over.

I've never worked hard for anything in my life before—until Daisy.

That girl makes me work. It's a struggle, one I'm willing to throw myself into. She's the one prize I'm determined to win. Forget being number one in my class. Forget being the most popular guy on campus. Who cares about any of that shit? Not me.

I want Daisy.

And nothing else.

I spot her bright blonde head exiting a nearby building, walking alone, the look on her face contemplative. Wait, I take that back. She appears worried.

Probably wondering where I'm at. I never got a chance to tell her I was meeting with the counselor because Peebles sent me a text early this morning, asking if I'd come see her first period instead of going to class. I was running late—as usual—and forgot to text Daisy like the asshole I am.

I run up on her, noting the way her face brightens when she spots me. Her golden eyes dancing as she tries to keep it together at my approach.

"Hey, Daze," I call to her.

"Hi." She smiles, slowing her pace. Ducking her head as I fall into step beside her. "You weren't in class."

"I had a last-minute meeting with Peebles." I shove my hands into my pockets as I walk with her to the admin building, nodding and smiling at people who pass by us, their gazes curious. People don't expect to see us together, despite me walking with Daisy to second period every single day for weeks.

"Oh yeah?" Curiosity rings in Daisy's voice, though I know she's not going to ask. She's not nosy like everyone else I know.

"She let slip a tasty little fact." I catch Daisy's glance over at me, her brows drawn together in question. "You don't know?"

"What are you talking about?"

I slow my steps when we reach the admin building and she does as well, turning to face me. "I'm not number one in our class anymore."

"You're not? Oh." Her frown deepens, realization hitting her slowly. "*Oh*."

"You're number one now." Reaching out, I tug on a piece of hair that whips across her cheek with the wind. It's getting cooler outside, especially the mornings. "Congratulations."

She averts her head, like she wants to hide the massive grin stretching her pretty lips, but there is no mistaking the pride on her face. The absolute glory at hearing she's number one. "Um, thank you?"

"Why do you say it like that?" We head up the steps, me glancing down at her, suddenly feeling protective. She's small and sweet and when she gets out into the real world, the lions are going to eat her whole. And there are a lot of lions out there, more than ready to take a bite out of her.

Why I'm thinking about lions, I'm not sure but damn it, I rub at the center of my chest to ease the sudden ache I feel there. The idea of not being with Daisy next year hurts. She has plans and goals, while I have nothing, and I don't think I fit into those plans of hers.

I don't know how I'll ever fit in.

"I've been working so hard, especially the last couple of years, to be number one in our class and now I am? It feels surreal." She sounds a little dazed too. Like she can't believe it's all happening.

We enter the building and head straight for the office, me breathing a sigh of relief that the room is empty and Matthews' door is closed. No Viv in sight, meaning I can make a semi-move.

I grab Daisy's hand and pull her into me, giving her a too brief hug. Wishing I could feel her cling to me versus quickly pulling away. "Congrats, Daze. If I had to be number two to anyone, I'm glad I'm number two to you."

"Thank you." She grins at me, barely able to contain her joy, and I don't think I've ever seen her so happy. And it's at my personal demise.

It doesn't even matter. I'd give up everything to see her smile like that at me again.

· · ·

"Sit with us," I practically demand as I steer Daisy into the dining hall. It's lunch hour and while I love being with Daisy alone, I realize we need to spend time together out in public. Amongst our class. My friends.

"Okay," she says, her voice light, though I see the flicker of panic in her gaze. I know why she's agreeing so easily.

She's still feeling on top of the world being ranked number one and she has every right to. I want my friends to see her at her best. I want to show her off.

But not too much. Those bastards even think about touching her and I'll crush them into pieces.

Jesus, I need to chill.

"I'm going to get a salad," she tells me, pausing when her gaze lands on someone standing behind me. "Oh hey, Edie."

"Hey, you two." I turn to see my sister's amused gaze locking with mine and I scowl at her. "Stop it, Archibald. Your fake grumpiness doesn't affect me."

Chuckling, I give my girlfriend a gentle push toward my sister. "Go get rabbit food together while I grab something with more substance."

Daisy waves at me, her expression helpless when Edie grabs her arm and steers her toward the salad bar.

I'm standing in line, placing two cheeseburgers on my tray when JJ sidles up next to me. "Bro, what's up?"

"Not much. I'm starving." I grab a basket of fries and pop one in my mouth. "What's going on with you?"

"Nothing much. Mya is talking about a party this weekend. You two need to come to it." He's meaning me and Daisy. "People are starting to talk, Lancaster."

"Talking about what?"

"You and Daisy. It's like you two are together, we can all see it, but you never go anywhere together socially."

"We spend time together."

"Alone. In hiding." JJ grins. "Come on. It's time to put yourselves out there."

"That's not on me. That's a Daisy thing." We pay for our food and I wait for Daisy and Edie before I head for our table, JJ waiting with me. "I can't push her too hard."

"Why not?" JJ frowns.

"She's not like that."

"What's she like then? What do you see in her?" He sounds genuinely curious. How do I explain to him that with Daisy, she doesn't care who I am or what I'm worth or any of that bullshit. She just accepts me for who I am.

"She's...sweet." She also kisses like a fucking dream and is always down to mess around with me. She's as into me as I am into her and the best part?

We don't argue. Well sometimes I'm a hothead and I set her off too but for the most part, we get along.

And I love it. She makes things easy.

"She's hot," JJ adds, making me frown.

"Stay the fuck away from her," I growl.

He laughs. "You've got it so fucking bad. Wish I knew what was so great about her."

If he's fishing for details, I'm not telling him a single thing.

My gaze snags on Daisy making her approach and I smile at her. "Ready?" I ask her.

She nods, Edie right beside her.

"You joining us?" I ask my sister.

"If you don't mind." She sends a scathing look toward the table she sits at most of the time, returning her attention to me. "I desperately need a new view."

We all head for our usual table, a few guys already sitting there, eating and shooting the shit. They all greet me enthusiastically when I join them and it hits me that it's been a while since I've sat with everybody. I hang out with JJ when I can, trying to make nice when I'd rather be with Daisy, so it's not often. Lately I've isolated myself and it looks like they've all missed me.

And it feels good, being missed.

"Where have you been?" someone asks me and I glance over at Daisy, who's sitting right next to me. Her smile is quick before she's returning her attention to Edie, who's talking nonstop.

"With my girl," I admit, grabbing my cheeseburger. "I've missed hanging with you guys."

"Your girl, huh?" I glance up to find Mya standing directly behind JJ. Thank God Cadence is nowhere in sight. "It's official then?"

I meet her gaze, noting the possessive way she touches JJ's shoulder. They've been looking pretty serious lately too, though he never talks about her with me. "Yeah. It is. You have a problem with that?"

"Hey. Ease up," JJ says, his stormy gaze finding mine.

"Sorry," I mutter, taking a big bite of my burger. It's only because Mya's so damn close to Cadence. I don't trust her motives.

Don't think I ever will.

CHAPTER THIRTY-ONE

DAISY

A week later and I'm in the dining hall by myself, contemplating where I'm going to sit. Arch isn't here. He went to a leadership conference with the student council in New York City for two days and I miss him terribly. He says he misses me too and texts when he can, but it's not the same without him actually being here.

I miss him so much it's like a part of me is lost and I'll only be complete when Arch is back on campus and with me.

Dramatic but true.

Schoolwork is keeping me busy. My class load hasn't let up whatsoever and I'm working as hard as I can to maintain my number one status.

Still can't believe I surpassed Arch. Things could still change once the semester is over, but I'm feeling pretty good. Even if I'm number one for only a short time, at least I did beat him at one point during our senior year.

It feels good, being on top. Feels even better when he's being so supportive.

He surprises me every day with the way he shows his support for me. How sweet he is. How thoughtful. Walking together in between classes while he tells me some entertaining story, greeting everyone as they pass by us. We always sit together at lunch, his chair beside mine, his claim on me clear.

Probably a tad archaic but I don't mind. I like being claimed by Arch Lancaster.

We work together on our homework in the library after school lately, but it's hard to concentrate when he sits so close, his leg pressed next to mine, his warmth seeping into me. That knowing look on his face just before he leans in to kiss me. Distract me…

Ugh. I miss him.

After I make myself a salad, I go in search of Edie, but can't find her anywhere. Instead, I head for my old table for two, wishing I'd brought a book with me to keep me occupied. I'm about to walk by the table where Arch and his friends usually sit when I lock eyes with Cadence who is of course, sitting at that table.

"Hey, Daisy! You should sit with us." Her smile is sickly sweet, the gleam in her eyes not so much.

I hesitate, my gaze going to Mya, who keeps her head down, her gaze on the table. "Um, thank you, but no."

Why am I bothering being polite toward Cadence? She's a snake. I should avoid her at all costs.

"Oh please. You can't say no." Cadence kicks the chair closest to me out so fast I have to jump out of the way before it nails me in the knees. "Join us."

My heart in my throat, I set my tray on the table before I sit down, scooting the chair close, leaving my backpack at my feet. I'm so nervous, my hands are shaking and I grip them together in my lap, trying to calm down.

I don't want to show them just how freaked out I am. They'll latch onto any sort of weakness I might show, and knowing Cadence, she'll never let it go either.

"Where's Arch?" Cadence asks me, her tone overly-friendly.

"He's at that leadership conference," Mya interjects, answering for me. "So is JJ."

It's hard for me to wrap my head around JJ being on the

student council with Arch, but it's true.

Cadence sends her a dirty look before turning her attention back to me. "I suppose Mya answered that question correctly since she's currently fucking JJ."

I blink at her, shocked she would say something so crude about her friend and JJ. "They're coming back tomorrow."

God, why did I tell her that? Though I'm sure she already knows thanks to Mya.

"Aren't you worried he might meet someone new while he's gone?" Cadence's brows shoot up and I say nothing. I've realized over the years that sometimes it's best to remain quiet. People can't use your words against you that way. "I suppose you two could be fucking, but I don't know. You seem more like the prudish type to me. There's got to be someone better out there for him, don't you think? There are hundreds of girls at that conference right now who are all probably gorgeous and smart. What if one of them—or more—caught his attention?"

My flinch at her words can't be helped and she spots it, the knowing look on her face giving me serious evil vibes. "I don't see how that's any of your business," I murmur.

"What? Him finding someone else? Or the fucking part? I mean...okay. Everyone knows you two are...together." She wrinkles her nose in seeming disgust. "So we can all assume he's fucking you. Or is he? I'm guessing you're the type who is saving herself for marriage."

Cadence giggles but Mya doesn't. Neither do I.

"You're just jealous because we're together and he's not yours anymore," I tell her, not holding back.

I'm tired of being quiet, especially with Cadence.

The incredulous look on Cadence's face switches to her bursting into shocked laughter, her elbow shooting out, nudging into Mya's side. "Please. Jealous of you? Give me a break."

"Is that so surprising? That he'd rather be with me than you?"

"Of course, it is. I mean, look at you." Cadence turns to Mya.

"Look at her, right?"

"Stop, Cadence," Mya says with a sigh, averting her head. She seems fed up, and I can't blame her. "You're being mean."

"She's being mean too." Cadence waves a hand at me.

"No, I'm not," I snap.

Cadence narrows her eyes as she studies me. "Look at Little Miss Virgin, speaking up for herself for once in her life. I'm surprised."

"How do you know I'm a virgin?" I challenge. I mean, technically I am, though Arch and I have done...a lot. We've just never done *that*.

"Come on, Daisy. You dress like a nun and no boy has ever noticed you the entire time you've gone here. I swear you're just some sort of—novelty to Arch." Cadence shakes her head, her lip curled in disgust. "I don't get it."

"Maybe Arch likes me for me and not because I just spread my legs for him on command like you did," I retort, not even knowing if that's true.

My words sober Cadence right up, her face turning red. "He doesn't actually like you."

"How do you know? You don't even talk to him," I point out. "Not anymore."

He can't stand her. He's implied that much to me. Not that we sit around and talk about her, though I'm sure she wishes we did.

"I do too. He came to my party," Cadence retorts.

"What party?"

Cadence shares another look with Mya, who I notice remains eerily quiet. "We got a house in town and partied all weekend. He was there with us."

I frown. He was with me last Friday night, but I don't know about Saturday...

He told me he went into the city with Edie. They had to go spend the weekend with their parents.

"We spent the night together." Cadence's smile is small, her eyes dancing. I'm sure she sees the uncertainty in my gaze and she is so enjoying this moment. "I'm used to him not being fully committed, but I don't know how you feel about that. I wanted to be a girl's girl and let you know."

A girl's girl. I know I don't have a lot of friends and would probably never be described as a girl's girl, but Cadence has a lot of nerve, dropping a bomb like that and trying to make it seem like she's just being a friend.

Please. More like she's my mortal enemy.

"I appreciate you telling me," I say, my voice flat.

"Anytime!" Her enthusiastic response almost has me rolling my eyes. "Us girls have to stick together, especially when it comes to Arch Lancaster, am I right? He's a total player. Good thing he has such a huge dick though. Makes up for all the shit he puts us through."

I cannot believe she's saying these kinds of things to me. And the expression of absolute misery on Mya's face tells me she's suffering too.

"I need to go." I leap to my feet and grab my tray, my appetite long gone and I didn't even take a single bite of my salad. "See you later."

I flee before they can say anything to try and stop me and I don't bother looking back, dumping my salad and setting my tray on top of the trashcan. From the sound of Cadence's tinkling laughter chasing after me as I exit the dining hall, I'm guessing she's feeling zero remorse over what she just said to me.

God, what a bitch.

I end up in the bathroom that's in the same building where my math class is, sitting in a stall but not using it, trying to keep it together. This is why I don't try to make friends. Allowing yourself to become close to someone is like opening a door to trouble. They'll end up disappointing you no matter what. Hurting you.

Abandoning you.

I feel abandoned right now, thanks to Arch being away, though I can't blame him for that. I have to deal with my own insecurities and get over them. Cadence is trying to get under my skin and it worked.

Now I'm full of doubt, and I hate it.

My temples throb with an impending headache and I take deep, almost gulping breaths, trying to calm my too quickly beating heart. Stupid Cadence and her rude comments. Talking about Arch's dick size and how she was with him recently. Is it true? Or is it a lie?

Everything she said is swimming in my head, her words and the visuals they conjured up turning into a muddy swamp of confusion.

No. It can't be true. He would never do that to me.

I can't let her get to me. That means she wins and I refuse to let that bitch win.

Ever.

The bell rings and I hurriedly exit out of the stall, stopping short when I see Mya standing just outside the bathroom, her expression full of sympathy.

"I thought you were in there," she starts but I keep walking.

I don't need to hear what she has to say. No false apologies or whatever it is she wants to offer me. Cadence is her best friend. In my eyes, they're together. A united front. What Cadence says, Mya believes.

She is not a friend. She's an enemy too.

"Daisy, come on. Let me explain," Mya pleads, and I only stop when I'm outside, whirling on her as multiple people walk past us.

"Explain what? That you hate me? That you think I'm stupid for spending time with Arch because he's still with Cadence or whatever? Don't worry, she said everything I needed to hear," I throw at her.

I'm about to leave, but Mya grabs my arm, stopping me, her gaze imploring. "You're not stupid. And I don't hate you. Cadence isn't with Arch. They haven't seen each other since he started hanging around you."

I gape at her, shocked she'd rat out her supposed best friend. "It doesn't matter."

"It does. Well, I'm guessing it matters to you." A sigh leaves Mya and she releases her hold on me, taking a step back, but I don't leave. Now I'm curious. "You were right. She's just jealous, Daisy. She had plans for her senior year and Arch smashed them all by ending things with her."

"What sort of plans?" I ask, unsure of what Mya's implying.

"She believed that she and Arch would rule the school." Mya rolls her eyes with a self-deprecating laugh. "I know it sounds silly, but she's the most popular girl and he's the most popular guy and they were a total power couple our junior year, remember? She believed they'd be a power couple senior year too."

"But he broke up with her on the first day of school," I point out. "We all witnessed it in the auditorium."

"That wasn't the first time he'd done that to her. She always believed she could win him back. Until you came along." Mya sounds vaguely surprised. Or impressed. I can't quite tell. "He hasn't tried to reach out to Cadence again."

"Really?" I hate how small my voice is. How hopeful I sound. I believe what Mya said. I do. Because I don't believe Cadence.

I hate that her words still filled me with doubt, even for a minute.

Mya nods. "Really. I just wanted you to know."

She's about to leave when my words stop her.

"Can I ask you a question?"

"Sure."

"Why are you still friends with her?"

Mya shrugs, staring off into the distance for a moment before she says, "I can't stand the thought of being alone."

I watch her walk away, her words repeating in my brain. Making me realize that at some point, all of us feel a little lonely. Like Mya. And even Cadence.

Some of us are just better at dealing with it.

CHAPTER THIRTY-TWO

ARCH

The moment we're hopping off the charter bus after getting back from our conference in the city, I'm headed for Daisy's house. School ended only a few minutes ago and we left earlier than originally planned, which worked for me.

I've been anxious to see my girl. Get my hands on her. We've texted pretty much nonstop since I left, and I know she's missed me too.

Once JJ and I go our separate ways, I move through campus like a man with purpose, only stopping at my room to drop off my stuff before I head for Daisy's house. Her dad is still on the clock and in her last text she told me he'd been dealing with a sprinkler system problem all day on the opposite side of campus.

Meaning we'll have some time together alone at her place.

I jog up the sidewalk, marching right up to her front door and start pounding on it, excited to see her.

Within seconds, she's answering the door, clad in a pair of black shorts and a matching black sports bra. I take her in, my gaze seeming to eat up her long, still tanned legs and when I finally look at her face, I see her lips are curved into a knowing smile.

"Finally," she murmurs, her gaze lighting up. "Come in."

I follow after her, shutting and locking the door behind me before I head deeper into the house, not stopping until she does in the kitchen. She turns on me, her lips parting, her eyes blazing with an unfamiliar emotion and before I can say a word, she launches herself at me, her arms slipping around my neck.

Automatically my arms go around her waist, my hands splayed across her back, touching bare, warm skin. She feels so damn good.

"I missed you," she murmurs, just before she kisses me.

I return the kiss, my hands wandering, my tongue curling around hers. Damn, this girl.

She's sexy as hell.

"I missed you too," I finally say when she breaks the kiss to press her lips to my neck. "I'm glad I'm home."

"I'm glad you're home too." She pulls away slightly so she can look into my eyes and we stare at each other for a moment, my heart pounding. When she reaches out and curls her fingers around the waistband at the front of my joggers, my dick twitches, eager to be set free.

Lust rushes through my veins, making my blood warm. My skin hot. All because of the way she's looking at me. How she's touching me.

Maybe I should leave campus more often.

"How was the conference?" she asks, releasing her grip on my joggers.

Disappointment floods me but I try to ignore it. "It was good. We had fun."

"Meet anyone new?" She arches a delicate brow and I frown in return, not sure where she's going with this.

"What do you mean?"

"I spoke to Cadence earlier—"

"When did you talk to Cadence?" I ask, interrupting her. I brace myself for her response.

My ex and my current girlfriend having a conversation? This

can't be good.

"We had lunch together."

"You willingly sat with Cadence at lunch?" I'm blown away.

"It's not like I had a choice." Daisy shakes her head, vaguely irritated. "She tried to imply I wasn't good enough for you. That you'd probably meet someone new while you were gone and forget all about me."

Fighting my anger at hearing what Cadence said, I reach out, drifting my fingers across Daisy's cheek. "I didn't even notice any of those girls at the conference. Don't let Cadence get in your head."

"She also said that you two hooked up recently at a party."

I'm frowning so hard my forehead fucking hurts. "What party?"

"I don't know. She claimed she was trying to do me a favor by telling me the truth." She shrugs.

From the look on Daisy's face, I can tell she's not hurt by what Cadence said. Nope, not at all.

My girl is pissed.

Hell, I'm pissed too.

"Did you believe her?" I yank her back into my arms, holding her close. "Because she's full of shit."

"I know." She plucks at the front of my hoodie, her gaze fixed on my chest. "She made me doubt you at first, but then I told myself she's just jealous."

"She is," I say without hesitation.

"And then I talked to Mya and she confirmed it was all lies." Daisy finally lifts her head, her golden gaze meeting mine. "I don't think their friendship is going to last much longer."

"Good. Cadence treats Mya like garbage." I thread my fingers through Daisy's hair, cupping the side of her face. "But I don't want to talk about Cadence or Mya."

Daisy tips her head back, her eyelids lowering to half-mast. She likes it when I stroke her hair. "I don't either."

"And I don't want you to ever doubt my feelings for you. I don't give a damn about Cadence. Or any other girl." I slip my fingers beneath her jaw. "I only care about you."

Her smile is slow. Dazzling. And I love how she clings to me. I want her to trust me. Believe in me. I never want to hurt this girl.

Doesn't she realize how much she means to me?

"I really hate it when you leave," she confesses, her voice low.

"I hate leaving you too," I murmur, just before I kiss her again.

We stand in the kitchen and kiss for long minutes, until she's grabbing my hand and leading me down the hallway toward her bedroom. I stumble after her, eager to get her on the bed and the moment we're in her room, I'm on her, gently pushing her against the closed bedroom door. I rest my hand on it, just above her head, my body pressed to hers. "How long till your dad gets off work?"

"I'm not sure," she whispers, her eyes glowing. "He usually goes and talks to Kathy for a while once he clocks out."

"We have a little bit of time then." I lean in and press my mouth to her neck, right at the spot where it meets her shoulder, and she sighs, her body melting.

"Definitely." She circles her arms around my neck and tilts her head to the side, giving me better access as I continue to kiss her throat.

Her scent hits me like a drug, sweet and floral, making my grip on her tighten. I want to devour her. Consume her until she becomes a part of me. Since I left for my trip, I've thought about nothing else but her. I was supposed to pay attention to lectures and presentations. Slide shows and video clips about the future of our youth and our country, and I couldn't focus.

All I could think about was Daisy.

I dip my head, my mouth finding hers, the kiss slow. All-consuming. I revel in the way she devours my mouth. Her eager lips and tongue. How it circles around mine while her hands slide down my chest until they pause in front of my joggers once again.

She wants me. And I want her too. So fucking bad.

Eventually I take over, cupping her face. Slowing the kiss, my tongue thrusting, plundering her mouth. I drop my hands, cupping her ass, teasing the hem of her shorts, the curve of her cheeks and she whimpers, that sound like a shot straight to my dick.

My hands shift to her hips and I steer her backward toward the bed until we both land on the mattress, our legs tangled. A soft huff of laughter leaves her, it turns into a moan when I kiss her deep. I keep her tucked beneath me, rising up to rid myself of my hoodie, tossing it on the floor. Pausing when I catch the way she's watching me, her gaze eating up my bare chest.

Her hands land on my stomach, the muscles constricting beneath her touch. Her fingers skim downward, pausing to curl around the waistband of my joggers yet again. "Take 'em off," I practically growl.

With eager, shaking fingers, she tugs them down, reaching inside to touch me, her fingers curved around my cock, giving it a squeeze just like I taught her. Hard enough to make my eyes cross. Firm enough to have me leaning in, kissing her again.

It's my turn to devour her. Consume her. And she lets me. We're lost in each other's mouths and hands. I've got her sports bra shoved up above her breasts, my mouth on her nipples, my hand cupping her pussy as she rocks into my palm. She's hot and damp and I'm dying to get beneath her shorts. Wondering absently if I have a fucking condom on me—

A door slams. "Sweetie, I'm home!"

I jerk away from her, climbing off the bed, Daisy lying there in the middle of the mattress with a dazed look in her eyes. All over her face.

And then she's moving, jumping to her feet and tugging her sports bra back into place. Smoothing her hair back with trembling hands, while I stand there like a fumbling idiot, looking around for my hoodie before I finally spot it and tug it back over my head, my dick practically hanging out of the front of my still tugged-down joggers.

Which hasn't caught on yet that her fucking father has just come home because I'm still as hard as a rock.

"Daisy, where are you?"

I'm shoving my dick back in my pants when the bedroom door swings open, revealing Daisy standing in the center of her room looking freshly fucked, offering an awkward little wave to her father in greeting.

"Hey, Dad," she says, her voice weak.

Ralph Albright steps into the bedroom, his gaze snagging on me at the last second. The disapproving look that appears on his face says it all.

He's not happy finding me in his daughter's bedroom all alone.

"Daisy." Ralph doesn't bother looking at me again, his focus solely on his daughter. "Explain what's going on."

Silence. The tick of a clock from somewhere in the house reminds me of a bomb about to go off.

"Um, Arch came over. He just got home from his conference and we were doing homework." Her voice is shaky, her eyes bright and her cheeks flushed. This is exactly what she looks like after she comes. I'm sure her father sees right through her.

Uh huh. Homework.

"I don't see a single book out." Ralph scans the room, his hands resting on his hips. "You know you should do your homework in the kitchen if you have—*guests* over."

Considering Daisy never has anyone over, I'm guessing she isn't aware of that rule.

"Sorry, Daddy," she whispers, her gaze sliding to mine for a brief second, silently pleading with me to understand.

And I do. I get it. This is the last thing I expected to happen.

Didn't expect her to try to jump me either so it's been a day of revelations.

"I think it's time for you to leave, young man." Ralph will barely look at me, his upper lip curled with obvious disgust, and I hate this is how he discovered that Daisy and I are a thing.

That we're together.

Any other girl, I wouldn't give a shit about her parents or what sort of impression I might leave on them. I've always been the mess around and leave them type because I've never wanted a relationship. Cadence was as close as I got to one and that was a fucking disaster from day one.

This girl and her dad, I want to impress. I want to do this right. I want to prove I'm not as bad as every adult in my life seems to think I am. Because they all think that. I know they do. I'm the reckless Lancaster. The kid who doesn't give a fuck. The one who doesn't have to worry about shit because Mommy and Daddy have got everything covered.

"Sir, if I could talk to you for a—"

Ralph holds up his hand, stopping me. "Spare me the details. From what I just saw, I can figure out what you two were up to."

I swallow hard. So does Daisy, our gazes connecting. Lingering.

"I'll see you later, Arch," she murmurs, her soft voice wrapping all around me.

Giving me no choice, I offer a short nod to her.

And leave.

CHAPTER THIRTY-THREE

DAISY

The moment Arch is out of the house, I'm following my father into the kitchen, unsure of how to explain myself.

"It's not what you think—"

He turns, silencing me with a look. "It's exactly what I think, Daisy. I have eyes. I saw the way you two looked. Guilty as sin. Both of you looked like you threw your clothes back on in a rush."

Oh God. I didn't even think about how we looked. I was so jittery, adrenaline pumping through my veins, nervous and excited over the idea of finally getting Arch naked.

I surprised myself.

"I'm glad I came home when I did or else you would be crying in your room by now. Just another girl used and abused by Arch Lancaster." Dad shakes his head, his disgust clear.

"He didn't use me. I-I like him. And he likes me. I know he does." Or maybe I'm an idiot who threw myself at the boy I'm in love with because I was terrified that he would walk out of my house and never want to spend time with me again.

I felt desperate in that moment. Almost unhinged. I couldn't stand the thought of him leaving me for good and so I did throw myself at him and he responded just as I'd hoped. When we ended up on my bed, I wasn't surprised. I wanted it. I didn't even care about moving on to the next level—oral—I just wanted to know what it would feel like, having him slide into me for the first time. Filling me up.

Making me complete.

"Please. He's definitely using you, sweetheart. Can't you see? Didn't I tell you that boy is no good? Reckless? Impulsive? He's doing dumb things around campus all the time and constantly getting into trouble, though he rarely receives any punishment. Did you know that?"

I don't bother answering him.

"I've never told on him because what's the point? Nothing's going to happen. That boy gets away with damn near murder around this campus almost every day and I'm sick of it. I should report him to Matthews. Say I caught him in my house, doing inappropriate things with my daughter," Dad continues.

"*No.* You can't do that. You'll ruin everything between us. For him." I go to my father and rest my hands on top of his, trying to clutch them, but he won't let me, shaking me off. But I'm persistent and I finally get a hold of his hands, my gaze locking with his. "I'm in love with him, Daddy."

The disgusted face he makes has my heart seizing in terror. "Don't say that."

"I am."

"You don't know what love is. You're too young. The first boy who pays a little attention to you and you're gone for him? *In love* with him? Grow up, Daisy Mae. Don't be so gullible. You can't fall for his bullshit."

I let go of him, backing away. Shocked he would be so dismissive of my feelings. "What he says to me isn't bullshit. He has feelings and an opinion, and he likes me. He might even be in love with me too."

Dad peers at me, his brows drawn low. "He hasn't told you that yet?"

I slowly shake my head, hating how shaky I feel.

"Then you don't know if he's in love with you. If he can't even work up the courage to say it, then he's not worth your time, darlin'." He starts to exit the kitchen. "I need to take a shower."

"We haven't even been seeing each other for that long," I blurt.

He stops in his tracks, facing me once again. "If you haven't seen him for that long, then how do you know you're in love with him? Like I said, you don't even know what that is. This is just—it's lust. You're full of hormones—and lord knows that boy is too—and he shows you a little bit of attention after you've been so shy throughout high school and now look at you. You're throwing yourself at that boy and letting him feel you up and God knows what else. I won't have it. He's not allowed to be in this house again."

"Daddy!" I'm crying. The tears are streaming down my face as if I have no control and I follow him through the house, stopping at the doorway of his bedroom. "You can't just banish him from our house."

"I can and I will. If I could, I'd do everything in my power to you keep away from him for good, but the more I tell you to stay away from him, the more you'll want him so that's pointless." His mouth thins. "If I don't want him in my house though, that's my right. He's a bad influence, sweetheart. You should steer clear of him. He'll only break your heart."

I'm still crying, shaking my head, unable to form words. My father approaches the doorway where I'm standing and grabs the handle. "I'm going to take a shower." He shuts the door in my face and I back away, covering my mouth so he can't hear my sobs.

Tears blurring my vision, I stumble down the hall and turn into my room, shutting and locking the door behind me before I land on the bed face first. Reaching for my pillow, I gather it in my arms and press my face into it, crying as hard as I want, as loud as I want, grateful it's muffling how noisy I am.

I cry and cry until it feels like there's not a drop of moisture left in my body. I'm dry, my eyes burning, my face swollen. I'm exhausted and I fall asleep, only waking up hours later, my bedroom shrouded in darkness. My father is in the kitchen, banging on pots and pans as he opens and closes cabinet doors, in search of whatever it is he needs to make dinner.

Rolling over onto my back, I stare at the ceiling, slowly coming back to life. My head is still foggy and my eyes still hurt but I sort of feel better. I roll back onto my side and reach for my phone, checking my notifications to find that I have exactly two. One from my father and one...

From Arch.

Dad's is simple.

I'm making dinner. It'll be ready in twenty minutes.

I check the time the text sent. That was barely five minutes ago.

Checking Arch's text fills me with a sort of nervous anticipation that leaves me jittery, and not in a good way.

Arch: *I hate what happened, and I wish your dad would let me talk to him. I hope you're okay. Text me when you can and let me know you're all right.*

I'm immediately texting him back, my fingers so anxious they fumble all over the screen, hitting the wrong keys over and over, making me have to correct myself.

Me: *I'm okay. Sorry I fell asleep.*

He responds almost immediately, like he was waiting to hear from me and I feel bad for not texting him sooner.

Arch: *Is he mad?*

Biting my lower lip, I decide to be truthful.

Me: *Yeah he is.*

I can't tell Arch that my father pulled the 'I'm disappointed in you' card on me. That will make Arch feel even worse. I know it worked on me. I'm still feeling guilty.

If Dad had come home any later, he would've caught us naked. In my bed. Having sex. We were well on our way there and I know we would've taken it all the way if we hadn't been interrupted.

Arch: *Think he'll ever talk to me?*

Me: *What could you say to him?*

Arch: *That I'm not a piece of shit like he thinks I am. That I care about his daughter and I'm not just fucking around with her.*

Swallowing hard, I stare at the words Arch just typed. I can't deny that my father thinks exactly that, which when you think about it, is funny.

Arch Lancaster is smart. Handsome. He comes from a wealthy family. He's got it all.

But he's still not good enough for my father. And if Arch isn't good enough...

Then who is?

CHAPTER THIRTY-FOUR

ARCH

Shit always has to hit the fan on a weekend, meaning I'll have to endure almost three whole days without seeing Daisy because I had to go home with my sister to spend a little quality time with Mom and Dad.

I'm going to hate every fucking minute of it.

Home is our parents' townhouse on the Upper East Side. It's been in the family for generations and the moment my mother moved in a few years ago—they wanted to move practically the moment they inherited the place from a dead relative—she went right to work. Hiring the best designers in the city to completely transform it.

Now it's bright and white with cool blue accents—I can hear my mother saying those exact words right now—and looks like every other place there is out there.

As I stare at the living room right now, I can't help but think, yet again, that it looks like they live in a museum, not a home. There's nothing cozy about this place. I'm afraid to sit on some of the furniture, it looks so delicate. Like I might bust the velvet blue chair with the spindly clear plastic legs.

"Darling, that chair was twenty thousand dollars. Please be careful how you sit on it," Mother says to me as I perch on the chair, obviously uncomfortable.

No wonder I'm scared I'll break it. Twenty Gs for an ugly ass chair? Damn.

"Want a drink?"

I glance up to find my sister standing at the bar in the corner of the living room, two glasses sitting on the counter, her fingers wrapped around the neck of a bottle of Tito's. Sixteen and she knows her way around the family bar. Terrifying.

"Please," I tell Edie, earning a hard look from Mother Dearest.

"It's so early," she scolds.

"It's five o'clock somewhere." Edie adds ice to each glass and pours the vodka almost to the rim, not adding anything else to it.

I start to sweat, taking the drink from her with a murmured thank you before I take a big sip.

I get the feeling I'm going to need as much alcohol as possible to get through tonight.

We got here Friday evening and I pretty much locked myself away in my bedroom, my thoughts focused on Daisy and nothing else. I still can't believe we almost got caught by her dad. Worse? I can't believe he said such shitty things to me. Ralph clearly can't stand me and that guy loves everyone on campus.

What the hell did I do to him to make him dislike me so bad?

Now it's Saturday afternoon and we're about to go to some high society dinner that's going to be boring as shit. I already tried to dip out but Dad said that was a firm no. Edie feigned a headache and they wouldn't let her bail either, so we sent each other a suspicious glance, unsure of what we're in for.

Our younger brothers—twins, nightmares, the two of them—are away at a boarding school in Switzerland where they belong. They need all the discipline they can get because if everyone thinks I'm reckless? Wait until they meet those two.

"It's almost four. Gimme a break," I mutter into my glass before I take a more fortifying swig. The alcohol burns going down my throat, but it's a pleasant sensation, coating my empty stomach with warmth. I haven't eaten much since I got here, too twisted up over what I'm going to do about Daisy. If I don't eat something soon, I'm going to be a drunk ass before we even leave for this dinner.

"Is that what you're wearing tonight?" Mother's snide tone tells me she doesn't approve.

I glance down at myself before lifting my gaze to hers. I'm wearing charcoal gray dress pants and a light blue button down that is ironed to a perfect crisp. There isn't a crease anywhere to be found in this damn shirt and that still doesn't please her. "What's wrong with it?"

"You need a tie," Father says as he strides into the room. Edie already has a glass out and is pouring him a vodka, which he takes from her with a smile, raising his glass in a toast to all of us. "Cheers to the family being together."

"We're missing two," Mother adds with a sniff.

I watch her, noting how her lip curls with disgust. She doesn't seem happy, but when does she ever? The Lancaster men never seem to pick nurturing women.

Well, I hope to break that mold. If I end up with Daisy, I'm fucking set and so are our future children because she's the sweetest person I know.

The realization that I can see Daisy as wife material has me sitting a little straighter. Like what the fuck? I'm eighteen and thinking of Daisy being the one for me?

Yeah.

Yeah, I am.

"Those boys don't count. They're heathens." My father chuckles, shaking his head, rattling the ice in his glass. "And they'd be pissed if they heard me say that."

"Hear, hear." I raise my glass in a toast and drain nearly half of it in one swallow.

"I'm texting them the transcript of this evening word for word," Edie adds with a faint smile.

Our parents ignore her, but I send her a pointed look. I wouldn't doubt for a fucking instant that she's doing exactly that. The girl has a vengeful streak running through her that goes deep. Don't mess with Edie.

I rarely do.

"You need a tie, Archibald," Mother says, busting out the full name to get my attention.

I send her a withering glare. "I'll grab one before we leave."

"And a jacket," Father adds as a reminder.

Edie giggles.

"What about her?" I wave a hand at my sister, sounding like I'm twelve and sick of her shit, which has been a constant pattern my entire life.

"What about Edie? She's dressed impeccably." Mother sends her an approving smile and Edie grabs the skirt of her simple pale yellow dress and offers a curtsey like Mom is royalty. "You, on the other hand, are far too casual for where we're going tonight."

Father starts talking, changing the subject, and I exhale softly, glad for the reprieve. I'm so tired of getting beat up all the time by my mother. The woman acts like she doesn't approve of anything I do and it gets old.

I check my phone for a text from Daisy, but I've got nothing. A few texts from JJ saying how he misses me, accompanied by a photo of him drinking straight out of a Jack Daniels whiskey bottle, Mya pressed against his side with her lips on his cheek. Oh, and there's what appears to be an endless string of texts from Cadence.

Where are you?

Are you out of town?

God I'm so bored when you're not around.

I miss you.

Do you miss me?

We should get back together.

We make such a good couple.

Arch, answer me.
Why do you always ignore me?
I'm so sick of your shit, Archie.
I won't be ignored.
FUCK YOU ARCHIE YOU DON'T DESERVE ME!!
I HATE YOU!!

The most recent text is a picture, her pouty face in the photo, anger filling her gaze while she gives me the finger. Her tits are pushed up so high out of the neckline of her shirt I'm pretty sure I can see a hint of nipple and Jesus, this is the last thing I want to see.

Infuriated, I block her, nearly jumping out of my skin when I hear Edie say something behind me.

"Who are you texting? Or should I say blocking?"

Fucking sneak. She's always been like that, ever since we were little kids.

"No one." I send her a look that hopefully says, *leave it alone.*

"Does her name start with a C?" Edie's eyebrows shoot up.

Guess my look didn't translate.

"She won't stop texting me." I shove my phone into my pants' pocket.

"She still believes she has a shot with you, Arch," Edie says, her tone wry. "You need to tell her you're done."

"I've told her that. Multiple times. She doesn't listen."

"Why is she sending you tit photos?"

Nothing is sacred when Edie is around, I'm telling you.

"Because she's still hot for me."

"I don't get why. You treat her like garbage. And it's really obvious, who you're into," Edie says.

"Right? Yet Cadence still doesn't get it." I'm already bored with this conversation. I don't want to talk about Cadence.

Ever again, if I had a choice.

"Exactly. Everyone knows you and Daisy Albright are together. Except our parents." Edie shakes her head, making a tsking noise. "When are you going to tell them?"

Like I want to tell my parents about my girlfriend. They probably wouldn't approve of her, yet they'd still force me to invite her over for Sunday dinner so they could silently pick her apart and mentally track all of her faults.

No one could possibly live up to my mother's expectations. Her question always is: is she good enough for my Arch?

It's true. I've heard those very words come out of her mouth before. And while Daisy is nice and polite and quiet, all qualities my parents would find acceptable, once they found out she comes from nothing and her dad is the groundskeeper at Lancaster Prep? Forget it.

They'd never approve.

"Arch, please go get a jacket and tie on. We're leaving soon," Mother says.

"Where are we going anyway?" I rise from the awful expensive chair and start to exit the living room.

"To a dinner, darling. There's a girl there I want you to meet."

I stop in my tracks, slowly turning to face my mother, who's already watching me, a smile curling her thin lips. "What girl?" I ask carefully.

"She's a lovely thing. From a good family. Graduating this year just like you and smart as can be. Just like you." Mother touches her pearls, her fingers tapping against them lightly. "Leslie O'Connor."

The name doesn't ring a bell and I glance over at Edie, who shrugs.

"She has red hair, Arch. Like that one girl you were seeing. What was her name?" Mother frowns.

"Cadence?"

She wrinkles her nose. "Yes. That girl. God, I could never stand her. So obvious. Always hanging all over you as if she had no control of herself. Not even an ounce of decorum in that girl."

I can't disagree with her. Cadence is the worst. But I'm not looking for anyone else.

I only care about Daisy.

"Maybe I'm seeing someone else," I start, but Mother waves a hand, dismissing what I'm saying.

"It's a high school relationship. We know how those work out." She rests her clutched hands in her lap, her legs crossed at the ankle, a serene smile on her face. "Leslie is lovely. Sweet. Well-mannered. Cultured. She will become a perfect wife for someone someday. I'm hoping that someone is you."

It's funny how the older generation Lancasters are always trying to match their children with someone for future marriage and it never works.

Like ever.

"I'm not looking for a wife," I say vehemently. "I'm only eighteen."

Mother's gaze lifts to mine, her expression smooth. Not bothered by my raised voice in the least. "Oh. Well, you should be looking for someone. Eventually. This girl is well-heeled. You best snag her up before someone else does."

"You talk about her like she's a dog."

The tiniest frown forms on her face. "That's rude, Archibald, and you know it. You shouldn't refer to women as dogs."

I roll my eyes. "And you shouldn't describe them as if they're a prize for a man to win either."

I could really use my father as backup right about now but he left the living room right at the same time I was about to. He was just lucky enough to get away.

"As the first-born son and oldest, I feel it is partially my responsibility to ensure you marry someone who's from good stock. Someone who isn't interested in you just for your money."

All the hairs on my body seem to stand on end at her words— and the meaning behind them. "Are you referring to someone in particular?"

Thick and imposing tension fills the room the longer neither of us says anything. Edie chooses that exact moment to sneak out, leaving Mother and me completely alone.

"Like I just mentioned, I know you're involved with someone currently," Mother finally says, clearing her throat. "And I know she doesn't come from—much."

I immediately feel defensive of her criticizing Daisy. "You don't even know her."

"I don't need to. I've got her all figured out. A sweet, smart girl with no mother and no feminine guidance. Her father is the groundskeeper at the school. We allowed her to attend for practically nothing and this is what I get for our charity." Mother waves a hand in my direction. "My son screwing around with the help."

I clench my hands into fists, anger boiling my blood and leaving me hot. "She's not the help. And we're not screwing around either."

"Tell me what it is then, hmm? I have eyes and ears on that campus, my darling. I know what's going on. Your father and I both know, even about the things you never bring up. Matthews keeps us informed in regards to your behavior. Your guidance counselor keeps us up to date on your grades. You've slipped, by the way."

"I know," I say through clenched teeth, flexing my fingers before I curl them back into fists. I'm tempted to punch a wall but I keep my anger in check.

"I'm sure this young lady—Daisy—is a perfectly nice girl, but she's not for you, Arch. Don't lower your standards." The serene smile is back, that impenetrable mask Mother wears so well. "I look forward to you having an open mind this evening when you meet Leslie. Do you understand?"

My spine stiffens and I glare at her, my mind automatically shutting down at her words. "Understood."

Fuck this.

CHAPTER THIRTY-FIVE

DAISY

The weekend was absolute torture and I only brought it upon myself. I needed time away from him so I could think. A little distance seemed necessary after everything that happened between us—and how we almost got caught by my dad. Plus, I didn't know what to say to Arch. Should I apologize? Tell him that my dad is mad at me? At him?

At us?

I wish he knew Arch like I do. He'd change his mind if he got to know him, I'm positive.

Early Saturday morning I woke up thinking I should invite Arch over so we could all talk it out but the first text I saw on my phone was from him.

Arch: *Have to go see my parents with E for the weekend. Talk soon?*

Disappointed that he left, I sent him a quick response.

Me: *Sure. Have fun.*

We didn't really talk the rest of the weekend and it…hurt. I recently started following Edie on social media and she posts constantly, which allowed me to keep track of Arch. I watched her stories religiously, torturing myself the entire time. Looking for a glimpse of Arch in every single one of them. He appeared here and there, always with a frown or scowl on his face, appearing irritated that she caught him on film. Never once did it look like he was having a good time.

I took a strange kind of satisfaction out of seeing that. His unhappiness. The dark look in his eyes.

His mood matched mine. He seemed miserable, and I was too. It didn't help, the guilt I felt every time my father looked at me over the weekend, his disappointment in me obvious. Like he believes I'm throwing my life away all over a boy, which is so not true.

I don't know what to do about my father and his obvious disapproval of Arch. I don't know how to change his mind.

Arch can be so sweet, so funny. So good to me. He makes me feel special. More than anything, he makes me feel *seen*.

I don't think there's been a person on this earth who makes me feel that way. Not even my mother did. She was too caught up in my dad, the two of them deeply in love.

Until Arch. He sees me. He notices everything about me and asks questions. He's curious about me and wants to know more, and I love that.

And when he kisses me? Touches me? I feel wanted. Cherished. It's heady stuff, being consumed by Arch Lancaster.

I never want it to end.

By the time it's Monday morning, I'm on campus early, lingering by the entrance to the main building, my gaze searching. Looking for his familiar face. He stands tall above everyone else, including the majority of the boys, but I don't spot him.

No surprise. He's late, always. I'm sure he was born late and he'll most likely arrive at his wedding late.

It's just Arch.

With a resigned sigh, I enter the building and head for our English class, keeping my head down, not wanting to gain anyone's attention. I wore my hair down again—I'm eighteen now, I think I should give up the childish braids once and for all—and

I keep feeling like people are staring at me as I walk past.

Or maybe that's just me being self-conscious.

I enter the classroom to find Mr. Winston already sitting at his desk, his gaze landing on me and a pleasant smile spreading across his face.

"Miss Albright. A pleasure to see you this fine Monday morning."

He is far too cheerful for me. It takes everything I've got to work up a smile for him. "Hi, Mr. Winston."

He frowns. "Rough weekend?"

"It wasn't the best." I settle into my desk, dropping my backpack at my feet.

"That's too bad. Hope you caught up with the reading."

I almost roll my eyes at him and I immediately feel terrible for being tempted. Maybe I spend too much time with Arch. But seriously. Leave it up to a teacher to be constantly teacher-ing. "I did, Mr. Winston."

His smile is one of pure relief. "Good. Can't have my best student falling behind."

The pressure is enormous, being considered the best student by all my teachers. It was probably good that Arch wasn't around this weekend. Having so much free time allowed me to work on my various assignments, every one of them difficult but they're all done.

Maybe my counselor was right. My school load this semester is really intense. Too intense.

The class fills up seemingly all at once, but still no Arch. The desk behind me remains empty when the bell rings and Winston goes to the door, pulling it shut. I duck my head, staring at the top of my desk, my mind racing.

Where is he? Is he still in the city with his family? Why isn't he in class? He's come in later, but this feels different. And I haven't heard from him since Saturday. We were all over each other Friday afternoon—I was going to let him have sex with me for the very first time—and now nothing.

Silence.

The tears threaten, welling in the corners of my eyes and I glance up, my gaze meeting Winston's.

"Can I use the restroom?" I ask.

He nods, the expression on his face full of concern.

Pushing away from my desk, I flee the classroom, running down the hall, my vision blurred with tears. I don't know where I'm going. Definitely not the bathroom. I don't stop running until I push through the double doors and I'm outside, the cool, early fall breeze smacking into me, making me shiver. I stand on the steps, my head swiveling left, then right.

That's when I spot him.

Arch, striding toward the building. Toward me. The expression on his face is grim, his mouth a thin line, his brows lowered. He walks with determined steps, clad in his full uniform, even the jacket.

He eventually spots me and the look of pure relief on his face when he does makes my heart trip over itself. I think to myself that I should remain where I'm at on the steps and wait for him to approach me but I can't take it.

I bolt into a run, heading straight for him, and he does the same, meeting me in the middle, reaching for me, pulling me into his arms. I cling to him, pressing my face against his chest, breathing in his familiar scent, my eyes falling shut.

I'm immediately calm, my earlier worry and anxiety evaporating at being in his arms. Being with him.

"I missed you," I tell him when I pull away so I can stare into his eyes.

"I missed you too, but I was with my family," he says, his troubled gaze making my anxiety return tenfold. "And I thought you might want some...space."

I blink up at him, unsure of what to say. Maybe he was the one who needed space? "Is everything okay?"

"Everything's good," he murmurs, his gaze searching my face. As if he's trying to memorize my features. "Why aren't you in class?"

"I couldn't stand being in there without you," I admit, briefly closing my eyes when he cups my cheek. I lean into his palm, savoring his touch.

"I was just running late," he admits sheepishly, his hand dropping to grab mine. "Come on, let's go before Winston gets pissed."

I let Arch lead me back into the building, the two of us entering the classroom together and when Arch walks in, Winston stops mid-lecture, remaining quiet until both Arch and I are in our seats.

"Glad you decided to show up this fine Monday morning, Mr. Lancaster," Winston says.

There are nervous titters of laughter throughout the class.

"I'm happy to be here, Mr. Winston. Sorry for being late," Arch says, sounding affable. Like his normal self.

But I can tell there's something troubling him. I need to know what it is. I need him to tell me everything.

• • •

"You're sitting with me in the dining hall today, right?" Arch asks, as if he can read my mind.

Nodding, I slip my hand into his as we make our way down the hallway. The bell just rang, indicating that it's lunch and I gave myself a mental pep talk that I was going to sit with him.

With his friends.

And if that includes Cadence and Mya, then so be it. I can handle them, especially with Arch by my side.

He's grinning, seemingly pleased with this bit of news. "You're not going to run off and read one of your sexy books by yourself and dream of me?"

"You wish I was dreaming of you," I tell him, making him chuckle.

"I know near the end of that last book you were. Have you read any other romance books since the one we shared?" He lifts his brows in question.

I shake my head, trying to fight the blush that wants to stain my cheeks. "I haven't had time lately. The homework is endless."

Arch frowns. "You're working too hard."

"I don't mind." My voice is overly bright and I can tell by the way he's looking at me that he sees right through it. I tug on his hand, needing to distract him. "Let's hurry. I'm starving."

Once we're in the dining hall, we separate, making our food choices. Once that's done, we walk together to the table where he always sits. JJ and a few of his other friends are there, including Mya, who's planted right next to JJ with Cadence sitting on her other side.

Both of them are watching me approach the table with shocked expressions, their eyes wide. They share a look, Cadence's lips curved into a sly smile, and I do my best to sit as far away from them as possible.

Arch seems to do the same, settling in a chair across the table and diagonal from where JJ is sitting, and I choose the chair on the other side of Arch. Still too close to them, though. I can feel their gazes on me as I grab my fork and stir the salad I just made around in the bowl, my eyes fixed on the vegetables inside and nothing else.

This is so awkward.

JJ asks Arch a question and they keep up a steady stream of conversation while I try to eat, not bothering to utter a word. I knew this would happen. The boys would get caught up in their conversation, the girls would watch me just waiting for me to fumble or do something stupid and I would be miserable.

But then Arch rests his big, warm hand on my thigh, his

fingers slipping just beneath my skirt. His touch is bold. A claiming.

As in he's claiming me.

"You all know Daisy, right?" he asks, his gaze sweeping across the entire table.

"Yeah. What's up, jail bait," JJ says with a grin, earning a hard scowl from Arch in return.

"Hey, JJ," I tell him, shaking my head.

He just keeps grinning.

"Are you two officially together or what?" Cadence asks, not holding back.

Arch sends me a quick look before he turns his attention to his ex, his hand still firmly resting on my thigh. I wonder if he's afraid I might run away and he feels the need to keep me in place. Maybe?

"Don't know how many times we need to say this but yes. We're together," he answers, his deep voice loud. Firm.

All I can do is sit there and smile, shivering when his thumb brushes slowly across my inner thigh.

"Isn't that sweet," Cadence says, her tone not very sweet at all.

More like it's extra bitter.

"We should all hang out this weekend," JJ suggests, glancing down at Mya who shrugs, remaining silent.

"It's only Monday," Arch reminds him. "Do we need to make plans for the weekend already?"

"Hell yeah. Aren't you bored yet?"

"For once in my life, no." The smile Arch sends my way makes my heart want to melt. "I'm pretty damn content."

Someone makes a gagging noise and I don't have to look up to know it was Cadence. She pushes away from the table, the chair legs screeching across the floor and she leaps to her feet, glaring at her best friend.

"Ready to go?" she asks Mya, her voice full of hostility.

Mya blinks at her, slowly shaking her head as JJ slips his arm around her shoulders. "I'm going to finish my lunch."

Cadence rests her hands on her hips, contemplating all of us, her expression incredulous. "Seriously, guys? You're just going to let Arch replace me with this shadow of a girl and forget I even existed?"

The table remains quiet and I can feel Arch stiffen at her insult directed at me.

"Watch what you say about Daisy," he bites out.

An aggravated noise leaves Cadence and her fingers curl into fists, still resting on her hips. "This is unbelievable! I'm the most popular girl on this campus, Archie, and you're really going to toss everything we've shared over the last year for this girl?"

She waves a hand at me, her nose wrinkled like she just smelled something bad.

"What we shared wasn't much, Cadence. Don't make me go there and let you know what I really think of our past relationship," he says darkly. "You don't want to hear what I have to say."

"You're a prick!" she screams before she marches away.

The table remains quiet for a few seconds, the tension Cadence created still radiating.

"Well, she's always fun," JJ finally says, making everyone crack up.

Including me.

Arch squeezes my thigh, his gaze warm and just for me. And as I stare into his beautiful blue eyes, I realize that I wish this could've happened sooner. That I would've been accepted sooner.

My high school life would've been so different.

I would've been different.

CHAPTER THIRTY-SIX

DAISY

I'm leaving my last class of the day when I see Arch waiting for me in the hallway, pushing away from the wall he was leaning against to approach me, taking my hand the moment he's close enough.

I smile at him, feeling a little dazzled at this new side of Arch. The attentive, always-wants-to-be-with-you boyfriend side. I didn't realize he had it in him.

"You busy?" he asks as we leave the building.

"Right now?" I think of all the homework I need to do. Plus, I have to study for a test and come up with the first paragraph of the essay that's due in English by midnight tonight. "No."

I shove all that work aside at the thought of being able to spend time with Arch. One on one time. Every other time we're left alone with each other, we end up doing...things. Sometimes risky things.

Like almost getting caught by my father.

I don't think I want a repeat of that moment. Talk about giving me near permanent heart palpitations.

"Come back with me to my room," he suggests, steering us toward the sidewalk that leads to the building where he lives. "You've never been there before."

"I know. You never let me in your private sanctuary," I tease him.

"Yeah, I'm not a big fan of bringing people back there. It's my private space, you know? I don't want JJ and the rest of my friends getting it all dirty with their shit." He shrugs, his focus straight ahead, allowing me to study his profile for a moment.

It's a beautiful profile. He is so attractive it's almost painful. The minute we're alone in his room, I'm going to tackle him. Kiss his firm jaw and his strong neck. That spot just behind his ear that makes him squirm…

I blink myself back into focus and smile. "Are you trying to tell me you're a neat freak, Arch Lancaster?"

"Busted." He smiles down at me and I swear my body feels light. As if I'm made of nothing but clouds and fairy dust, and that is the silliest thought I think I've ever had, but it's true.

This is how he makes me feel, being in his presence. When he smiles at me. Like I have no problems and nothing could get me down. Not when I have Arch standing beside me.

I follow him into the building, noting how empty and isolating it feels in here. It's not really used by the school anymore except for storage, and where the Lancasters live when they're in attendance. At least he has his sister in this building too. Otherwise, I think I'd be way too lonely here by myself.

We stop in front of a closed door and Arch taps at the keypad just above the door handle, the light turning green once he's put in the code. He leads me inside the cavernous room, the door falling closed behind me with a quiet click and I stop, looking around, taking it all in.

The room is huge. He could probably have our entire senior class in here for a party and we'd all fit. There's a giant bed against one wall and a desk against another. A massive dresser and a full-length mirror stand in the corner of the room. There are two windows, both of them big, one of them overlooking the cottage where I live with my dad.

I turn to Arch, who's dropping his backpack on top of his desk. "You can spy on me."

"Yeah." He unzips the front pocket of his backpack and pulls out a lip balm, uncapping it and slicking it on his lips. "I can."

"Do you?"

"Not really." My brows lift and he drops the lip balm on top of his desk, though it falls on its side and rolls right onto the floor. "Fine. I do. Sometimes."

"If I find a pair of binoculars in this room, I'm going to freak out," I threaten him with a smile, marching over to the window and studying my little house. The massive garden and my rose bushes, their branches waving in the breeze as usual. It's getting cooler at night and the new buds aren't popping up near as often as they used to.

Soon, there won't be any flowers at all.

"There aren't any binoculars in here," he reassures me. I can feel him approach me from behind, the heat from his body suddenly right there, seeping into me, and I suck in a soft breath when he wraps his arms around my waist from behind. "Besides, I don't need to spy on you anymore when I've got the real deal right here in my room. In my arms."

He kisses my neck, his lips warm and persistent and I tilt my head to the side, giving him better access, resting my hands on top of his. I know why he brought me back here. Why he wanted us to be alone.

I want the same thing. I'm not scared anymore about it. It's all I thought about over the weekend, and I wonder if he did the same.

"Did you miss me?" I ask, immediately hating how needy I sound.

"Yes," he breathes against my neck, his hands wandering, sliding toward the front of my shirt, his fingers already undoing the buttons. "All I could think about was what we were doing before we were—interrupted."

By my father, I think, shoving all thoughts of him right out of my brain. I don't want to think about that moment. Not now.

For once in my life, my father's opinion doesn't matter to me. This is my life, not his.

"I couldn't stop thinking about it either," I admit, tilting my head down and giving Arch the room to push my hair away from the back of my neck.

"I like that you wore your hair down today," he murmurs against my skin, making me shiver.

"I'm tired of the braids," I admit.

His hands settle on my hips, slowly turning me so I'm facing him and when I look up, the warm glow in his eyes makes me momentarily breathless. "I like them." He curls his fingers around the ends of my hair, giving it a tug. "I miss pulling them."

A soft laugh leaves me and before I can respond, he's kissing me. Pushing me gently so my back hits the wall, his busy mouth never straying, his tongue tangling with mine. I slide my hands up the solid wall of his chest, curling my arms around his neck, burying my fingers in his hair. Clinging to him.

Silently hoping he never, ever lets me go.

We're quiet, too wrapped up in each other's mouths, his hands wandering to dangerous places. Places he's touched before, stroked before, kissed before. I go easily when his hands dip beneath my skirt and wrap around my butt, lifting. I wrap my legs around his hips, marveling at his strength when he carries me over to his bed and drops me onto the center of the mattress, where I land with a bounce.

There's no opportunity to give him any grief for dropping me though. The next thing I know he's crawling on top of the bed, on top of me, his mouth finding mine once more as he settles his weight more firmly on me. I welcome it, reveling in the sensation of his hot, solid body pressing against mine. He's hard where I'm soft, and it's like we just...fit. Two pieces of a puzzle coming together, clicking into place.

It's like this for long minutes, his hips rocking against mine, his erection nudging a certain spot that increases my heart rate and makes my blood run hotter. I eventually get his shirt unbuttoned, my hands roaming across his chest, fingers tracing across his pecs, smiling when I feel him shiver.

He shifts down, his mouth raining kisses across my chest before he moves lower, licking my stomach, his hands beneath my skirt, fingers curled around the sides of my panties. I wait, breathless, a gasp leaving me when he flips my skirt up, his lips blazing a trail across the waistband, coming closer and closer where I feel the neediest.

Oh God, if he goes down on me, I don't know what I'll do. I can only imagine how good it will feel, and when he places his hands on the inside of my thighs and spreads them wider, I know what's coming.

Swallowing hard, I close my eyes, waiting. All of my focus on that one spot. He runs his fingers just along the inside of my underwear, brushing against my sensitive skin and I hiss in a breath. Waiting.

Waiting.

He tugs the cotton aside, pausing for a bit, and I lie there in tense anticipation, waiting to feel his mouth on me down there for the first time.

But he doesn't do it. It's like he's come to a complete stop and I crack open my eyes to find he's watching me. My face.

The moment our gazes connect, he smiles, the sight of it making my heart tumble over itself. "Don't want you to forget who's about to do this to you for the first time."

"How could I forget?" I ask, my voice weak. This boy...

"Didn't want you thinking it was one of your fictional book boyfriends." He dips his head and before I can say a single thing, he's pressing his tongue against my clit.

And like the greedy person I am, I'm lifting my hips, practically smashing myself against his face, seeking more. More,

more, more.

He gives it to me, his tongue searching everywhere. Leaving no spot untouched. I'm gasping for air, struggling to breathe, my eyes tightly shut and my hips moving in tandem with his thrusting tongue. He licks one spot in particular and a loud moan escapes me. He licks it again.

Another moan falls from my lips and I arch my back, lift my hips. Seeking more.

He concentrates on that spot, licking and sucking so enthusiastically that maybe I should be embarrassed but I'm not. It feels too good, too magical, too otherworldly. Like I'm about to have an out of body experience. And when he slides his finger inside me, slowly thrusting in and out, the suction of his mouth right *there*, that's all it takes.

I'm falling apart. Broken into tiny little pieces, my body shaking almost violently. He never lets up, his mouth zeroed in on that one spot still, his fingers thrusting hard. Harder. A keening cry sounds and I realize it's coming from me.

When I collapse on the bed, I have a hard time catching my breath. I lie there like my body has turned to liquid. A puddle of bones and flesh in the center of the mattress. He eventually lifts away from me, his mouth gentle. Dropping little kisses on the inside of my thighs, making me tremble. A kiss for one hipbone, then the other. Until he's sliding up, up. His face in mine, his mouth on mine, the taste of me still on his lips.

I kiss him as if I can't get enough, my tongue licking, teeth nipping at his bottom lip. He pins me down and I revel in the sensation of his fingers clamped tightly around my wrists, my arms above my head. When he lifts away, he stares down at me, his brows lowered, his gaze roaming over my face. Like he can't quite believe he's got me in this position.

"You liked that." It's not a question.

My nod is slow, my body suddenly languid. Like my limbs are made of concrete and I can't lift them. He kisses me again and I let him, lost in the glide of his tongue, the way I can still taste myself on his mouth and it tugs at something deep inside me. Making me want him again.

Making me want to do the same for him that he just did to me.

Reaching out, I rest my hand on his belt buckle, somehow undoing it with still quaking fingers. He doesn't stop me. I know he wants me to do this. He's been wanting it for what feels like forever, but he's been so patient with me. He cares about my feelings and my wants and needs and my fears and insecurities. He's the most thoughtful person I've ever met, which is hilarious because our first interactions? He was terrible. A nightmare.

A menace.

Mean and cruel, he said the worst things. Lashing out at me for whatever reason until eventually...

He became—direct quote from his mouth—*obsessed with me*. And I, in turn, have become obsessed with him.

Arch rolls over onto his back, folding his arms behind his head, watching me with an almost amused expression on his handsome face as I fumble with the front of his uniform pants. He doesn't offer to help and I don't expect him to. I'm full of too much determination to make this happen on my own, without his assistance.

Why, I'm not sure, but I can stand on my own two feet and I want to prove that to him.

Eventually the belt is undone and so is the button and the zipper. He's lifting his hips, kicking off his shoes and when he's finally lying there with the unbuttoned shirt still on along with his boxer briefs and socks, I can't help but think he's the sexiest man I've ever seen.

He's all mine too.

Greedily, I run my hands all over him, shoving at his shirt until he's shrugging out of it, tossing it on the floor. I map his flesh with my hands and fingers, silently marveling at the defined muscles of his arms and shoulders. His chest and stomach. His body is beautiful.

Perfect.

I touch him everywhere I can with my mouth. My tongue. Nip at his flesh with my teeth. I wish I could take a bite of him. Consume him...

I'm too caught up in my thoughts and my wants and needs to focus on much else, but he doesn't seem to mind. He's reaching for me too. His fingers sift through my hair, getting tangled in the strands, and I savor the gentle tug. The soft massage of his fingertips on my scalp, until I'm out of his reach and I mourn the loss of his touch instead. I race my lips across the flat expanse where the waistband of his briefs lies against his flesh, feeling him tremble beneath my mouth. Does anyone ever kiss him there?

I hope not. I want it to be my spot. Mine.

Just like he is.

CHAPTER THIRTY-SEVEN

ARCH

I lick my lips, the taste and scent of Daisy's pussy still lingering, and I close my eyes, concentrating on how good it feels, her hands and mouth all over me. She came to me with zero expertise and while we've messed around pretty often, this is the first time we've ever gone this far.

Her excitement and eagerness more than make up for any lack of experience she might have and I lie there and take it. The soft strokes and the gentle touches. Her fingers streak across my rib cage and stomach, her index finger circling around my navel. Most of my clothes are off, while most of hers are still on and I screwed up there. I should've stripped her naked. But I'd been too eager to get my mouth on her pussy to think about all the small details.

It had been worth it, my eagerness. Watching her come undone was the hottest thing I've ever witnessed. It always is. I think back on the other girls I've been with. A couple of quick fumbles and maybe three pumps before I was coming in my very early days of sexual activity. I was sixteen and had no idea what I was doing.

Gathered some finesse as I got older but I'm starting to realize that the other girls—cough—Cadence—cough, were faking that shit when I went down on them.

Not Daisy. She's so fucking responsive, just hearing her moan nearly has me jizzing in my pants. The girl is teaching me that I need to learn how to control myself.

It's tough though. All I want to do is unleash on her. Fuck her until she's crying out my name and clinging to me. Whenever I slide a finger inside her, she's so damn tight, I can only imagine what will happen when I finally push inside that tight little pussy. I'll probably come in seconds.

Talk about lacking in finesse. It'll probably be like doing it for the first time all over again.

I'm currently trying to keep my cool with my arms folded behind my head, keeping a firm eye on Daisy as she basically mauls me with her mouth. When her lips drifts across the spot right above the waistband of my boxer briefs, my cock surges against the cotton, eager to escape.

She lifts her head, strands of blonde hair tumbling over one eye as she contemplates me. Her fingers curl around the waistband, gently tugging down, and our gazes stay connected as she pulls the fabric down, down. Until my cock essentially pops out, waving in the air, eager to greet her.

All the air lodges in my throat when she glances down, her eyes on the head of my cock, her lips parting. She's touched me bare before. Plenty of times. But her mouth has never been that close.

My muscles tense in anticipation and she reaches for me, her fingers curling around the base, giving me a firm squeeze, just like I taught her. I was always worried she'd want to do this sort of thing at night. In the dark. Too afraid to let me see anything.

But she likes to watch. To see everything and I'm so fucking grateful for that. It's like my own personal porn, watching her stroke me, feeling her fingers press and squeeze. And when she dips her head, her soft, wet lips brushing against the tip of my dick, I can't help the groan that leaves me.

Daisy glances up, her eyes still on me as she sticks out her tongue and licks me, swirling it around the head before dragging it down my shaft. Another groan escapes, this one louder and I close my eyes for a moment. Savoring the drag of her tongue up and down the length of my dick, tickling just underneath the flared head.

"Am I doing it right?" she asks at one point, lifting her mouth away from me completely.

My eyes pop open and I take her in. The disheveled hair and swollen lips. The half- unbuttoned shirt with her tits straining against the front. The skirt hiked up past her hips, exposing her pretty pink panties.

"You're doing it so right," I rasp, my breaths coming fast. Like I just ran ten miles. "Take off your shirt."

She shrugs out of it immediately, the bra still on.

"Take that off too," I encourage, needing all the visuals I can get.

The bra is gone in seconds, her perfect tits on display and I watch as she bends over me once more, taking me fully into her mouth.

Within minutes, I'm ready to come. Fucking dying to come. Reaching for her, I shove her hair away from her face so I can watch, my hips lifting in rhythm with her busy mouth, panting. My heart feels like it could beat straight out of my chest and when she draws me as deep as possible, her cheeks caving in like she's turned into a human vacuum, I hiss out a breath.

"I'm fucking close," I warn her, but she doesn't acknowledge me. Just keeps sucking and stroking and licking and driving me out of my fucking mind. "Daze. I'm gonna come."

Still no acknowledgement. And I can't take it any longer. My orgasm is eminent, pressing down, until I can't control myself any longer.

I groan her name, my hips bucking when the orgasm hits me, pulsating through every part of me. She never pulls away from me, swallows as much down as possible before she removes me from her mouth, semen dribbling past her lips and down her chin.

Fuck, that was hot. My body is still shaking when I collapse on the bed and I close my eyes, trying my best to calm my still racing heart.

She gets up from the bed and I crack open my eyes, watching her as she stands, the skirt falling at her feet in a heap since I unzipped it earlier. She kicks it away along with her loafers, the heavy shoes thunking on the carpet as she pads across the room, her head swiveling like she's in search of something.

"Where are you going?" I ask.

Daisy turns toward me, her breasts bouncing, nipples hard as can be. "You have a bathroom?"

I wave my hand to the right. "It's over there."

She heads in without a word and I can hear water running for quite a while. When she comes back out, she's got a washcloth clutched in her hand and she crawls back onto the bed, hovering next to me on her knees. "Can I clean you up?"

Her sweet voice and innocent question just about do me in. I'm tempted to grab hold of her, crush her to me and never let her go, but instead I nod, biting down hard on my lower lip so I don't say anything stupid like, I'm madly in love with you. You can't ever leave me.

Instead, I remain quiet, grateful the washcloth was soaked in warm water, twitching when she touches me in sensitive places. When she's finished, she climbs off the bed once again and disappears back in the bathroom before she returns, crawling onto the bed and cuddling up right next to me.

I immediately grab at the throw blanket that somehow still remains draped across the corner of my bed, pulling it over us and tucking her in close. She's got her head under my chin, her face pressed against my neck. Her leg is draped over both of mine and I plant my hand right on her ass cheek like I own it, my fingers slipping just beneath the thin fabric of her panties.

She doesn't say anything for so long, I'm afraid she might be having second thoughts. I'm about to ask when she finally speaks.

"Why didn't we do that sooner?"

Chuckling, I squeeze her shoulders with my arm and she tips her head back, allowing me to dip my head and press my mouth to hers in a soft kiss. "I tried to tell you."

"No, you didn't. You always talk about respecting me and not wanting to push."

"I'm an idiot," I immediately say. "Next time I'll fuck you until you can't walk if that's what you want to hear."

Her eyes go bigger and her lips part. I stunned her silent.

"Unless that's not—"

She rests her fingers against my still moving lips, shutting me up. "That's exactly what I want."

"Seriously?" I ask when her hand drops away from my mouth.

Nodding, she buries her face against my neck, going shy again. "I should go soon. But yes. I want it. I want you."

I close my eyes and gather her close, the heat of her pussy pressed against me, causing my dick to rouse, clearly ready for round two.

"Can't you stay a little longer?" I ask, not caring if I sound whipped.

I can face facts. I'm a complete goner for this girl. My face is currently buried in her hair and I'm getting high off her scent. Thinking about the next time I can get her alone. The next time I can go down on her and make her come with my tongue. Get her nice and wet and loose and ready for me to actually slip inside her for the first time—

"I can't." She pulls out of my arms and disappointment fills me. I watch as she puts her uniform back on while I remain in bed like a lazy idiot, too blissed out to stand and put my clothes on. "I have to start dinner soon."

"Do you cook your dad dinner every night?" I rise up on one elbow, watching her slip her skirt back on, enjoying the visual she's giving me. How she slides the little plaid skirt up and over her perfect ass.

Hot.

"Not every night. Sometimes he cooks. Sometimes I just grab a sandwich or whatever. Especially lately. He's not home as much as he used to be in the evening." She sounds a little disappointed by that.

"Out with Kathy?" I ask.

"Yeah." She pulls her shirt back on, quickly doing up the buttons, hiding all the good stuff from me, which is a bummer. "I should be happy for him that he found someone."

"You should," I agree, only because she's found someone too.

Me.

"It's still weird though."

I sit up, push my hair back before I reach down, swiping the sweats that I left on the floor this morning and shoving them on real quick. Essentially hopping into them as I stand. Daisy watches me with an amused expression, shaking her head as I make my way toward her, protesting only a little when I sweep her back into my arms and deliver a smacking kiss on her lips.

"You're kind of hot in just the sweats," she admits breathlessly, her hands pressed against my chest.

"Didn't the dude in that romance book we read wear gray sweatpants and nothing else at some point?" I kiss her again because I can, but she dodges away from my lips and disentangles herself from my embrace.

"He did. That's romance readers' crack," she admits, slipping her loafers back on her feet.

"Gray sweatpants?"

Daisy nods. "You're the epitome of that scenario right now. The sweatpants and nothing else. No underwear so you're all... uncontained under there." She waves her hand toward my crotch.

I glance down at myself before I return my gaze to her. "The big swinging dick theory?"

"Yeah." Her cheeks turn pink. "You really think you have a big swinging—dick?"

Hearing sweet little Daisy refer to my dick like that is making me hard, not gonna lie. "You tell me if I have one."

Her cheeks are now bright red. "Okay, I should go."

I grab hold of her before she makes her escape, pulling her into my arms and kissing her. Again. Like I can't help myself.

I can't. I can't stop kissing her. She's too delicious, too sweet.

"Text me later?" I ask the question with my lips still pressed to hers.

She nods, nipping at my lower lip with her teeth. "I will."

I watch her go, lifting my hand in a wave right before she turns away from me and exits the room, the door closing softly behind her.

The moment she's gone, the stillness returns, louder than ever, though I can't hear a damn thing. It's too quiet, too boring, too empty without her here.

Fuck I've got it bad for this girl.

So bad.

CHAPTER THIRTY-EIGHT

DAISY

I hurry home and take the quickest shower, washing every bit of Arch that still lingers on my skin away. I'm disappointed that I have to do this, but I can't have my dad come home and suspect I've been up to something because he can smell the scent of sex on me.

That would be embarrassing. And horrible. I want to respect my dad's wishes, but I want Arch more.

So, I'm defying my father. He might not know it but I do, and while I have some guilt over what I'm doing with Arch, ultimately, I can't let my father control me.

I'm going after what I want. And what I want—*who* I want—is Arch Lancaster.

By the time I'm in the kitchen and prepping dinner with my hair still wet from the shower, Dad finally waltzes in, whistling an unfamiliar tune, a broad smile on his face when he enters the kitchen.

"Smells good in here, sweetheart," he announces, pausing right beside me as he stares at the chicken sauteing in the pan. "I didn't realize it was your turn to make dinner."

It wasn't. I have ulterior motives. "I was starving so I thought I'd get it started."

"I appreciate it." He washes his hands, the running water along with the sizzling pan of chicken both so loud he has to yell to be heard. "Just to let you know, tomorrow night I'm going out."

Huh. I guess I don't have to come up with an alternate plan after all. "Oh?"

He turns off the faucet and dries his hands on a towel. "I'm going over to Kathy's house for dinner. As long as you're okay with it, of course."

Asking my permission. Something he really doesn't have to do.

"I don't mind if you have dinner with her." I turn over each chicken breast, pleased to see the cooked side is nice and brown.

"Do you want to come with me?" He sounds so hopeful. And that's the last thing I want to do.

"Sorry, I can't. I have plans." I don't sound sorry at all and I purposely try to sound more cheerful. "I appreciate the offer though."

"Uh huh." He sounds distracted. Like he might not even care.

Which is fine. I don't want him to care.

"I'm going to study in the library with a group of people from my advanced physics class," I tell him.

There *is* a group getting together tomorrow in the library to study and I should be one of them because I need as much help as I can get, but I'm not going.

Hopefully, I'll be with Arch in his room.

Alone.

"That's good." He blinks me back into focus. "Your class load getting to you yet?"

I like how he uses the word yet. Like he was fully prepared for me to hopelessly flail with my intense class schedule.

"It's intense," I answer, deciding to be truthful. "But I can handle it."

I sound more confident than I feel. I have to handle it. There's no choice.

"Good." He nods once, pushing away from the counter. "I need to go change real quick. I'll be right back."

"Dinner will be ready soon," I call after him, my phone buzzing where I left it on the counter. I grab it and check my notification, smiling when I see who I have a text from.

Arch: *I miss you.*

I send him a quick reply.

Me: *I miss you too.*

Arch: *We should do it again tomorrow. Same time, same place.*

I press my fingers against my lips to stifle the laughter that wants to spill.

Me: *It's a date.*

He sends me a string of flaming heart emojis in response and I can't help but wonder what I did in a previous life to earn Arch Lancaster's attention now. He is just…

Perfect.

"Smells like something's burning in here!" Dad proclaims, striding into the kitchen.

"Oh no!" I drop my phone and go to the stove top, immediately turning off the burner under the pan of chicken. The meat is sizzling and some of the pieces looked faintly charred but it's nothing I can't salvage. "It's not so bad."

"Good, I'm hungry." Dad kisses my cheek but I don't react, too distracted by my almost burning chicken.

By the burning I feel deep in my soul—it's because of Arch. How he touches me. The way he makes me feel. What we're going to do tomorrow. Just the mere thought leaves me giddy. Breathless.

If this is what it feels like to fall in love, I never want it to stop.

Ever.

• • •

He's waiting for me at the front of his building the next morning, falling into step beside me on the pathway as we make our way to the main campus. It's cooler this morning and I'm wearing my uniform jacket, as is he and he keeps his hands in his pockets for the entire walk, making conversation about nothing in particular.

It's weird, how we can get naked with each other and do things to each other that we do with no one else, yet here we are walking together to class like we're just friends who don't maul each other behind closed doors. But what are we supposed to do? Wear signs around our necks declaring our sexual ties to each other?

Of course not.

I wonder if he knows how important he is to me. How I'll never, ever forget him.

Arch is my first in every single thing. Kisses. Touching.

Sex.

I watch him as we walk. The way his mouth moves when he talks. How he keeps pushing his hair away from his eyes because it's getting long and he probably needs to get a haircut, though I don't want him to. I like how it's a little longish and tinged gold by the sun.

I enjoy the sound of his voice. How deep it is. How it seems to reach inside me and grab hold of my heart whenever he speaks, leaving me enraptured with every single thing he says.

It's a beautiful day. The sky is clear. I can smell fall in the air and there are birds chirping merrily, singing us a song.

I can't even focus on the weather or the beauty of the day. All I can see is Arch.

"You're looking at me funny," he says as we begin our ascent up the stairs that lead into the main building where our English class is.

"I am?" I know I am. I jerk my gaze away from his profile and stare straight ahead, murmuring a thank you when he holds the door open for me. "Sorry."

"You got a thing for me, Albright?" He's teasing. I can see it in his eyes. The tone of his voice.

"Not really," I say, trying to sound serious, but I can't help the smile that stretches across my face.

He's reaching for me, his hand about to snag mine when we hear someone make a gagging noise. Glancing up, I see that it's Cadence.

Of course, it's her.

She's standing in front of a row of lockers, watching us with Mya by her side, who shoots us a sympathetic look before she walks away, abandoning her. Cadence never lets up, keeping her gaze on us. I glance over at Arch to find him glaring at her in return.

"Get a life," he calls out.

She gives him the finger, mouthing 'fuck you' before she flounces off.

A ragged exhale leaves Arch as he glances over at me, the apology gleaming in his gaze. "Sorry about that. She sucks."

"Yeah, she does." This time I'm the one who's reaching for his hand and I take it, interlocking our fingers together. "Sometimes I wonder what you're doing, spending so much time with me."

The look on his face, the intensity I see in his gaze, takes my breath away. "If you can't figure it out by now, then I don't know what else to tell you. I think it's kind of obvious, what I'm doing, but maybe I'm wrong."

Without warning, he leans in and kisses me. Right there in the main hallway, where everyone who's passing us by can see. Lancaster Prep doesn't have an overly-strict PDA policy among the students, but they don't love it when couples blatantly make out in the halls.

And we're pretty much making out.

"You're my favorite person," he whispers against my lips at one point, just before he moves in for another too-quick kiss. "No one gets me like you do, Daze."

I walk on air for the rest of the morning, my giddiness Arch-induced. Enjoying how he tugs on my hair in English, his fingers brushing across the back of my neck. We flirt throughout second period in the office, Vivian barely tolerating us, Matthews nowhere in sight. In all of the classes we have together, we share secret smiles and quick glances. By the time lunch rolls around, I'm in a constant state of anticipation. Of the next time I get to feel his eyes on me, his hands. If I'm lucky enough, his mouth.

This probably…isn't good. I'm too far gone over him. I can't concentrate. I'm not listening to what the teachers are saying and this is the semester where I have to stay on top of everything. If I get even a little bit behind, it could get difficult for me. Difficult enough that I won't be able to come back from it.

He's a complete and utter distraction, and the old me would tell him that maybe we need to stop seeing each other so much. Actually, the old me would've never paid much attention to Arch in the first place. I avoided him—everyone—at all costs. I didn't allow myself to get close to someone for exactly these reasons.

Not just the distraction part, but I know, deep in my heart, that this can't last forever. Nothing ever can. School will end and we'll graduate and I'll go away to college and Arch will do whatever it is he's supposed to do. We won't be together anymore. He'll leave me.

Eventually everyone leaves.

And that's a fact.

CHAPTER THIRTY-NINE

DAISY

After school is finished, Arch and I go to the library where we do our homework. There are a lot of students in the library, lots of conversations happening, and while Arch is easily distracted—and untouchable thanks to the librarian loving him so much—he keeps wandering off to talk to his friends.

Me? I have to concentrate. Once we get through this semester, I can relax. By then my grades won't matter as much. I'll have all of my college applications sent in and some of that pressure will be relieved.

Still want to come out on top though. If I have to lose to anyone, I wouldn't mind it being Arch.

"Want to go back to my room?" His voice is casual as we exit the library, but I can hear the subtle meaning behind his question.

Go back to his room and mess around is what the plan is.

"Yes," I tell him firmly, because that sounds perfect to me. A little reward for getting my work done. Even Arch settled down eventually and completed a few assignments.

His grin makes my heart trip over itself. "That's the answer I was looking for, Daze."

We hurry back to his room, not talking much. The two of us eager to be alone. I love that this doesn't feel one-sided.

He seems just as into me as I'm into him.

The wind has picked up and the sky is heavy with dark clouds. A storm must be rolling in and I swear right before we enter the building, I feel a couple of rain drops hit the top of my head.

The door clangs shut behind us, shrouding us in silence, the only sound our clipped footsteps on the floor. I follow him to his room, taking everything in, wondering where Edie might be.

"Where's Edie's room?" I ask once we're inside his room.

He locks the door and turns to face me, leaning against it. "Just down the hall on the right side."

"Ah." I nod, going to his desk and setting my backpack on top of it before I start to take off my uniform jacket.

"Already stripping?" His teasing tone has me looking over at him again.

"Tired of the jacket," I say as I slip it off and drape it across the back of his desk chair.

"Same." He shrugs out of his jacket and lets it drop on the floor.

I drink him in as he approaches. How his shirt fits a little snug across his chest, the sleeves emphasizing the sheer size of his biceps. I rarely hear him speak about working out beyond going for a run here and there, but he has to go to the gym. There's a two-story one on campus where all the boys like to go and I'm sure he's one of them, lifting weights with his friends' encouragement and posing in front of the mirrors afterward.

I've seen the stories on social media. I know what they like to do in the gym.

"How long until you have to go home?" He comes to a spot in front of me, just out of reach.

Reaching behind, I clutch the back of the desk chair, hoping I look nonchalant. Like what's about to happen is no big deal. "I don't have to be home until later."

His brows lift. "Define later."

"Sometime later in the night." He frowns. "My dad is going

to Kathy's tonight for dinner."

"Ah." The frown is gone, just like that. "So we have hours to ourselves?"

I nod, clutching the back of the chair tighter. My heart starts to beat faster at the look on his face. "I'm thinking I should be home around nine."

He checks his phone. "It's four-thirty."

I nod again, not saying anything this time.

"That's over four hours."

"Glad to see you can count." I smile, unable to help myself from giving him a hard time.

"All those math classes over the years, you know?" He steps closer, his arms sneaking around my waist, trapping me. Not that I mind. "There's a lot we can do in four hours, Daze."

"You think so?" I tip my head back, the heat I see in his gaze taking my breath away.

Arch nods, touching my face. His fingers drift across my jaw, his thumb pressing gently into my chin. "You tortured me in the library."

"You tortured me too, you know. But I had to get my homework done," I remind him. "I would've felt too guilty otherwise."

"Always such a good girl. Doing what she's supposed to." He leans in, kissing me and it's shockingly dirty. His tongue is thorough, searching my mouth in a way that leaves me breathless and when he breaks away, I'm grateful I'm still holding onto the chair. "With the exception of being with me."

His words make me think of my father's disapproval, and that's the last thing I want to focus on. "Don't worry about that."

"I look good on paper. Don't see what his problem is with me." He's joking. Or at least he's trying to sound like he's joking, but I can hear the hurt there, lingering beneath the words.

"He just doesn't know you," I say, and he frowns.

"Why don't you ever wear the earrings I gave you?" The hurt is still there in his voice, stronger now and I shrug, feeling bad.

"They're so beautiful. I'm afraid I'll lose them." It's not just that. The earrings are expensive, so obviously not fake. My father will see them and question me. Anyone would ask about them, they're that stunning. Vivian. Matthews. Any of my teachers. Maybe even Edie. And I wouldn't know how to answer them. Wouldn't know what to say.

I keep the earrings in the box they came in, stashed in my sock drawer, and I'll pull the box out almost every day, staring at them, remembering how he gave them to me. How pleased he was when I put them on. They're beautiful.

Too beautiful.

"You won't lose them," he starts but I cut him off, not wanting to have this conversation anymore.

"Kiss me," I demand, trying to get his mind off the stuff that doesn't matter.

The only thing that matters right now is me and him. In this room together.

Completely alone.

He does as I ask without hesitation, the kiss this time gentle. Almost sweet. Our lips meet and break apart over and over, leaving me needy. My knees wobbly. I finally let go of the chair and run my hands up his chest, savoring the hard, hot wall of his chest, burning my palms through the fabric of his shirt. When his tongue finally curls around mine, I whimper, returning the kiss, my body aching for more.

I want to feel his hands all over me. In all of those secret places only he's touched. I grab fistfuls of his shirt, tugging on the fabric as he devours my mouth and his hands slide lower, gripping my butt. Gathering my skirt, lifting it and diving beneath, his hands now on my flesh.

"This skirt drives me fucking insane," he murmurs against my lips, his fingers slipping beneath the thin fabric of my panties, brushing against my sensitive flesh. "Watching you walk all over campus in it. Knowing what it's hiding."

A throb starts lower in my belly. My panties are wet. Just by his words alone. His barely- there touch.

"Did you think about this all day?" His mouth shifts to my throat, his lips hot, his tongue wet as he licks me there. "Imagine me doing this to you?"

"Yes," I whisper, his words reminding me of my earlier thoughts. Of us acting so normal when we share something so... intimate.

He cups the neediest part of me between my thighs, his fingers pressing, making me shiver. "Are you going to give this to me, Daze?"

I nod, my breath hitching in my throat. "Y-yes."

"I want it." He kisses my neck. Bites it, the sting of his teeth making me cry out. "I want you to be mine."

"I am yours," I say without hesitation.

He lifts away from my neck and I crack my eyes open to find him watching me, his searing gaze roaming all over my face, a pleased smile curling his lips. "I'm taking another one of your firsts."

"I want you to be my first," I tell him, my eyes falling closed when he pushes my hair away from my face, his fingers threading through the strands. My breaths are coming fast, everything inside me throbbing, and when he leans in, his mouth brushing against mine, I kiss him hard, needing more.

Needing everything he can give me.

"You're so beautiful, baby." His compliment, the rough tone of his voice, makes my bones turn to liquid. "I could look at you all night."

I don't want him to look at me all night. I need him to touch me.

His mouth is still on mine, barely moving, almost as if he's breathing me in. I'm trembling and he seems so in control. So perfectly composed. And when he grabs my hand, placing it on the front of his trousers, I curl my fingers around the hot, hard length of him, pleasure rippling through me at the physical proof that he wants me. "Feel that?"

I nod, squeezing harder, making him groan.

"It's all for you."

I part my lips, ready to speak, but I forget what I wanted to say when Arch kisses me, his hands moving to slide up and down my butt, making me shiver. We stand and kiss like this for what feels like forever, his hands never moving from my backside, my hands eventually going to the buttons on his shirt, undoing each one with shaky fingers. I touch his bare chest, streaking my fingers along his hot skin, smiling when his muscles constrict beneath my fingertips. I love that my touch affects him.

I love so much about him.

I'm in love with him.

Anyone would probably say I'm in love with Arch only because he's the first boy to actually pay attention to me and maybe they're right. Maybe he finds me a novelty, a mystery. The girl no one knows except for him.

But it feels like we share more than that. We're more than that. I feel everything more intensely when I'm with him. He's not just the boy I'm in love with. He's also my friend. My confidant. He makes me laugh and he brings me pleasure and gives me comfort.

I didn't know it could be like this. Feel like this. I've read enough romance books in the last couple of years to have a sense of what a romantic relationship might be like, but in the books it all feels heightened. Unbelievable. No one can find a perfect love like what exists in books. That sort of thing is for fairy tales.

What Arch and I share feels like a fairy tale. Fantastical. Unbelievable.

The best thing I've ever experienced.

He picks me up with ease and carries me over to the bed, carefully depositing me onto the mattress versus dropping me like he did last time. Something has shifted in the air between us.

This moment we're about to share feels serious and that leaves me more jittery than normal.

But he calms my nerves, joining me on the bed and slowly undressing me. Everywhere his hands touch, his mouth follows, delivering sweet kisses on each newly exposed piece of skin. I close my eyes, lost in the sensations only Arch's lips and hands can give me, lifting up when he tugs my skirt around so he can unbutton it. He slips it off, murmuring, "Unbutton your shirt for me, Daze," in this deep, sexy voice that has me automatically reaching for the front of my shirt.

I undo the buttons with shaky fingers, a trembling exhale leaving me when he takes over, removing the shirt from my body. I reach for him, eagerly trying to shove his shirt off of his shoulders and he shrugs out of it, tossing the fabric aside.

Soon we're both naked, getting tangled up in each other, our mouths fused. He rolls me underneath him, his big body covering me as he rocks his erection against my throbbing center and I spread my legs wider, wanting more.

Needing more.

He continues teasing me, the head of his erection brushing against my wet flesh as he thrusts his hips. Like he's already trying to slip inside of me. I tense up when I feel just the head broach my entrance, my hands going to his broad shoulders, holding him off.

"Relax," he whispers against my lips and I nod, wishing it was that easy. I want him, but I'm also scared. It's going to hurt. I know it is.

He continues kissing me, his mouth insistent. Needy. I slowly relax with every sweep of his tongue, losing myself, my earlier nerves dissipating.

"I have condoms," he tells me at one point and I can't help but smile.

"Condoms? Plural? Are you hoping for more than once tonight?" I tease.

"Always," he says with a chuckle, kissing me deep.

He breaks away from my lips to kiss me everywhere. My shoulders and chest and breasts and stomach, his mouth lingering on the best parts, his hot tongue bathing my skin. I'm shaking from his attention, anticipation curling through my blood when he shifts lower, his mouth blazing a trail all over my stomach.

Cracking my eyes open, I watch, entranced by the sight of him kissing my body, his gaze lifting, meeting mine. We stare at each other as he licks at the sensitive skin just above my pubic hair and I swear my entire body throbs from the look on his face.

In his eyes.

I squirm when he slips even lower, his shoulders parting my legs. He spreads me wide open, palms braced on the inside of my thighs as he studies me there for a moment, making me sling my arm over my eyes, unable to take it anymore.

He's torturing me. As if he's getting off on driving me out of my mind with lust and I suppose he is. He has more experience, is always much more patient and in control compared to me, and when he finally licks me between my thighs, his tongue teasing my entry, testing me, I cry out, unable to help myself.

"You taste so good," he tells me in between hot flickers of his tongue against my clit. "Look at me, Daze."

I drop my arm to my side and open my eyes, caught up in the intensity of his gaze, unable to look away. His mouth on my flesh, his own eyes falling closed as if he's completely enraptured with me, his lips closing around my clit. Sucking.

It's too much. Not enough. I shudder and shake beneath him when I come seconds later, the orgasm sweeping over me, leaving me a moaning mess.

"I think you're ready," he murmurs against my still throbbing flesh, shifting up the length of my body to press his lips to mine before he leans over me, yanking open the drawer in his nightstand and reaching inside.

He pulls out a condom and I watch with blatant curiosity as

he shifts into a kneeling position, his erection thrusting outward as he tears open the condom wrapper before rolling it on. When he catches me staring, he gives himself a stroke and I nearly pass out from wanting to watch him do that again.

Would he want to do that? Masturbate in front of me? I suppose he would, only if I did it in front of him, and I don't know...

I think I'm a little too shy for that.

"You look scared," he observes.

"I'm just..." I shake my head, trying to find the words. "A little overwhelmed, but not too scared to go through with this."

"Yeah? Good." He crawls back on top of me, kissing me soundly, his lips and tongue helping me forget any fear that still lingers within me. The more he kisses and touches me, the more I want him and when he rocks his hips, his cock nudging against me once more, this time I arch against him, feeling hollow. Needing him to fill me.

I want him. So much.

He shifts his position, grabbing the base of his shaft and guiding it slowly inside me. I immediately tense up, hissing in a breath when I feel him broach my entrance, so wide and thick.

"Relax," he whispers in my ear before he blazes a path of hot kisses down my neck. "It's going to feel good. I promise."

I take deep, fortifying breaths, willing my bones and muscles to ease. The more he kisses me, the more relaxed I feel, and when he sinks deeper, I spread my legs wider, both of us moaning when that sends him even farther.

We both lie still for a moment, me needing to get used to him. His cock throbs within my body and I wiggle beneath him, an undeniable pinch making me twinge.

He's so freaking thick, I feel as if I'm impaled on him. It's not that it feels bad, it just feels...

Odd. Being connected like this. His flesh in mine.

His hips flex and he lifts up, the slow drag of his cock

withdrawing from my body, lighting off sparks deep within me. When he thrusts back in, I gasp at the delicious friction, needing more, and thank God, he gives it to me.

Our pace is slow at first as we learn our rhythm with each other. He's so careful with me, his touch gentle, his thrusts not too hard. Like he doesn't want to hurt me and I appreciate that.

But as we continue, I can tell he's holding back. I bet if I had more experience, he'd be moving much faster, and I'm curious.

I want him to unleash on me. Lose all control.

That's what I want to see the most. Arch losing control. On me.

With me.

I try to urge him on by racing my hands up and down his back, resting them on his very firm ass. I push him deeper and when he kisses me, I break away first, opening my eyes to find he's already watching me.

"You don't have to be so—gentle," I say, my cheeks burning.

Everywhere I'm burning. I'm willing to ask for what I want despite my embarrassment. And I shouldn't be embarrassed with him. We've done everything together.

Everything.

"You sure?"

I nod.

"Okay." He visibly swallows. "I warned you."

CHAPTER FORTY

ARCH

I've been restrained around Daisy pretty much since the day I actually looked into her eyes and spoke to her. Despite trying to deny the attraction I felt toward her from day one, how mean I was toward her, how fucking obsessed I've become with her, I'm funneling it all into this moment.

Showing her exactly how I feel about her. How much I want her.

It's too much. It might scare her but fuck.

Too late now.

She doesn't try to push me off her so I take it as a good sign. I give in to my baser instincts and let go. Grunting with every thrust, pushing my cock into her again and again, still careful, always careful with Daisy. She moves with me, hooking her long legs around my waist and tilting her hips, which sends me even deeper.

I give up trying to kiss her or touch her and just grip her hips while I thrust inside her, my orgasm barreling down upon me. Robbing me of thought and breath. All I can focus on is getting that satisfaction I know is just on the horizon.

And when I feel her inner walls tighten, squeezing around me in a stranglehold, that's what sends me over the edge, making me come with a shout.

"Fuck," I groan, pressing as deep as I can get as the shudders wrack my body. Until I collapse on top of her in a boneless heap, my mind spinning. My body still shaking.

Daisy runs her hands up and down my back, tickling my skin, making me shiver. I lie there for I don't know how long, a big sweaty mess dripping all over her, but when I try to lift away from her, she presses her hands on my back, keeping me in place.

"Don't go yet," she whispers, and so I don't.

I savor the feeling of her beneath me. Naked and sweaty and so fucking beautiful, it hurts to look at her. Hurts worse that I didn't make her come when I was inside her, but I know she did earlier, when I went down on her. I'm going to rest for a little bit, and then I'm going to make her come again.

If I could, I'd make her come all night. With my mouth and my fingers and my cock. Giving her as many orgasms as she could stand until she couldn't take it anymore.

That's all I want. To give my girl pleasure. To hear her sob my name. To know I'm the only one who can make her feel like this.

The only one.

"You okay?" I finally ask, choking out the words.

She nods, her hands drifting up and down my back still. "Definitely okay."

"You didn't come."

"You did."

Lifting up so I can look at her face, I see that she's smiling. "Kind of hard to hide it."

Her smile is tremulous, her eyes brimming with emotion that makes my heart pang. "It was perfect."

I kiss her forehead. "I hurt you?"

"Only for a little bit. It truly wasn't that bad."

I kiss her lips, searching her mouth with my tongue, and when I break away from her, she's breathless, her body wiggling beneath mine. "What are you, some sort of perfect girl or what?"

"Only for you," she whispers, the look on her face serious. Well hell.

"I'll be back," I tell her, pulling out of her body before I crawl off the bed. "Gotta get rid of the condom."

I practically run into the bathroom and shut the door, flicking on the lights so I can look at myself in the mirror. Completely naked with a deflated dick and a condom still on, all sweaty and with my hair sticking up everywhere, I look like a nightmare.

Jesus.

I dispose of the condom and grab a clean washcloth, running the water until it's warm before placing the washcloth under the water, getting it wet. Once that's done, I wash my hands, staring at my reflection in the mirror. I look like a mess and I try to smooth my hair out by finger combing it, though I realize quick that's a waste of my time.

The longer I stare at myself, the more changed I feel, which is ridiculous but damn. What Daisy and I just shared...

Such a cliché, but she rocked my world.

It's okay to tell her how you feel. She won't throw it in your face later like everyone else in your life. She's a good girl. Probably feels the same way you do.

Nodding once, I turn off the light and exit the bathroom, joining Daisy where I left her: in my bed.

She's sprawled across the mattress, lying on her stomach, her hair messier than mine, the covers kicked off to reveal her perfect body. I'm seized with the need to worship all of that naked skin on display and I press my knee onto the mattress, studying her for a moment longer before I slowly crawl onto the bed.

"You awake?" I murmur, my hand hovering above her calf.

She nods, her hair rustling against the sheets. "I'm tired. I think you wore me out."

Daisy doesn't even know the lengths I will go in order to wear her out. It's my dream to fuck her into oblivion for the rest of our days.

The realization is like a smack across my face and I pause, letting my thoughts sink deep into my heart.

I care about this girl more than anyone else I know. Could probably fall in love with her, if I haven't already.

"Let me clean you up," I whisper.

Another nod is her answer, her hair rustling against the pillow.

Letting my hand drop, I smooth it up the back of her leg, squeezing her thigh. She wiggles her ass and my gaze drops to the perfect round shape, suddenly tempted to sink my teeth into the fleshiest part of it.

Shit. Not yet. I don't want to scare her.

"Turn over on your back," I urge and she does, a faint smile curling her lips when her gaze meets mine. "Spread your legs, baby."

Suddenly looking shy—hilarious considering she's naked—she averts her gaze and spreads her legs, all of that glistening pink flesh on display. I take the warm, wet washcloth and dab it between her legs, my gaze on her face the entire time.

She winces when I touch a particular spot and when I finally finish, I check the washcloth, not surprised at all to find tiny streaks of blood on it.

Shit. I hurt her. But she was a virgin. I was bound to hurt her.

Feeling guilty, I throw the washcloth on the floor, kicking it under the bed.

"Roll back over on your stomach," I tell her and she does without saying a word, clutching the pillow, her arms stretched over her head.

I resume stroking her legs, my cock rousing, Daisy stirring beneath my hands. Like I'm working her up too. She's restless, her legs shifting, and I catch glimpses of her pretty pink pussy, still soft and glistening.

I shouldn't do anything to her. I should leave her alone. She's probably sore and achy and doesn't want me to touch her.

But my cock's standing at attention now and it's an insistent fucker. Carefully I lock my fingers around both of her ankles. "Get on your knees."

She could tell me no. Or beg off by saying she's too tired. Too sore. Over it.

Daisy does none of that. There's no hesitation when she drags her legs toward her and rises onto her knees, her upper half still pressed into the mattress. What a sight she makes. Ass straight up in the air, her pussy on display just for me.

Leaning in, I press my face against her, making her jolt. Her musky scent drives me fucking wild and I brace my hands on either side of her ass, gripping her tight so she can't move. I tease her pussy with my tongue, searching every part of her on display.

Daisy cries out, her voice muffled thanks to the pillow that she's clutching to her face, her knees spreading open wider. Her silent invitation that she wants more.

I will more than gladly give this girl whatever she wants just to make her moan my name and shudder in pleasure.

I lick her everywhere I can touch, my fingers drifting upward, until I've got my thumb pressed against her asshole. She bucks against my mouth, basically sobbing into the pillow, and when I suck her clit between my lips, she cries out my name, her entire body shaking. I don't let up my ministrations on her clit until she's trying to pull away from me and when I back up, she collapses onto the mattress.

Without hesitation, I go to her, wrapping her up in my arms and clutching her close, spooning her. She shifts closer, her ass right on my dick, her body still shaking, and I press my lips on the spot where her neck meets her shoulder, her pulse pounding beneath them.

"Oh my God," she finally whispers, making me chuckle.

"Liked it?" I kiss her neck.

"That was…"

"Fucking hot?" I supply for her.

"Yes." A nod. "Definitely."

We lie in silence and despite the raging hard-on I'm still sporting, my eyelids eventually close and my thoughts start to drift. I can hear the rain falling outside, the drops hitting against the windows whenever there's a gust of wind and it's soothing.

So soothing, we both eventually fall asleep.

• • •

I wake up to complete darkness, slowly realizing I'm alone in the bed. I sit up quickly, pushing my hair out of my eyes to find Daisy moving about the darkened room, running into furniture.

"Ow," she mutters when she smacks into the corner of my desk.

Reaching toward my nightstand, I turn on a lamp, illuminating the room. Daisy is standing in the middle of it clad in just a pair of pale blue panties, her uniform shirt clutched in her hand.

"Oh. Hey. I didn't realize you were awake."

"What time is it?" I grab the phone and answer my own question. "Shit, it's already nine."

"I know. I need to go home. I can't believe we slept that long." She swipes her bra from the floor and puts it on, then slips her shirt on over it. "The light is on at my house."

My gaze goes to the window but from where I'm at, I can't see her cottage. "Your dad is already home?"

"That or he left a lamp on. I don't know." She sounds nervous and her movements are almost frantic as she tries to get her clothes on.

I climb out of bed and go to her, pulling her into my arms and giving her a hug. "Hey, it's going to be okay."

She sags against me, her forehead pressed against my chest. "I don't want to lie to him."

"You want to tell him the truth, but you know he won't like it," I warn her.

Daisy pulls out of my embrace, turning her back to me so she can slip on her skirt and I immediately miss her. "I don't care if he doesn't like it. I'm not a liar, Arch. I can't lie to him. He's all I've got in this world."

I'm standing in front of her with nothing on and in this moment, I feel like I've got nothing to lose.

"You've got me."

She yanks her skirt into place and buttons it before turning to face me, buttoning her shirt. "I know." Her voice is small, and the sound of it makes me feel small too.

Like she doesn't believe me, which is just mind blowing. Doesn't she see it? How gone I am for her?

"Do you really, Daze?"

"I do." She tucks her shirt back into place before settling onto the edge of my bed, slipping back on her socks. "I'm feeling— guilty, is all."

Ah, shit. That's the last thing I want her to feel.

Spotting my boxer briefs, I slip them back on, not about to have this discussion with her while I'm naked. I feel vulnerable enough already.

She's trying to put on her loafers when I kneel in front of her, my hands on her knees, my gaze imploring as I stare up at her. "Don't feel guilty, Daze. What we just shared...it means everything to me."

"It means everything to me too," she whispers, and I can tell she feels as vulnerable as I do.

"Don't feel guilty." My voice is firm. "You're eighteen. Teenagers have sex. It's what we do."

Daisy smiles, her hair falling around her face. "Is that so?"

"Yeah. Look at us. I'm already thinking about how I can get you naked again."

She stares into my eyes, her lips still swollen from my kisses, and I swear I see a mark on her neck, also probably my fault. I've marked her, yet she can't see it.

Daisy Albright is mine. All mine.

"I like you, Daze," I admit. "A lot."

Her smile is faint. "I like you too, Archibald."

I'm frowning, but I can't keep it going. I'm too damn happy. "I don't like it when you call me that though."

"Why not? It's your name, after all."

"A name I don't particularly like." I rise up and kiss her, my lips lingering. "Want me to walk you to your house?"

"I can go by myself."

She stands, going to my desk chair and grabbing her jacket, pulling it on, then slinging her backpack over her shoulder. "I'll see you tomorrow?"

"Yeah." I go to her again, pressing her against the door, kissing her hard. I can't stop kissing her. I wish she didn't have to leave. We need to try and plan some sort of weekend getaway soon, though I'm sure her dad won't let her go.

Fucking sucks, having to deal with an overprotective parent. That's a first.

"Bye," she whispers, kissing me one more time.

"I'll miss you."

She smiles. "You'll see me in the morning."

"I'll still miss you. I like having you in my bed."

Her cheeks turn pink. That this girl can still blush after I went down on her from behind and made her scream into a pillow—I don't get it. "I like being in your bed."

We kiss—and we don't stop. Until she's eventually pushing me away and I stumble backward, not ready to quit but doing it for her.

Always for her.

"I'll see you later," she says, her voice firm as she turns her back to me and unlocks the door.

"Text me when you get home."

"I will," she promises, opening the door. "Bye, Arch."

"Bye, Daze."

I watch the door shut, hating how empty my room feels with her gone. I immediately go to the window, pissed at myself for not walking with her. Thankfully the rain stopped, but the sidewalks are wet and what if she slips and falls?

Jesus, I sound like a protective papa bear. I need to chill.

Within seconds, Daisy appears walking down the sidewalk, headed to her house. I watch her go, my chest aching, worry filling me though I don't quite know why.

That's a lie. I know. It's her dad. I'm worried he'll overreact when she comes home and make her feel guilty for being with me. I don't want to lose her, and I definitely don't want her father convincing her that I'm a piece of shit she should steer clear of.

I don't get his hatred toward me. I need to talk to him. Show him how much I care about his daughter. Because I do. Care about Daisy.

Pretty sure I'm falling in love with her.

CHAPTER FORTY-ONE

DAISY

I enter the house quietly, glancing around the darkened living room, looking for any sign of life. I realized as I approached the house that the light is actually coming from the kitchen, the little lamp that sits on our table that my dad uses sometimes when he pays bills and has trouble reading the fine print. I don't remember leaving that light on when I left this morning, but maybe my dad did because it's awfully quiet in here.

Thank God he's not home.

Shutting the door, I turn the lock and am about to switch on the lamp when I hear my father's voice break through the silence.

"Where the hell have you been?"

I flick on the lamp, shocked when I see my father sitting in his recliner, his head tilted to the right, his intense gaze locked on me. He's leaning forward, his elbows resting on his knees and his hands clutched together, his expression stormy. I remain rooted to the spot where I stand, clutching my backpack strap so tight my fingers start to ache.

"Um—"

"Were you with that boy? Arch Lancaster?"

Here's my chance. I told Arch I didn't like lying to my dad and I meant it.

"Yes." I lift my chin, trying to look strong, though I feel like I could crumble completely apart inside.

A ragged sigh leaves him and he leans back in his chair, staring up at the ceiling as if he's asking for help from God. I don't know what to say. Or how to act. I'd give anything to take a hot shower and wash my troubled feelings away, but I know he's not going to let me go without an explanation or a lecture. Most likely both.

"You had sex with him, didn't you?" It's more a statement than a question.

"I—"

"Don't bother denying it. Look at you." The disgust in his voice is obvious.

I clamp my lips shut, fighting the humiliation that spreads all over my skin. The guilt. I'm eighteen and it's normal to be a teenager who has sex with her boyfriend, which I'm pretty sure is what Arch is to me now. We haven't made anything official yet, but I know in my heart, it's true.

It is.

"You really believe you're in love with him?" he asks, when I still haven't said anything.

I stare at my father, ready to answer yes, despite knowing that will upset him even more when he interrupts me yet again.

"Be careful if you say yes, sweetheart. Because if you do, I'm going to do everything I can to convince you to stay away from him," he spits out.

"Why?" I ask incredulously, hating how confused I feel. How can my father make this seem so wrong when being with Arch feels so incredibly right?

"He's reckless. Foolish. Selfish. A taker, Daisy Mae. That's all he'll do—take and take and take until you've got nothing left to give and then he'll move on to someone else and forget all about you. Look what he's already done! He got you suspended. You don't ever get in trouble, Daisy, and now you're getting suspended and sneaking around behind my back. Lying to me. I don't even know who you are anymore."

I flinch at his cruel words. His opinion of Arch—even of me—is so awful and I don't know what Arch ever did to him to make him feel that way.

"You're being unfair," I tell him. "I've never had anyone in my life but you since Mom died, and now I finally find someone I care about—someone who cares about me, and you're telling me I'm not allowed to go out with him? I'm eighteen years old! It's okay if I have a boyfriend."

"You can have boyfriends. You can choose any kid at Lancaster Prep, but you had to go and choose that one? The richest one? Frankly, Arch Lancaster is an asshole, sweetheart. He doesn't have any feelings. None of the Lancasters do."

"That's not true," I start to tell him, but he's not listening to me.

"That boy doesn't know what he has in you. You're just like your mother. Special. Bright. Brighter than sunshine. You light up every room that you walk in, just like she did, and I knew it from the start. I cherished her from the very first time I met her. I knew she was special."

I think of how terrible Arch was to me when we first met. He didn't think I was special and he definitely didn't cherish me. If I were ever to tell my father that, he would just use it as evidence against Arch.

"No one is special to him. Arch is the center of his own universe. And when he's through with you, he'll just discard you like trash and diminish your brightness, Daisy. Do you want that? Is that what you want for your life? Because you deserve so much more." He slumps against the chair, as if he's exhausted by his own speech.

"You don't even know him and you're already judging him. Can't you just let me have something for myself for once?" With a childish huff, I march out of the living room and head for the kitchen, hating how ridiculous he's being.

He's treating me like a child. As if I can't make my own decisions. He's coddled me for far too long and I'm over it.

"You're my daughter and if you're living under my roof, you will do as I say!" he screams after me.

Ignoring his outburst, I flick on the kitchen light, desperate to get something to drink to ease my dry throat when I pause, staring at what's sitting on the table next to the lit lamp. I didn't even notice when I first walked into the room but now it's all I can see.

A vase sitting in the middle of the table, filled with roses. From my rose bush. The orange ones my mom liked best.

I blink at the arrangement, shock coursing through my blood, leaving me cold. I stare at the vase, at the roses. They're going to die now.

They're going to die. In a vase instead of outside where they belong.

Like a zombie, I turn and slowly walk back into the living room, my heart in my throat, my head pounding. I stare at my father, unable to form words, my heart threatening to fly out of my mouth.

"Daisy, what in the world is wrong with—"

"Why did you cut my roses?" My voice is eerily calm.

He blinks at me, his brows lowering. "What do you mean?"

"The roses, on the table." I inhale, but it's not deep enough. I can't catch my breath and I fight the panic that wants to overtake me. "Did you cut those? Why?"

"I knew that the storm was coming and when I came home for lunch, I clipped some to take to Kathy when I went to her place. And then I forgot them. I'm going to take them to her tomorrow."

"No."

"No? You can't tell me who—"

"*NO!*"

The scream rasps at my throat, making it hurt, but I don't

care. I don't care about anything. I can't feel anything. My head, my heart, my everything...

Numb.

I march back into the kitchen and grab the vase, clutching it in both hands, the water jostling out of the top, it's so full. I can't believe he cut my roses. No one ever does. He knows this. He knows how I feel about them and for him to want to take that specific color to stupid Kathy when it was Mom's favorite, I just...

I can't believe it. I can't believe *him.*

"Daisy, calm down right now!"

I glance over my shoulder to see my father approaching me and I turn toward the sink once more, lifting the vase and throwing it into it with all my might. On impact, the glass shatters everywhere, water splashing in my face, the roses scattering, petals shaking loose. I'm screaming at the top of my lungs, over and over, and when my father tries to grab hold of my shoulders, I shake him off.

"Get away from me!"

I fall to the ground sobbing. My vision blurred, my head swimming. "Those were Mom's flowers. You can't just give Kathy my mom's roses. They don't belong to her! You know how I feel about cutting them!"

"Daisy. Sweetie. I knew the storm was going to bring cold temperatures this week and that your roses wouldn't live much longer outside, so I thought I'd bring a few inside. I didn't think you'd mind," Dad pleads.

"You brought them inside for Kathy, not for me or for you. For *her.* They're not yours to cut, Daddy. They're *mine.* And they deserve to live. Everything deserves to live." I'm sitting in the center of my own destruction, rocking back and forth, unable to stop the tears. My stomach hurts and I curl my arms around my middle, clutching myself, my hair hanging in my face, sticking to my cheeks because they're wet with my tears.

When I reach up to push my hair out of the way, I wipe the

tears from my eyes, glancing down at my hands.

My fingers are streaked with blood.

I touch my cheek, wincing when I feel the gash in my flesh. And when I draw my hand away, blood coats my fingers, bright red and thick.

I cut myself. Most likely on the glass from the broken vase when it shattered everywhere. And I don't even care.

"If this is some sort of distraction to make me forget what you just did with that Lancaster boy, it's not working," Dad starts out, but I leap to my feet with a shriek, thrusting my face in his.

"This has nothing to do with Arch and me. It has everything to do with you." I burst into tears again, the salt getting in the cuts on my face, bringing me pain. Everything hurts. All of it. It feels like a betrayal, what my father did, wanting to give the roses to his new girlfriend. She doesn't deserve them. He barely knows her. I don't even know her, not that well.

How dare he do this? I'm probably being completely irrational, but I don't care.

What he did, how thoughtless he was—it cuts to the bone.

"Me? You're upset because I cut roses for Kathy?"

"You cut my roses and didn't ask for permission. You chose the exact color that was Mom's favorite, and planned on giving them to another woman. You say Arch is thoughtless and careless, but you just proved to me tonight that you're exactly the same way," I tell him, surprised by how calm I sound.

How calm I suddenly feel.

I exit the kitchen without another word and Dad lets me go, also remaining silent. I keep my posture rigid, my steps slow as I make my way to the bathroom, shutting the door behind me and turning the lock before I hit the light switch.

My reflection nearly takes my breath away. I'm a mess. My hair is everywhere, my face bleeding in multiple spots. My eyes are swollen and I close them for a second, hoping it'll all go away because it's just a dream.

But when I open my eyes again, I'm still in my bathroom and I'm still a disaster. This isn't how I thought the night would end. At all.

CHAPTER FORTY-TWO

ARCH

I've been up since six—unheard of for me. I can't get what happened between Daisy and me last night out of my mind. I can't get her out of my head, not that I want to, but fuck.

I'm obsessed.

The sound of her voice, the taste of her mouth, her skin, her pussy...

Having sex with her for the first time was like nothing I've ever experienced before. All of the sexual encounters with Daisy feel different. It's like I care more. It means more.

Shit, I *am* in love with her. Helplessly, completely in love with her.

I've already taken a shower and ate a protein bar. Again, completely unheard of for me. I'm eagerly waiting for Daisy to come out of her house, still lingering in my room and staring at the cottage through my window. It's getting late. First period is going to start any minute and I'm dressed and ready to go for once in my life.

Looks like waiting for Daisy is going to actually make me late. This is a first.

When she still hasn't come out and there's literally three minutes before the bell rings, I'm texting her, pissed at myself for waiting this long.

Me: *Are you okay?*

Two freaking minutes pass and she finally answers me.

Daze: *Can you take me somewhere?*

I don't even hesitate.

Me: *Where?*

Daze: *Come pick me up please. My dad is already gone.*

I leave my room and sprint over to Daisy's place, ready to barge right in when she opens the front door, surprising me. She's not in her uniform. She's wearing dark gray sweatpants and a big black hoodie with the hood completely covering her head. Like I can't even see her eyes or nose, just her mouth.

"Daze?"

She opens the door wider. "Come in."

I walk inside the house, glancing around the room, unable to shake the weird feeling creeping over me. Something's wrong.

I can sense it.

"Tell me what's going on," I demand as soon as she approaches me.

With shaky fingers, she reaches up and tugs the hood back, revealing her face.

With jagged cuts all over it.

"What the fuck, Daisy? What happened to you?" I reach for her, my touch gentle as I carefully cup her cheeks and examine her face with my gaze. The biggest cut is on her cheekbone and it looks deep, but not deep enough for stitches. I don't think. There's a tiny butterfly bandage on it, keeping the wound together, but it still looks like it's bleeding.

"A vase broke last night," she says, her voice flat. "I cut myself."

"You broke the vase?"

She nods.

"How? What happened?"

"I don't want to talk about it." She lifts one shoulder in a halfhearted shrug, staring off into space like she's not even paying attention to me.

Or anything.

Fear ripples through me and I drop my hands from her face, stepping back. "Where do you want me to take you?"

"To the doctor. That urgent care in town? Maybe they can help me."

"You don't want to see the nurse on campus?"

Daisy shakes her head. "I don't want to answer her questions."

What the hell?

"I'll take you," I say firmly.

"We'll have to miss class."

"I don't care."

She waves a hand at me. "Do you want to change out of your uniform?"

"It's fine. Come on, let's go. I'm worried about you."

She lets me take her hand and lead her out of the house, and we stop by my room to grab my car keys. I end up getting rid of my jacket and tie and pull on a sweatshirt, my movements hurried, my brain scrambling.

Something is definitely up, and I wish she would just tell me what it is. I watch her out of the corner of my eye and she's not paying any attention to me. She just stands there quietly, her eyes glazed over, her movements slow. Almost as if her arms and legs are weighted down and it's freaking me the fuck out.

Daisy isn't acting right. At all.

We're in my car and halfway to town when she finally murmurs, "I should call Vivian and tell her we're not going to be at school today."

"Don't worry about it," I reassure her, reaching out to settle my hand on her knee. She flinches at my touch and I immediately remove my hand, confused at her reaction. Her mood. Something is definitely wrong, but she's not talking.

She's not listening either.

I try to concentrate on the road, but I can't help trying to sneak looks at her every few minutes. She stares straight ahead, her expression blank, her skin pale, the red jagged cuts standing out. A million questions run through my head, but I can't work up the nerve to ask her, too worried over what she might say.

Or what she might not say. I don't know what's freakier.

We finally arrive at the urgent care clinic in the town closest to campus, and the moment I park the car, Daisy opens the passenger door and walks right out, not saying a word. I scramble to grab my keys and follow her out, walking right past her to open the door to the building. She enters and makes her way to the front desk and I hover behind as she speaks to the receptionist. Hating how the woman eyes me suspiciously, like I'm the reason all of those cuts are on Daisy's face.

This is fucking killing me. The not knowing, the suspicion that's being cast upon me.

I'm just trying to support Daisy during her time of need. It's like she's purposely keeping me in the dark and I don't get why. I deserve to know what's going on. I don't buy her story that she did this to herself. What changed between her going home last night and her texting me this morning? Did she get into a fight with her dad?

Alarm fills me. Did her father do this to her?

No. Ralph is a good guy. A calm, nice guy. He wouldn't harm a hair on Daisy's head. He loves her.

"I need to fill this out." Daisy clutches a clipboard in her hands with a bunch of forms clipped on it and I follow her to the waiting area, both of us settling into chairs right next to each other.

While she fills out the forms, I'm texting with the attendance office at school, letting them know I'm out with Daisy and I took her to the doctor. Of course, the lady who works in the office told me I can't excuse Daisy, that she'll have to call in, and I said I'd have her call soon.

Road blocks all morning, I swear.

It takes Daisy forever to fill out the forms and finally she

326326

gives them to the receptionist and we wait some more. My girl remains quiet, unfocused, reaching up to touch her cheek every couple of minutes, wincing. The cut on her cheekbone looks worse than I thought and maybe she will need stitches.

"Does it hurt?" I ask, leaning in close so I can murmur into her ear.

She pulls away a little, like she needs the distance. "Yeah. I didn't even realize how bad it was until I woke up this morning."

"Why?" *Tell me, Daze. What happened?*

"I did something stupid." She shakes her head, her gaze lifting to mine, and fuck, there are tears shining in her eyes. "I got mad."

"Mad at who, baby?" I touch the side of her head, my fingers tangling in her hair and this time she doesn't pull away.

"My dad." She closes her eyes, taking a deep breath. "Myself."

"What happened?"

"Daisy Albright?"

We both glance over at the woman in dark pink scrubs with a file clutched in her hand, holding the door open that leads to the examination rooms.

"That's me," Daisy says weakly as she stands up.

"Come on back, hon," the nurse chirps cheerfully.

"Want me to go with you?" I ask.

Daisy shakes her head, smiling down at me. "No. I'll be okay."

"I'll wait for you."

"You can leave if you want. There's a good coffee shop down the road."

"I'm staying," I say firmly.

"Okay."

I watch her walk across the waiting area and through the door the nurse keeps open for her, my heart panging the moment the door slams shut. I glance over at the receptionist who greeted us, catching her watching me, and she looks away hurriedly.

Damn it, I hope like hell she doesn't think I hurt Daisy. Does that chick recognize me? I am a fucking Lancaster, which right now isn't working to my advantage at all.

Lancasters don't go to the local urgent care to take care of their medical emergencies. We have private doctors and top of the line insurance coverage because money isn't a factor. We can afford whatever we need and a Lancaster always gets the best medical care.

I have zero experience in situations like this. I've never been to a chintzy urgent care like this before in my life. What am I supposed to do?

How am I supposed to act?

Leaning back in the chair, I kick my legs out, watching the mother sitting across from me holding a fussy toddler. The old man sitting in the next row of chairs over, his head hanging, mouth partially open.

Pretty sure he's asleep.

Reaching into the front pocket of my hoodie, I find my AirPods case, and I slip them into my ears, turning on some music.

Tuning out the world.

CHAPTER FORTY-THREE

DAISY

The nurse is kind, with her gentle voice and gentler questions. I do as she says, standing on the scale. Letting her take my blood pressure. Answering her questions about my health.

"What about your mental health, Daisy?" she asks—the thin gold badge pinned to her shirt says her name is Carmen—and I lift my gaze to hers. "How have you been feeling lately?"

"Happy. Stressed." I take a deep breath, wondering how much I should reveal. Carmen doesn't know me. She's just asking questions because she's required to, not because she cares. "I have a boyfriend."

Her smile is soft. "Your first?"

I nod. How did she know?

"The young man waiting for you?"

I nod some more.

Carmen's voice gets a little louder. "You two didn't have a—fight, did you?"

"No."

"So, he didn't do this to you?" She inclines her head toward me, indicating my injuries.

"No, no, no." I shake my head, hoping I don't sound too defensive. I'm just shocked she would even think that. "I did this to myself. I got mad last night."

"At your boyfriend?"

"At my father," I whisper, closing my eyes, the humiliation returning. When I woke up this morning—late, which never happens—I realized my father was already gone. He didn't leave me a note, nothing. No apology given, and I couldn't say sorry to him either.

I hate that we're fighting. That I lost my temper and acted like a toddler having a tantrum. I don't know how to make this right because I never do this.

Ever.

"Your father didn't do this to you, did he?" Carmen asks gently.

"No." The tears are streaming down my face and I close my eyes, hating that I'm crying again. "He's a good person. My boyfriend is too. They just want what's best for me. I'm the one who lost it."

Carmen pats my knee and I can't help it.

I begin to cry harder. Hard enough that she pulls me in for a hug and lets me sob against her shoulder. We stay like this for an embarrassingly long amount of time until I finally pull away from her, wiping at my face with the back of my hand, wincing when I drag my fingers across my wounds.

Carmen offers me a box of tissues and I take the entire thing, grabbing a few and blowing my nose.

"Your cuts are pretty superficial but I do worry about the one on your right cheekbone. The doctor will be here in a few minutes and she'll take a look at it," she explains.

I grab another tissue and carefully dab at my face. "Thank you."

"You're welcome, Daisy. And here." She pulls a business card out of her pocket and hands it to me. "Call this number or visit the website if you ever need to. The services they provide are free."

Carmen leaves me alone in the examination room and I study the card. It's for a mental health website aimed specifically at teens.

Right after my mom died, I went to counseling, and continued to do so for about six months. One day my father asked if I felt okay about Mom dying and I said yeah because how else was I supposed to answer? Because of that, I never went back.

I probably should have. Maybe my dad couldn't afford it. He has decent health insurance, but there are some things that aren't covered. I don't know what happened, but I never saw that counselor again. I can look back now and see it was probably too soon for me to quit, but I was twelve and I just did what my dad said.

I never questioned it. I never thought I could.

There's a knock on the door and then it swings open, revealing the doctor. She has a friendly face and long dark hair that's pulled back into a low ponytail. She has kind eyes. They're big and brown and her smile is pleasant, as is her demeanor.

"Looks like you had a run-in with a rose bush," the doctor says jokingly.

"Actually, you're kind of right," I say, holding very still when she comes close to examine me.

"Tell me what happened." She presses her fingers against my face.

"I got into an argument with my father and I threw a vase full of roses at the sink," I explain, wincing when she gently prods at my cut.

"Uh huh. That doesn't sound so good."

"It wasn't." I hiss in a breath when she removes the butterfly bandage that I put on my cut earlier. "The vase shattered when it hit the sink and glass went flying."

"Into your face," the doctor says.

"I have some cuts on my arms and legs too," I admit.

She pulls back, her gaze narrowed. "Let me see."

The humiliation is back, twenty-fold. I feel so stupid as I shove up my sleeves and show her the tiny cuts on my forearms. And the ones on my legs too. She deems all of them superficial and that I'll be okay.

"The cut on your cheek though." She shakes her head, her gaze trained on it. "You're going to need stitches."

Fear trickles through my blood, leaving me cold. "Will it scar?"

"Not if I can help it. I'm pretty good at this." She smiles reassuringly. "And the cut only needs about four stitches, so not too bad. It'll be over before you know it."

"Will it hurt?"

"No." She shakes her head. "The worst part is the shot I'll give you to numb the pain."

"Can my boyfriend come in here and be with me when you stitch it up?" I ask, suddenly needing Arch with me.

"Absolutely. I'll have Carmen go fetch him." She pats my shoulder. "Let us get some things together and then I'll do the procedure. It won't take long."

I watch her go, wringing my hands in my lap the entire time while I wait for Arch. When the door finally swings open and he's walking into the room, I start crying all over again.

I'm so tired of crying. Of being sad. Of beating myself up over this. I had an outburst and I'm acting like it's the end of the world.

Arch doesn't say a word. Just takes me into his arms and holds me close, his hand running up and down my back, soothing me. The tears dry up as fast as they spilled out and I finally pull away from him, tilting my head back so I can meet his gaze.

"What's the verdict?" he asks, concern filling his blue eyes.

"I need stitches."

His smile is faint. "You're going to look like a badass."

The laugh is automatic. Small but there, and my heart immediately feels lighter. "Please. I will not."

He nods, his eyes dancing. "Hell yeah, you will. That's all

I wanted when I was a kid. Stitches. And on my face? That would've been so cool."

"Why would you want stitches on your face?" I'm still laughing, shaking my head, smiling at him.

"Because like I said, you'll look like my favorite badass. Especially where the cut is, right on your cheekbone." His smile fades, his gaze turning serious. "You going to tell me what happened?"

"It's dumb," I say on a sigh.

"Aren't accidents usually dumb?" He goes quiet and I realize he's waiting for me to explain.

"My dad and I got into an argument."

He averts his gaze like he's staring out the window, though he can't see anything because the blinds are closed. "About me?"

"It started out about you." I clamp my lips shut when the doctor walks back into the room, Carmen, the nurse, trailing behind her.

Arch and I share a look and I realize we're going to have to talk later.

About everything that happened.

. . .

After the procedure, Arch takes me to the café I mentioned to him earlier, and I order a vanilla latte and a cinnamon roll while he gets a white chocolate mocha and a breakfast sandwich. He insists on paying and I let him because I didn't even bring my wallet with me. Plus, I think it makes him feel good, that he's taking care of me.

My face is still numb from that terrible shot—the doctor was right, it was horrible and painful—and I feel like I'm eating weird. Drinking weird. Arch even grabs me a straw to use to sip my hot coffee from the to-go cup, and while I feel dumb, it does help.

I feel dumb about a lot of things, including the argument with my father. The way I acted last night. It's like I'm having an emotional come down and I'm regretting everything I did yesterday, with the exception of one thing.

I don't regret having sex with Arch.

We make small talk and it's almost as painful as the shot the nurse gave me. Until finally, Arch balls up the wrapper his sandwich was in—he consumed it in less than five minutes I swear—and tosses it on the table so it bounces against my cup.

"Are you going to tell me what happened last night when you went home?"

Taking a deep breath, I tell him everything. How my dad scared me. How mad he got when he found out that I was with Arch. I don't mention Dad figuring out we had sex because that's just embarrassing, but I tell him how angry I became when I saw he cut the roses. How upset I was at the idea of him giving the flowers to Kathy.

"My mom's favorite color too," I add, my voice small.

Arch reaches out and rests his hand on my forearm, giving it a gentle squeeze. "I'm sorry, Daze."

"I am too." I drop my gaze to where his hand rests on my arm, noticing how big it is, how long his fingers are. How his touch gives me so much comfort—and pleasure too. And how that feels like a very grown-up thought to have.

"Have you talked to him?"

"He was already out of the house by the time I woke up," I admit.

"You should probably have a conversation with him."

"I don't know what to say. I want to apologize, but I think he should too, you know? I can't believe how mean he was. He said terrible things about me and you and—us." I whisper the last word, feeling silly.

"I don't know what I did to him to make him hate me." Arch removes his hand from my arm and leans back in his chair, kicking his legs out. His frustration is clear and I wish I could reassure him. "Be real with me, Daze. Am I that bad?"

No. He's perfect—perfect for me. But how can I tell him that? How can I say the words out loud when we haven't discussed what exactly our relationship is? He hasn't asked me to be his girlfriend. Is that how it works? Do we need to make it official? We spend all of our time together and I could assume that's what we are, but I never want to assume.

I never want to be made a fool.

"You're not that bad. You're not bad at all," I murmur, thinking of all the wonderful, thoughtful things he's done for me lately. "You're a good boyfriend."

The word falls from my lips without thought, hanging between us, and Arch's gaze flicks up to mine.

"I didn't mean that," I say when he remains silent. "I mean— you've been a great friend."

Okay that sounds lame.

One side of his mouth kicks up in a closed-lip smile. "You really calling us friends right now?"

"I don't know." I shrug, tearing my gaze away from his. I am squirming in my chair, and I think he's enjoying it. "What do you call what we're doing?"

"Well, I know one thing." He scoots close to me, crowding me until he's all I can see and smell and hear. "We know each other pretty damn well, wouldn't you agree?"

I duck my head, nodding. I breathe in his clean, masculine scent, my body leaning into his. "Very well."

"We haven't made anything official." He's touching my hair. The side of my face, careful not to brush his fingers against my wound. "But I think we should."

His fingers curve around my neck, tilting my head up so our gazes meet. He looks so serious, and I'm suddenly scared. "Wanna be my girlfriend, Daze?"

I nod.

He smiles.

And the relief I feel at hearing him call me that, at feeling his lips brush against mine immediately after...

I'm not scared anymore.

Of anything.

CHAPTER FORTY-FOUR

DAISY

We skipped school for the rest of the day, something I've never done in my life, and I can't believe I don't feel even a twinge of guilt over it. It's impossible to worry for too long when I've got Arch distracting me.

Dragging me in and out of all of the cute shops downtown, trying to get me to pick something out so he can buy it for me. I don't want anything. I'm perfectly content just spending time with my boyfriend.

Hmm. That's going to take some getting used to.

"I like this necklace." We're in one of the stores that sells a variety of knickknacks including jewelry, and he's standing over a glass display case, pointing.

I stop beside him, laughing when I see the charm on the necklace—a tiny letter A. "You would like it. That's your initial."

"You could wear my initial." He glances down at me, smiling. "Then everyone would know you're my girlfriend and that you belong to me."

Thank God I'm gripping the edge of the counter. Otherwise, I'd swoon and faint, falling to the floor in a heap at the sweet look on his face and the words he just said.

"Does it matter if people know I'm yours or not?" I ask, my

voice soft.

"Yeah, it does to me." His tone is fierce, the look in his eyes possessive. "I want the whole world to know, Daze."

He leans in and kisses me, his lips so soft and tender, I almost want to cry. It's like he's able to reach inside of me, grab hold of my heart and squeeze until I can't take it anymore.

Eventually I convince him to leave the store without the necklace because I need nothing from him. Just his time.

That's what means the most to me. We only have so much time on this earth and we have to make the most of it. Just basking in Arch's presence calms me. Makes me feel special. Makes me feel...

Loved.

Eventually we end up going to the beach, not too far from campus, and we take a walk, the wind whipping against us, making it a struggle. We give up pretty quickly and end up back in his car in the parking lot. There's no one else around since it's in the middle of a weekday.

"The clouds are so dark," I observe as I peer out the windshield, noting the storm heading toward us in the distance. "And that wind is fierce."

It howls outside as if in answer, making Arch's car rock.

"Gonna rain again." He reaches for me, tugging, like he wants me closer but I don't really budge. "How's your face?"

The numbness has worn off mostly. "It hurts a little."

"They prescribe you any painkillers?"

I shake my head. "No and I really wouldn't take them if they did."

There's a glow in his eyes that leaves me fluttery inside. "Always such a good girl."

"Drugs and alcohol aren't my thing." I wrinkle my nose.

"Funny because I'm pretty sure I'm addicted to you," he says with utmost sincerity.

I burst out laughing. "That was so corny."

"Look at me. I become your boyfriend and turn into a complete idiot." He's grinning, reaching for me again, and this time, I don't resist.

I let him pull me into his lap, readjusting me so I'm straddling him. I curl my hands around his broad shoulders, my knees slipping so they're on either side of his hips and when he tilts his head back, I lean in, pressing my forehead to his.

"Can I tell you something?" he asks.

"You can tell me anything," I whisper, my heart aching at the truth of my statement.

I just want this boy to confide in me, to tell me everything that he thinks. His hopes and dreams. His worries and fears. I want to know all of it. All of him.

"You're my favorite person in the whole world," he admits, his gaze locked on mine. "If I could spend every minute with you, I would."

"You're my favorite too," I whisper, my throat aching with the admission. It feels like we're talking in code. As if we don't want to say the biggest, most meaningful word to each other.

Yet.

"You scared me this morning." His fingers are tangled in my hair and a soft murmur of appreciation escapes me when he combs it out. "I was worried about you."

"I was—numb. Like I felt nothing." And I'm so tired. Emotionally worn out. I could probably fall asleep like this if he keeps stroking my hair...

"I bet I could make you feel something," he says, like my words are a dare.

And when he kisses me, I forget all about sleep. All I can focus on is the needy press of his lips. The easy way his tongue slips into my mouth, sliding against mine. I kiss him back with everything I have, trying to show him how much I appreciate him. Care about him.

I wish I could say it. I wish I could tell him I've fallen in love with him, but it's so hard. So scary.

His hands fall to my hips, holding me in place as he continues to kiss me. I can feel him in between my thighs, hard and throbbing already, and I can't help myself. I rock against him, pressing against his erection and he groans.

We kiss and kiss, drowning in each other, his hands slipping beneath my sweatshirt, fingers pressing into my bare skin. Now that we've had sex, he doesn't hold back like he used to. His touch is bold, his hands moving up until they're undoing the clasp on my bra, his fingers seeking as he brushes them against my nipples. I can't stop shivering and when he tugs on one nipple extra hard, I whimper against his lips, surprisingly enjoying the pain.

He finally tears his mouth from mine, his breathing ragged, his hands still on my breasts. "I'm not fucking you in my car, Daze."

I'm breathing hard as well and it takes me a few seconds to speak. "Why not?"

Arch leans back against the headrest, his lids at half-mast as he studies me. "First, I don't have a condom, and second, I have a perfectly good bed we can make use of. Like we did yesterday."

"Maybe I want to do it in the car." It's so hot in here and when I quickly glance over my shoulder, I notice the windshield is fogged up. "I don't want to go back to campus."

He's frowning, his hands cupping my breasts, his thumbs brushing back and forth across my nipples. "Someone could catch us."

"They'll catch us wherever we are." I lean in and kiss him, my tongue searching his mouth this time around and his hips lift a little, his erection pressing against me. "Let's do it here."

"Daisy..."

"Please." I reach between us, my fingers brushing against his erection. "You can pull out right before you come."

"Holy shit. You can't say things like that." He sounds like he's in complete agony and I can't help the tiny thrill that pulses through me. Knowing that I'm the reason he sounds like this. Feels like this.

It's all because of me.

I'm already undoing the front of his uniform trousers, grateful he's not wearing a belt. Makes it far easier for me to access him and when I slip my hand inside, my fingers drifting across the front of his cotton boxer briefs, a soft, breathy sigh escapes me. He's so hard and thick and perfect.

Knowing he's my boyfriend makes me bolder too. Like I have every right to touch him. He's not stopping me either. Not when I pull down the front of his boxer briefs and expose him, making him hiss out a breath. Not when I curl my fingers around his shaft and begin to stroke. I don't recognize who I am in this moment or what I'm becoming, but I like her.

I like me.

"Daze, Daze, Daze." He locks his fingers around my wrist, stopping me, and when I look up at him, I find he's watching me with a serious expression on his face. "You gotta stop."

"Why?" I'm confused. Doesn't he like this?

He licks his lips, his gaze wild. A little unfocused. "Because if you keep doing that, I'm gonna come all over your hand."

Leaning in, I press my lips to his and say, "Maybe that's what I want."

I kiss him, essentially shutting him up, and we get a little lost in each other for a bit, until I feel his other hand on my shoulder, gently pushing me away so I have no choice but to break away from his lips.

"What the fuck, Daze?" He sounds bewildered, but I ignore his confusion and kiss him again. His fingers on my wrist slowly loosen and then I'm kissing his neck. Behind his ear. Breathing into his skin, stroking him, my pace increasing.

I have no real idea what I'm doing. I mean, we've been messing around for a while so I have a sense of it. I know what he likes. But I'm also winging it, just giving into my urges and letting myself do whatever I want.

Within reason of course.

"Baby, you gotta slow down," he chokes out at one point, his hands returning to my hips, tugging down on the waistband of my sweatpants. His words don't match his actions, but I don't bring that to his attention.

Instead, I let him do it, inhaling sharply when he dives his hand down the front of my pants, his fingers brushing against my panties.

The next thing I know, I end up with my sweatpants pushed to my ankles and my panties tugged to the side. I'm rubbing against him, skin on skin, bathing the head of his cock with my wet heat and he's groaning. And when just the tip slips inside me, I don't hesitate.

I sink all the way down on him, ignoring the slight pinch of pain. My inner walls clamp tight around him, our bodies connected as one and I rise up, my lids cracking open to find he's already watching me.

"Fuck," he bites out as he flexes his hips. "You feel so good without a condom."

I start to ride him, knowing this is reckless. The most reckless, impulsive thing I've ever done. If my father knew that I was having unprotected sex, he would be so disappointed. I'm taking a risk. Risking my future and Arch's.

But right now, I'm too caught up in how good he feels to care.

• • •

We drive back to campus mostly in silence, but it isn't uncomfortable or tense. More of a satisfied...quietness. A contentedness I haven't felt in I don't know how long. Arch is listening to a playlist, while I drift in and out of sleep, his hand rarely leaving where it rests on my thigh. His touch grounds me, reminds me that I have him in my corner, which I desperately need.

Eventually I give up on sleep and stare out the passenger side window, absently chewing on my lower lip. The closer we get to home, the more anxious I feel. I can't ignore the nervous sensation swirling in my stomach, making me faintly nauseous.

I need to talk to my father and I don't want to do it with Arch as a witness. My dad will be hostile toward him and it would all just fall apart. I need to try and reason with my dad first before I bring Arch into it. It's going to take a while, but I'm patient.

I have to make this work.

"You okay?" Arch asks when we finally pull into the school parking lot.

"Nervous about seeing my dad." I release a shaky breath, sending him a quick smile.

"It'll work out," he says with all the confidence I wish I felt. "He'll listen to you and you'll listen to him. He'll apologize and so will you. And then all will be forgiven."

"I hope so," I whisper, glancing down at my lap to see my hands all twisted together. I unlink them, shaking them out, noting how sweaty my palms are.

We get out of the car and walk across campus. It's late afternoon and it's mostly empty. I'm searching in every corner for my father, hoping he's with Kathy or preoccupied with a work task. I'd prefer him being at home waiting for me versus just stumbling upon him while I'm walking with Arch.

God, I really don't know which scenario is worse. They're all terrible.

"Want me to walk you to your door?" Arch asks when his building looms ahead of us.

I slowly shake my head. "I should probably go home alone. I don't know how he'll react, seeing you with me."

Arch's jaw visibly tightens and the scowl on his face is almost scary. "I hate that he doesn't like me."

"He just doesn't know you," I reassure him. "Once he actually spends some time with you, he'll see just how great you are."

"If he'll even give me a chance to get to know me," he mutters.

The skeptical look on Arch's face says he doesn't really believe me, but I try to ignore it, offering him a shaky smile. "Thank you for helping me today."

He hauls me into his arms, kissing me without hesitation. "I would do anything for you, Daze. I hope you know that."

I touch his jaw, and I swear I can feel the tension easing from him. Do I calm him down like he does for me? When things get rough, he's the perfect person to have by my side. I never want to lose him.

Ever.

"I know," I whisper, leaning up on tiptoe to kiss him one last time. "I'll text you later."

"You better." He says it like he doesn't believe I will, and I think of how I never texted him last night when I promised I would.

I hate breaking promises. Especially to Arch.

Reluctantly, we part ways and I head for my house, my stomach pitching and rolling like I'm on a freaking boat. I stand up straighter and increase my pace, faking confidence. Hoping it'll turn into real confidence but my shoulders sag when I see that my father is outside, like he's waiting for me. In the garden, a giant pair of clippers in his hand.

His gaze is directed on me as I approach and he looks away as if he's disgusted, striding over to the rose bushes. Panic rises, clogging my throat, and I break out into a full run, not stopping until I'm standing between him and the line of rose bushes that belong to me.

I'm the one who nurtures them, not him. They're mine.

"I know you were with him all day. Don't bother denying it. I just saw the two of you together." His face is contorted into an ugly mask to the point that he's downright unrecognizable. "All day, Daisy. You skipped school! You *never* do that."

"I had to go to the clinic. I needed stitches." I point at my face, relieved when Dad drops his arm, the clippers hanging at his side. "Arch took me there. He helped me when I needed him."

"He helped you screw around and forget all about your responsibilities. What about school? What about getting into college? Skipping school and getting behind is only making it tougher on yourself." Dad's tone is bitter. "I'm disappointed in you, Daisy Mae. You know how I feel about Arch Lancaster and yet you still ran away with him."

The disappointed remark isn't going to work on me like it did last time. His feelings about Arch don't affect mine.

"What I don't get is why you hate him so much. Maybe he wasn't that nice to me at first, but he's changed. He cares about me. I know he does." I glare at him, wishing he would actually listen to me. "Us not being at school had nothing to do with 'screwing around,' as you call it. I needed to see a doctor."

Dad's mouth sets into a firm line, his displeasure more than obvious. "I would've taken you. It's my duty to take you—you're my daughter. At the very least, you should've seen the nurse on campus first and gotten permission to leave and see a doctor."

"Why bother when she would've sent me to the doctor anyway? What's done is done. I don't know why we're arguing about it." I try to walk past him but he shifts to the side, blocking me from going any farther. "Daddy, please. I want to go inside. I need to take a shower."

"No. You listen to me." His voice lowers and when I meet his gaze, I physically recoil. I don't think I've ever seen my father look so...mean. "You two are done. I forbid you from seeing that boy."

What? "But—"

"No buts. And I don't have to give you an explanation. I'm your father and I know what's best for you. And I don't care to hear you defending him either. If you'd only open your eyes, you would see that he'll bring you nothing but trouble. Look at you now. You start hanging around him and you've turned into a different person. I still can't believe your attitude last night. I don't even recognize you anymore."

I feel the exact same way about him. Who is this man, and what has he done with my thoughtful father? "You're the one who cut my roses—"

"They were going to die anyway!" He inhales sharply, averting his gaze. Like he can't stand to look at me. "You're being ridiculous. Way too focused on the damn roses when they're not the issue. They've never been the issue. That boy is the problem, Daisy. You just can't see it."

He's too stubborn to see that Arch makes me happy. That he's bringing me out of my shell and helping me discover I can stand up for myself. "Why can't you trust me? It's like you don't even think I'm capable of making my own decisions."

"When it comes to him, I don't trust you. You're too dazzled by his wealth and his good looks. You can't see beyond that. The boy has faults. Lots of them," Dad mutters.

"Don't we all?" I ask incredulously. "And that's not true." I can't deny that Arch is gorgeous but it's more than that. *He's* more than that. "I like him for more than his face. He's a good person."

"Who's using you," he practically spits.

"How? He doesn't need to use me. He could have any girl he wants and he chose *me*. Because he cares about me."

"He uses you for—sex." He bites out the last word with disgust.

My entire body flushes with embarrassment at my father uttering that word. Like that's all my relationship with Arch is about and nothing else. He doesn't understand.

He most likely never will.

"This is the last time we'll have this conversation." My father's voice breaks through the silence. "I forbid you from seeing Arch Lancaster. End of story."

I glare at him, my chest aching, the tears threatening yet again. I am so tired of crying. "You can't make me stop seeing him."

"Oh yes, I can. I'm your father and as long as you live in my house, I have every right to tell you what you can and cannot do. If I have to, I'll even go to Matthews myself and tell him that Lancaster is harassing my daughter. Matthews will make his life a living hell for the rest of the year. Might even kick him out of school."

Shock courses through me, leaving me breathless. "You wouldn't."

"I would." The determination that appears on his face is downright frightening. "Don't test me."

"You would *lie* to get rid of Arch?"

"I would do whatever it takes to protect you from harm, and that's all he'll bring you. You just can't see it. See how terrible he is. He's a horrible person, sweetheart. Mark my words if I let this continue, he will ruin you. Now go inside."

The tears fall from my eyes and streak down my cheeks soundlessly. I just stare at my father in disbelief, my mind scrambling, unable to come up with a response.

He nods curtly, stepping aside so I can head into the house. "Someday you'll thank me for this."

Thank him for destroying the one good thing that has ever happened to me?

I don't think so.

CHAPTER FORTY-FIVE

ARCH

I'm restless. Anxious. Two emotions I rarely deal with but shit. It's late. Past ten and I still haven't heard a peep out of Daisy. I'm tempted to go over to her house and make sure she's okay, but I don't want to cause any unnecessary drama with her dad so I remain in my room, pacing the floor. Hoping like hell Ralph wasn't too upset with her when she came home.

He probably was.

And it's all my fault.

I'm in bed when the text finally comes and I check it immediately, frowning when I read what she said.

Daisy: *I can't see you anymore.*

Wasting no time, I immediately call her. She answers on the fourth ring, her voice the barest whisper. So low, I can barely hear her.

"Please don't call me anymore, Arch."

My heart seizes in my chest, threatening to stop beating. "What the fuck, Daze? What are you talking about? Why can't you see me anymore?"

She remains quiet and I swear I hear her sniffling. Like she's crying.

"Is it your dad? Did he tell you that you can't see me?" I press when she doesn't say anything.

More crying.

I sit up in bed, my gaze going to the window. I wish I could see her house from here. See her bedroom window and the light on inside and know that she's safe and sound. That she's still mine.

"This is bullshit. Your dad can't tell you what to do. You're eighteen and almost done with school. If you want to be with me, you can."

"I can't. I can't do this," she croaks into the phone, and fuck, I can literally feel how sad she is. It's washing over me, leaving me wrung out. "Everything's too complicated right now, and I don't see how we can fix it. It's probably for the best anyway. We're too different. We would've never worked."

"You really believe that?" I retort, letting my frustration shine.

None of this sounds like Daisy. More like it sounds as if someone—her dad—fed her a bunch of lines and she's regurgitating them.

She goes silent and I wait for her to say something.

Anything.

"I have to," she finally says on a sigh. "There's someone better for you out there, Arch. And I don't think it's me. Goodbye."

The call ends.

She's gone.

I pull the phone away from my ear and stare at the screen like she's going to magically call me back and yell, "got ya!"

Of course, this doesn't happen.

Without even thinking, I throw my phone across the room. It hits the wall and bounces off, skidding across the floor and I shove my hands in my hair. Pulling.

Hard enough to make it hurt.

But I still don't feel a single fucking thing.

. . .

'm up at the butt crack of dawn because I couldn't sleep and I'm striding across campus by seven-thirty, making a stop in the dining hall to pick up a coffee and a blueberry muffin. I'm starving since I didn't eat dinner last night and I need a hit of caffeine to function.

I'm also hurt. So freaking hurt that she'd dismiss me from her life that easily. I don't care if her dad says she can't see me. The fact that she's agreeing with him is what kills me.

This is some straight-up bullshit. Doesn't she know how much she means to me? How much I need her in my life?

Fuck this. She can't just dismiss me. Doesn't she know who I am?

Yeah, I sound like an arrogant asshole even in my own head, but come on. I'm fucking Arch Lancaster. I run this school. Who gave her the right to just kick me aside and tell me it's over?

The moment the thoughts cross my mind—and this isn't the first time that's happened either—I know it's just my ego talking. It's easier to be all, *do you know who I am,* rather than focus on the pain that's currently growing inside me like a living, breathing thing. My heart is shriveling, shrinking in size every second that I continue to exist and Daisy isn't mine. Pretty soon it's going to be gone completely.

What's crazy is I finally give it to someone for the first time in my life and she immediately throws it back in my face.

Like what the actual fuck?

My luck is for shit.

"You look like you want to kick someone's ass." I turn with a snarl on my face, my mood not easing whatsoever at finding JJ standing in front of me. He immediately takes a step back, holding his hands in front of him. "Damn, bro, who shit in your bed?"

Fucking disgusting, what he just said. "Bad morning," I mutter.

"I'll say." He falls into step beside me uninvited. "Seriously, what's wrong?"

"Nothing." My world is just imploding. It's no big deal. "I don't want to talk about it."

JJ is frowning, practically jogging beside me to keep up. "You don't want to talk about it?"

I glare at him. "Isn't that what I just said?"

"Yeah, yeah. Sorry, man. I just—" He clamps his lips shut, facing forward as we keep walking, heading toward the library. There's a bench in front of the building where you can see everyone coming and going on campus. The perfect spot for me to drink my coffee, inhale the muffin and watch for Daisy.

"You just what?"

"I just...haven't seen you look like this before." He hesitates. "Or act like this before."

"Like what?" I lift my head, squinting against the sun. It's so wild how your life can take a completely different turn, leaving you ragged and questioning everything, yet the world just keeps on turning.

Life goes on. It doesn't stop for your pain or suffering. It skips right past it, leaving you and all that pain in the dust.

I hate it.

"Like someone kicked your dog and killed it," JJ says, as blunt as ever. "You're rarely in a bad mood unless Matthews decides to give you shit."

"For once in my life, I'm not pissed at Matthews," I say truthfully, falling onto the bench and pulling the muffin out of the small white bag. I take a big bite and practically choke it down. So fucking dry.

"A miracle has occurred." JJ settles onto the bench next to me, his gaze lingering on my face. Like he's trying to figure me out. "Girl trouble?"

I exhale loudly, hating that he nailed it. "Yeah."

"But you don't wanna talk about it."

"Considering you're messing around with my ex's best friend,

I definitely don't want to talk about it," I say, sipping from my too hot coffee before I take another bite of my too dry muffin.

I can't win today.

"Hey, I take offense to that. I won't say shit to Mya if you don't want me to. Though they aren't as close as they were. I think Mya is sick of her shit."

"Really?" I'm not that shocked. Cadence has treated Mya terribly for years.

"Yeah, she's over Cadence. And just so you know, I consider you one of my best friends. I can keep a secret." JJ actually sounds hurt.

And I immediately feel bad.

"Look, I'm sorry. I'm all wound up over this and I wasn't trying to insult you, I swear. If Cadence ever found out I was having trouble with Daisy, she'd gloat like the bitch she is."

"I won't tell her anything. I won't even mention it to Mya," JJ promises.

"Thanks, man." I take another sip of coffee, scanning the area for Daisy. No sign of her yet.

"Did you and Daisy break up?" JJ's eyebrows shoot up when I glance over at him.

"She dumped me."

JJ's mouth drops open. "Seriously?"

I nod, a lump sticking in my throat, making it hard to speak.

"I'm—surprised." He shakes his head. "You spent a lot of time with her. Seemed like you were into each other."

His words make my chest ache. We were totally into each other. I was into her.

I had it bad for her.

Hell, I still do. My feelings for Daisy can't change overnight. I'm not a fucking machine.

As if she could sense we were talking about her, Daisy appears out of nowhere, walking across campus, heading for the building where our English class is. Her head is bowed, her hair pulled back into a single braid just like she used to wear it, and it's like what happened between us never existed.

I'm back to being me and she's back to being the little ghost that floats around campus, everyone looking right through her.

Except for me. I see her.

"Yeah, well, it didn't work." I flash JJ a smile but it feels more like a baring of teeth so I let it fade quickly. "Maybe I'm not meant to be in a relationship."

That's a complete lie. I'm dying to be in a relationship with only one girl. She just chooses not to be in one with me.

I rub at my chest, hating how down I am. Knowing that nothing will fix my mood except for Daisy.

"Me either." JJ chuckles, holding up his hand for a high five.

I don't give it to him, a scowl forming on my face. "What about Mya?"

He drops his hand, shrugging. "What about her?"

"You two aren't together?" I'm so fucking confused.

"I haven't made anything official, and she hasn't asked. We're just hanging out and fucking around. Why can't it just be that?"

Because if you were into her, you wouldn't want it to be just hanging out and fucking around. You'd want to be with her all the time. Your thoughts would be consumed with her. You'd see things, or something would happen to you, and you'd immediately want to tell her. Because she's it for you. You can't see or think or taste anything else.

Just her.

Her.

"I can't take anything seriously," JJ continues, clearly on a roll. "Just like you."

His words haunt my thoughts when I leave him on the bench a couple of minutes later, right before the bell rings. When I'm walking down the hallway and pausing in the open doorway of Mr. Winston's classroom. I stand there and watch Daisy sitting in her usual spot, pretending to read the open book sitting on her desk in front of her.

I know the truth. I see the way her eyes flicker up and immediately glance down when she catches me watching her. I don't care if she sees me staring.

I want her to see.

"Are you joining us today, Mr. Lancaster? Or do you prefer to remain in the doorway?" Mr. Winston asks good-naturedly.

I enter the classroom without saying a word, heading straight for Daisy. She keeps her head bent and I swear her shoulders visibly shake, which makes me feel like shit.

Of course, I feel bad. I'm not a monster.

I keep walking past her, not sitting in the desk behind hers. I choose not to torture myself today. Sitting behind her, smelling her, having to resist reaching out and touching her silky hair...

My self-restraint isn't that strong.

Instead, I sit in the back of the class like I used to. Kicking out my legs and nudging the chair in front of me, crossing my arms in front of my chest. The look of pure disappointment on Winston's face doesn't faze me. I'm sure he's bummed I'm not sitting at the front like before. The happy, pussy-whipped chump I was not even twenty-four hours ago.

This is the new me. The old me.

The still fucked-up over Daisy me.

CHAPTER FORTY-SIX

DAISY

He's so angry, the emotion practically radiates off of him. Though what did I expect? For him to be happy and excited that I dumped him? I'm sure no one dumps Arch Lancaster. He's the dumper, never the dumpee.

When he stood in the doorway of our English class watching me, I could feel his stare, hot and penetrating. I could barely look up, not brave enough to face him. But when I finally did, I saw the flash of emotion in his gaze. I know what it was. I recognized it because I feel the same way.

Pain.

Sadness.

Immediately replaced by false indifference.

After Mr. Winston called him out, he walked by me casually, like I didn't matter, when we were everything to each other only yesterday.

Yesterday.

Now I'm once again persona non grata on campus. No one my age notices me. They look right through me, as if I don't even exist. I would've thought I'd be used to it. It's how everyone treated me for the last three years, so why does it hurt so much worse now?

Because, for a fleeting moment, I basked in the glory of Arch's attention. Having him smile at me, chase after me, flirt with me, kiss me and everything else that followed after those kisses, it was like living in the sun. So bright and glorious and beautiful.

Now I'm in the clouds. Dark and dreary and heavy.

Dramatic but true.

I didn't go to the admin office for second period. Couldn't stand the thought of facing him, though I know Vivian would've shoved him back into that tiny office and made him staple paper packets, and he probably would've gone without protest. I'm sure he's furious with me, and I can't blame him.

In his eyes, I did him dirty. I did him wrong. If he only knew the truth, that I'm protecting him from my father, but I can't tell him that. He wouldn't understand.

So, I didn't put myself in that situation. I'd already gone to the office before school started and told Vivian I couldn't be there during second period and did she mind if I went to the library instead? She said it was no problem and the moment the bell rang, indicating first period was over, I was up and out of my desk in an instant, practically running to the library, isolating myself completely. It was much easier hiding away in there, than facing the boy I've fallen in love with.

It's true. I've fallen in love with him, but it's too late for us.

When it's lunch, I dash into the dining hall and grab one of those pitiful sandwiches and a bag of chips, nervously standing in line to check out. Hoping against all hope that I don't run into Arch or anyone else from his friend group.

"Oh God, so is the rumor true? You and Arch actually broke up?"

I briefly close my eyes at the sound of Cadence's whiny voice coming from behind me. She would be the person I have to actually face first.

"Can't speak? What's your problem? Too scared of me?" she taunts.

I whirl around to face her, the sight of that petty smirk on her face filling me with anger. Balling my hand into a fist, I keep it at my side, secretly wishing I could punch that smug expression right off her face.

No other person makes me feel violent like Cadence does.

"What happened between Arch and me is none of your business," I say through clenched teeth.

Her smile is small, her eyes flickering with what I can only assume is victory. "I'm sure he figured out what a boring lay you are and dumped your ass immediately. He should've done that a long time ago if you ask me. I never understood what he saw in you."

"Right back at you," I toss at her. Her eyes go wide. I can tell she didn't like that, but for once I don't care. "And by the way, I'm the one who broke up with him."

Cadence bursts out laughing. "You're a liar."

"It's true." I shrug.

She tilts her head to the side, contemplating me. "I could ask him, you know. He wouldn't lie to me."

He might just to save face but maybe not. This is Cadence, after all. I don't think Arch really cares what she thinks of him.

"Go ahead and ask him." I lift my chin, trying to appear strong. Hoping against hope that I don't fail. "Though I'm not lying. I ended it between us last night."

Not my proudest moment, or my easiest. I still can't believe he called me after I sent that text, but I should've known. Arch wouldn't accept a breakup over text.

That's not his style.

"I think you're full of shit so I'm definitely asking him. He's right over there. Arch!" Cadence waves her hand above her head and if I could melt into the floor, I so would. I do not want to have this confrontation right now with him, while Cadence is watching. I'm trying to avoid him, not actually speak to him.

But I don't even need to look to know he's drawing closer. I can feel his presence, and when I glance to my right, I find he's standing right there between Cadence and me, a little frown forming between his eyebrows.

"What do you want, Cadence?" Arch sounds exhausted.

He won't even look at me.

"She said she broke up with you, but I don't believe her." Cadence points at me like she can't even acknowledge me by my name or treat me like a human being. God, I really can't stand her and I try my best not to dislike anyone.

Cadence though? She's the absolute worst.

"It's the truth." Arch's gaze barely flickers in my direction, like I've become subhuman to him once again too.

Cadence gapes, her mouth hanging wide open, and it's not a good look for her. "You're serious? Come on, Arch."

"Dead serious." His gaze finally slides to me, so intense I feel like I can't move. I can't even breathe when he murmurs, "Daisy Albright broke my fucking heart."

And with those final words, Cadence and I watch Arch walk away without a backward glance.

The moment he's out of earshot, Cadence scoffs, her incredulous gaze meeting mine. "What, did you pay him to say that?"

"I don't have any money, remember? I'm just the broke scholarship girl." I leave my sandwich on the counter and flee the dining hall as well, making sure I go in the complete opposite direction of Arch, though he's nowhere to be seen, so truthfully, I have no idea where he's gone.

Instead, I head back to my house, the need to spend a little time outside in our garden nearly overwhelming me. There's no one out here. Just me and the wind coming in off the ocean in the far distance, the garden and the leftover roses still clinging to life, their heavy, wilting blooms bobbing and dancing with the breeze.

I sit on one of the old outdoor chairs we keep in the yard,

dropping my backpack on the ground, a startled noise leaving me when I hear a cat's meow.

My little tabby friend that I found is now currently rubbing against my backpack, purring loudly. I bend over and rub my fingers together and the cat meanders toward me, rubbing his cheek against my fingers and letting me scratch under his chin.

"Aw, at least you're my friend, huh?" I pet him for a while until a door slams somewhere in the near distance, the loud bang startling the cat and making him dart away.

Looks like my last friend ditched me too.

It's hard to believe only twenty-four hours ago I was with Arch. We were at the little café by now. Or maybe we'd already left and were wandering in and out of the shops, looking at everything. Laughing and smiling at each other. He distracted me from my misery and he was just the shot of happiness I needed to forget what happened to me.

To forget what I did to myself.

I reach up and draw my finger across the stitches on my cheek, wincing when I touch a tender spot. The doctor promised she'd do what she could for the wound not to leave a scar but I don't even care anymore. Give me a scar and make me a hideous troll, what does it matter?

"I still think you look like a badass."

I open my eyes to find Arch standing on the walkway that runs past our yard, his hands in his pockets, his gaze on me. I stare at him for a moment, my entire body aching to go to him, but I remain in the chair, unable to move.

"How are the stitches?"

Automatically, I touch my face again, tracing my index finger over the stitched skin. "Still hurts a little."

"I bet."

We can't look away from each other and I jump to my feet, why...I'm not sure. I even part my lips, but no words come out. I don't know what to say. I don't know how to express my feelings for this boy who was everything to me.

Who is still everything to me.

I wish I could tell him the truth. That my father threatened to ruin him.

I can't risk Arch getting into trouble for something he didn't do. I won't be responsible for that.

"I know you want me to leave you alone, Daze, but I wasn't lying when I said you broke my heart." He visibly swallows and I know that took everything inside him to admit that. "I didn't say that just to wreck Cadence, though I hope I did wreck her."

My smile can't be helped at his irritated tone—not because he confirmed that I did indeed break his heart. That was something I didn't need to hear. But I do love that he still can't stand Cadence. "She accused me of paying you to say that."

"She would," he says with a chuckle that dies quickly and he glances over his shoulder, like maybe someone his waiting for him. "I should go."

"Wait—" I start toward him and he goes still, waiting for me just like I asked. I don't stop until I'm standing directly in front of him and when I do pause, I realize he's blocking the sun. The wind. He's blocking everything and he's the only thing I see.

"What's up?" he asks softly, his gaze roaming over my face, as if he's trying to memorize it one last time. I do the same to him, mentally cataloging his handsome features, and a tiny voice buried deep inside my brain starts asking me all sorts of questions.

That's it? That's all that's going to be said? You're just going to let him walk away and not tell him anything? But what can you tell him?

"I'm sorry," I whisper, my body swaying toward him as if I have no control over myself. "For breaking your heart."

He blinks once. Twice. His lips part and I wait for him to say something to change all of this.

But I don't know how it can be changed. What's done is done.

"I've never met someone like you, Daze," he murmurs, slowly shaking his head. "It didn't have to be like this."

"Be like what?" My throat aches and I swallow hard, trying to hold back the sob that lingers there.

"Like you took the best part of me and stomped all over it with your loafers." He actually smiles, but it's the saddest smile I think I've ever seen. "You own my heart, Daisy Albright. You can kick it, throw it in the trash, do whatever you want to it, but it's yours. Whether you want it or not."

CHAPTER FORTY-SEVEN

ARCH

It's been over a month since the day Daisy broke up with me over the phone with no real explanation. A month without hearing her laugh or seeing her smile at me. A month without holding her in my arms and kissing her. Touching her naked body and slipping inside of her.

I didn't get to be with her nearly enough. What Daisy and I shared, it was more than fucking.

And I've turned into a complete sap, but only when it comes to her.

I miss her.

I've tried to move on. To carry on with my life and pretend she never came into it. I tell myself it wasn't even that big of a deal. I barely knew her. We spent...what? Almost two months together? If that?

That's nothing. Just a blip of time. A mistake that should've never been made. I pretend that I'm over her and that I'm the same carefree jackass who gives in to his impulses and does whatever the hell he wants, whenever he wants to, but those closest to me know the truth.

I'm not the same. I haven't really returned to my old self. That part of me feels like a stranger that I don't want to reunite with. I'd rather be the guy who felt on top of the world because he had Daisy by his side.

Fucking Daisy and her cute ass name and cute face and hot as fuck body. With the braid and the skirt and the loafers and the white lacy socks. The girl whose body belonged to me. I stole every single one of her firsts and I feel like I earned them. They're mine.

Just like she is. She always will be.

She doesn't realize it yet.

It's late October and everything's shifted. The mornings are crisp and cold and we've had a few rainstorms come in. We just finished midterms and I aced everything. I didn't even have to apply myself—it's all too fucking easy. I went home over a long weekend and essentially begged my parents to let me leave Lancaster Prep after the fall semester, but they refused.

"Enjoy your time at Lancaster Prep while you can," Dad said with a sly smile. "You're only young once."

"I have expectations once you graduate," Mother said with a tiny sniff. "Familial obligations that only you can fulfill."

What the hell my mother was referring to, I have no clue. She probably has me married off to at least three different girls and I could give a shit about any of them. Besides.

The only girl I'm interested in won't even look in my direction.

We haven't really talked since that day when I followed her to her house during lunch. When I told her she owned my heart. That wasn't a lie. She's still got it, though she probably doesn't realize it. Hell, she might even believe I've moved on. From her viewpoint, I've fallen back into my old habits. Hanging out with JJ and the rest of the guys. Cadence and Mya and a few of their friends all sit with us at lunch. Or get together with us after school. We party sometimes together on the weekend, but I haven't touched anyone.

Not a single girl.

Though they've all tried—minus Mya, who's still messing

around with JJ. And especially Cadence. She's been throwing herself at me whenever she can, and I constantly push her away and tell her no. I'm not interested.

Not at all.

Think she'd get the hint, but I'm starting to believe that Cadence is a glutton for punishment.

After the tension that midterms always brings, we're all looking for an opportunity to party and the annual Halloween bash is this weekend. We've been planning it for weeks, me and all of my friends. Edie and her friends too. If there's a Lancaster in attendance at the school, then it's up to them to organize the party.

It's been the distraction I need. If I'm with my friends and my sister putting together an epic blowout then I won't find myself glancing around in search of Daisy. Though she's not easy to find. She's in hiding most of the time nowadays. I'm guessing in the library or in the admin office—which I'm not working at anymore. I got called into Matthews' office later that day, after I talked to Daisy by her garden, and he told me I had to work in the library with Miss Taylor during second period from now on. She has me shelving books every single day and it fucking sucks.

I'd rather torture myself by staring at Daisy in the office for a solid fifty minutes, knowing I don't have the right to touch her or kiss her any longer.

I'm also a glutton for punishment, I swear to God.

It's Tuesday afternoon and the last class of the day. Statistics with Mrs. Nelson. The moment I settle into my desk, I peek underneath it, always hoping I'll find a book that Daisy left behind. It never happens.

Wait a minute…

Until now.

Glancing around, I make sure no one is paying attention to me before I pull the book out and settle it into my lap. I stare at the cover. It's another one of those cartoonish illustrated covers, and this one features a couple standing next to each other, him looking down at her while she smiles up at him. She's blonde and has braids. He's tall and has golden brown hair.

Huh. The resemblance is pretty spot on.

Nelson is talking to a couple of students who surround her desk, so I thumb through the book, checking to see if she's left me any notes. I know this is Daisy's book. She's annotated a few passages and she's doodled in the margins. There's one section that gets me near the end of the book. It's highlighted in pink and pretty simple, but it feels like a swift kick to my heart.

I realize that in this very moment I still love him. I'm still in love with him.

And I don't know what to do about it.

She's drawn little hearts all around the two sentences, and every single one of them has a jagged line down the middle.

All the hearts are broken.

Did she mean for me to see this? Did she want me to know? Or was this an accident and this all means nothing? What if this isn't even Daisy's book at all? Hey, another girl could sit at this desk and like reading romance books. She could even enjoy drawing inside them and highlighting all of her favorite parts. You never know.

Weirder things have happened.

"Hey, Mrs. Nelson," I call to the teacher when the students leave her desk and she's all alone.

"Yes, Arch?"

"Who sits in this desk sixth period?" I shove the book back into the storage slot. No way am I going to show it to her. She'll probably try and take it and return it to its rightful owner.

"Daisy Albright." She tilts her head, her gaze narrowing. "Didn't you two have a little…thing going on?"

I shrug, playing it cool. "We were friends. Now we're not."

A frown forms. "That's too bad. I like the idea of the two of you together."

"Why?"

She seems taken aback by my question. "Why?"

"Yeah, why do you like that idea?" I need to know her opinion.

"Well...she's quiet. You're not. She's sweet. You're not."

"Hey," I protest.

Nelson smiles. "I'm kidding, but you know what I mean. You two are opposite personalities and I think you would balance each other out nicely."

"I'm not her type." I lean back in my chair, kicking my legs out. "She wasn't into me."

"Really?" She sounds like she doesn't believe me.

I nod, enjoying this conversation. Nelson seems a little stunned by my confessions, and it goes to show that faculty gossips about us. Not that I'm surprised. "Sometimes people can be a little too opposite, you know?"

Her smile is thoughtful. "Interesting."

The bell rings and she immediately starts talking, asking for last night's homework. I pass mine up, my thoughts going to the book seeming to burn a hole in the desk, and I pull it back out, staring at the cover, knowing Daisy's hands were just on it.

It's definitely her book. Now the question is, did she leave it behind by accident or on purpose? And if it was on purpose, then she most likely meant for me to see that message via the passage she highlighted.

I lean back down and peer into the storage slot, spotting something else in there. Reaching inside, I wrap my fingers around it and pull it out.

A pastel blue highlighter pen.

Hmm.

This is definitely not an accident.

The teacher starts talking about a new section from the textbook and I tune her out, flipping through the romance book Daisy left for me, my eyebrows climbing when I find an extra hot scene.

This book has some spice. And I almost laugh out loud at a part Daisy highlighted.

Good girl.

She swallowed every drop.

Shit, I'm sweating.

I skim the scene, shifting in my seat, hoping no one notices I'm getting all fired up over a sex scene in a book. But it's not even the words that are getting to me. It's more the knowledge that I know Daisy read this and liked it and highlighted it. Is she still getting off while reading this stuff? Does she touch herself and think of me?

Yeah, can't think about things like that right now. Way too distracting.

Instead, I uncap the highlighter pen and run it across a few sentences that I hope will get a rise out of her. Once I'm finished with that, I grab a piece of paper and write a note to her, feeling like I'm living in a goddamn movie. Most people would just send each other a text saying, *I miss you* and discuss things like two modern people who aren't afraid of a little confrontation.

But this is Daisy who I'm dealing with. She's not big on confrontation.

After reading over the note at least five times, I fold the paper and place it in the book, and then stash it away where I found it. I'm impatient for the rest of the period, relieved when the bell finally rings, signaling the day is over.

Thank God.

I'm walking across campus, feeling aimless when I run into JJ, who for once in his life doesn't have Mya with him. He may claim he's not in a relationship, but they sure act like they are, and every time I see them together, I feel a pang in my chest. I don't like to identify what it is, but deep down, I know.

Jealousy.

"Wanna get the hell out of here?" JJ asks, glancing around like he's afraid someone is going to spot him.

"Sure. What are you thinking?"

"Anywhere but here." JJ starts walking. "Come on."

I follow him to the parking lot, noting his determined steps and the scowl on his face. JJ seems pissed, and he's rarely angry.

"What's your problem?" I ask once we're in his car and he's starting the engine.

"Fucking Mya." He shakes his head, his hands gripping the steering wheel so tight, his knuckles go white. "We got into an argument."

I don't ask him what about. If he wants to volunteer that information to me, he will.

He drives in silence for a few minutes, turning so we're headed into town and finally, he speaks.

"She said she's tired of me not fully committing to her and if I can't do it, she'll go find someone else who will." He pauses for only a moment. "I told her to go ahead and find someone else then, if she believes I'm not good enough for her."

"I don't think that's what she was saying…"

"Felt like it," JJ says, speaking right over me. "I've told her from the start that I don't do serious. She knew this and she's still wanting more from me than I can give."

"Why can't you give it to her?" I think of Daisy and how I believed I wasn't someone who could be serious either. Though really, I was committed to Cadence, even though I regretted that decision pretty quickly. But I stuck it out.

I guess I'm a commitment type of guy, which is a little fucking mind-blowing.

"I don't know. Because I saw the way my parents fought when I was a kid, before they finally got a divorce. How they used their kids like weapons against each other. Love is bullshit, man." JJ hits the steering wheel.

"It's not so bad if you open yourself up to it," I say, sounding like the sap I've become.

"Please." He makes a dismissive sound. "I had a front row

seat to the disaster that was your relationship with Cadence. That was a nightmare."

"My relationship with Cadence doesn't count."

"For real. What other relationship are you talking about?" He sends me a quick look, his eyebrows rising. "You and jail bait?"

Fury fills my blood, leaving me hot. "Don't call her that."

"You still hot for her? You don't talk about her."

I can't. I don't want to. "I'm in love with her."

JJ goes completely silent. It's not until he's pulling up to the curb downtown and parking the car that he finally speaks.

"In love? You?"

Nodding, I avert my gaze, staring at a store I ran into with Daisy. The day before our world imploded. "Tell me I'm an idiot."

JJ doesn't say a word and I turn to face him, only to see the sympathy flickering in his eyes. "You're an idiot."

"I am." I nod. "I fell in love with her and she ended it with me."

"Why?"

"She said we were too different." That's not the only reason though. I have suspicions and maybe that's why I don't push.

I think the breakup has everything to do with her dad, and while I probably can't change his mind, I'm still tempted—a month later—to go to Ralph and ask him what the hell is up.

Why does he hate me so much that he doesn't want his daughter to come near me? He must think so low of me, and I don't get it.

I'm a fucking catch.

I treated his daughter like gold.

Daisy makes me want to be a better person. I still want to be a better person, even though I'm not with her. I still want to do it for her. In the hopes that she'll see and realize that she misses me.

Pathetic. That's me. I'm not an idiot. I'm a pathetic fool who's hung up on a girl who's so closed-off, she's probably already forgotten all about me.

"Women," JJ mutters, shaking his head and I can't help it.

I start to laugh. Because he's right.
Daisy's my favorite person in the whole world.
But she's also become my worst nightmare.

CHAPTER FORTY-EIGHT

ARCH

I find him out in his workshop, puttering around in front of a massive red tool chest that's as tall as he is, going through a drawer full of wrenches. I pause in the open doorway, fearful for a second that he might take one look at me and grab a wrench to use as a weapon against me.

Then I tell myself I could take the old man and I clear my throat to get his attention.

Ralph Albright glances over his shoulder, his brows lowering when he sees me. He faces his workbench once more, grabbing a faded red rag and wiping his hands with it as he turns to face me fully.

"Been waiting for you to make an appearance." His voice is flat, his expression devoid of any emotion. He's not welcoming, but he's not openly hostile either and I take that as a positive sign.

"Didn't figure you wanted to talk to me." I take a step inside the workshop, coming to a stop when I see the way his gaze flares. He doesn't want me any closer and I'm encroaching on his territory so I stay put.

"Still don't."

I don't let his words discourage me. "I wanted to explain some things."

"Like what? How you used my daughter? How you took advantage of her kindness and now she's a shell of her former self?" The frustration in his voice is clear.

"She broke up with me because of what you said, sir. I'm not the one who took advantage of her kindness." I pause, deciding to go for it. "That's on you."

His gaze narrows and he goes silent. Taking the rag he's still clutching, he tosses it hard on the workbench, the fabric snapping. "You don't know her."

"I do."

"Not well enough. You're too self-absorbed to see her for what she really is." His tone is dismissive and he turns his back on me once more.

I stare at him, my frustration building. "I know she's sweet and smart and kind. She's funny and she loves roses because of her mom and you. She likes to read, especially romance books. Even though she loves Lancaster Prep and has lived most of her life here, she wants to go away to college because she wants something better for her life and to make you proud. She's so damn beautiful she makes my heart hurt every time I look at her, but I'm trying my best to respect her wishes. She'd rather give up on me to please you because you mean the world to her. You're all she has. I want to be there for her too, but you won't let me, which means she won't let me, and I don't get why, sir. What did I do to make you hate me so damn much?"

His shoulders rise practically to his ears, reminding me of his daughter, and he exhales raggedly before he turns to face me yet again. "You're not good enough for her."

"I know." I don't even hesitate with my response and I can tell I surprised him.

"You live a different type of life. She's not used to that sort of thing."

"I'd do whatever it takes to make her comfortable."

Ralph stares at me, his gaze hard, as is his expression. "It's not that easy. She's...shy. It's hard for her to open up to new people and experiences."

"She's not shy with me. I know how to get her to open up." Another hesitation on my part. I don't know if I should say this, but fuck it. "She's going to graduate soon. Do you want her to be miserable for the rest of the school year or happy? Because I can make her happy, sir. You can't keep her to yourself forever."

"You have no right saying that to me." He looks pissed.

But I don't back down. "I'm not trying to be rude. I'm just—stating facts."

Another ragged sigh leaves him and he drops his head for a moment, rubbing the back of his neck. "She's a good girl. A sweet girl, like you said. I just don't want her to become jaded and spoiled like the rest of you."

I don't take offense at what he said. "I would never let that happen. The best thing about Daisy is how good she is. She has a pure heart."

Normally I would never say stuff like this because it sounds like a bunch of bullshit. But when it comes to Daisy, it's all true.

She is pure of heart. I miss her so damn much it physically pains me not to have her as a part of my life.

"I will do whatever it takes to prove to her—and to you—that I deserve her. I know you might think that'll never happen, but I want nothing more than to have her in my life. By my side. I'm in love with your daughter, sir. I need your approval before I can see her again, and I'm begging you to give me a chance." My voice shakes and I clear my throat, not wanting to seem weak.

I sure as hell feel weak. My heart is racing and my head is spinning. I brace myself for him to tell me no. And he's quiet for so long, I'm positive he's going to kick my ass out of here when he finally speaks.

"I said some things about you to Daisy that...weren't kind. Now I wish I could take those words back, but I can't. And that's why she ended things with you. I made some—threats." He shakes his head and I wait for him to continue. "I'm not proud of what I did, but I was trying to protect her and that was the only way I saw I could do it."

Pretty positive I don't want to know what he said about me.

"I'm not too sure if you even deserve my approval," he continues, and I close my eyes, waiting for my heart to shatter completely.

"But my daughter has been miserable since she's stopped seeing you, and I know why. I'm pretty certain she's in love with you too." I open my eyes to find him staring off into the distance, as if he can't quite meet my gaze. "If she's willing to give you another chance...I suppose I am too."

What the fuck? Did he just say what I think he said?

"That's if she still wants to be with you," he tacks on.

I rub at my chest, my heart feeling like it's being stitched back together. "She wants to. If she cares even half as much as I care about her, then she definitely wants to be with me."

He slowly shakes his head, as if he finds that unbelievable. And maybe he does, but I don't give a damn. I'm just glad he gave me his approval, however reluctant it might be. "Just...be careful with her, Arch. Don't break her heart. It's already fragile enough."

"I know what it feels like, to have your heart broken, and I wouldn't do that to my worst enemy, let alone to the girl I love." I stand up taller. "I will protect her with everything I've got. She means more to me than anyone else."

Ralph smiles and it looks a little sad. "Don't ever forget that."

"I won't." I finally smile, truly happy for the first time in what feels like forever. "I promise."

CHAPTER FORTY-NINE

DAISY

I stride into the admin office just as the second period bell rings, tossing my backpack on the desk before I turn to face Vivian and blurt, "I'm in love with Arch Lancaster."

Vivian blinks, seemingly taken aback, and I almost feel bad about my outburst but oh my God.

It feels like I've been holding that in for so long, and it's a relief to say the words out loud.

"Honey." Vivian rests her hand against her chest, like this is all too much for her heart. "I thought you two were just friends."

"Yes. We were. And then we got...closer. The problem is I like him too much. I love him." I fall into a chair and prop my elbows on the desk, burying my face in my hands. "I'm in love with him and I'm miserable because I broke up with him."

"You two were actually together?"

I drop my hands from my face, thankful I don't feel any tears trying to form. The last thing I want to do is cry. I'm so over crying. "For a little while."

"I'm so confused," she murmurs to herself, shaking her head. "Why would you end things with him if you're in love with him?"

"Because." A sigh leaves me and I hang my head. "My father made me."

"Ralph?" Now Vivian really sounds surprised. "Why would he make you break up with Arch?"

"He doesn't approve."

"Well," Vivian's mouth sets into a firm line, "I can see why."

My heart drops. Vivian's opinion of Arch has never been high. She always acted as if she was merely tolerating him.

"But I saw the way he behaved around you, and I liked it. He was kind and considerate of you always. Flirting all the time too. The boy can be quite charming. I can see how you fell for him."

My heart soars back into place. "He was, wasn't he?"

Vivian nods. "Why don't you tell him how you feel?"

"I'm scared." It was scary enough just telling Vivian how I feel about Arch, and she wouldn't judge me for this. At least not to my face. "What if he doesn't feel the same way?"

"You won't know unless you ask him?" Her smile is gentle. "Though I know that won't be easy for you."

A sigh leaves me and I shake my head. I feel dumb. I have no friends and I'm talking about boy troubles with the headmaster's secretary. It's like I've hit a new low and I'm pretty certain I can't get any lower.

I truly believed my feelings for Arch would lessen over time but no. They've gotten stronger. To the point that I'm overwhelmed with love for him. I can't think about anything else. Or anyone else. I'm not doing as well at school. I can't concentrate. I'm mad at my father for keeping us apart, and he knows it. He tries to make conversation with me, but my answers are always short, and I don't spend as much time with him like I used to.

In turn, he's now officially together with Kathy so he's not around much anyway, and that fills me with resentment. It's okay for him to move on and find someone new, yet I can't?

That's not fair.

Recently I picked up a romance book and of course, the entire time I'm reading it, all I can think about is Arch. How the main male character reminds me of him. The things they do remind me of us. I started highlighting and annotating and…

Yes. I left my book in the desk on purpose, hoping Arch would see it and read it. Maybe even annotate and highlight parts with the pen I left for him.

Pathetic? For sure. I'm a mess over this boy, and I'm tired of holding back. I'm tired of being the good daughter and doing what my father wishes. I'm tired of making myself sick with misery over not having Arch in my life.

I deserve happiness. I deserve love. And Arch brings me both things. I need him. I want him.

I'm in love with him.

And what's so wrong with that?

Vivian and I talk a little more about my issues but then the phone starts ringing and eventually Matthews comes in, asking us to do a few administrative tasks for him. Vivian has me filing papers and it's just the mindless distraction I need.

The rest of the morning goes like it's gone for the last thirty days or so. I ignore Arch in every class we share together and he does the same. Sitting with his friends. Stretching his legs out like he always does, laughing and sounding full of joy while I sit alone with my misery. I feel pitiful. Invisible.

But what did I expect? That Arch would read the passages in my book and feel the need to approach me today about it? Of course, he wouldn't. Even if he did find my book, he probably thought my little idea was stupid. Cowardly.

I spend lunch outside, soaking up the sun, knowing we're nearing the end of days like this. Soon it'll be cold and rainy, and then cold and snowy. I don't bother going to our garden though. The roses are all gone, which makes me sad. The only evidence that remains is the dried-up petals scattered across the ground. The garden has gone dormant. What was beautiful and blooming is now dried up or dead.

Even the roses Arch gave me for my birthday have stopped

blooming, though that's normal. I miss seeing them. Like I miss seeing Arch's face, the intimate smile that would stretch across it. The one that was just for me.

My chest aches at the mere thought of it.

When I walk into my statistics class, I'm relieved to find Mrs. Nelson isn't at her desk yet. I go straight to my desk and peek inside to see the book still sitting there. Trying not to get my hopes up—he might've never noticed it in the first place—I pull the book out, realizing that there's something inside of the pages. I flip the book open to find a folded piece of paper.

My heart thumping wildly, I take the piece of paper out and unfold it carefully, my breaths coming faster when I see Arch's bold handwriting.

Daze,

If you're trying to tell me something with the passages you highlighted in this book, then I've got the message loud and clear. There are a few things I need to tell you too and I used the highlighter you left for me (thanks for that BTW) so read them and think of me.

That's what I did. When I read those parts you highlighted, I thought of you. Nothing else but you.

I know it's hard for you to confront your problems and share your feelings. I know you've spent the last six years isolating yourself and there's a big part of you that prefers living that way, but I also know there's a tiny part of you that liked the attention I gave you.

You're like your roses you love so much. They can only grow when they're fed and watered and basking in the light.

Let me be your light, Daisy. And you can be my rose.

That was really fucking corny but you know what I mean.

Love,

A

A huff of laughter leaves my lips and I press shaky fingers against them, trying to contain the tears that want to fall. Though they're not sad tears. Not even close.

I'm happy.

He gets me like no one else does. He sees me when I'm positive I'm invisible. He's the only person who truly understands me, and I don't know how I let my father deprive me of being with Arch for this long.

Students start to enter the classroom and I ignore them. I'm flipping through the book, searching for any trace of blue highlighter and when I find the first one, I read the line he highlighted with my heart in my throat.

I am a patient man, but I can wait for her for only so long.

Oh my. If that isn't an ominous message.

There's only one other part he highlighted, this one a little dirtier. Much like the slightly dirty one I highlighted for him.

She tastes like heaven. And when I make her come with my lips and tongue, when I clutch her hips and she grinds her face against my mouth, I immediately want to make her come again.

I never want to stop.

This girl is mine, whether she realizes it or not.

All.

Mine.

"Daisy, are you okay?"

I jerk my head up, my gaze meeting Mrs. Nelson's, who's watching me with concern. Her brows are lowered and she's frowning and I blink at her. "I'm fine. Why do you ask?"

My voice is shaky. I don't sound fine, but hopefully she doesn't notice.

"You're flushed. Your face is so red. Are you feeling okay?"

This is embarrassing. I'm flushed from the words I just read. Knowing Arch wanted me to read that part has me flustered.

"I'm okay. Really." I duck my head, my vision blurry, and thankfully someone approaches, distracting her completely. I pull out a piece of lined paper and a pen and start writing my response to Arch.

Arch,

No one understands me like you do, and while this is the most cowardly way ever to reach out to you, this was the only way I could do it. I love the parts you highlighted, and one in particular reminds me of what we've done together.

I want to do that with you again. And just to let you know, when I read the part earlier, Nelson asked if I was okay because I was all flushed. I lied when I reassured her that I was fine.

I'm not fine. I miss you so much. I let my father control me but I've learned that no one really watches out for me except for... me. And for the first time in my life, I want to defy my father and do what I want.

Be with who I want.

But I'm scared. I need to know you're all in. And you're probably scared of me because of what I did before, which I totally understand.

Just know I'm all in this time around. I promise. And I don't break promises.

You told me once that I was your favorite.

Am I still?

xoxo,

Daze

I don't bother highlighting any other parts. I told him everything that I feel and that's enough.

Folding the paper with still shaking fingers, I shove it back in the book and put it away in the desk. I'm keeping the note Arch wrote me. No way do I want that to get lost. It's probably the most meaningful thing anyone has ever given me. I'll cherish it forever. But for now...

I wait.

CHAPTER FIFTY

ARCH

It's Friday. The Halloween party is happening tonight. And while I've been working hard all week putting together this party, my thoughts have been preoccupied with other things as well. Specifically, one thing. One person.

Daisy.

I can't wait to see her, and this is my best opportunity to talk to her, during this period where I've left her alone for weeks, always spending it in the library instead of torturing myself in the office. Even Matthews let me go easily, which is unusual for him.

I think we've come to some sort of peaceful coexistence, Matthews and I. I'm not sure, and I don't want to test it. Afraid I might jinx everything.

I walk into the administration building right as the bell rings, indicating the start of second period. Daisy is already sitting at the desk chatting with Viv, her gaze finding mine the moment I enter the office. Her lips curl into the faintest smile and I return it, slowing my steps as I make my way toward her.

Once we exchanged the secret messages in her book, we turned to texting each other every day after school, long into the night. Basically ignoring each other in class during the day like we're not together. As if we're scared. She probably is.

I know I am. I don't want to fuck this up.

But this morning, I can't take it anymore. That's why I'm in the office. I can feel it when Viv notices me, her eyes widening as she takes me in, sending a quick look in Daisy's direction before she returns her attention to me.

"Arch. It's been a while." Vivian smiles, her expression nervous. "We haven't seen you in here lately."

"Been keeping away from Daisy to give her some space." I send her a look and Daisy's golden eyes go wider than normal. "Right, Daze?"

"Um, right." She nods, slowly rising to her feet. "Hi."

Her attention is all on me, and I swear to God, my heart threatens to beat right out of my chest, it's pounding so hard. Having her in front of me and not looking like she wants to run feels like a major accomplishment.

"You two are good?" Viv looks between us, her head bouncing back and forth like she's at a tennis match.

"We're—good." Daisy smiles.

"Yeah." I smile back.

"I've been busy planning the party tonight," I start but Viv immediately sticks her fingers in her ears and starts chanting "la-la-la" over and over.

I send an amused look Daisy's way, who's watching Viv with a shocked expression on her face.

Viv drops her fingers from her ears the moment I go quiet. "I can't hear any details about that particular event, Arch. We try to ignore it as much as possible."

It's not school sanctioned and everyone who works here looks the other way, pretending the annual Halloween party doesn't happen.

Including good ol' Viv.

"Well, I need some help with party stuff and I was hoping I could steal Daze here." I incline my head toward the love of my fucking life, shoving my hands in my pockets so I don't do something crazy like grab hold of Daisy and never let her go again.

Hope lights up Daisy's eyes and she turns toward Viv. "Can I help him?"

Viv releases a great big sigh, checking on Matthews' closed office door. "He's currently not on campus. As a matter of fact, he's gone all day."

She should've never admitted that. I'm already lunging toward Daisy, grabbing her hand and dragging her out of the office without a backward glance. Lifting my hand in a wave, I call out as we exit through the door, "Thanks a lot, Viv! See you Monday!"

We're outside in seconds, Daisy's warm hand still clasped in mine, and it feels so good, so fucking right, I yank her closer, wrapping my arm around her waist, pulling her to me.

She gasps, her hand resting against my chest as she tilts her head back, her lips parted. "Arch…"

"I've missed you." I squeeze her close, my hand around the back of her head, her face tucked against my chest. Her body molding to mine like we're a perfect fit. "Don't say anything, Daze. We don't need to have a serious conversation right now. I just want to spend time with you for a little bit. Is that okay?"

She nods, her hair brushing against my jaw. She's got it in a high ponytail today and I miss the braids. "It's what I want too."

Pulling away from her slightly, I kiss her forehead before releasing my hold on her completely. "By the way, I lied."

Daisy frowns. "About what?"

"Needing help with the party. I don't need help. We've got it all figured out. Everything's handled. I just wanted to spend some time with you outside of the office." I grin at her. "Want to go grab a coffee downtown?"

Her eyes light up, though I see the caution in her gaze too. "What about our classes?"

"We could be gone all day and it doesn't matter. The teachers don't really care with the party going on tonight, especially with the seniors. Not like we're paying any attention anyway." I shrug.

"That sounds fun." She doesn't bring up her dad or worry about getting in trouble for skipping class, which is a relief. And then she says the craziest thing. "Maybe we should invite JJ and Mya to hang out with us."

The words hang in the cold air between us, shocking me silent for a few seconds.

"Seriously?" I thought she hated JJ.

"Sure." She shrugs. "Mya and I have been talking more."

"You have?"

She nods. "At lunch, I sometimes sit with Mya and Edie."

"You do?" I've been laying low since Daisy ended things with me, hanging out with my friends mostly, avoiding any common area where Daisy might have been, like the dining hall. I'd grab lunch but I rarely sat inside. It was easier avoiding her than watching her and making myself sick over the fact that she wasn't mine.

And my sister has never mentioned to me that she's been spending more time with Daisy and Mya. Figures she wouldn't tell me something so important.

I like it though, that they're becoming friends. Even Mya. I could tell she wasn't happy hanging out with Cadence. I'm glad she got away from her.

"Yeah." Daisy shrugs, smiling. "I actually have friends now."

She sounds so pleased with herself, and I'm happy for her too. This is all she's ever wanted. She just didn't know how to get it.

And look at her now.

"Text Mya," I tell her, pulling my phone out and sending a quick text to JJ and then—fuck it—to my sister.

Once the bell rings, Edie, JJ and Mya meet us out at the G Wagon in the parking lot and I drive us all to that coffee shop downtown. The one Daisy and I went to the day I took her to urgent care when she got her stitches.

That feels like a long time ago. Things have changed—definitely for the better. And while I wish Daisy was sitting in the passenger seat instead of JJ while I'm driving, she wanted to be in the back with the girls. I'm just so damn thankful she's in my car and we're acting like everything's normal, I don't protest.

I'm the happiest I've been in a long ass time.

Once I park my car on the street, we make our way to the coffee place and order our drinks and food, sitting at a small table outside, people watching and making idle conversation. Daisy sits to my right, Edie on the other side of her and while they're engrossed in conversation for most of the time, she does send me the occasional smile that reassures me she's in this.

She's into me.

All I can do is watch her talk, admiring her beauty like a lovesick fool. Pleased that she's made friends, that her and my sister are laughing and joking with each other while JJ hauls Mya into his lap and delivers a smacking kiss to her lips. It's almost surreal, how great this moment is. How happy everyone seems.

"Let's go to that one store," I tell Daisy after we've gathered all of our stuff and tossed it in the trash. Edie suggested we should wander around and look in the shops, and I have to agree with her it's a good idea.

Daisy frowns. "Which store?"

"The one with the jewelry."

We find it quickly, sneaking inside while everyone else goes into another shop next door, and I'm dragging Daisy over to the counter where the initial necklaces are, fighting the disappointment rising inside of me when I realize they don't have the necklace I was looking for on display anymore.

"Did you sell the necklace with the A charm?" I ask the sales lady when she comes over to help us.

"Ah, I'm afraid we just sold it." The woman glances over at Daisy, doing a double take but Daisy turns away, heading for another display across the store. The women offers me a sympathetic smile. "We don't have any more at the moment, but I'm sure we'll get a new shipment in soon. You should check back if you can."

"Okay, thank you." I nod at the lady before I go in search of Daisy, who I find at the front of the store, spinning around a rack that's loaded down with various pairs of oversized earrings. "Why'd you take off?"

"I thought these earrings were cool," Daisy says, keeping her focus on the ugly ass earrings like she's unable to look at me.

"You've gotta be kidding me," I tease her and she flashes me a smile, laughing. "Come on, Daze. Let's go find our friends."

. . .

We return to campus during lunch, Daisy and I parting ways with a wave and a smile, JJ watching us the entire time with a confused look on his face.

"What the fuck is going on with you two?" he asks me once all the girls leave us.

I shrug as we walk across campus. "Trying to take it slow."

He snorts. "You take nothing slow."

"With Daisy, I do," I say firmly.

The look on JJ turns thoughtful. "I think she's good for you."

"You do?" I turn to him, surprised.

JJ nods. "Hell yeah. I know you were all twisted up over her a while ago, but you seem...calmer now. More like your old self but better, if that makes any sense."

"It makes sense." I feel better knowing Daisy and I are going to make this work. It helps that I spoke to her dad. Having his approval means the world to Daisy.

And to me.

After the final bell rings, a bunch of us go to the ruins and help set up the party. There's so much booze, it's ridiculous.

Kegs and bottles of liquor everywhere. A few guys have set up a makeshift bar and we even have a decorating committee who has decked out the old burned-out building with all sorts of Halloween-themed stuff. It looks pretty amazing.

Since this is my last Halloween party at Lancaster Prep, I want to do it right. All Lancasters throw an epic Halloween bash. I remember hearing about my cousin and the sex-tape scandal that was exposed at this party a few years ago. Carolina got suspended over that whole mess, so at least I wasn't the first Lancaster to get busted. Not that I plan on getting busted tonight.

No bad vibes are coming from this party. It's going to be a good time and that's it.

The best fucking time, if I have my way.

When I return to the ruins, it's dark, the strings of orange and purple lights strewn about everywhere giving off a decent amount of light, and there's music playing. There are a few people already hanging around the bar, red cups clutched in their hands. The beer is flowing, a group of girls just showed up in sexy costumes and the air is filled with promise.

I'm nervous though. If Daisy doesn't show up...

Oh come on, what am I thinking? She's definitely coming.

It's happening.

"What the hell, bro? What's your costume supposed to be?"

I turn to find JJ approaching me, clad in black pants and a white shirt with black suspenders. He's got a hat on and there are fake bullet holes in his shirt, fake blood oozing from them. Mya is beside him in a clingy white sweater and a long, tight black skirt with a black beret on her head. She's carrying a toy gun and she's got bullet holes oozing blood on her sweater that match JJ's.

"Who are you two supposed to be?" I throw back at him, frowning. They look great, but I can't figure them out.

"Bonnie and Clyde," Mya answers, smiling up at JJ, who gives her a quick kiss.

Shocking. These two finally seem like they've got it together.

"The criminals? Cool costumes." I nod.

"You don't think we're pushing it with the bullet holes?" Mya looks worried and I suppose I can't blame her.

"Nah, it's Halloween. I can guarantee someone is going to show up dressed like a pimp. Does that mean he's pro-prostitution?"

"Well, maybe…" JJ starts, Mya jabbing him in the ribs with her elbow to shut him up, but all he does is laugh.

"And who are you supposed to be again?" JJ's gaze sweeps over the suit I'm wearing and I get it. I don't look like I'm actually wearing a costume.

I readjust my fake glasses on my face and unbutton my suit jacket, tugging at the front of my button-down shirt, which is fake. It's really got snaps and I undo them quickly with both hands to reveal what I'm wearing underneath.

The Superman emblem makes an appearance and JJ smiles. "Clark Kent!"

I slap his offered hand in a high five. "Superman, bro."

We chat for a bit, Cadence coming into view at one point wearing a sexy Cinderella costume and she brought some dude who's dressed as her Prince Charming.

The poor sucker. He's screwed.

More and more people begin to arrive and I'm checking on each group like I'm hosting this event, which I sort of am. The costumes are killer and I take a lot of photos, realizing quickly that I'm grateful that I am the host and completely preoccupied. Otherwise, I'd be sweating over the fact that Daisy still isn't here.

Where is she?

I grab my phone to check it for the millionth time, tempted to text my sister and ask where they are, but I resist the urge. What if Edie tells me something I don't want to hear?

I'd rather not risk it and pretend that Daisy is definitely coming. After everything we did earlier today, and how easy it was between us?

She has to.

CHAPTER FIFTY-ONE

DAISY

"You're going to the Halloween party?" The skepticism in my father's voice is thick. "You sure that's a good idea?"

We're in the living room and I just told my father what my plans are for tonight. I've been hinting at this for the last couple of days, so he has to know that I'm going for Arch. My feelings are fairly obvious.

My nod is firm. "It's definitely a good idea. Plus, it's my last chance to go since I'm a senior. I want to see what it's all about."

And, of course, I want to spend more time with Arch. I'm still shocked that we left campus today and hung out with our friends. When he hugged me, it felt so good to be back in his arms. That's all I want. For Arch to be in my life. To be my boyfriend.

I love that I've made friends too, and that Mya and Edie and I are close. It might be risky, letting Mya into my life knowing how close she was with Cadence, but it's a risk I'm willing to take. Besides, I don't think she likes Cadence anymore.

Mya never talks about her. At all.

After all the text conversations Arch and I have shared lately, I know that he's into me. And I'm into him. We're going to make it work this time, but there's one thing I still really need to do.

I have to tell my father that I'm getting back together with

Arch, and I'm not going to let him stop me.

I've already mentioned to him that we're talking again, and have even dropped Arch's name here and there in conversation lately. Dad doesn't say much when I do mention his name, but at least he doesn't tell me that I can't see him at all, which is major progress.

"I'll be with Arch the whole night, so he'll take care of me," I reassure my dad, wanting him to know that's exactly what Arch will do. My father can trust that Arch will always watch out for me. He's so protective of me and it's sweet. I like it.

I like him.

More than anything, I'm in love with him. I want to tell him that tonight, and while that's scary, I can do it.

I know I can.

A ragged sigh leaves my father and he turns to face me, his gaze going to the tote bag I've got slung on my shoulder, filled with the stuff I need for my costume. I hope Arch likes it. It's simple, it might even be a little dumb, and I really hope he gets it, but we'll see.

"You really care about him, don't you?" Dad asks me.

"I do. I'm in love with him," I tell him, but he's already talking, cutting me off.

"What do you know about love, hmm? It's just infatuation," he mutters, scrubbing a hand across his face.

"You and Mom got together when you were young," I point out.

The tiniest flicker of guilt appears in his gaze because he knows I'm right. "That was different. We were, what? Nineteen? Twenty?"

"It's not that different at all. Plus, it's not fair that you judge him so harshly when you don't even know him." I straighten my spine, hoping my voice doesn't waver when I speak. "I'm in love with Arch Lancaster, Dad. And I want to be with him. He wants to be with me. If you would just give him a chance, you would see that he's a pretty great guy. Don't you trust my judgment? Don't you believe in me? I wouldn't choose a total jerk to be my boyfriend."

He studies me, resting his hands on his hips. "I spoke with him, you know."

My jaw drops open and I struggle to find words, I'm so shocked. "W-what? When?"

"A while ago." He shrugs, like it's no big deal.

I blink at him mutely, shocked Arch went to him and they talked. He never mentioned it to me once. Not in any of the texts we shared. "What did he say?"

"He told me some things that you should probably hear from him and not me." My dad's smile is a little sad. "And that he wants to protect you and take care of you. He knows what kind of girl you are, Daisy Mae. You're a good one, and he doesn't want to let you go. I can't blame him."

Tears shimmer in my eyes and I blink, causing them to fall and I let my bag drop to the floor. "Daddy."

"I gave him my approval to see you, though it was a bit reluctant—*whoa*."

I tackle-hug him before he can say another word, squeezing him tight. His familiar smell surrounds me and I pull away slightly, giving him a kiss on the cheek. "Thank you."

"For what?"

"For giving Arch a chance." I release my hold on him and take a step back, grabbing my bag once more and slinging it over my shoulder. "He really is a good guy."

"He must be if you love him." He shakes his head, running a hand along his jaw. "Kathy did tell me I wasn't playing fair when it came to you two."

More shock courses through me at Kathy coming to my defense. I'm not outwardly mean toward her, but I'm not overly warm either. She's come over to our house a couple of times to spend time with my dad and the three of us have even gone out to dinner together, but I don't open up to her too much. Not yet.

"What do you mean, she says you don't play fair?" I ask.

"You've accused me of holding you back, and Kathy agrees with you. She told me I have to let you grow up sometime, and all I'm doing is making you resent me."

It's like he plucked the words from my brain.

"I just worry about you, honey. You're my little girl and I don't want you to get hurt. That's all," Dad admits, pain flashing in his eyes. "That's why I did it."

"I'm not a little girl anymore. You can't keep me one forever." I go to him, throwing myself at him once again and he automatically wraps me up in another hug. "I know what I'm doing. Mostly."

He chuckles and I laugh too because it's true. I sort of know what I'm doing, and what I don't know, I'm learning. My father can't protect me for the rest of my life. I have to go out and live and make mistakes.

"I want to be with Arch. He wants to be with me. Please don't tell me I have to choose between you two, because I'm afraid I wouldn't choose you." I tilt my head back so I can look into my father's eyes. "I need both of you in my life."

"I won't make you choose," he murmurs, his thumb brushing against my chin. "I love you, sweetheart. You're all I've got in this world. I just want what's best for you. Guess I've been a little overprotective of you."

"A little?" My brows shoot up and we both laugh again. "More like a lot."

"I already lost your mom. I didn't want to lose you too." His eyes are brimming with tears and I give him another hug, hiding my face against his chest, fighting my own tears again. I don't want to cry. Not tonight. It's a happy occasion, not a sad one.

"You haven't lost me, Daddy. I love you," I tell him, my voice muffled. When I lift my head to meet his gaze, I see the tears are already gone. "I have to go. I'm going to get ready with Arch's sister."

"With Edie?" When I nod, my dad smiles. "She seems like a nice girl. One of the nicer Lancasters."

I roll my eyes and withdraw from his embrace. "You need to get over the grudge you have against the Lancasters."

"I will, darlin'." He winks at me. "Eventually."

. . .

"Oh God, we're so late. My brother is going to kill me." Edie grabs my hand and drags me down the damp grass path that leads to the ruins, where the party is being held. We're still pretty far out, but I can already hear the bass of the music playing. The sound of people talking and yelling, having a good time. Excitement and nerves make my stomach churn and I'm glad I'm not wearing heels like Edie is. I don't know how she's running so easily across the mushy lawn.

"He won't kill me," I say with confidence, making Edie laugh. We've just spent the last two hours together getting ready for this party and while I don't know exactly what she did to me makeup-wise, when I looked in the mirror after she was done, it was like I was staring back at a different person. My face was completely transformed. I somehow still looked like me, but an enhanced version. It's wild.

I hope Arch likes it.

"No, he definitely won't kill you. More like he'll take one look at you and want to drag you away so you two can be alone. You look cute, Daisy," Edie says for about the thousandth time.

"You really think so? You don't think my costume idea is dumb?" I'm second-guessing myself constantly tonight and I'm starting to annoy even myself.

"Not at all. Once he figures it out, he's going to love it," Edie assures me.

I hope she's right.

When the ruins come into view, I go instantly into search mode, looking for Arch. There are so many people here, and while there are some I recognize, a lot of them are wearing masks, or a wig, or a lot of makeup, which makes it hard to figure out who they are. And all of the costumes are so clever that I doubt my choice yet again, especially when I glance over at Edie and see how great she looks in her red 1920s flapper costume. She's got so much fringe on her dress that shakes when she walks, ropes of long pearls around her neck and a feather in her hair. She looks amazing.

While I just look like myself with a bunch of makeup on my face. Big deal.

"Your nerves are showing," Edie says, bumping her shoulder into mine.

"What do you mean?" I turn to her, my steps slowing, dread coating my insides. I'm tempted to bolt. I feel like a fraud. Like I don't belong here.

And then I remember that I've made friends and I've got Arch and I need to get over my old anxiety once and for all.

"You look scared to death." Edie wraps her arm around my shoulders and gives me a squeeze. "We need to find Arch before you run away and never come back."

How can someone I've only known for a little while already have me so easily figured out? Maybe I'm just that obvious.

"I'm not going to run away," I say firmly. "Maybe I should drink something. It might calm my nerves."

"Liquid courage?"

"Yeah." I laugh. "I think I need it."

Putting on a brave smile, I let Edie take my hand and lead me up the rickety old stairs of the building. All sorts of people greet her and I realize she's the star of tonight. A Lancaster in her element.

I'm sure that means Arch is a star too. He always is. Everyone wants to be around him. With him. I get it. I'm drawn to his magnetism and when he flashes that secret smile that seems to be only for me? I want to melt.

I *do* melt.

God, where is he? I need to see him.

Once we've gone through the house and there's no Arch in sight, we go get something to drink at the temporary bar that's been set up by the side of the house. I take a cup of beer and when I sip it, I get nothing but foam, which is gross. I toss the cup in a nearby trashcan.

Pretty sure beer isn't for me.

There are so many people here and they all enthusiastically greet Edie, and some of them even greet me, saying my name and everything.

"I figured they didn't know who I was," I say after about the tenth person said hi to me.

Edie rolls her eyes. "You've gone here the entirety of high school. They definitely know who you are."

I take a step back when a huge group of people head in our direction, all of them pushing past us to get to the bar. I lose sight of Edie at one point, there are so many people between us, and my heart drops when I hear a familiar voice.

"Edie! Fucking finally. Where's Daisy?"

Edie's laughter is coy. "She's around."

The crowd dissipates slowly, revealing Arch standing between us, his back to me. He's wearing a charcoal gray suit that fits him to perfection and I wonder what he's supposed to be when he turns and faces me. The tamed hair, the fake glasses and his slightly undone shirt, revealing the hint of an S on the shirt beneath gives it away.

My Superman.

"Daze..." His voice drifts as he drinks me in, his gaze touching me everywhere, all at once. His brows draw together and I can tell he's trying to figure out what I'm supposed to be and coming up with nothing.

I glance down at my Lancaster Prep sweatshirt. It's not a part of our uniform rotation. They sold this particular shirt in the student store our sophomore year and I've always loved it. It's got the giant Lancaster family crest on the front of it with Lancaster written beneath it. It doesn't even say Prep anywhere on it, which I thought was perfect for tonight.

"You look...amazing." He approaches me and everything else fades. All I can focus on is him. His beloved face and his comforting presence and also the fact that he's so gorgeous, he makes my body ache.

"Thank you." I'm feeling shy, which isn't abnormal but God, I really wish I could get over this.

"You wore your hair down." He reaches out, brushing a few strands from my shoulder, and tingles break out all over my skin. "For me?"

"This entire costume is for you," I admit. "But I don't think you figured it out yet."

His gaze sweeps over me, lingering on the sweatshirt. The necklace I'm wearing. Realization hits and he meets my gaze. "You're wearing that necklace. The one we saw at the store. The one I checked on earlier."

Reaching up, I brush my fingers over the tiny gold A charm. I had money from my birthday and I spent it on this necklace. I wanted to wear his initial on a chain around my neck to please him. To show everyone that he belongs to me. The daisy earrings he gave me for my birthday are in my ears, their solid weight reminding me that daisies are his favorite. That I'm his favorite, just like he's mine. "I am."

"You're the one who bought it?" He chuckles, shaking his head. I can tell he's pleased but still a little confused. "I give up. Who are you supposed to be?"

I take a step forward, our bodies gently colliding and he automatically rests his hand on my hip, keeping me in place. Pressed right next to him. "I'm Arch Lancaster's girlfriend."

The joy sparkling in his blue eyes has my heart racing. "Hell yeah, you are. That's your costume? You dressed up as my girlfriend?"

"Well yeah. I wore my hair down because you like it, but I kept a couple of small braids because you seem to like those too." I point at the braids on either side of my head. "The sweatshirt has your name on it and nothing else. And the necklace." I'm rubbing the A charm again, the nerves coming back when he still hasn't said something.

"Maybe it was a stupid idea," I tell him when he remains quiet. "I thought it would be kind of fun, but it's also a little lame, huh. I'm so—"

He kisses me, cutting off my rambling, and I fall into his kiss, returning it with all of the pent-up emotion I've been keeping to myself for way too long. He coaxes my lips apart and our tongues glide against each other, and when he slips both arms around my waist and clutches me close, I cling to him, relieved that he likes it.

That he likes me being his girlfriend.

CHAPTER FIFTY-TWO

ARCH

I crush Daisy to me, pressing my face against her soft hair, breathing in her familiar floral scent. She smells good, she feels good, she looks so fucking good. Wearing my initial and the Lancaster sweatshirt and telling me her costume is Arch Lancaster's girlfriend.

It's perfection. She's perfection. And she was so damn nervous too. I could see it written all over her. Her voice was slightly shaky and fuck.

I love her.

Kissing the top of her head, I pull away slightly so I can stare into her beautiful golden- brown eyes. "I'm glad you came."

"I had to." Her smile is tremulous, and I don't know how she can still feel doubt over me. Over us.

Can't she see it in my eyes? My actions? Feel it when I touch her? She owns me. She's owned my heart since she broke it. Now she's put the pieces back together and I feel whole.

Only with her.

"You're beautiful." She has a lot of makeup on her face and I know that Edie worked her magic. She's always been good at this kind of stuff. And while I think Daisy is stunning with it on, she's just as beautiful with no makeup at all too.

"So are you," she whispers, her arms tightening around me. "Superman."

"Is it too cheesy?"

"No." She tips her head back, laughing. "I think it's perfect."

She tugs at the front of my fake button-up shirt, the snaps undoing with ease, revealing the Superman shirt completely. With her fingers she slowly traces over the giant S in the middle of my chest, her touch making me shiver.

Glancing around, I wonder if anyone would notice that we took off. Fuck this party.

I want to get my girlfriend alone. Just the two of us.

"Want to get out of here?" I whisper, cupping her cheek, my gaze heavy. Hoping she understands what I really mean.

I'm desperate to get her naked.

Her brows draw together. "No way, Lancaster. This is my last chance to go to this epic Halloween party and I'm going to enjoy it. All night long."

I groan. Is she for real right now? "Come on, Daze."

"No, you come on, Arch. Let's go have fun." She withdraws from my arms and takes my hand, leading me into the fray.

And damn it, she's right. We have a blast. We drink and dance and talk to people. Well, Daisy talks to people. I watch her in amazement as she chats animatedly with people we've gone to school with for years. People who didn't know her, who had no clue what she was like or what she's into, and my heart swells with fucking pride.

She's trying to come out of her shell and she's doing a damn good job of it. She's so beautiful and smart and I don't think it hurts that she's had a couple of drinks. I got her to ditch the beer and convinced her to drink a flavored seltzer and she loves them.

Maybe a little too much, but there is something to say for liquid courage.

Her confidence is attractive. Everything about her is attractive, and knowing she willingly went and bought that necklace with my initial on it and is proudly wearing it makes me feel like I can conquer the entire damn world as long as I've got this girl by my side.

And I've already conquered her. She's mine.

Only when the party starts to dwindle and people are leaving does Daisy finally look at me and whisper, "Maybe we should go."

"We're leaving," I announce to anyone who's listening, taking Daisy's hand and dragging her out of the mostly empty building.

Edie is still here. We walk past her sitting with a small group of friends outside and she calls out to me, "Better come back tomorrow morning and help us clean this up!"

"That's your job," I yell back at her, earning a glare from my girlfriend.

Don't think I'll get over calling Daisy that. At least for a while.

"We'll help!" Daisy says, squeezing my hand and lowering her voice to say, "Right?"

I bring our linked hands up to my mouth and drop a kiss on her knuckles. "I'll go if you go."

"I want to." She smiles, yanking her hand out of mine and doing a twirl in the grass, stumbling and nearly falling over. "I had the best time tonight!"

"Socializing with people your own age isn't so bad, am I right?" I raise my brows, reaching for her when she stumbles again and tips over into me. I help right her and she darts away, skipping ahead of me.

"It was great! I think I made friends. Even with Mya!"

I noticed they had their heads bent close together during one point of the night and I wonder how authentic Mya was with her. Though I do know Mya's been sick of Cadence's shit for a while. And speaking of Cadence...

"Did you see Cinderella get into an argument with Prince Charming?"

Daisy laughs, turning so she's walking backward and facing

me. Probably not the smartest thing, considering her current state. "I did. Why is she so mean all of the time? I think she's a miserable person."

"She's not happy with anything or anyone," I agree, ready to change the subject. "I'm glad you had fun."

She runs toward me and I stop, grunting when we collide, her arms coming around my neck, her fingers sinking into my hair. "I had the absolute best time of my life. Now, where are you taking me?"

"Where does your dad think you are right now?" I have all sorts of ideas of where I could take Daisy. On my bed.

Against the wall.

In the shower.

The possibilities are endless.

"Spending the night with Edie." She grins up at me and I lean down, dropping a kiss on her nose. "That's what I told him. And he has Find my Phone, so if he checks, I'll be in the building where Edie's room is."

"You are so fucking smart," I murmur, kissing her for real. But she's withdrawing from me way too soon, breaking out into a run, and I chase after her, catching up with ease because my legs are longer and really? She's not that fast.

"I'm so tired," she whines, leaning into me. "And we still have to walk so far."

This girl is all over the place. I blame the alcohol. "I'll carry you."

"What?"

"Get on my back." I turn and bend over. "Hop on."

She does as I say so quickly, I nearly fall over, but slowly I rise up, her arms going around my neck in an almost chokehold while I grab the back of her legs. I carry her the rest of the way home like this, her mouth at my ear, her body wrapped all around my back and I can't wait to drop her on the bed. Fall on top of her. Kiss her senseless.

When we get to my building, she hops off my back and the moment we're locked away in my room, she's on me. Knocking me back so I fall onto the bed with my girl straddling me, her arms around my neck, her forehead pressed to mine.

"I missed you so much," she whispers. "I was so stupid, breaking up with you like I did."

"You thought you had to," I whisper back, slipping my hands beneath the bottom of her sweatshirt, encountering nothing but bare skin. "Your dad told you so."

"I shouldn't have listened to him. He feels bad about it by the way." She dips her head, pressing her mouth against my neck.

I hiss in a breath at the contact, feeling it right down to my balls. "He's going to give me a chance, huh?"

"He was just being overprotective." She reaches for the front of my suit, pushing it open. "I don't want to talk about him right now."

"Whatcha want to talk about, Daze?" I'm teasing her. The liquid courage is carrying over to her basically mauling me, not that I'm complaining.

"I don't want to talk." She pulls away so she can look into my eyes, her expression serious. "I want to feel you inside me."

I groan, shocked yet pleased by her response. "You are a different person when you drink."

"I kind of like who I am right now." Her smile is small. "I feel more like my real self."

"Keep it up, baby." I grab hold of her and gently shove her to the side so she falls onto the bed then stand, getting rid of my jacket and the costume button-up shirt immediately. "I'll give you exactly what you want."

She leans back on the bed, her hands braced on the mattress, her legs dangling over the edge. She toes off her shoes, the movement causing her sweatshirt to ride up, revealing a sliver of pale skin.

My hands literally itch to touch her, I want her so fucking bad.

Within seconds I've shed everything I was wearing, save for my boxer briefs, while she's still struggling to take off her jeans. I take over, helping her get rid of them.

"Sit up," I tell her and she does what I ask. "Lift your arms."

I take the sweatshirt off, pulling it up and over her head and tossing it on the floor. She's sitting in front of me in just her bra and panties, and my dick surges against the front of my boxers, eager to get inside her.

"You're not too drunk, are you?" I ask.

"No." She giggles, shaking her head.

"I don't take advantage of drunk girls."

"How can you take advantage of the willing?" she asks, genuinely serious.

I chuckle, leaning in to brush her lips with mine. "Guess we can go through with this then."

She smiles, nipping at my bottom lip with her teeth. "You better go through with this."

"Don't ever doubt me, Daze." I kiss her. "I'm going through with this over," I kiss her again, "and over," another kiss, this one with tongue, "and over again. All night long if you'll let me."

Her laugh is as eager as her hands, which are currently sliding all over me. "I'll let you do whatever you want to me."

"Promise?" I guide her so she's lying on the bed with me on top of her.

The glow in her eyes when she looks at me makes my heart feel like it just grew twice its size. "Promise."

CHAPTER FIFTY-THREE

DAISY

His touch is so gentle, his fingers skimming over my skin, making me shiver. I lie there in the middle of his bed and bask in his attention, my eyes closed, my heartbeat fast as I try my best to calm my breathing.

But it's no use. He's got me worked up and twisted over this moment, the two of us finally together again. When he removes my bra, his lips automatically finding my nipple and drawing it into his mouth, I thrust my hands in his hair, holding me to him like I never want him to stop.

I don't. I would be perfectly content if we could stay in this bed forever, wrapped up in each other. I'm so in love with him I can't even see straight, and what's so crazy?

We haven't even confessed our feelings to each other yet.

"Arch," I whisper as he drifts his mouth across my chest, kissing me everywhere. "Arch, I need to tell you something."

"What do you want to tell me?" His lips move against my skin when he speaks, tickling me, making me squirm.

"Um." I press my lips together, the words sticking in my throat and I immediately feel stupid.

He lifts his head, his heavy gaze sexy. Even a little sleepy. I touch his face because I can't help myself, savoring the way he's looking at me, his hands still on me. He's beautiful. And all mine.

"I want to tell you something too," he murmurs.

"You go first." I may be coming out of my shell, but I'm still a little shy about the important stuff. I can't help it.

"Daisy Mae Albright." I told him my middle name recently and I hope I don't live to regret it. "I'm in love with you." He drops a kiss on my rib cage, leaving me trembling.

"Archibald Lancaster." His parents didn't give him a middle name, which I thought was surprising. "I'm in love with you too."

He smiles. So do I. We stare at each other for a moment, soaking up the words, the feelings we just confessed to each other, and then he shifts into action. Tugging my panties off, his lips pressed against the inside of my thigh in an open-mouthed kiss. I struggle to take off his boxer briefs and he eventually takes over, getting rid of them completely until we're both naked and wound around each other. His erection presses against my core, throbbing and insistent, and I press my hand against his chest, stopping him just as he's about to reach for a condom from his nightstand.

"I got on birth control," I admit.

"You did?" His brows lift in surprise.

Nodding, I let my hand drift down, my fingers streaking across his stomach. Then lower, curling around his shaft. "I liked it that one time when we didn't use a condom."

He's actually grinning. "I fucking loved it."

"I know." I roll my eyes, a gasp escaping me when he knocks my hand away from his erection and wraps his fingers around the base, guiding himself inside me. Pushing all the way in until I'm filled completely.

I tense up, closing my eyes and inhaling deeply. He goes still too, and I can feel him watching me. Can sense the question on his lips.

"Are you okay? Did I hurt you?"

"I'm good." I nod. "You didn't hurt me."

Slowly he starts to move, pulling almost all the way out before he pushes back in. His pace is steady. Patient. He rocks into me, his hips thrusting, his mouth seeking mine in a dirty kiss. It's all tongues and lips and teeth, and when I sling my legs around his hips and send him deeper? We both groan.

Loudly.

Our movements go from slow to frantic in seconds. He rises up on his knees, bringing me with him, my legs still wound around his hips, though my back is still on the bed. I watch as he fucks me hard—there's no other way to describe what he's doing—his gaze locked on the area where our bodies are connected. Just watching him watch us, feeling what he's doing to me, the now familiar sensation rises up within me.

The tingling low in my belly. The throbbing. My breath catches with his every thrust and I arch my back, lifting my hips. He touches me there, his fingers rubbing my clit, making me whimper. With one final push, he fills me deep, hitting a spot that has me crying out, the orgasm slamming into me so hard, I can't breathe.

Can't see or smell or hear. I can't do anything but ride the wave, my inner walls squeezing around his shaft, milking his orgasm right out of him. His groan is loud, his body shuddering over mine until he collapses on top of me, breathing so hard I get kind of worried about him. I rub my hands up and down his muscular back, enjoying the weight of him on top of me.

"I'm crushing you," he finally says, shifting like he's going to roll off of me and I hold him tighter.

"Don't go yet," I murmur against his neck. "I like how you feel."

He smiles. I can feel it. "That ended way too quick."

"It was still amazing." Because it so was.

He lifts away slightly so he can kiss me. "We need to do it again."

I can't help it. I start to laugh. He just grins at me, dipping his head to kiss me, his lips lingering on mine. "I love you," I whisper, overwhelmed with emotion for him.

"I love you too." Another kiss, this one soft and sweet. "Have I told you today that you're my favorite?"

"No," I lie, needing to hear it again.

"Well, you are." He kisses my chin. My jaw. My throat. "You are my favorite person, Daze."

"You're my favorite too," I confess, clinging to him.

"Really?" He sounds shocked.

"Definitely."

"More than your roses?"

"Remember what you said?" When he slowly shakes his head, I continue, "I'm the rose. You're the sun."

"I said that?"

"Oh, come on, don't play like you didn't."

His expression turns serious. "Well, I meant it. Let me be your sun, Daze."

"Only if you'll let me be your rose."

He's laughing. So am I. "This is some corny ass shit."

"You're the one who said it in the first place."

"Yeah, still can't believe that." He shakes his head. "Love you."

"Love you too."

"Want to do it again?" His tone is hopeful.

I stretch beneath him. "Most definitely."

CHAPTER FIFTY-FOUR

DAISY

THANKSGIVING

I'm nervous. My palms are sweaty and I'm tempted to rub them on my skirt but that's gross and I don't want Arch to notice.

But he grabs my hand, clutching it tight as we ride in the swiftly rising elevator to the penthouse apartment where his parents live, and he notices.

Of course, he does.

"Nervous?" He squeezes my fingers.

I withdraw my hand from his, vaguely embarrassed. "Your parents don't like me."

"They just don't know you." He tosses my own words back at me. I remember saying that to him about my dad. "Once they meet you, they're going to fall in love with you. Just like I did." He snags my hand again, pulling me to him and kissing me soundly, just as the elevator doors swoosh open.

I pull away from his still seeking lips quickly, my cheeks flooding with heat, but no one is there. All I see is a pristine white wall and a gold console table.

"Come on." My hand is in his yet again and he leads me out of the elevator and into his parents' apartment.

All I can do is stare, my head tilted back as I take it all in, Arch dragging me deeper into the plush, beautiful apartment. Everything is white and the palest blue, vividly colored landscape paintings are on the wall. Expansive windows that show off the city spread out before us. Light fixtures that look more like pieces of art shine down upon us, and I reach for my ear out of habit, my fingertip drifting across my diamond daisy earring.

"It's beautiful," I whisper, afraid to speak in a normal tone, it's so quiet in here. "Where is everyone?"

"In the dining room. We're late."

I don't think Arch knows the meaning of being on time. I wonder if his parents realize this.

They have to.

When I asked my father if I could spend Thanksgiving with Arch and his family, I was worried he'd say no. A big part of me didn't want to leave him alone during the holidays, but he said I should go, that Kathy invited us to spend the day with her family already and he'd said yes.

I'm relieved he's with Kathy and her family. I don't feel as guilty leaving him alone to be with Arch, because he's not alone.

And no one should be alone during a holiday.

"Is your mother upset with you?" *With us?*

Worry gnaws at me. I'm desperate to make a good impression and Arch warned me already that his mother might not be exactly...warm towards me at first. Her expectations are high when it comes to her children and the people they date, and nothing makes her happy, according to Arch.

And also Edie, who warned me I shouldn't take her mother's potential attitude toward me personally.

But I'm me, and I'm definitely going to take it personally. I just want his mother to like me.

I want his family's approval. I can't help it.

"I'm always late, so she's not upset." Arch grins, as casual as ever, but I suppose he has every right to be. This is his home, his family, and he's not nervous at all. But he must notice the fear in my expression because he sobers right up, stopping us in the middle of the living room. "Daze, don't sweat it."

"Easy for you to say." I shake out my sweaty palms, gasping when he yanks me into his arms and kisses me, like that's going to make it all better.

Which it does. For about ten seconds. Then the nerves are back, roiling in my stomach, making me nauseous.

I don't know how I'm going to be able to eat a single bite of food during this meal.

Resting my hand on my stomach, I take a deep, steadying breath, Arch watching me, affection shining in his eyes. "You're going to be great. Just be yourself."

I nod once and we head for the dining room. The apartment is gigantic, a maze of rooms and wide corridors, until finally we're standing in an open doorway, staring at a giant table that's covered with huge autumn-colored floral arrangements and beautiful table settings placed in front of each chair. Almost all of the seats are occupied, his family chatting pleasantly amongst themselves.

A man who resembles Arch spots us first, a pleasant smile stretching his mouth. "There you are. Glad you finally showed up. We're starving."

"Sorry, Dad. You know how it is." Arch glances over at me, his expression warm as he says, "Everyone, this is Daisy."

There are murmured greetings, Edie louder than the rest and I shoot her a grateful smile, my nerves easing some when I spot an empty chair right next to hers, with another empty chair across from it.

"Sit by me, Daisy," Edie encourages, and I go to the empty chair, settling in as carefully as I can, flashing a timid smile at the older woman sitting on the other side of me. "You look beautiful."

"Thank you." I give her a quick hug, thankful for the ally at the table that's not just Arch. I love my boyfriend, and I know he loves me, but it's nice having someone else who likes me too.

I think I'm going to need as many allies as I can get, dealing with the Lancasters.

Arch introduces me to all of his relatives, including his little brothers, who are sitting close to their dad and have matching sullen expressions on their faces.

They look like trouble. Arch tells me they're little heathens and I don't doubt it.

There are a few cousins here, including a beautiful blonde named Charlotte and her equally beautiful husband, Perry. I stare at them like I can't help myself, which I sort of can't because they're sitting next to each other and across from me. He looks at her with so much love filling his eyes, and they're constantly touching each other like they can't help themselves.

It's sweet.

My gaze slides over to Arch to find he's already watching me, his lips curved into a closed mouth smile and my skin goes warm.

He looks at me like I matter too. I might watch Perry and Charlotte, wishing I had the same kind of love…

But I already do.

• • •

Once the plates are cleared—I was able to eat after all, Edie's constant chatter putting me at ease—all of the women end up in a sitting room while the men are in the room with the giant big screen TV, watching a football game. I guess even rich guys enjoy football, which is silly of me to think but it makes them seem more human.

Being alone with the women though, is a little intimidating, especially when Edie excuses herself and rushes off to use the bathroom.

"So." Miriam Lancaster studies me, finally engaging me in

conversation. She's been pleasant, welcoming me to her home when Arch specifically introduced us at the table, but otherwise she hasn't said a word to me.

Which is fine. I'd rather be ignored—I'm used to it after all—than have her attention on me like it is now.

I shift in the uncomfortable chair I'm sitting in and smile at her, curling my hands in my lap, waiting for her to drop a verbal bomb. Bracing myself.

"Arch has told me about you," Miriam finally says, her tone even. There's not much emotion showing on her face either. "Are you still ranked number one in your senior class?"

Does that impress her? I hope so. "I am," I say with a nod.

"Do you plan on going to college?"

"I do." Lately though, Arch and I have been talking more about the gap year plan and I want to do it. He does too. Traveling is an education in itself, isn't it?

That's what I tell myself.

"Where do you want to go?" She sounds genuinely curious.

I rattle off my usual list, some of them state universities I know I can get into, the rest Ivy League schools that are tougher to get admission. She nods, looking impressed and when I finally go quiet, she says, "Perhaps you'll be a good influence on my Arch and convince him to go to college."

My Arch. She's possessive of her children, I can tell. It's the way she looked at them at the table while we were eating, how she engaged in conversation with them. Arch says she's a pain in the ass who never lets up on him but maybe his mother just wants the best for her children. And who can blame her for that?

"Maybe," I hedge because I can neither confirm nor deny my influence over his future choices is that strong.

But we'll see.

"I know you and Edie have become closer. I think that's wonderful. Edith has never had a lot of friends. Her circle is tight." Miriam tilts her head, contemplating me. "You don't come from much, do you?"

No one else is paying attention to our conversation, thank goodness. Everyone is broken off into smaller groups, chatting among themselves, the occasional tinkle of laughter filling the room and right now, I'd give anything to be a part of that conversation. The one where they're laughing and most likely having a better time than I'm having.

I shift in my chair, my hands twisted together. "My father works at Lancaster Prep."

"I know. Ralph. The groundskeeper. And your mother…I'm sorry that she's no longer with us."

My hand automatically goes to my ear, tracing over the earring Arch gave me. Touching them calms me sometimes, eases my racing heart and nervous stomach. "Thank you. I miss her."

"I'm sure you do," she murmurs. She studies me for a moment, her gaze intense. Like she's trying to make me break.

I sit up straighter, my hand dropping back into my lap.

I'm not going to break. I refuse to.

"Arch mentioned you had a strong spirit, though I don't think he phrased it quite that way." Her smile is small. "I think he said that when you believe in something, you don't back down from it."

My heart starts to pound harder. Where is she going with this?

"And I get the feeling that you believe in my Arch," she continues, a delicate brow rising. "You're in love with him?"

I can't answer. The words get stuck in my throat. All I can manage is a nod.

"He's in love with you. I see the way he looks at you. You could break his heart, I think. And that's a powerful position to have." She leans forward, as if to share a secret, and I find myself leaning forward as well, eager to hear what she has to say. "When a Lancaster falls in love, they tend to do it when they're young and passionate, and they put their whole heart into the relationship. You'll be overwhelmed by their love, but in the best possible way." She pauses. "Consider yourself lucky, Daisy."

Edie returns to the room, plopping herself onto the edge of the chair I'm sitting on and I scoot over, giving her more room. "What did I miss?" she gushes.

Her mother leans back in her chair, sharing a secret look with me. "Nothing, darling. Daisy was telling me about her future college plans."

The conversation shifts back to college, Miriam drilling Edie on what she might want to do and I watch them speak, replaying what Miriam said in my mind.

Consider yourself lucky, Daisy.

I am.

I'm the luckiest girl in the world.

EPILOGUE

ARCH

GRADUATION DAY

"Congratulations to the graduating class of Lancaster Prep!" Headmaster Matthews yells into the microphone, a big grin on his face.

I'd bet good money the only reason he's smiling is because he's glad my ass is finally out of here.

Feeling is mutual, Matthews.

We all leap to our feet, tossing our graduate caps into the air, hundreds of them flying, spinning in the sky. I turn to Daisy and haul her into my arms, hugging her tight and she squeezes me right back, her arms around my neck in an almost stranglehold. I pull away slightly, pressing my lips to hers and she kisses me back with just as much intensity, her happiness bleeding into me.

Mine seeping into her.

"Was the speech really okay?" she asks me at one point as we're wandering around the field, taking endless photos with friends and family and staff members. Viv even took a photo with us, standing in the middle, a giant smile on her face.

I think she believes she somehow had a hand in our getting together and I don't mind giving her a little credit.

"Your speech was amazing." I slip my arm around her shoulders, kissing her cheek. "Best valedictorian speech this school has ever seen."

"Okay, no need to exaggerate." She rolls her eyes but I can tell she's pleased. And that's all I want.

To please my girl. Make her smile. Make her moan.

Whoops. My thoughts just veered into dirty territory, which is a chronic problem, I can't lie.

"Seriously, Daze. It was perfect. And you did great." Her voice only a shook a little in the beginning but then she glanced down at me, like she sought me out to give her a little strength and I nodded. Gave her a thumbs up gesture which made her smile and that seemed to take care of her nerves.

People cheered and clapped for her when she was finished and I've never seen her look prouder. I was proud too. My girl is smart. Strong. She's going to do amazing things.

In a year though. After we travel the world together.

Our parents were kind of pissed but eventually, they let up on us and said they couldn't control us. Even her dad, who is a lot more relaxed now that he's in a serious relationship with Kathy. When we leave in a week, Kathy is moving into the cottage on campus with Ralph. He's asked her to marry him. She's got a diamond on her finger and everything.

I think Daisy is relieved, knowing her dad has someone. Then she doesn't feel like she's abandoning him.

My parents like Daisy—fucking shocker because damn, they're judgmental—and while they weren't thrilled with our plans at first, they've come around. Dad more than Mom, which is what I expected. Mom is just glad I'm talking about attending college next year, which is something I never mentioned before. She also gives Daisy all the credit for mellowing me out and getting me where I need to be on time.

Like today's graduation ceremony.

"Don't forget we're going out for a late lunch," Dad tells me when we come across him out on the field. "Your mother made the reservation for two-thirty."

"We'll be there," Daisy reassures him, curling her arm through mine. "Right?"

"Definitely," I say to her.

Dad smiles. "Congrats you two. Enjoy your time out here with your friends."

"We won't be late," Daisy calls as he walks away, smiling up at me once he's gone. "I need to keep impressing them."

"They're already impressed. You can relax." I kiss her like I can't help myself, laughing when I hear JJ make a disgusted noise.

We take photos with JJ and Mya, and at one point I spot Cadence in the distance, watching us with envy shining in her gaze. If I could give her the finger I would, but there's no need to antagonize her further.

I'm glad I'm out of this school and won't have to see her face every day.

The crowd slowly dwindles and eventually we head for the parking lot, shedding our graduation gowns before we climb into the G Wagon. I reach for a gift bag I left behind the passenger seat and hand it to Daisy, who takes it with wide eyes.

"What's this?"

"Open it and find out." I'm trying to be cool but I'm nervous. I want her to like this present, though I don't know why I'm worried.

She's going to love it.

Daisy is as slow as my grandma on Christmas morning opening presents. She carefully removes the tissue paper Edie stuffed inside, laughing when she keeps pulling out more and more. Until finally the pale yellow bag is empty save the box sitting at the bottom. She pulls the black velvet box out, staring at it.

"It's bigger than the box you gave me for my birthday."

I nod, wishing she'd just open the damn thing.

She slowly cracks the lid open, gasping when she sees what's inside. "Oh, Arch."

Tears spring to her eyes and I reach for her, cradling her cheek, smoothing my thumb across her soft skin. "Don't cry, Daze."

Her tears get to me. I never want my girl sad.

"It's just so beautiful." She reaches for the necklace she's currently wearing. The one she bought with my initial on it. "But I don't want to take this off."

"You can wear both." I gave her a necklace with a daisy pendant that matches the earrings I gave her for her birthday. I bought it at the same time, knowing even then she'd flip out just over the earrings.

I thought it best to save the necklace for another special occasion. I almost gave it to her for Christmas, but held off. Instead, I took her to that giant bookstore on Fifth and told her she had three minutes to grab as many books as she could and I'd buy them all for her.

The girl is faster than I anticipated. I spent a small fortune on a mountain of books, but I just handed over my credit card with a smile while my girlfriend stood by my side, panting and wiping her hair away from her sweaty face, making conversation with the cashier.

That was a good moment. A fun memory. But this one is good too. Maybe even better.

I'm glad I waited until graduation to give her the necklace.

"I love it so much." She lifts her gaze to mine, her eyes shiny with tears. "It's beautiful."

"You're beautiful," I murmur, pulling her into my arms, my mouth finding hers.

We kiss for long, tongue-filled minutes, until the jewelry box falls into my lap, right on my semi-hard dick. I finally break the kiss, pulling away from her, noting how flushed her cheeks are. Her swollen lips. The dazed look in her eyes.

"We should go," I say, clearing my throat. I hand her the box with the necklace and she takes it, carefully pulling the necklace from within before she holds it out to me.

"Will you put it on me?"

Nodding, I take the necklace and she turns her back to me, lifting her wavy blonde hair so I can stare at her neck. She's wearing a simple white sundress that exposes her back and shoulders and I can't wait to get her alone later. We're staying at a hotel for the night, just the two of us.

If all goes to plan, I'll be keeping her awake all night long.

I place the chain around her neck, my fingers brushing against her skin, making her shiver. I do the clasp, and she immediately reaches up, her fingers brushing over the white and yellow diamond pendant. She glances at me from her over shoulder, her eyes shining with so much love for me I'm almost overwhelmed.

"It's so beautiful, Arch." She turns to face me fully, and I like the way the daisy looks next to my initial. As if we belong together.

Which we do.

"I'm glad you like it."

"Thank you," she whispers, leaning in to kiss me again. "I love you."

"I love you too." I kiss her, my lips still clinging as I murmur, "We should probably go."

She kisses me over and over, breaking only to say, "We have a few minutes."

"We'll probably be late," I warn her, leaning back to let her crawl over the console and settle in my lap.

Daisy straddles me, her dress riding up, offering me a glimpse of her long legs. "I don't care. It's what they expect, right?"

"What about your dad?" He's going to meet the rest of us for lunch at that Italian restaurant downtown, with Kathy accompanying him.

"He'll be fine. They'll love him." She kisses me again, her

lips hungry, her tongue insistent. "I just want to kiss you for a little while longer."

I rest my hand on her chest, just above her breasts, my fingers toying with the necklaces she's wearing. "My mom might get annoyed."

"No, she won't. She's used to you being late. Come on, Arch." She smiles, looking pleased with herself. "Don't be so uptight."

"Sounds like something I would've said to you, once upon a time," I tease.

Her mouth rests against mine, breathing me in. "You've changed me for the better."

"You've changed me too, Daze." I kiss one corner of her mouth, then the other. "I think we make each other better."

"We do," she says, a sigh leaving her when my hand drops to her breast, kneading her, my thumb rubbing across her nipple, which strains against the fabric of her dress. "Are we really doing this in the school parking lot?"

Her words snap me out of my Daisy-induced spell and I break out into laughter. "Not like Matthews can bust me anymore. What's he gonna do, kick me out of school?"

"Make you repeat senior year?" she teases, her eyes dancing.

I press my finger against her lips. "Never say that again. Promise?"

She nods, her expression solemn. "Promise," she says once my finger falls away from her mouth. "You're my favorite person, Archibald Lancaster."

I groan, my hands sliding up to cup her face just as our lips meet. Daisy kisses me and I can feel those same words in the way her lips move.

I'm her favorite.

And she's mine.

Forever.

EXCLUSIVE
BONUS
CONTENT

DAISY

"I don't want you spending a lot of money on my present," I warn my boyfriend, trying to keep my voice firm, my expression serious.

It's still weird to think that Arch Lancaster is my actual boyfriend. That he loves me and I love him and we don't see a future without the other in it.

It may be weird, but it's also the best feeling ever.

Arch smiles, and I can tell at once that he's humoring me. "Okay. Sure."

We're walking along Fifth Avenue hand in hand, the sidewalk practically bursting with people, it's so crowded. It's five days before Christmas and the air is bitingly cold, the sky heavy with dark clouds. It's supposed to snow in the next couple of days, which means we could have a white Christmas.

Something that used to happen more often when I was younger, but not lately. I'm kind of looking forward to spending snowy afternoons locked away with Arch at his parents' apartment, staring out at the city lights while drinking a mug of hot chocolate, the Christmas tree twinkling in the background.

Knowing Arch, he'd rather drag me away to his bedroom while his parents are out at yet another holiday party and give me at least two orgasms before they return home. If I'm lucky, maybe even three.

The man is insatiable and I'm not complaining. I like the idea of both scenarios if I'm being truthful.

"I'm serious, Archibald. I don't want some lavish piece of jewelry or a designer bag." I glance up at him, loving how delicious he looks with the black wool coat on and a black beanie on his head, his hair curling from beneath it.

"Ooh, you're busting out the full name. That's when I know you're serious." He grins, swinging our linked hands between us before he yanks me in close, his arm curling around my shoulders. He drops a kiss on my temple, his lips grazing my hat more than my skin. "Just let me do what I want, okay, woman?"

I say nothing because I don't want to look ungrateful, but the earrings he gave me for my birthday are so expensive I still haven't told my father about them. I could probably pay for my entire college education with those earrings.

At least a year of tuition, I bet.

Once Arch releases my shoulders, he grabs my hand and we stroll along the street in companionable silence, occasionally stopping in front of a window display to admire the decorations. Christmas is my favorite time of year. Though I'm always missing my mom around the holidays, it has become a little easier as every year passes.

It's also easier when I have a boyfriend that I'm in love with and completely wrapped up in. The holidays are a lot more fun with Arch around.

"The bookstore is right up there," he says at one point, his tone nonchalant and I glance up at him, smiling.

"Are you taking me to the bookstore?" I can't hide my excitement. I don't even bother trying to.

His grin is devastating. "Of course, I am. I'm not stupid."

I practically skip to the flagship store, getting so ahead of Arch, he has to hurry to keep up with me. I let go of his hand to push through the doors and I come to a stop at the entrance, my gaze eating up the space.

The store is huge and there are books everywhere. People everywhere.

"I need to find the romance section." I take a step, ready to go on the hunt, but Arch snags hold of my hand, stopping me.

"I have a plan."

I turn to face him fully, frowning. "What do you mean?"

"This is your Christmas gift." He inclines his head forward, like he's indicating...wait a minute.

The *entire* store?

Oh my God. That is so very Lancaster of him.

"Arch, there is no way you bought me this bookstore," I say, my voice so low I'm sure he can barely hear me.

He bursts out laughing, shaking his head. "No, I didn't buy you the bookstore, though I probably could."

I rest my free hand on my chest, breathing a sigh of relief. "Oh, thank God. Yeah, I definitely don't need to own a bookstore. I'm perfectly fine just visiting them."

"Yeah well, what would you say if I bought you as many romance books as you could grab in say...three minutes?"

I blink at him. "Three minutes?"

He nods.

"As many as I can grab?" I turn the idea over in my head. I bet I could snag a lot of books in three minutes.

"Whatever you've got in your arms when your time is up, I'll buy for you."

I start bouncing up and down, giddiness making my heart race. "Holy crap, are you serious?"

"Dead serious, Daze. Come on." He squeezes my hand as we both start walking. "Let's go find your favorite section."

We wander through the store, my gaze catching on so many gorgeous covers. Interesting, bold titles. If my funds were unlimited, there would be so many books I'd buy. I'd probably never get around to reading them all.

Once we arrive in the romance section, I stare greedily at all the covers that are faced out, spotting more than a few books that I've been dying to read. School has kept me occupied and so has Arch, so I haven't been reading as much as I used to. Plus, my funds are limited.

But right now...for three minutes?

I can grab whatever books I want, and they'll be all mine.

"What if I drop one?" I ask him.

"Then you grab another or you let it go." He tips his head. "I wouldn't bother to stop to pick it up. What if all the books fall out of your arms?"

I imagine exactly that happening and a shiver courses through me.

"Oh, that would be awful." I tap my index finger against my pursed lips. "Okay, give me a few minutes to strategize."

He lets me do exactly that, watching me with amusement as I wander through the section, scanning my choices. I mentally lament the fact that the section isn't that big but doesn't romance always get the shaft? I don't understand why. They're the best kind of stories. Always full of love and positivity.

Well, for the most part. I do love those dark romances where the guy has morally gray values and is vaguely terrifying...

"You ready?" Arch asks, his deep voice breaking through my thoughts.

I turn to face him and nod. "Definitely."

"Okay, get into position."

I love that he's taking this seriously because I am too. I shake out my hands and put my right foot out in front of me, ready to leap forward the minute he gives me the signal. I feel like I'm in a race. With myself.

Finally, he speaks.

"You ready, Daze?" When I nod, he starts the countdown. "3-2-1—go!"

I'm off, frantically scanning my options, reaching for one book, then another. I make a base within my arms and start stacking, my pile growing scarily fast. Arch follows along with me, laughing and calling out my time to let me know how much longer I have.

"Two minutes!"

That minute came on way too fast and when I reach for another book, two fall out of my arms, landing with a thud on the floor. I'm about to grab them when Arch screams at me.

"Keep going! Ninety seconds!"

I go back to the shelves and pick up the books I just dropped, my mind racing as fast as my heart. When he yells "sixty seconds" I'm in full panic mode and just grabbing books without looking at their title or who wrote them.

I'm past the point of caring. I'm just getting what I can, my arms aching, the sharp edge of a hardback nudging my chin when I walk. My pile is that freaking high.

"Thirty seconds!"

My knees wobble and I worry for a hot second I'm going to pass out but I stop in front of a table piled high with gorgeous, colorful covers and I just start adding them to my stack until Arch finally yells, "Done!"

I sag against the stack of books that now rest on top of the table. "Oh my God."

He's grinning, eyeing my book stack. "Impressive."

"I went a little crazy," I admit.

"That's what I'd hoped for. Come on." He stops directly in front of where I'm standing, his fingers slipping beneath my chin to tilt my face up. "Let's go pay for your Christmas presents."

I stare at all the books I get to take home, wondering where I'm going to put them all. "I don't even want to know how much this is going to cost."

"Don't worry about it. My Christmas gift, remember?" He's smiling, looking so pleased with himself that I slap my hand on top of the pile to keep the books in place and rise up on tiptoe, giving him a quick kiss.

"I love my Christmas gift," I murmur. "This was fun. Even if it felt like a sporting event."

He chuckles and kisses me again. "I love you, Daze."

"Love you too, Archibald."

He scowls just before he kisses me again, so deeply I sort of lose myself until I'm brought back to reality when the books tip over, scattering all over the table and floor.

Making Arch laugh.

"Oops." I stare at the mess on the floor, and Arch immediately starts picking them up. I help him, snagging a basket that I spot just magically sitting under the table and I shove as many books in there as I can before I rise to my feet, brushing the hair out of my eyes.

"You're looking a little sweaty," he teases as he takes the basket, and I grab whatever books remain and head for the cash register.

"That was hard work." I smile at him. "But worth it."

His expression turns serious. "You're worth it, Daze."

My heart threatens to leap outside of my chest and I can't help but wonder...

Is it always going to feel like this between us?

My guess is yes.

ACKNOWLEDGMENTS

Oh this book put me through it. When I wrote the first draft, I thought it was magical. I was in love. Back at Lancaster Prep, whoo hoo! Then I turned it in and traveled to a couple of signings over two weeks and came back to major edits waiting for me in my inbox. Major notes. The book was a mess.

I tore this baby apart and put it back together and now I can finally say I truly love it. Arch and Daisy - they are a different vibe from the other Lancaster Prep books. There's a hint of sadness thanks to Daisy's circumstances, and they are opposites in every way, with only a few similarities. But they are so good for each other...

As I must always do, a huge thank you to everyone who reads my books. I wouldn't have this career without you, and you mean so much to me. I need to shout out again a special thank you to Rebecca Hilsdon and the rest of the team at Michael Joseph/Penguin Random House UK for bringing the Lancasters to the UK Commonwealth. Thank you for touring me around London in July and the Waterstones appearances in London and Liverpool with Tillie Cole. I had such a great time and met so many wonderful UK readers.

Everyone at Valentine PR, I need you. Please never leave me. Nina, Kim, Valentine, Daisy, Sarah, Meags, Kelley, AMY (my kid, ha) - you ladies are the best! Nina, your notes for this book helped me so much. You made the book better so thank you.

Always must thank my editor Becky and to my proofreader Sarah. You guys are the best. And I need to thank Emily Wittig for the gorgeous Lancaster Prep covers. Your endless support for the romance reading community is so appreciated.

p.s. - If you enjoyed *You Said I Was Your Favorite*, it would mean so much if you left a review on the retailer site you bought it from, or on Goodreads. Thank you!

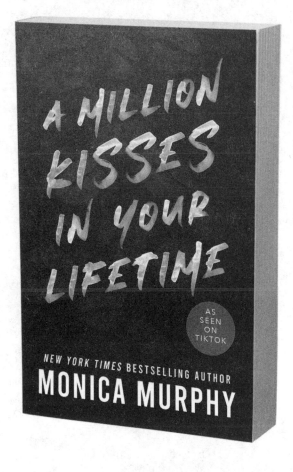

I've got ninety-nine problems and my brother's snarky, smart-mouthed best friend Sam is tangled up in every last one of them.

livy hart

When it comes to firefighter Sam O'Shea, absence—and a regime of tactical avoidance—has been working for me *juuust* fine. But when the audition of a lifetime falls in my pathetically broke lap, he's the only one who can help me land the job. But I'm willing to make a deal with the devil if it means I can kickstart my career as a narrator for audio books.

The problem? We'd have to actually *do* the job. Together. And *then* we're told it's for an erotic romance. Narrating steamy lines in a tiny studio with a man who lights a fire under your skin? An occupational hazard. Accidentally inciting a town scandal when your erotic audiobook clips wind up on the radio? A crisis. And falling for the *one* man I promised my brother—and my heart—I wouldn't touch?

A disaster—and temptation—I can't resist.

Twenty years as an army brat and Ember Howard knew, the soldiers at the door meant her dad was never coming home.

FULL
MEASURES

REBECCA
#1 *NEW YORK TIMES* BESTSELLING AUTHOR
YARROS

She knew. That's why Mom hadn't opened the door. She knew he was dead.

Twenty years as an army brat and Ember Howard knew, too. The soldiers at the door meant her dad was never coming home. What she didn't know was how she would find the strength to singlehandedly care for her crumbling family when her mom falls apart.

Then Josh Walker enters her life. Hockey star, her new next-door neighbor, and not to mention the most delicious hands that insist on saving her over and over again. He has a way of erasing the pain with a single look, a single touch. As much as she wants to turn off her feelings and endure the heartache on her own, she can't deny their intense attraction.

Until Josh's secret shatters their world. And Ember must decide if he's worth the risk that comes with loving a man who could strip her bare.

*Lyla Wilder is done being the shy,
chemistry nerd extraordinaire.*

GETTING *Lucky* NUMBER SEVEN

A Taking Shots Novel

CINDI MADSEN

While every other college student is out having fun, Lyla is studying.
With her cat. Well, she's played it "safe" quite enough, thank you. So
she creates a "College Bucket List" with item number seven being
a night of uninhibited, mind-blowing sex...

Now she just needs some help from her best friend.

Hockey player Beck Davenport thought Lyla's transformation would
be subtle. Man, was he wrong. With every item she ticks off, Beck
finds himself growing seriously hot for his sweet, brainiac best friend.
And if he's not careful, he'll end up risking their friendship in order
to convince Lyla that he might just be her lucky number seven...

You Said I Was Your Favorite is a romantic and angst-filled new adult romance. However, the story includes elements that might not be suitable for all readers. A death of a parent, off page, is included in the novel. Readers who may be sensitive to these elements, please take note.